DEAD HARVEST

DEAD HARVEST

A PAUL ONDRAGON MYSTERY

ANETTE STROHMEYER

Podium

Translation from German edited by Sarah Rimmington

Cover design by James Iacobelli

ISBN: 978-1-0394-5665-5

Published in 2025 by Podium Publishing
www.podiumentertainment.com

DEAD HARVEST

PROLOGUE

January 12, 2010
South Haiti, Route 208, heading toward Nan Margot
4:25 pm

The sky was heavy with the threat of rain. The clouds hung over the mountains as if they wanted to devour them. Gray haze was eating its way down the steep slopes, blotting out the rocks and trees.

Christine Dadou moved fast. She didn't want to get wet. She didn't want her beautiful new school uniform, a pink dress her mother had saved up for, to get spattered with mud from the dirt track. When it rained, it turned into a sludgy river within seconds.

Her head bowed, Christine hurried on, thinking of her father. Since his disappearance three months ago, the life of her small family had become even more difficult. His meager income as a tinsmith had gone, and Christine and her little brother often had to help their mother work in the fields after school. Christine was nine and her brother seven. They didn't own much, living in a small hut made of boards and corrugated metal on a tiny piece of land where they grew corn, bananas, and squash. Fortunately, a small stream ran behind the property, so at least they didn't have to carry their water a long distance like some of their classmates. That was the only luxury they had.

Christine turned onto the steep, narrow path that cut across the switchbacks of the mountain pass. It led through a forest of kapok and rubber trees. Christine knew every stone and every turn, but today, in the mist of the low-hanging clouds, the track seemed eerie and strange. Like a path into the spirit world.

Into the world of loas.

The girl shivered, although the day was tropical and sultry. Normally, she would have been out with the other schoolchildren from the village. They all took the same route to school and always walked together, but today she was feeling unwell and the teacher had allowed her to leave class early. Christine felt sadder and sadder lately, and often cried; she missed her father.

Unconsciously, she raised her hand to her chest and clutched the gris-gris she wore around her neck. Her mother had bought the amulet from the mambo in the village. It held protective magic. Her mother and brother also wore one.

The haze grew thicker, creeping down the mountain between the tree trunks. Fearfully, Christine lifted her eyes to the branches. She feared that Marinette Bras Chech might be on the prowl. A vicious female loa who liked to eat human flesh. Marinette flew through the woods disguised as a barn owl and silently swooped down on her victims to devour them.

Christine's steps quickened. The forest was full of ghosts. They lived in the trees and the ponds, and under the ground. Werewolves also lurked here. Her mother had warned her anxiously not to go with strange women, even if they seemed really nice and offered to help her. They usually concealed a *loup garou*, who was on the lookout for little children.

Christine's heart beat harder and harder against her ribs. Her thin chest rose and fell with each frightened breath. Her mother also said there was a bokor in the area, an evil sorcerer. People in the village also talked about it. They claimed that the *blancs*, the Whites who had settled up in the abandoned mine in the mountains three years ago, were working with the bokor. Ever since the strangers had arrived, people from the surrounding villages kept disappearing. So had Christine's father, Etienne Dadou. One day he had not returned from Jacmel, which he visited regularly to sell his homemade tinware at the market. It was immediately clear to the villagers that the whites' bokor was involved. But no one did anything about it. Everyone was afraid. Even Christine's mother did nothing. There was nothing that could be done against a dark wizard, except cast spells to protect yourself, she said. This was why she had taken three of her best chickens to the temple and traded them for the gris-gris pendants.

Christine didn't know what the whites were doing up there in the mountains, and it was also forbidden to approach the buildings they had put up. But naturally, she had been curious. She had never seen a person with white skin before, so she had defied the prohibition and secretly climbed into the mountains.

Christine listened. Somewhere ahead of her in the forest, she had heard a crackling sound. In the fog, the outlines of the bushes and rocks looked like terrifying creatures, but she knew her imagination was just playing tricks on her. There was no one there.

Her thoughts drifted back to the strangers in the mountains. Meeting them had been frightening at first, but her fear had quickly turned to disappointment. She had crept very close to the camp, right up to the long, sharp fence. Lying under a bush, she had waited for something to happen. After quite a while, two figures had come out of one of the buildings. They had lit cigarettes and talked in a foreign language. What had been frightening was that they were white from head to toe. They wore white pants and shirts and strange hoods, and their skin was as pale as the bones the mambo used to summon spirits in her temple. The figures looked like the living incarnation of the two spirits of death—the collector of crosses, *Ramasseur-de-croix*, and General Fouillé, who was said to ransack graves in cemeteries at night.

Christine would have liked to run away, but her curiosity was stronger. And the longer she watched the two white-skinned creatures talking and joking with each other, the clearer it became to her that these were not gèdè ghosts. They looked like skeletons come to life, but they turned out to be merely men. Men made of flesh and sinew. Disappointed, Christine left.

Another noise brought her back to reality.

Was that a groan she had heard?

Nervously, Christine looked around. The mist had become so thick by now that she could taste it. With each breath, it flowed over her lips into her lungs, moist and earthy. *Like the breath of the grave,* she thought, and shuddered. She quickly started to move.

When the path finally led downhill, she began to run. The worn soles of her sandals clattered on the hard ground, pounding along with her heart. It was not far to the place where the path rejoined the road. You could see her village from there. Just through the narrow gorge and over the bare hump and then . . .

Suddenly, a figure was standing before her, jutting out of the earth like a tombstone.

Startled, Christine came to a halt to avoid colliding with it. In the process, she lost her balance and fell over backward. She tried to break her fall, but her slender wrists simply buckled. A sharp pain shot up her arms, and her new dress landed in the dirt. Tears sprang into Christine's eyes. She looked up, her lips quivering. She had to blink to make out anything through the veil of tears.

In front of her stood a man. A Black man, but strangely his skin seemed less black than gray. A deathlike pallor covered his arms and hands, almost like a paleface. He was barely skin and bones and wore tattered clothing that hung from his limbs like tattered gauze bandages. He was stooping, his face covered in buboes and disfigured.

Swaying slightly, as if he had drunk too much clairin, he came toward Christine. One arm lifted mechanically and an indefinable sound escaped from his throat. The smell of decay rose to her nostrils.

Hastily, Christine got up and wiped her eyes to allow her to see better.

Her breath caught.

More tears welled up in her eyes.

"Papa?" she breathed in disbelief as the damp mist allowed her some air to breathe.

The man she recognized as her father said nothing. His eyes were milky, as dull as those of a sick dog, and were staring past her. Yellowish saliva dripped from his mouth. He took another faltering step toward her. His fingers, the nails splintered, bent themselves into claws.

"Papa?"

Suddenly, a hand shot forward and wrapped itself around Christine's neck.

"Papa! What are you doing?" she said with difficulty. Horrified, she stared at the disfigured face. The hand was brutal, squeezing the air out of her. Black dots danced before her eyes.

"Papa, it's me!" It was a soundless croak. Christine was gripped by desperation. Then she remembered the gris-gris and groped for it with one hand. She felt her strength fading. Why was her father doing this?

But she had known the answer long ago.

He was no longer her father.

He was a *zombi cadavre*—a reanimated corpse!

With the last of her strength, Christine tore the protective amulet from her neck and stuffed it into the mouth of the zombie, which had come so close that its foul stench was enveloping her.

With a shrill scream, the zombie let go of her, trying to get the gris-gris out of its mouth. It spun around in a wild frenzy, giving out a strangely distorted scream. Acrid smoke came out of its mouth. It smelled of charred flesh.

Gasping for breath, Christine watched as the zombie violently tore at its lower jaw. Bones cracked and the joints gave way. But the zombie raged on, feeling no pain, until finally it held the gris-gris in its pale hand.

In that moment, Christine managed to tear her gaze away from the horrifying sight. Without paying any heed to the small bag on the floor that held her school materials, she ran. She stumbled down the path in reckless leaps, hastily turned onto the street, and ran in the direction of the village. Behind her there was silence. Still, she did not dare to look around. She ran until her lungs threatened to burst. Her muscles were burning like fire. Soon her legs would no longer be able to carry her.

The first raindrops hit her forehead as she used the last of her strength to reach the cluster of shabby huts. She screamed, but no one came to her aid. The village was deserted. Where had they all gone?

In a panic, she ran to her house. "Mama!" But that too was empty. Christine slammed the door shut and locked it. Quickly, she hid under the bed. Listening to the drumbeats of her racing heart, she looked toward the door.

Silence.

Then a pawing sound. Was that her mother? She was about to call out to her when she heard the moaning. Sweat froze on her skin. *It* was there, outside the door. The horrible image of the grotesque ashen face with the dislocated jaw made her tremble all over. Christine knew there was nothing she could do now if the zombie came into the cabin. Her gris-gris was gone. She had no more protection.

A scraping sounded at the door. Splintered fingernails on rough wood.

The zombie tried to open it, but could not. It let out a frustrated gasp. Gurgling, inarticulate.

Then silence again.

A scrape on the side wall of the hut.

Christine hardly dared to breathe. The blood was still rushing in her ears from her wild escape. In the darkness of the hut, her eyes sought out a weapon. Rain began to drum loudly on the corrugated iron roof.

Another scrape.

Suddenly, the door flew open. A black shadow stood in the bright square of light. A shadow with a dislocated jaw. Christine cried out and tried to crawl even farther under the bed. She heard the heavy footsteps of the zombie. They approached the bed.

Bondieu, she thought, *please protect me*. Then she heard only a deafening clap of thunder. Something heavy crashed onto the bed above her, and her mouth and nose filled with dust.

The world swayed. The ground reared up, as if trying to throw off humanity. All the spirits of the earth had awakened in anger from their sleep.

4:53 pm.

In the capital, Port-au-Prince, the government palace collapsed, along with countless other buildings. Tens of thousands of people were buried alive under the rubble.

4:54 pm.

Silence.

CHAPTER 1

February 4, 2010
Los Angeles, California
7:25 am

The morning was hazy and the visibility over LA was lousy. Despite that, Paul Ondragon peered through the arm-thick telescope. The high-powered eyepiece caught the shadowy twenty-eight–story skyscraper on Sunset Boulevard at the foot of the western Hollywood Hills, and Ondragon brought it into focus.

The individual windows on the north facade of the Golden State Credit Bank building were clearly visible. Behind some of them, he could already see people at work, their computer monitors giving off a bluish glow. Those were the early birds. He would join them in a moment. But before that, the same procedure as every morning.

Ondragon panned the telescope to the top floor, to the office window on the far left. He glanced at the clock. Not quite half past seven. He let a minute pass. Then he saw the lights in the office come on, and a smile settled on his lips. Shortly afterward, Charlize Tanaka appeared at the office window, watering the yucca on the windowsill with a red watering can. That was the signal they'd agreed. All was well. No irregularities.

For a moment, his assistant looked out the window and then sat down at her desk.

It was no coincidence that Paul Eckbert Ondragon had his office on the top floor of that bank building. The entire high-rise was as secure as Fort Knox against break-ins (like Fort Knox itself, you might say) and, more importantly, it was easy to observe from his villa on Doheny Drive. The building was the ideal place for him to work—although, ironically, it was a bank and his principles forbade him from ever working *for* banks. Still, there was nothing to stop him from working in the same building as a bank. After all, banks were protected by state-of-the-art surveillance technology, and this particular bank had several ingenious escape routes for him and Charlize—should things ever get dicey. But who would break into the top floor of a bank when the vault was in the basement?

Satisfied, Ondragon turned away from the telescope, which was set up in front of the large picture window in the living room, and went to the counter in the open-plan kitchen, where the triple espresso he always had in the morning was waiting for him. He emptied the cup in one big gulp, reached for the jacket hanging on the back of a chair at the dining table, and routinely felt in his pants pocket for the car keys. As he did so, his fingers touched the talisman hanging from the key chain, a kitschy Berlin bear that had saved his life a few years ago.

Everything was in its place, so he could calmly make the short trip to work. Just as he was about to open the front door, his cell phone rang. Frowning, he fished his iPhone out of his jacket and looked at the display, his frown deepening. The area code showing was for the United Arab Emirates, but he didn't have any business there at the moment.

After another ring, he decided to answer. "Ondragon!"

"Hi, Ecks. Are you on a job right now, or can we talk?"

Ecks—that was a somewhat peculiar abbreviation for Eckbert. And only one person in the whole world called him that. Ondragon's features brightened. "Rod! Well, I'll be! It's good to hear from you. No, I'm free, you can talk. What's up? And why are you calling from the UAE?"

"Oh, you know, I moved the main office of DeForce Deliveries from Mombasa to Dubai two months ago. They just offered me better terms here. So, where are you hanging?"

"You won't believe this, Rod, but I'm home."

"I don't believe it. That hardly ever happens."

"You can say that again. Business has been pretty good lately. I see the American Airlines gals more than my assistant in the office. How are things at DeForce?"

"Can't complain. The world's got more trouble spots than ever, and our specialized transport services are needed everywhere. But that's not why I'm calling you, Ecks. I mean, to talk business."

Perhaps Ondragon had imagined it, but his old friend suddenly didn't sound quite so cheerful. "What, then?" he inquired.

"Well, Ecks, it's like this . . . I need your help."

Ondragon put his jacket aside and sat down on the chair at the big dining table. If Roderick DeForce needed his help, he really had to be in deep shit. "Shoot," he said.

"One of my mailmen has disappeared. You don't know him; he's only been with us for four years. But he's a very good man. Reliable. Tyler Ellys is his name and he lives in Tucson. He works Central and South America with a couple of other colleagues."

"I didn't know you had expanded to this continent as well."

The boss of DeForce Deliveries laughed. "Well, we move with the times, although most of the business is still in the Arab world and Africa. That hasn't changed since you left us, Ecks. Which I'm still sorry about, by the way. But you were always on a completely different track. On an express train with faulty brakes."

"Charming, Rod."

"You know how much I appreciate you, Ecks."

Ondragon did know. Fifteen years older than Ondragon, Roderick DeForce had taken him under his wing when, in the confusion after his studies, he hadn't quite known what to do with himself and had had an almost pathological compulsion to solve every problem that presented itself to him. The British-born Rod had recognized Ondragon's unusual talent and brought him into DeForce. Rod had not only given his protégé unrestricted confidence in his abilities, he had also been something of a father figure.

More father than the man who raised me, Ondragon thought bitterly. His time at DeForce Deliveries had been damn good. He had learned a lot of "useful" things that were helpful to him now.

"So what's the deal with this Tyler Ellys guy, then?" he asked his former boss.

"Well, like I said, he's disappeared. I don't know exactly when, but he didn't show up for work yesterday. He had gotten his assignment via the bulletin board on the internet as usual, but the other guys were left waiting for him at the Buenos Aires airport. Ellys was always reliable. It's not like him not to show. I sent a floater to his place in Tucson to find out what had happened. His house is empty, his car is in the garage. No sign of Ellys."

"And what do the police say? You must have called them."

"There was no getting around it. The cops did a cursory search of Ellys's house but found nothing. The neighbors didn't see anything either, anything at all."

"And what are the police going to do about it?"

"Oh, you know what they're like," Rod snorted angrily. "If there's no evidence the person is in danger, the case goes onto the discard pile. And it sits there with all the missing persons cases the United States has had since the beginning of the last century."

"Maybe Tyler Ellys got out," Ondragon mused. "This kind of thing happens all the time, doesn't it? Guys can't take what they see on the job and quit."

"Not Ellys. He's an ex-Navy SEAL. A real tough guy. I'd stake my life on him. He's done the dirty stuff too, without batting an eye."

"Where was he last?"

"In Mexico, corpse transport from Monterrey to Nuevo Laredo on the border."

Corpse transport. Ondragon knew all too well what that meant. A critical commodity was transported in a coffin through unsecured territory, camouflaged by a real corpse until it reached its destination. Difficult terrain, hostile forces, dangerous cargo—no problem. This sort of thing was DeForce Deliveries' bread and butter. A private delivery service, so to speak. Their customer list was long and illustrious. Businesses used DeForce mailmen, but so did government agencies when the conventional means wouldn't do the job. Ondragon had undertaken such transport himself, in Somalia and Afghanistan under contract with DeForce in the early 1990s. Risky missions that had cost more than a few men their lives. But back then, he had prided himself on being one of those tough mailmen—because Rod employed only the best and most hardened men.

Contrary to all expectations, DeForce was a legal business. A service provider like FedEx, only with more extreme cargo. Roderick DeForce was the founder and principal owner of the company he had established in 1989 when the Berlin Wall came down, initially based in Cairo. And even if Rod didn't go out on assignment himself, he still held all the strings like a spider in a web and supervised all contracts from his office. That's why Spider was his code name within the company.

Spider heard everything and saw everything, because he had access to several private as well as government satellites. He always knew what was going on where and which crew it involved. Ondragon suspected that was the very reason the disappearance of Tyler Ellys was upsetting his friend. Rod had lost track of an employee and that meant he no longer had control over him. Ondragon knew how much Rod hated it when anyone or anything was outside his control.

"And what exactly do you want from me?" he asked his old mentor.

Roderick DeForce hesitated, as if it was difficult for him to ask a favor of his former employee. Ondragon wondered what had prompted his friend to contact him of all people. After all, Rod had plenty of capable people within his own ranks.

Maybe it's something internal, he thought. *Something that only an outsider can handle. Someone he has complete confidence in.*

"Ecks, this may sound a little trite, but I want you to find Tyler Ellys for me," Rod said finally. "My people aren't trained for this. They're not detectives."

"Neither am I."

"I know, Ecks, missing persons cases are way too trivial for you; you need more challenging nuts to crack."

"Rod, for the love of God, I—"

"I'm asking as a friend. And I'll pay your usual fee, of course. Besides, the case does indeed present something of a challenge, as you'll see when I tell you what my floater found in Ellys's house before the police got there."

Ondragon sighed. Could he refuse his old friend a favor? Of course not. Besides, as always, his curiosity won out. "Agreed, Rod. Let's get on with it, then. What did he find?"

"Thank you very much, Ecks. I am deeply in your debt."

"It's okay; just invite me to your new office in Dubai sometime."

"Consider your flight booked!" Rod gave a short laugh. He seemed relieved. Then he grew serious again. "Well, my floater gained entry to the house. It looked as if Ellys had just left. The TV was on in the living room and there were three empty beer cans next to a dozen full ones. There was nothing else out of the ordinary, but the guy searched the house carefully, as I had instructed him. In the trash can he finally found a crumpled letter. It was a white envelope with only one sheet of paper inside. On it was written—and this is strange—in French: *Tyler Ellys, your body shall be an empty bottle.* Underneath was a painting of a coffin."

"And what's that supposed to mean? Is it a death threat?" Ondragon was not particularly impressed by this revelation. He couldn't quite get up the motivation for this case.

"I don't know. The floater has the letter. You should get in touch with him in Tucson; I'll text you his number. He can tell you everything he knows."

Ondragon pondered. A missing mailman, a letter in French, no leads. That didn't sound very exciting. But Roderick DeForce was personally asking for his help and that alone made the case interesting. "All right," Ondragon agreed, "my Mustang could do with another run anyway. I'll be on my way as soon as I can. I'll be in touch when I get to Tucson."

There was a relieved sigh from the other end of the line. "Thank you, Ecks."

"You're welcome."

"And take care of yourself!"

After hanging up, Ondragon stared at the phone. In all the time he had worked for Roderick DeForce, his boss had never said *"Take care of yourself!"* Strange that he should do so now, of all times. But maybe his friend was just getting old. And age, as we all know, brought with it not only physical infirmity, but also the specter of fear. And once it appeared, it clung to you like a disease.

The longer Ondragon thought about it, the more he was overcome with the feeling that there might be more to Tyler Ellys's disappearance than he had first assumed. And more too than Rod had wanted to admit on the phone.

He hit the menu button and called Charlize. Today he would not be coming in to the office.

CHAPTER 2

February 4, 2010
somewhere on Interstate 10, heading east
3:40 pm

It was exactly 501 miles to Tucson. Eight hours of driving through the driest, most hostile environments on the continent—the Mojave and Sonoran Deserts. But his aging '69 Mustang bravely ignored the fact that its black exterior literally absorbed the sun's rays while the heat conjured shimmering mirages on the dead-straight road. Inside, in the cool breeze of the air-conditioning, Ondragon sat at the wheel, chewing gum and listening to "Easy" by Faith No More with the volume turned up. His right cowboy boot rested loosely on the gas pedal and there was a relaxed expression on his face.

The reason he liked the desert was that it was nature, but empty. There was nothing here to get on your nerves. No mosquitoes, no larger animals like bears or wolves to mistake you for a morsel of salmon, and no treacherous weeds looking to trip you up. And best of all, you had a clear view in all directions! So enemies would have a hard time sneaking up on you unnoticed. No water also meant no life. No life: no nasty surprises. The desert was a very clear, simple place. Not like the forest, where everything was overgrown and impassable.

Ondragon reluctantly recalled his stay in Minnesota last summer. There, the forest had revealed its malevolent nature to him. It was a green beast that devoured people and did not spit them out again. And then the creatures there . . . No, if he was going to be out in the open, let it be the desert! Although the Arctic certainly had some advantages too. Cold, white nothingness. Wonderful!

Lost in thought, Ondragon cruised along in his Mustang, nearing his destination a mile at a time. In the rearview mirror, the sun sank lower and lower over the horizon, and the barren, cactus-covered landscape all around him became a fabulous interplay of colors, like the photo wallpaper from the eighties, before an impenetrable darkness descended.

The city of Tucson emerged from the desert night like a safe harbor in a dark sea. A shining oasis in the void. The lights glowed invitingly, promising good company and cool drinks. Everything a lonely desert rider could want after a dusty day on the trail.

Ondragon checked into the Hotel Congress downtown. It was a little noisy and uncomfortable, but the bar and the food were reputed to be of the very highest quality. More importantly, the hip 1920s brick building was always bustling, so you could come and go without attracting attention. Even late at night. So Ondragon was willing to accept the inconvenience of the small, not too luxurious room. Normally, he only stayed in the best hotels. When you were constantly on the road like he was, a clean, comfortable bed and good service were essentials.

After taking his travel bag up to his room and checking the floor for potential escape routes, he went down to the lobby, ordered himself something to eat, and allowed himself a whiskey sour at the bar. That was enough for today. The monotonous drive had worn him out. He would contact the floater in the morning and then inspect the Tyler Ellys house for himself. A quick preliminary check from a distance before he proceeded to a more detailed search.

"Yes?" asked a brittle male voice on the other end of the phone when Ondragon dialed the floater's number in his room that morning.

"Kaplan Bolič?"

"Yes."

"This is Mr. O. I have been instructed by Spider to contact you about the case of the missing mailman." He used the DeForce cover names as a precaution.

"He told me. I'm at the Arizona Hotel, room 506. Drop by and see me, Mr. O."

That's not far away, Ondragon thought. *Just a couple of blocks.* "All right, I'll be there around noon," he said.

"I'll be here. I feel like shit anyway. Probably caught the flu or something. Headache and aching limbs. That's why I'm staying in the room."

"I wanted to look at the Ellys house first. Is there anything I should know in advance?"

Bolič coughed loudly. "I searched everything thoroughly. Except for the letter, I found nothing. The only thing I noticed was that the curtains were drawn and the TV was on when I arrived. Oh yeah, and the open beer can."

"Could mean Ellys went missing in the evening or at night."

"I think so too."

"And the police?" continued Ondragon.

"They think he's run off. Who knows why. They say it happens more often than you think. Debt, woman problems, or just desert fever."

"Desert fever?"

"Yes, I hear there are people who can't stand the endless sun and the barren landscape here after a while."

"Did Tyler Ellys own the house?"

"Yes, he bought it three years ago, shortly after he started at DeForce."

"Where was he born?"

The man on the other end coughed again. "Denver. Oh man, I'm all dizzy."

Ondragon pursed his lips. The whole thing seemed strange to him. Nobody just left his house behind, desert fever or not. The police seemed to be on the wrong track there, as they so often were. "And the letter?" he asked.

"Nothing special, except the words."

"I'll pick it up from you later."

"Stop by anytime, Mr. O. Also, would you be kind enough to bring me some painkillers?"

"You got it." Ondragon put his cell phone away and checked his pistol. The lightweight Sig Sauer, used as a police weapon in

Europe, was always in a holster under his jacket. Today, however, he had swapped his finer getup for a beige windbreaker and jeans. It wasn't a good idea to walk around a simple residential neighborhood like Tyler Ellys's in a tailored suit, even if that was his preferred work attire. Ondragon placed a lot of importance on a neat appearance, but he also knew what clothing was appropriate when. This had been indelibly drilled into him by his father, a German diplomat with almost military manners. Diplomacy and polish were everything—if his old man was to be believed. But one thing Ondragon had learned in the course of his life: It was much more important to be inconspicuous. For some things, it was essential to become one with one's surroundings. Ondragon liked to compare himself to a tiger. Outside the bamboo forest, he was colorful and conspicuous, but when he moved around in his territory, his stripes merged with the tangle of the jungle and he became invisible.

Ignoring Arizona's legal requirement to carry his gun openly, he tucked it in his waistband. Then he rose from the edge of the bed and went to the tiny bathroom to check in the mirror that his appearance gave him the bearing of a desert dweller, as he wanted. Then he turned out the light and left the room.

He took a cab to the nearest car rental agency, where Charlize had reserved a car for him the day before, and picked up a boring silver Chevrolet Impala with local license plates and tinted windows. He headed east on the highway, where he took the exit for the Pima Air & Space Museum, the largest airplane graveyard in the world, and almost in the center of Tucson. Mile after mile, he followed the road, which was lined on both sides by retired military aircraft behind long steel fences, before finally turning left onto Escalante Road. Tyler Ellys's house was on East Barrow Street, which ran parallel to it. Slowly, Ondragon steered the car through the meticulously laid-out residential neighborhood, looking closely at each house. When he arrived at Ellys's address, he carefully noted the surroundings of the building and continued at the same pace to avoid attracting attention.

Back out on Escalante Road, he parked the Impala at the side of the road next to a couple of tourists who were murmuring to each other as they photographed the decommissioned lords of the skies through the wire mesh, and pretended to be as interested as they were in the heaps of light metal scrap. His eyes concealed by his sunglasses, he looked around discreetly.

Across the street was the residential neighborhood where Ellys's place was located. The house didn't look very inviting; the vegetation in the front yard had withered away to yellowish skeletons under the desert sun.

After a while, Ondragon broke away from the group and crossed the street. He made his way along a small path between two houses without cars in front of their garages, and then to the back boundary of Ellys's property and squeezed through a bush-covered gap between the high picket fences surrounding the properties. Through a knothole, he observed the garden and the back of Ellys's house. The lawn was dead, and had been for some time, although there was almost certainly an underground sprinkler system. Tyler Ellys probably didn't set much store by a green yard. The house didn't make too fresh an impression either. Although it couldn't have been more than ten years old, it was in desperate need of a new coat of paint, the wood poking out through the chipped light brown paint like pale bones under withered skin. Ondragon noted that there was no fence between the Ellys and Diego properties. Obviously, Ellys got along quite well with his neighbor. Only when it came to lawn care, Mr. Diego apparently was a bit more conscientious. Bright green and freshly sprinkled, the Bahama grass on his half of the garden shone in the morning light. The facade of the Diego house had also been painted recently.

Ondragon again examined the missing man's home. The curtains at the windows were still closed. The police had apparently changed nothing.

Suddenly, a shadow flitted past Ondragon's eyes at the knothole. He quickly moved back from the fence. Was there someone else watching the house?

He heard quiet footsteps on the other side. The person seemed to be standing right by the fence. Ondragon held his breath, fearing they might hear him. There were a few scrapes on the wooden slats, then more footsteps. What the hell were they doing?

Only when someone began to sing softly behind the fence did Ondragon realize who was on the other side. He relaxed. It wasn't an invisible enemy; it could only be Mr. Diego's daughter. Kaplan Bolič had told him about Ellys's next-door neighbors. Mr. Diego was a widower and lived with his two children, five-year-old Maria and three-year-old Xavier.

Ondragon approached the knothole and could now see the little girl. She was hopping happily from the withered Ellys lawn to the fresh green grass on the Diegos' side. Like a little world traveler, she strode between the realm of the dead to that of the living.

Maria was barefoot and wore a blue dress. Her dark hair was tied in two cute braids and around her neck dangled various homemade necklaces made of nuts and seed pods. Ondragon watched her disappear into the Diego house through a back door.

He remained behind the fence for another half hour, but observed nothing worth mentioning. Shortly after eleven, he left his hiding place and returned discreetly to the car, on which the dust of the desert had already settled. Switching on the air-conditioning, he jotted down his latest findings in a small notepad and then drove back downtown. At the Tucson Mall, he parked and walked into the huge complex. He needed some equipment for his nighttime excursion.

Once he had everything he needed, he returned to the hotel and had an excellent lunch in the restaurant.

A short time later, he made his way on foot to the Arizona Hotel. Entering the lobby through the main entrance, he passed the front desk with a nod and headed for the elevators, where he adjusted his freshly purchased baseball cap to hide his face from the omnipresent security cameras. Then he pressed the button for the seventh floor. Once there, he slipped into the adjacent stairwell and climbed back down two floors to the fifth. Some would say he was paranoid, but in Ondragon's experience you could never be too careful. So he knocked on the door marked 506 only after he had made certain no one was in the hallway.

At first all he heard was silence, but then, finally, a muffled groan came, followed by "Who is it?"

"Mr. O," Ondragon said softly.

On the other side, the security chain rattled and the door opened. Ondragon stepped past the tall, hunched figure into the room, where he immediately looked around but saw nothing noteworthy.

The floater closed the door, put the safety chain back in place, and shuffled over to the bed, dropping weakly onto it. He was dressed only in a bathrobe and looked ghastly. His unshaven face had the gray tinge of liver sausage that had been left out too long, and a thin film of sweat gleamed on his high Slavic cheekbones. The dark eyes lay reddened in their sockets, gleaming feverishly. Kaplan Bolič really seemed to be ill.

Ondragon pulled the small paper bag from his jacket pocket and tossed it to him. "The painkillers."

"Thank you." Bolič caught it and extracted the box of pills with shaking fingers. He took two pills right away, washing them down with a glass of water. Afterward, he lay back on his pillow with a groan and looked intently at Ondragon. "So you're the famous Mr. O! You're still considered something of a hero at DeForce. Even Spider speaks highly of you."

Ondragon was silent. He was uncomfortable with the DeForce people talking about him as if he was a fucking legend. Instead, he tried to size up the man in front of him. According to Rod, Bolič was a native Bosnian and had learned the art of war at the age of twelve after escaping the Srebrenica massacre in 1995. After that came the Foreign Legion and private personal security. For the past four years, he had been working as a so-called floater for DeForce, based out of Moscow. Floaters were not part of the regular crew. They were free-lancers who filled the gaps when regulars dropped out for whatever reason, or when an extra pair of hands was needed. Floaters worked all over the world; they didn't specialize in any particular area. They were the mercenaries at DeForce, the men for the rough stuff. Bolič was weakened by illness, but otherwise did not give the impression of being particularly squeamish. Beneath his robe was a brawny, well-toned body that undoubtedly bore a scar or two, like souvenirs.

That's exactly what I look like under my clothes, Ondragon thought. *No one would suspect we were battle-scarred men who would go to extreme lengths to achieve our goal.* And he knew that killing was purely a question of self-preservation for anyone who worked at DeForce. On a mission, you had to see that you stayed alive and delivered the cargo. Nothing else mattered. In this respect, he and Bolič were the same.

"All right, Kaplan—"

"Captain!"

Ondragon looked at him, frowning.

"Call me Captain. I prefer that name." He waved his hand for Ondragon to continue.

Ondragon was already pretty irritated by the Bosnian's airs and graces, but continued the sentence he had started: "*Captain* . . . you'd best show me the letter you found in Tyler Ellys's trash now." He pulled up a chair while Bolič groaned and leaned over to rummage around in the nightstand drawer. As he did so, Ondragon tried not to glance at the obligatory Bible in the drawer. He was deeply averse not to religion, but rather to the book itself. Although his phobia of books had begun on the very day he had also lost his faith in God, the revulsion against everything printed and bound between two covers was stronger than his anger against God. After all, it had been the tons of books, and not God, that had killed his twin brother, Per Gustav, at the age of ten.

"*Ovdje molim,* here's the letter." Bolič held a transparent ziplock bag under his nose. Inside was a crumpled and re-smoothed piece of paper and a blank envelope.

Ondragon, who was happy to be pulled out of his depressing train of thought about his dead brother, took the plastic bag and turned it back and forth in the light of the bedside lamp.

"Was under a layer of brushwood and a dead bird in the barrel behind the house."

Ondragon read the line aloud, "'*Tyler Ellys, son corps doit être comme une bouteille vide*'—your body shall be like an empty bottle. Strange. Do you speak French, Chaplain? Uh, *Captain*?"

"*Bien sûr.*" His accent was terrible.

Ondragon himself spoke French and many other languages fluently, but he wanted to know what Bolič thought of it. After all, the man worked for Rod and might have an idea whether the letter had something to do with a DeForce job. He looked at the awkward drawing under the block capitals. It was an oblong hexagonal structure with a cross on it. Probably meant to represent a coffin. "What do you think it could mean?"

"I haven't the faintest idea. Most likely a threatening letter and Ellys got the jitters and bailed, or he's already in hell."

"You think he's dead?"

"Yes, vulture food."

"Did you know Tyler Ellys?"

"No. But that's what I think, Mr. O. He's dead." Bolič folded his massive forearms in front of his chest. "Tyler Ellys is out there in the desert somewhere with a bullet in his head, and we're just wasting our time here!"

"But who would have a reason to kill him?" Ondragon didn't let up, which visibly annoyed the Bosnian.

"How should I know? I'm not a private dick, I'm a soldier! Maybe the damn Yankee stepped on someone's toes one too many times, him and his charming manner. Or maybe somebody had a score to settle with him, which can happen in this job. Anyway, I don't care; you're on the case now. You can deal with it. I'm off the case!" He rubbed his forehead. "If only I could get rid of these fucking headaches! Ever since I went to the Ellys place, I've felt like shit. You'd think there was a curse on the house. I can hardly see straight anymore." He cursed fiercely in Bosnian and slammed his fist into a pillow, and Ondragon noticed the tattoo on the inside of his forearm that all DeForce members got sooner or later: Bugs Bunny as a mailman, holding a package. Luckily, he did not have this work of art himself, because it would have literally "bitten" the Japanese dragon he had had on his chest since he was eighteen.

"Does Ellys have any friends?" he asked the pale floater.

"I've already checked them all out. They're guys from his crew, but they don't know anything. You're welcome to call them again. Here are the numbers." Bolič tossed him a notepad. "That's everything I found out. Take it; I don't need it anymore."

Ondragon flipped through the pages. There wasn't much information. He put the pad in his jacket pocket. "Is there anything else I should know?"

"Nothing that I can think of. Just take the letter with you."

"Has it been dusted for fingerprints?"

"Nah, you'll have to do that, I don't have the equipment. But Rod told me he did."

Well, well, Rod knows more than I do, thought Ondragon, and put the letter in his pocket.

"Now get out of here, Mr. O! I need my rest."

"How can I reach you?"

"I'd prefer it if you didn't, but I think I'll be hanging around here for a while until I'm fit to board a plane."

Or until Rod allows you to, buddy! Ondragon tapped a finger on his forehead in farewell and left.

"Good luck!" called a Bosnian voice as he closed the door behind him.

CHAPTER 3

February 6, 2010
Tucson, Arizona
1:05 am

Ondragon waited awhile, gazing out through the car's windshield into the darkness, which had an almost tangible quality in the desert. Despite the streetlights, he could make out little more than the ghostly facades of the neighborhood houses. There were no lights burning in the windows. All good citizens were asleep at this hour.

Quietly, he opened the car door, got out, and ran, crouching, between the houses. In the shadowy, narrow path that led to the backs of the properties, he pulled the softshell face mask over his mouth and nose, making him look like Hannibal Lecter's little brother, but ensuring he would not be easily recognized. He was dressed in black pants and a bomber jacket of the same color that he had bought at the mall. He also carried Scotch tape and a large bowie knife on his belt. His hands were in thin, dark leather gloves.

Endeavoring not to make any noise, Ondragon climbed over the picket fence into Tyler Ellys's backyard and scurried to the back porch, where he fiddled at the door with a lock pick. The lock clicked and Ondragon pushed the door open, but he couldn't open it more than an arm's thickness. At least four security chains on the inside prevented him from getting any farther.

Damn it! Of course, he hadn't brought a bolt cutter. Why hadn't the floater told him about the security chains? Now he had to go in through the front door.

Cautiously, Ondragon crept around the house, peered out onto the empty street, and finally pushed his lock pick into the lock, which gave way after only a few seconds. The door swung open and Ondragon slipped into the even blacker darkness of the house. Having closed the door again, he flicked on a tiny diode lamp with a small rubber loop and slipped it over his index finger.

In the matte, bluish glow of the lamp, he first checked whether the curtains were indeed all closed and then began to look around the living room. Almost timidly, he let the light glide over the furniture and other objects it contained. A sagging brown couch, a low table in front of it with a multitude of dark rings on the wooden top that had likely been made by well-chilled bottles or cans. Across from the couch was an expensive Sony flat-screen TV with a Blu-ray player. This was where Tyler Ellys had kicked back and relaxed.

The light darted on. Above the television hung three framed photos. One showed Ellys with a GI crew cut, red cheeks, and blue eyes. His muscular torso was covered by a Hawaiian shirt. A beach with palm trees was visible in the background. Ellys was grinning, holding a cocktail in one hand, his other arm around a blond man. The next picture was another classic of American amateur photography, an essential feature of every living room: Ellys with a fishing rod and a massive fish on a hook, sunglasses on his nose and cigar in the corner of his mouth. Ondragon wondered where you could catch fish here in the desert. The third photo again featured Ellys and the blond guy. With orange oversized cowboy hats on their heads and so many Mardi Gras beads glittering around their necks that they rivaled the Masai women in Africa, they grinned, obviously drunk, into the camera. What a great guy!

Ondragon illuminated the shelf next to the pictures, whistling softly through his teeth when he discovered a thousand DVDs. Now, that was the kind of library he could get on board with. There wasn't much else in the room; only a brand-new Dolby Surround Sound system, like the one Ondragon himself had at home, confirmed the image of a movie lover. How lucky the guy didn't collect books! But he wouldn't have expected that from a mailman either.

For a while, Ondragon let the impression of the room sink in. Actually, he was very reluctant to do house searches. The reason was not only his fear of a possible encounter with the paper products he hated, it was also that he always felt like a burglar, even if he didn't steal anything. There was something humiliating about riffling through someone's private belongings. Nevertheless, Ondragon often had to bite the bullet. After all, the motto of his small company promised that they could solve any, absolutely *any* problem. So he had to live up to it. He also knew that, among many other talents, he had a special gift for spotting glitches in patterns, even the tiniest pixel out of place. In simple terms, this meant he could find the flaw in the image. Unfortunately, in the image he had in front of him at the moment, everything was in place. There was not one irregularity to be seen.

Ondragon went over to the TV, turned on the Blu-ray player, and opened the tray. He took out the disc and read the title. The latest *Star Trek* movie. With one hand, he took the Scotch tape out of his pocket, pressed a small strip of it to the disc, and slowly pulled it off. In the light of the diode lamp, the fingerprint was clearly visible. Ondragon needed it to compare with the prints on the letter later.

He put the disc back and moved on to the next room. A dining room with an open kitchen. The furniture looked cheap and run-down, the kitchen dingy. Apparently, Ellys invested most of his money in high-end gadgets. Ondragon made a mental note to be sure to look for the computer Tyler Ellys used to keep in touch with DeForce. First, however, he rummaged systematically through all the drawers and cabinets in the kitchen, tapping everything for hidden compartments. He found nothing, only breadcrumbs. He even felt the underside of the dining table and *bingo* . . . a 9mm Beretta-92FS semiautomatic. It had been held to the underside of the table with duct tape. *Bolič hadn't been very thorough with his search*, Ondragon thought, putting the gun in his jacket pocket.

Next, he did the same in the bedroom, hallway, bathroom, storeroom, and a study where there was a bare network cable sticking out of the socket, but no PC or laptop. Ellys or someone else had pulled it off the cable along with the router and taken it with them. Unfortunately, it was the same with the cell phone. No trace of it. Ellys had to have one, because he didn't have a landline. Perplexed, Ondragon looked up at the ceiling. Was there an attic in the building?

He went out into the hallway and found the hatch. Using the bar provided, he opened it, folded down the ladder, and climbed up into the dusty hideaway of forgotten things. The floorboards creaked softly under his soles as he searched through the boxes and plastic bags under the low ceiling. But here too he found nothing out of the ordinary. Dissatisfied, Ondragon climbed back down and stood in the hallway for a while, chewing on his lip.

Where did you hide it? he mused. Ellys was a mailman. And a mailman had a whole arsenal of guns and equipment that a cop would call illegal. But the police had found no weapons, not even the pistol under the table, and the floater hadn't said anything about a stash or a safe, which at least reflected well on Ellys, who had been conscientious when hiding his equipment. Because in the day-to-day lives of people who worked for DeForce Deliveries there should be no clue that their job was of a somewhat more "unusual" nature.

That only leaves the garage, Ondragon thought irritably. Might he leave here without having found out anything worth mentioning? Had he rummaged through someone else's garbage for nothing?

"Waste of time!" he grumbled in a muffled tone, checking the door that gave on to the garage from the hallway. It was fitted with as many brand-new security locks as the house and porch doors. What had an intrepid mailman like Ellys been so afraid of that had led him to barricade himself in like this? Ondragon opened one lock after another and peered into the dark garage, ready to draw his gun at any moment.

But everything seemed calm, and he slipped inside.

Tyler Ellys's dark blue pickup truck stood like a giant, silent, shiny beetle in the spacious extension. The Dodge was freshly washed and unlocked. Ondragon got in, checked the glove compartment, and behind the sun visors. *Nada.* He rummaged through the side compartments. Lots of junk, a lighter, a pocketknife, a heavy Maglite flashlight, nothing else.

Ondragon got out and leaned inside the car again, shining his lamp under the seats. Crumbs, sand, a dried-up piece of gum, Velcro.

Aha. At least Ellys had another weapon hidden here. Suddenly, a sound reached his ears and he paused. It had come from the garage's roll-up door. A soft scraping. Very soft. Nevertheless, he had heard it.

The sound came again. This time it was a few yards away, at another point on the door. A scraping, as if something was brushing fleetingly against the metal. Ondragon waited. But when no further sound came, he turned back to the vehicle. It was probably just a cat or a coyote that had strayed into the suburb to rummage through the garbage.

After checking the back seat of the pickup, the cargo box, and even the underbody, he straightened up and looked at the vehicle, his hands on his hips. It was damned clean too!

He looked around the garage. Tools hung neatly on the back wall; in the corner next to them stood gardening equipment that had certainly never seen any action—the clichéd epitome of an American garage. Ondragon's gaze slid over the workbench and the gas cans beneath it, and caught on a scrap of gum wrapper lying under the workbench. Suddenly, he felt a tingling in his fingertips; an unmistakable sign that something was wrong with this picture.

He went over to the workbench, squatted down, and looked at the silver paper.

It was stuck under the right front leg of the workbench. How could that be?

Ondragon pulled on it. It tore.

He straightened up and felt the wood of the table. His fingers found an indentation at the edge of the top and pressed it. There was a soft click, and the table swung forward weightlessly. Ondragon stepped aside and pointed the glow of his small lamp into the cavity that appeared in the wall behind the table.

So here was the hiding place. The garage had a double rear wall. Tricky.

Ondragon crawled into the opening. Behind it was a narrow room lined on both sides with steel shelves, just wide enough for a man to squeeze through. He looked at the shelves. They were filled with a multitude of numbered aluminum suitcases, wooden crates marked US ARMY that he suspected held weapons and ammunition,

and . . . Ondragon forgot to breathe and stared at the shelf . . .
books!

He suddenly broke out in a sweat and his scalp contracted as if an
ice-cold gust of wind were sweeping over him. He swallowed, feeling
his fingers dampen in his gloves.

Goddamn fucking books! Why can't I cope with this? he thought
irritably, trying to get his panicking metabolism under control. Involuntarily, he recalled his dead brother. Like a mirage, the image rose
before his mind's eye. Per Gustav Ondragon.

It had taken him thirty-one years to remember.

That had been last summer, at that creepy psycho clinic in Minnesota, where he had drifted into a really strange case, downright
mysterious, even. And since then, he hadn't been able to get his
deceased brother out of his mind. Per Gustav had become a silent
companion who always showed up when he was least welcome. Like
an admonishing archangel.

He had been under the treatment of Dr. Arthur back then; the
doctor had dragged his forgotten brother back from the decaying
depths of his subconscious into the light . . . and with him the ominous ghosts of a past Ondragon would rather have banished again,
sending them back to the depths where they had been resting.

He bit his lower lip until he tasted blood. The pain helped to clear
his mind. He forced himself to look at the books in the back corner
of the shelf and read the titles, puzzled: *Mein Kampf* in German and
in English translation, plus miscellaneous biographies of Nazi crimi-
nals and a myriad of White Power pamphlets. On the wall behind the
books, a swastika flag hung resplendent, with a runic crest beneath it.

Ondragon wondered if Roderick DeForce knew Tyler Ellys was
a closet neo-Nazi.

He took out his iPhone and photographed the spines of the
books, including the titles, and then turned to the aluminum cases.
Grabbing the handle of case number one, he pulled it from the shelf.
From the signs of wear and tear, Ondragon guessed this was Ellys's
first choice when he traveled for work. He snapped open the catches,
lifted the lid, and peered inside. A strangely misshapen form lay on
top of the black foam padding in the interior. Ondragon took it out

and turned it back and forth in his gloved fingers. A small sack of dirty linen, tied at the top with coarse black yarn that formed a large loop, as if the thing could be hung around your neck. Caught in the knot on the sack were black bird feathers and what Ondragon thought was a dried chicken foot. The brown stains on the cloth could therefore be blood. Ondragon held the thing up to his nose. An overpowering stink was emanating from it, dull and sweetish, like patchouli and decaying flesh. Disgusting. What did Ellys want with something like that? Was it an amulet? A fetish?

He tossed the souvenir back into the case and searched the rest of the contents, which were nothing special. The pistol-shaped recesses in the foam were empty. So was the ammunition compartment. Ellys must have taken both weapons with him.

Ondragon opened three more cases containing all kinds of well-maintained weapons: knives, grenades, handguns, and a sniper rifle, like the one he always kept in the Mustang—just in case.

He closed the cases, put the Beretta from the dining room on the shelf, and left the secret room. The workbench swung back across the opening when he pressed the button, unobtrusively preserving the illusion.

After going through the house several times, Ondragon glanced at the clock and declared the search at an end. At 2:20 am sharp, he made his way back to his rental car. As he turned on the ignition and drove out onto the street, he reconsidered. He had left no trace at Tyler Ellys's house, merely photographing any items of significance with his iPhone. Still, he had a feeling he hadn't done a clean enough job and had missed something. The inkling hovered behind him like an eerie shadow on the back seat. But when he turned around, it was empty.

Of course.

He drove back to the hotel via the highway and arrived in the lobby at 2:45 am. A crowd of young students, noisy and boisterous, was having a party there. Ondragon made his way through the alcoholic twenty-year-olds and slunk upstairs. He was unnoticed, at least.

The next morning, Ondragon entered the hotel restaurant just as the swing band in the lobby was taking a break. There was a brunch and so the restaurant was full. Good thing he had reserved a table. He took a seat with his back to the wall, facing the entrance. It was pure instinct; he always had to be able to see everything, especially the people who came into the room.

He ordered a triple espresso from the waitress and, instead of his usual Swedish-style porridge, muesli with yogurt and fresh fruit. While he ate, he looked at the photos from the search on his iPhone and let the *centrifuge* circle gently: This was how he referred to the thinking that mostly started up of its own accord in his head. If anyone was watching, they would think he was a businessman conducting his affairs via his smartphone. No one would guess he was a special person with a special job.

Aware of the uniqueness of his profession, Ondragon glanced up briefly at the people chatting at the next table. The early desert sun cast sharp shadows on their faces and warmed the right side of his body. He had to be on his guard all the time, and it was only rarely that he felt any longing for a normal life. To be like them, the ordinary people, chatting and enjoying a breakfast with friends, innocent and completely relaxed. Ondragon sipped the triple espresso. Luckily, today was not one of those days. Today he loved his job; after all, he had chosen it himself. Amused, he pursed his lips. What was he thinking, "chosen"? He had created it! There was not a job in the whole world that would have suited Paul Eckbert Ondragon. So he had invented one, he had invented *himself*. He couldn't even say what his official job title was: problem solver, spy for hire, professional assassin, consultant, private agent? He was probably a little bit of each.

He turned back to his iPhone screen. It showed the photo of the Nazi flag, and Ondragon wondered if Tyler Ellys's views might have something to do with his disappearance. He looked at his watch—it was now eight o'clock in the evening in Dubai—and dialed Roderick DeForce's number.

A friendly female voice told him that the subscriber was not available and referred to a voice mailbox. Ondragon hung up. He never left messages.

To review all the information again, he pulled his small notepad out of his pocket and leafed through it. He had transferred all the entries from Bolič's notepad into his own yesterday. The bumbling floater had put together very little. On this point Roderick had been right, his people were not trained for this. At least Bolič had taken the time to look through Ellys's papers. A note said he had found neither Ellys's passport nor his driver's license, nor any old airline tickets. Ondragon could confirm this: He had not been able to find any documents in the secret room in the garage either. He scrolled back to the list of Ellys's friends. There were only two names on it. Ondragon was not surprised, because mailmen were loners. Next to the names, Bolič had noted that they were colleagues from the DeForce unit Tyler Ellys belonged to, the Central and South America Crew.

Ondragon finished his espresso and went upstairs to his room. First he dialed Bolič's number. No answer. Next, he tried the first number from the friends list. It belonged to a certain Alejandro Green from Miami. He didn't answer either. Same with the second friend, Sylvester Stern, who lived in Chalmette, Louisiana, near New Orleans. Irked, Ondragon looked at his cell phone. Had he missed something? A strike by cellphone workers or something? Oh well, the two DeForce employees could be on a job just then and therefore unavailable. Ondragon tried Roderick again, the person who could have given him the best information, but unfortunately got the woman's voice again instead: *The person you have dialed . . .* Fuck! He threw the phone down on the bed. How was he supposed to do any work?

Once he had calmed himself down, he set to examining the letter again, though he didn't expect it to tell him much. He sat at the small table and pulled the ziplock bag out of his carry-on. Pulling on latex gloves to protect his hands, he opened the plastic bag, took out the crumpled letter, and held it up to the light. The paper was of the cheap variety from the supermarket and the words had been written with a conventional black felt-tip pen.

"Your body shall be like an empty bottle." Ondragon still had no clue what it could mean. He typed the phrase into Google on his iPhone, but got no useful result. Sighing, he fished a small aluminum case out of his travel bag and opened it. It contained his detective gear. He carefully applied a forensic film to both sides of the letter—the film was also great for "faking" fingerprints that could be used for digital scanners. The wafer-thin gelatin layer on the flexible surface captured the prints well, and all you then had to do was photograph them and feed them into a database. Unfortunately, he didn't have a database.

Ondragon examined the three isolated but incomplete fingerprints through the magnifying glass and compared them with the one from the Scotch tape. Then he leaned back. It was no use. He would have to ask his FBI friend to run them through his scanner in a quiet moment.

Although his motivation was decreasing, Ondragon next picked up the envelope. It bore no stamp and no addressee, and had merely been torn open along the top edge. Ondragon looked inside. Nothing. Or was there? He turned the envelope over and tapped the open side on the table. Some powder trickled out. Not much, just a few tiny grains. Ondragon bent and scrutinized the residue on the tabletop with a magnifying glass, his breath bated. Brownish, crystalline, mixed with amorphous globules.

Maybe it was a drug. Coke? Crystal meth? Suddenly, Ondragon remembered the Bosnian's flu symptoms and hastily stepped back from the envelope.

You blockhead!

Powder in envelopes! What was the first thing that usually came to mind? Anthrax, of course! But did *Bacillus anthracis* cause the kind of symptoms the floater had been displaying? Ondragon quickly shoved the remains back into the envelope and triple-sealed it in plastic bags. Only a lab examination would tell him what it really was. Drugs, anthrax, or simply dust.

He sat there a while, staring at the closed curtains. What the hell had he gotten himself into? And what had Tyler Ellys gotten himself into? Was he a member of a neo-Nazi terrorist cell planning an attack? But then why attack Ellys with the letter? Ondragon gave himself a shake. Hysteria was never a good counselor. He put his concern aside. Who could have sent Ellys an anthrax letter? And why? It was completely absurd. The letter had been in the trash, after all. The sand had likely gotten into the envelope there. Harmless desert sand. But he wanted to be on the safe side. He would send the powder to his crazy chemist in LA. If he sent it by express courier, it would be there tonight. But for now, he moved on to his next task: questioning the neighbors.

CHAPTER 4

Ondragon adjusted his aviator sunglasses and pressed the doorbell. A small sign next to it read DIEGO. Loud Mexican music from inside the house fell silent and the door opened. Standing before him was a stocky man in his mid-forties wearing track pants and a ribbed undershirt. *Lucky today is Saturday*, Ondragon thought, and asked, "Mr. Osvaldo Diego?"

"*Sí. ¿Quién es?*" Diego eyed him suspiciously. He was a little chubby, short black hair, a three-day beard, brown skin, and dark eyes. Not unlikeable. Ondragon held his fake ID under Diego's nose. "FBI, Special Agent Otter," he said briskly. "I'm here to ask you some questions about your neighbor, Mr. Tyler Ellys." In a slightly friendlier tone, he added, "Perhaps we can discuss this inside?"

Diego nodded distractedly and let Ondragon in. Immediately, two children came running up curiously to ask who the visitor was. "The man just wants to talk to me about Tío Tyler; why don't you go out into the garden and play? Come on, *en marcha!*"

Uncle Tyler? Ondragon raised an eyebrow.

"Would you like something to drink, Mr. Otter?" asked Diego after the children had disappeared through the back door.

"No, thank you, I'd rather get right to the point."

Diego nodded and invited his visitor to take a seat on the couch. Ondragon sat down, pulled out his notepad, and pursed his lips. Most people had only come across FBI agents on television. So obviously he too should behave like one of those TV G-men. CSI and all that nonsense, but people believed it, because hardly anyone ever had anything from real life to compare it with; and in this case the fake created more trust than the original would. Ondragon had even matched his disguise to the TV image. He was wearing black pants, a white shirt with a tie, and over it a dark windbreaker with FBI printed in big white letters on the back. On his head sat a baseball cap with the same lettering. Ironically, you could get all these items at the nearest mall. Except for the ID, of course.

"Mr. Diego," he began in a professional tone, "how long have you and Mr. Ellys been neighbors?"

"Since this neighborhood was built, for ten years now," Diego said frankly. He seemed cooperative.

"How's your relationship with Mr. Ellys? Functional or friendly? I noticed there's no fence between your properties."

"*Muy bien*, Señor Ellys is a very nice person. We got along very well. He was always friendly with the children too. He never minded them playing on his porch or in his garden. He likes Xavier and Maria very much and"—Mr. Diego smiled—"that's why they call him Tío Tyler."

Uncle Tyler . . . to some Latino kids! What kind of neo-Nazi was Ellys anyway? "Mr. Diego, do you know what Mr. Ellys does for a living?"

The chubby Mexican frowned very slightly. "He said he was in sales for a logistics company, like UPS or FedEx, and that he had to travel all around the world."

That was close to the mark.

"Sometimes he brings back something for the children. He's really very nice, Señor Ellys."

"Have you ever been to his house?"

"Yes. We often got together, for barbecues, when he had time."

"Did any of the other neighbors come?"

"No, just the kids and me. Sometimes a friend of Señor Ellys from the company. His name was Sly or Sylvester, I think."

"Where is your wife?" Ondragon had deliberately chosen this style of interrogation. Quick questions usually yielded quick answers and prevented the interviewee from suspecting he had an ulterior motive.

Diego lowered his eyes, distressed. "She died three years ago. Cancer."

"My condolences. Do you have any idea where Mr. Ellys might have gone? Without his car and without telling anyone?"

"No. I don't know."

"Did you notice anything strange about Mr. Ellys lately? Was he acting differently? Had he had any visitors or gotten any mail, anything that was troubling him? Did he mention anyone breaking into his house? Was Mr. Ellys feeling unwell? Had he had any arguments? Think, Mr. Diego, any kind of clue could be important."

"You know, Mr. Otter, I hadn't even noticed he was gone. I had thought he was just out of town again. It wasn't until the police showed up at my door that I realized something was wrong. Do you think something bad happened to Señor Ellys?" Diego crossed himself.

"That's what we're trying to figure out. Well? Did you notice anything?"

Diego pondered, chewing his lower lip. "Hmm, I don't know. Señor Ellys was away twice in the past two weeks. Where he went, I don't know; we didn't talk much, I had a lot of work, even on weekends. Today is my first day off, Mr. Otter."

"That's everything? Nothing else?"

"*Perdón*, I . . ."

"But, *papá*, Tío Tyler scolded us! Don't you remember?"

Diego turned around on the armchair toward his daughter, who had come in unnoticed. Maria bit her lower lip sheepishly and grinned. She was wearing the blue dress again, her bare legs sticking out from it like brown matchsticks. Around her neck dangled the homemade seed necklaces. Behind her, her little brother had put both hands on the screen door and was looking in at them.

"Ah, you're right, *corazoncita*. Come, Maria, say hello to Mr. Otter."

"*¡Buenas tardes!*" Maria bowed courteously, which elicited a grin from Ondragon.

"Why did Mr. Ellys scold you?" he asked the girl.

"Oh, Señor Ellys thought my children had smeared his car with paint," Diego replied instead of his daughter.

"And had you?" Ondragon asked Maria.

"No, it wasn't us. Word of honor. *¡Sinceramente!*"

"Then who was it? Did you or your brother see anyone?"

The girl shook her head shyly, but Ondragon could see that something was bothering her. He put on a friendly face and asked, "What was smeared on Mr. Ellys's car?"

"Kind of a pattern. Squiggles and crosses with white paint. On the doors."

"A pattern? Could it have been one of the neighbor children?"

Maria shrugged her shoulders.

"Did you notice anything else? You play outside a lot, don't you?"

The girl nodded. "All I know is that Tío Tyler was out of town, then he was back, then he was gone. Then there was the dead bird on his porch and after that he was sick."

"Sick?" asked Diego and Ondragon at the same time.

"Yeah, Xavier and I were playing on his porch and that's when he came out of the house and told us to go back home because he was sick and he didn't want us to catch it."

The anthrax letter! Ondragon thought. Spontaneously, his fingers began to sweat. "What did Mr. Ellys look like? Was he pale, did he have a cough?"

Maria nodded at both questions.

"When was this?"

The girl looked up at the ceiling, thinking. "Monday."

Roderick DeForce had called Ondragon on Thursday. At that point he'd had no contact from Ellys for two days. If the girl had been with him on Monday, she might be the last person to have seen him.

"And what about the dead bird? What kind was it?"

Another childish shrug of the shoulders. "A black one, maybe a crow. Tío Tyler threw it in the trash."

"And when was that?"

"Sunday."

Then the strange letter had arrived before that, Ondragon thought; at least, the floater had told him he had found it *under* the bird. "Have you noticed anything else, Maria?"

"No, señor."

"Can you describe to me again the pattern on Mr. Ellys's car?"

"Yes, it was squiggles and crosses. Come with me, I'll show you."

Ondragon looked at the girl in amazement, and Maria laughed. "It's on Tío Tyler's porch too!"

They hurried out into the garden together and over to Ellys's porch. As they stood in front of it, Ondragon saw in the light somewhat smudged squiggles and lines. They had been applied to the floorboards in white, glittering paint, probably with a finger. He had not seen them the night before because he had not turned on the outdoor light. The pattern was about one pace long and was right in front of the door. In the center was an equal-armed cross, the ends of which split into squiggles and smaller crosses; around these were naive skulls and the coffin-shaped objects again. Below it was written the word *SAMEDI*.

"Can you write?" asked Ondragon to the girl, who shook her head. "I guess that would also prove that your daughter did not do this, Mr. Diego." The Mexican nodded in agreement. Little Xavier, clutching his father's leg, looked up curiously at Ondragon. "How long has this pattern been here?"

"Since the bird. It was there." Mary pointed to the center of the large cross.

"Have you ever seen anything like this before?" Ondragon turned to Diego again.

"No, I didn't even know the scribbles were here too. I had only seen the ones on Señor Ellys's car. But it looked just like that."

"What could that mean?"

"It's not Mexican. Maybe Candomblé?"

Ondragon nodded and photographed the pattern. Candomblé, he recalled darkly, was a Brazilian religion that combined African and Christian elements, much like Santería in Cuba or Voodoo in Haiti. But what did that have to do with Tyler Ellys, a White neo-Nazi?

Ondragon urgently needed to speak with Roderick DeForce. He put his phone away and looked at Diego. "Thank you so much for taking the time to answer my questions."

"*No problemo*. I hope Señor Ellys shows up again soon." Diego sounded genuinely concerned.

"We hope so too. Have a nice day." Ondragon went with him out of the house. He waved goodbye to the two young children and walked over to his car, which he had parked on the street this time.

On the way back to the hotel, he took off his baseball cap and jacket and thought about the conversation with the Diego family. One thought worried him the most: Tyler Ellys had been sick too! He fished the cell phone out of his back pocket and dialed Bolič's number. It went to voicemail. Ondragon hung up, cursing. Where was the guy? Why couldn't he answer his fucking cell phone?

When neither Tyler Ellys's two friends nor Rod picked up, he thumped the steering wheel in anger. He had had enough. This case was like a stubborn donkey that he had to drag forward step by step. He had found out nothing so far. Not the faintest trace. There was no hint of where the damned mailman could have gotten to.

At the hotel, Ondragon parked in the underground parking lot and went for lunch in the restaurant. The excellent food calmed his mind, which had been spinning wildly. He had also googled *anthrax* and found that the pathogen was very rare and extremely difficult to obtain unless you knew a chemist in a US military lab. So, no need for hysteria. Besides, the letter was already on its way to his chemist. He would know by tonight, and then there would still be plenty of time to pop some antibiotics. He ordered himself an espresso for dessert, and an idea occurred to him. He knew someone who might be able to help with the pattern. A very learned man he had met a few years ago on a job in Africa.

He dialed the number, wondering if the professor would be in.

"Ludewig."

"Good evening, Günther!" said Ondragon delightedly, in his best German. He was half-Swedish and half-German and spoke both languages fluently. He also enjoyed the game of communication, and depending on the role he was adopting, he spiced his words with the appropriate accent. For Günther Ludewig, he played a German management consultant.

"Paul. Well, this is a surprise. Where are you right now?"

"In the States."

"Too bad, I thought you might be paying me a visit in Hamburg."

Ondragon thought he really should do that sometime. "I'm afraid not, Günther. I'm calling because I need your advice as an expert."

"Well, well, as an expert. What about?"

"I'm sending you a photo on your phone. Take a look at it and tell me what you think."

"You're making things exciting again, Paul. All right, send me the picture and I'll get back to you." Ludewig hung up, and Ondragon sent him the MMS.

He had to wait for the answer and used the opportunity to think about his friend in Germany. Prof. Dr. Günther Ludewig was kind of his Phone a Friend. He had called him on countless occasions when he needed scientific advice, and so they had always remained in close contact over the years. The sixty-seven-year-old anthropologist and explorer still worked at the University of Hamburg and simply knew everything. In his adventurous life, he had taken part in a multitude of expeditions on all seven continents and had amassed such a phenomenal wealth of experience that he made the Encyclopedia Britannica look like a picture book. To Ondragon, his friend's brain seemed like a terabyte of hard drive, full of information and with capacity for more. Ludewig was a gifted scientist and lived for his research. He was happy to share his knowledge with others. And—even more importantly—he never asked questions.

After ten minutes, however, Ondragon became impatient. What was taking Ludewig so long? He finished his coffee edgily. This case was a pain in the butt!

A pain in the butt!

A pain in the butt!

I should take up yoga or something again to improve my patience, he thought.

Suddenly, the phone rang and he picked up.

"Sorry it took so long, Paul. But I called a colleague in Atlanta who knows more about this particular area than I do."

"And what area is that?"

"Voodoo. Or, rather, Vodou, as it is practiced in Haiti."

Voodoo, Ondragon thought. What the hell did Tyler Ellys have to do with this kind of nightmare?

"The pattern in the photo is a vèvè. A ritual drawing that represents a particular loa. Loas are Voodoo deities with a wide variety of personalities that you invoke depending on their characteristics and let them possess you or ride you, to fill you with their life force. That then becomes a trance. This drawing represents the vèvè of Baron Samedi. As you'll see, the name is written in capitals under it. My colleague explained to me that Samedi is the Lord of the Dead. He walks abroad in graveyards and is a feared gèdè loa, a kind of devil or evil spirit."

"And what does it all mean?"

"Well, it can have many meanings. I don't know the context, unfortunately. The only certainty is that black magic is involved. Only a dark sorcerer would use the vèvè of Baron Samedi."

"Black magic?"

"Yes, the followers of the Voodoo cult differentiate between black and white magic. Black magic, of course, is used to bring evil on people or to influence them. So a love charm could also be categorized as black magic, because the result is usually less pleasant for the bewitched person; after all, they are deprived of their free will."

"And there are people in this day and age who seriously believe in this kind of thing?"

"In Haiti, yes. And also in other countries in South America and Africa, because parts of the religion originated on that continent. It came over with African slaves who were brought to the plantations run by White overlords. Even in industrialized nations, in the USA and in Europe, there are people who practice Voodoo. It is a spirit religion, and is in vogue among people who are weary of civilization and inclined toward the esoteric. The practices with Voodoo dolls are particularly popular, although they have precious little to do with actual Voodoo beliefs." Ludewig laughed softly. He didn't seem to think much of such hocus-pocus either. But the mystery remained of how the Voodoo signs had gotten onto a porch in Tucson, Arizona.

"You are silent, my dear Paul. That is rare." Ludewig laughed again.

"I'm as puzzled as ever." Ondragon was irked by this, but kept it to himself.

"I'm very sorry. But perhaps I can offer you a little more help. My colleague from Atlanta gave me the name of a specialist in New Orleans, and I'm sure she can tell you more about the vèvè."

"New Orleans, of course!" sighed Ondragon. He didn't like the way the Tyler Ellys case was going at all. Voodoo magic. Black magic. Such nonsense.

"You'll find the lady at her store, Captain Zombie, on Bourbon Street. Ask for Madame Tombeau. Apparently, she's an experienced mambo—an initiated Voodoo priestess. She knows all about black and white magic."

"The Witch Queen of New Orleans," Ondragon sang sarcastically. How often had this myth been sung about? It couldn't be any more cliché!

"I'm serious, Paul, she was recommended to me by a reputable colleague. Why don't you give it a try first, then you can judge."

"You're right. After all, I wouldn't want anyone to accuse me of not having tried everything. So why not Voodoo?"

Günther Ludewig sighed. "I'd better give you the number of my colleague in Atlanta. I've already warned him you'll be calling him at some point."

"I probably won't," laughed Ondragon. "The Witch Queen is enough for me. But thanks for your help, Günther. I'll be in touch."

"When you're Hamburg, maybe?"

"Quite possibly. See you then." Ondragon hung up. His expression darkened. Magic, spells, monsters. Such nonsense. But somehow these ghost stories seemed to haunt him. Just last summer in the clinic in Minnesota, he had been on the verge of being mauled by an Indian forest monster that existed only in Ojibwe legends. The Wendigo. For a legend, the beast had been damn real. Today, however, he was no longer sure he had not merely imagined the whole thing. In his wretched mental state back then, he could have imagined the whole *Dance of the Vampires* business and thought it was real. Ondragon rubbed his eyes, but quickly opened them again because the image of his brother had appeared in his mind's eye. Son of a bitch! Voodoo. Of all things!

Back in his room, Ondragon dialed his assistant, who was holding down the fort in LA.

"Yes, boss?"

"Charlize, be a doll and book me a hotel in New Orleans on Bourbon Street. Somewhere nice, huh? Arriving the day after tomorrow—two nights for now, plus parking. I'll take the car and stop at a motel on the way."

"*Hai, Paul-san,* I'll do it right away. So how's it going?" Ondragon loved her Japanese-Brazilian accent.

"Hmm, not especially well." He was always honest with Charlize, because he knew he could rely on her. Not least because she had rescued him from so many dicey situations. "Is there anything else, Charlize?"

"No, everything's quiet. Dietmar is in Iraq and Achille's in Algeria. The jobs are going to plan. *Good,* thought Ondragon. He was glad to have outstanding people like Dietmar Hegenbarth and Achille "the French secret weapon" Mercier working for Ondragon Consulting. These were two of his four employees—not counting the freelancers. "Well then, I'll head out to search for flying pigs again."

Charlize giggled. "Good luck with that, Chief."

Good luck! Ondragon hung up. How many times had he heard that in the last few days? He looked at the clock. No way, it was the middle of the night in Dubai. And the matter wasn't urgent enough for him to get Rod out of bed. So he tried Bolič. Nothing.

That's enough! I'm going over there!

Ondragon ripped open his travel bag and donned his businessman's disguise: elegant suit, tie, briefcase, Ray-Bans.

Twenty minutes later, he arrived at the Arizona Hotel on foot. He avoided the surveillance cameras by keeping his head down and pretending to be busy with his smartphone. Up on the fifth floor, he knocked at room 506, but there was no sign of life. "Hey, Bolič, open up. It's Mr. O!" he called mutedly at the door. "Damn it, man, open the door!" But the room remained silent.

Ondragon took out his lock pick set and opened the lock. Fortunately, the security chain was not on. He was greeted by a musty, sour rush of air. Entering quickly, he closed the door behind him. Turning around, he saw Bolič. He was lying on the bed under the covers, asleep.

"Hey, Bolič! Wake up. You can sleep later. I have something important to discuss with you!"

Bolič did not move. Ondragon went over to the bed and shook the floater's shoulder. But Bolič's eyes remained closed. Ondragon frowned and put a finger on the Bosnian's muscular neck. No pulse. He lifted one eyelid, but the brown eye just stared back at him expressionless, the pupils unreactive. There was no doubt about it, the floater was dead!

Ondragon pulled back the blanket and looked at Bolič, who lay curled up like an embryo. He was wearing only boxer shorts. His pale skin was reddened in places, but otherwise showed no signs of violence. Bolič's face was also ashen and he wore a strangely relaxed expression. In a fit of sudden realization, Ondragon stepped back from the bed, slapping his tie over his mouth and nose for protection.

Panic seized him. Had Bolič died of anthrax? He himself had touched the letter. Shit! He looked around frantically. He had to get out of here! But first he would be wise to eliminate all traces that could lead to him. He located the Bosnian's cell phone and gun and pocketed both. In the process, he found a laptop in its case and took that as well. All links to DeForce also had to be eradicated, he owed Roderick that. Once Ondragon had rummaged through everything, he opened the door to the hallway, peered out, and fled at a moderate pace out of the hotel onto the street, where he took a deep breath.

Fresh, germ-free air at last!

He looked up at the bright blue desert sky above the city. To calm himself, he counted to ten in Japanese, as he did during his martial arts sessions: *ichi, ni, san, shi, go, roku, shichi, hachi, kyuu . . . jyuu . . .*

Take it easy, Paul. There's no proof of anything yet. You'll know more tonight. So pull yourself together. He started moving and made his way inconspicuously back to the hotel. Bolič's death would not be discovered until tomorrow morning, when room service arrived. He had plenty of time to get out of Tucson before that.

After taking a long, hot shower, he sat down on the bed and dialed Rod's number. No matter what time it was in Dubai, it was now important enough!

"*The person you want . . .*" Ondragon clenched his cell phone so hard his hand hurt. Why wasn't anyone answering their fucking phone? How was he supposed to tell Rod his floater was dead in the hotel and that he himself might also have inhaled the anthrax powder?

"Man, calm down, you're acting like a rookie," he said to himself quietly. "Rod can't help you from Dubai. You'll have to help yourself." With difficulty, he loosened his grip on the cell phone and sent Rod a text message with the old DeForce code word *carwash*, which meant get in touch with the sender immediately. Then he set his iPhone aside and noticed how shaky his hands were. Was that his imagination or the first symptoms of the pathogen? He clenched his hands into fists again. The first thing he had to do was get out of there.

He quickly packed up his things and checked out downstairs at reception. He took the car to the rental office and a cab back to the hotel, where he retrieved his Mustang from the underground parking garage. At just after three o'clock in the afternoon, he left Tucson in the rearview mirror and steered his car east onto Interstate 10, heading deeper and deeper into the desert. Fourteen hundred miles lay ahead of him.

CHAPTER 5

February 7, 2010
Kerrville, Texas
the middle of the night

Dead tired, Ondragon fell onto the bed in the motel room he had rented. He had been driving for nine hours, which was a pretty good time for the distance he had covered—thanks to speed limit violations and the luck that no sheriff had crossed his path. But his matte-black Mustang was also almost as invisible as a bat in the dark.

After one last look at his phone, he closed his eyes in exhaustion. Still no word from Roderick or Charlize. But what worried him most was that his chemist, Fresenius, had not yet gotten back to him. The twenty-four-year-old doctoral student in chemistry had confirmed the arrival of the sample at seven that evening, but he had also disclosed that the device for carrying out a rapid anthrax test was not located in his lab. He would have to go to the university for it, and even there it wouldn't be easy to get to it. "Dr. Strangelove," as he styled himself, was a highly gifted research prodigy, and spent all his savings on a private laboratory that filled almost his entire apartment. Most nights, he tinkered with his projects there, on the trail of new breakthroughs and discoveries. But Strangelove wasn't just a brainiac, he also had that crazy something that could make him a truly brilliant scientist. Ondragon was sure that one day the young man would make a breakthrough. Unfortunately, Strangelove was permanently broke. He had a scholarship, but ran up enormous expenses for his private research. So Ondragon kept hiring him for small jobs and paying him well. This assured him not only of excellent results, but also of the discretion of the young Fresenius. In this sensitive matter too, though the young chemist sounded audibly agitated on his cell phone. "I'll do my best, Mr. Ondragon. I'll go to UCLA right away and feed your sample into the Bioflash. You'll get your results, I promise you!" Those had been Strangelove's last words, and Ondragon wished the damn phone would ring already.

He opened his eyes again. He just couldn't sleep, not with this uncertainty. The day after tomorrow, he might be dead! Just like Bolič . . . and Ellys.

But Ondragon wouldn't have been Ondragon if he hadn't long since begun to pull on other levers. On the way here, he had made several phone calls to Charlize, instructing her to go to Tucson to be on the scene when Bolič was found. His body would almost certainly be autopsied and that might produce a usable result. Ondragon had tasked Charlize with monitoring the police radio and staying as close to Bolič as possible. Of course, she had been horrified to learn about the anthrax. But Ondragon had stone-walled her pleas that he should go to the hospital immediately. If he had done that, he might as well have put an announcement in the paper detailing who he was and what his mostly illegal business consisted of. No, he had to remain the great unknown in the book of world history. An anthrax case and the press hype that came with it could destroy his life's work.

"It could be your death too!" Charlize had berated him, and secretly he agreed with her, but there was no other way. After that, she had promised she would leave immediately, and Ondragon trusted her to get the information he needed sooner or later. Charlize could . . . well, be very convincing. But unfortunately, he also had to wait for her to deliver results.

A glance at the clock told him it was still six hours until sunrise. Goddamn it! Ondragon rose. He was still fully dressed. He had to do something to distract himself. Swaying slightly, he left the room, crossed the deserted lobby, and headed for his car. Where was the nearest 24-hour liquor store?

Ondragon awoke in his car in a supermarket parking lot. He was sitting at the wheel, a half-empty whiskey bottle and a tube of aspirin between his legs. The sun was shining brightly through the dusty windshield, causing stabbing pains in his retinas.

He looked at the clock. Half past ten.

"Well, I could have saved myself the cost of the motel room," he muttered, coughing and rubbing his stiff neck. Finding his sunglasses and rinsing the bad taste from his mouth with a sip of water, he started the engine and drove back to the motel.

There, he freshened himself up as far as he could, checking his cell phone every five minutes.

Get back to me, Strangelove! Or Rod! One of you, at least!

Frustrated, he packed his travel bag, left the room, and went to the breakfast room for a coffee, whose awful taste alone was enough to wake him up.

A short time later, he was in his car, heading down Interstate 10. He wouldn't be able to speed in daylight like he had last night, so he turned on the cruise control and rocked through Texas at an enervating 75 miles per hour. As the landscape flattened and became greener on either side of the highway, he kept glancing at his phone, but there were still no messages from Strangelove, Charlize, or Rod. Ondragon stared at the shimmering two lanes ahead of him. Except for the hangover, he was actually feeling pretty good. Even the trembling in his hands was gone. But maybe it was just the painkillers suppressing the symptoms. He had to know what had been in that letter!

Shortly after passing Houston and treating himself to a decent coffee and two bagels at Starbucks, his cell phone rang while he was driving. Hastily, he reached for it, but it slid off the passenger seat into the footwell. Cursing, he fumbled for it as trucks thundered past on his left. He got hold of it just as the ringing stopped. He pressed recall.

"*Hai*, Chief?" his assistant's voice announced. "Are you all right?"

"It depends," Ondragon growled. "What's up?"

"So, I took up my post at the Arizona Hotel last night at seven, room 510. Since then, I've pretty much been sitting down here in the lobby or marching up and down the hall outside Bolič's room, but so far nothing has happened!"

"Has housekeeping been around yet?"

"No, they're not exactly quick off the mark here; my room hasn't been done yet either. So I'll have to wait. Or I can give the police an anonymous tip, and things'll move faster."

Ondragon checked the time and saw it was two in the afternoon. "I'd rather not, Charlize. Wait till housekeeping gets there. A tip is too much of a smoking gun, plus it might throw the cops off the scent."

"All right, Chief. Has Strangelove reported in yet?"

"Unfortunately, no."

"*Kuso!* Oh, *gomen nasai*, Chief, I'm sorry about that. But if I get my hands on the guy who's messing around with this dangerous stuff, I'll cut off his thumbs and make him eat them as sushi." She cursed again in Japanese and Ondragon had to grin. Charlize was truly adorable, and at that moment he would have liked to take her in his arms and kiss her. He listened patiently as she made another attempt to convince him that it would be better to consult a doctor after all, and sensed that she was afraid. For him. This was really (and he meant *really* really) touching. No one had been worried about him for a very long time. Nevertheless, he could not respond to it, much as he would have liked to do what she said.

"I've explained why I can't, Charlize. Don't worry, I won't die." Ondragon wasn't sure he believed his own words; he was scared shitless. But he didn't want his assistant to keep freaking out over him. "Focus on Bolič, and call me the minute you find out anything new. In a few hours I'll be in New Orleans—The Big Easy. I can have a little fun there and distract myself."

The silence on the other end made him suspect she still had something on her mind. "Ask me, Charlize!"

"So . . . um, aren't you contagious? Shouldn't you be staying away from other people? I mean, if you're infected."

"I did the research. Anthrax isn't contagious, at least you can't pass it from person to person. Does that reassure you?"

"*Hai, Paul-san.* You'll let me know when you get the results from Strangelove? After all, I want to keep working for you for a while yet, Chief!" Charlize laughed, but Ondragon could hear the strain in her voice. He said goodbye and then went on staring at the road . . .

thinking with every minute that passed, of course, about the results of the biosensor test.

While he was taking a break a few miles out of Baton Rouge to buy water and pop more pills for his headache, his cell phone rang again. The sun was blazing down, and Ondragon moved to the sheltering shade of a tree. There he answered the call. "Yes?"

"Alejandro Green here."

"Hello, Mr. Green, good of you to call back. I'm sure you got the message from Spider that I need to talk to you urgently."

"Yes. Is this about Ty?"

"In a way." Ondragon glanced across the parking lot to the gas station, wondering how to phrase the story without giving too much away. "Do you know if anyone might be targeting your colleague Ellys?"

"Targeting? Ty? Is he dead?" Green sounded neutral. Ondragon blamed it on the tough-as-nails work environment; after all, as a mailman, you got unpleasant surprises all the time. And dealing with them was one of the many survival strategies you had to adopt at DeForce.

"We don't know, there's still no sign of him," he answered truthfully.

"I have no idea if Ty had any enemies, Mr. O. Sure, he hung around with dodgy types sometimes, but—"

"With people from the White Power movement?"

"Exactly, with them, but he never brought anything like that into any jobs. I don't know why Ty gets together with those Nazi nutcases. After all, he isn't that extreme himself. Ty has always been cool and reliable, you know. He's a comrade and a friend you can count on, even when the going gets tough. You already know what I'm talking about." Green paused, then said abruptly: "Spider tells me you're the legendary Mr. O."

Ondragon rolled his eyes and wished Rod had kept quiet. He ignored the undisguised admiration in Green's voice and asked him about Tyler Ellys's most recent assignments.

"Spider said you have his absolute trust. I will help you, Mr. O; after all, I want to know what happened to Ty as well." Ondragon heard the sound of typing in the background, then Green continued. "On the fourth of January we were in Colombia for three days; on the sixteenth of January, right after the big earthquake, we were in Haiti, and then in Mexico, transporting bodies. You know the drill."

"What was the job in Haiti?" *This fits with the Voodoo hocus-pocus,* Ondragon thought.

"It came in right after the earthquake, on January 12. CSAC got the instructions . . ."

"CSAC?" interrupted Ondragon.

"The Central and South America Crew."

"And that consists of how many people?"

"Tyler Ellys, Sylvester Stern, and me."

"Okay."

"We were instructed to go to an underground research facility that had been destroyed in the quake. After the severe earth tremors, there had been no radio contact with the lab's staff, so it was assumed they had died. Our task was to check whether this was actually the case and how much of the laboratory had been destroyed. If it was still accessible, we were to blow up the shaft and seal it permanently. That was all."

"And what about the lab staff? Were they really all dead?" asked Ondragon.

"We found four bodies on the surface and no sign of any other survivors, and then, per our instructions, we blew up the entrance to the shaft where the facility was located. It won't be easy to get in there now."

"There might have been survivors in the shaft." Ondragon watched a Chrysler station wagon pulling in next to the Mustang. A family with two children got out.

"That wasn't part of the assignment," Green replied icily.

"And you didn't transport anything either?"

"What do you mean?"

"Well, DeForce Deliveries, as the name implies, as far as I know, specializes in transportation, but not demolition squads. Didn't that strike you as odd?"

"No, not at all. We delivered the bomb."

"I see. Could one of your colleagues have had a special assignment? Tyler Ellys, perhaps? Was he transporting something . . . out of Haiti?"

"I would have known about it because I got the plan of action from Spider. It didn't say anything about transportation. Our job was just to do the blasting. Besides, Ty was always near me."

"Then you are the Head?"

"Yes, I'm in command of the operations. Ty is the Neck, Sly is the Body."

"It's okay, I just wanted to make sure." Ondragon soothed the now slightly irritated-sounding mailman and changed the subject. "What kind of lab do you think it was? Was it legal? If you ask me, your account sounds suspiciously like drugs or forbidden experiments." Ondragon thought of the anthrax. "Maybe bioweapons?"

"I don't know, Mr. O. I don't care. My comrades and I did our job, and we did it well. But if it makes you feel any better, it looked like any other lab to me. Besides, we were assured beforehand that there was no *biohazard.*"

Green was already a little naive. Truth was a rare commodity, especially in these circles! Ondragon knew the next question was pointless but tried it anyway. "Who was the client?"

"Mr. O, I don't think I have to explain the DeForce rules to you. After all, you were a mailman yourself; you know we merely act on behalf of the client. Only Spider knows the principal." Green was right; that was standard practice at DeForce. That way, no one could spill the beans. He asked Green how CSAC had gotten into Haiti and whether the operation had gone undetected.

"It was all very smooth. We landed by speedboat and went straight into the mountains. It went very quickly: in, blast, and out again. Two days later we were already back home. The earthquake did a great job on the island, I can tell you. All the villages around the mountains where the underground laboratory was located were completely destroyed. Nothing but rubble and debris. There was total chaos there, which was ideal for us because we like operating in chaos. It's our best friend. But the people there are really screwed!"

As if that would bother a mailman!

"And what about your colleague Stern? Why isn't he getting back to me?" Ondragon wanted to know.

"Maybe he's just wasting his money on the broads again. He likes to do that; it's his way of enjoying life. I spoke to him on the phone last night. He didn't say anything about you. Maybe he didn't recognize your number and that's why he didn't pick up." Green paused. "The next time I speak to him, I'll tell him to call you, Mr. O. But I can tell you right now, Sly won't have a clue where Ty might be either."

Ondragon felt a hunch rising inside him. There was another reason why Stern might not be responding. What if he and Ellys had long since shared the same fate and were lying in a ditch somewhere, dead as doornails?

"I'll give you a piece of advice, Mr. Green," he finally said to the mailman, "leave your mail unopened until you get the green light from me! And as a precaution, put all letters in airtight bags."

"Why?"

"Because *I'm* telling you to!" replied Ondragon brusquely. He had no desire to argue with the guy.

Green cleared his throat. "Of course, Mr. O, I understand."

The surprising subservience of the DeForce mailman pleased Ondragon and he permitted himself a smirk. At least there was one good thing about being a legend. Your reputation preceded you and you were shown the appropriate respect!

"One more thing, do you still use the codeword *carwash*?"

Green seemed unsettled; he didn't answer right away. Only after some hesitation did he say, "No, it's changed several times now. It's *Coca-Cola* at present."

Maybe that's why Rod isn't responding, Ondragon thought, a little annoyed his friend and client had obviously neglected to tell him the new code. He said goodbye to Green and immediately dialed his friend's number in Dubai. He needed more specific information about the Haiti job.

When the woman's voice came on again, Ondragon let out a loud curse and kicked a trash can, startling the family eating hot dogs next to his car. He stomped angrily back to the Mustang and got in. He needed the air conditioner! The heat out here just irritated him all the more. He started the engine and was backing out of the parking spot when his cell phone beeped. Another frantic grab for the phone. It was a text message! Strangelove!

Going to have to wait! Can't put sample in the Bioflash till this evening.
Sry, that's the best I can do. ☹

Ondragon suppressed the impulse to hurl the iPhone out the window. Instead, he slammed his fist against the dashboard a few times. Then he pressed his foot down on the gas pedal and, tires screeching, drove out of the gas station parking lot.

He'd scarcely driven a mile when his cell phone rang again. First no one answered for hours and then they all rang at once!

"Charlize, any news?" he asked, more irritably than he'd intended.

As usual, his assistant didn't let his moods bother her—or at least she didn't let on. "You bet, Chief!" she said meaningfully. "House-keeping's been in, but they didn't raise the alarm."

"But they must have found Bolič's body!"

"They didn't."

"How so? The guy is dead and happily stinking away! How can you not notice something like that?" Ondragon couldn't believe it.

"I can tell you why!" Charlize paused. "Because there's no body in that room!"

CHAPTER 6

February 7, 2010
the village of Nan Margot, South Haiti
3:25 pm

Christine Dadou stood by the grave, staring at the whitewashed wooden cross, on which was written, *Ici repose Frédéric Dadou* and below it, *05/20/2002–01/12/2010.*

The cemetery, which was shared by the three villages in the area, was located on the northern edge of Nan Margot, where the dusty slope began to climb toward the mountains. It had doubled in size in recent weeks. Christine looked up from the many fresh crosses to the sky, where a few white clouds were drifting. A light breeze was making the tops of the few surrounding trees whisper, and the air smelled unusually light and clean. For the first time since the terrible accident, Christine felt she could breathe properly again. But this was not due to the friendly weather; it was rather that now all the bodies had been recovered from the ruins of the village and buried . . . and the sea breeze was finally dispelling the omnipresent stench of decay.

Christine's thoughts went back, as they always did, to the day when the earth had opened up as if to swallow all humankind. At least that's how the priests had always described it when celebrating the Mass: God would one day wash the earth clean of all sin.

Christine was glad that God had spared her. But what had her brother done to Him that meant he had to die? She still blamed herself terribly because she had been alone on the way home that day—without her brother. Although there was not much she could have done about it, since the teacher had only allowed her to leave early because she had felt unwell.

Frédéric had been forced to stay at school and had been in a mathematics class when it happened. He and his twenty-one classmates had been killed by the collapsing concrete ceiling of the classroom, as had most of Christine's classmates in the next room. It had been a week before they had finally found Frédéric under the mountains of rubble. His small body had shown barely any injury under the white layer of dust covering his dark skin. Her brother looked as if he were asleep. If it hadn't been for his crushed skull. A chunk of concrete had hit him in the back of the head and pushed the bones into his brain.

Christine remembered the sight of the crater of the wound and the dried blood in it, mixed with the dirt and the yellowish mass that had leaked from Frédéric's head. She had cried a lot since then, had mourned her brother and the fate of the people from her village, but now her tears had dried up. On other days, her eyes had always welled up when she read Frédéric's name on the cross, but for some time now she no longer had the strength for that. She saw so much suffering every day, and in the course of that the healing source of her grief had simply dried up without her really noticing. Her feelings were numb, but she could do nothing about it. She worked every day with her mother to rebuild their hut and to conserve what little they had left.

Silently, Christine thanked the Good Lord and Bondieu, the chief of all the loas, that at least she still had her mother and had not become an orphan. She had heard about the many thousands of children who had lost their parents in the terrible catastrophe and were now wandering helplessly through the streets of the destroyed cities. For Christine, that would be a nightmare. But fortunately, her mother was still there.

Cécile Dadou had told her daughter she had been gathering wood in the forest when the ground beneath her feet had turned to surging earthen waves, sweeping her off her feet. The trees around her had also started to sway, flapping their branches at her like drunken giants. She had crouched, frightened, as some of the trees had been uprooted and fallen to the ground with a loud crash. Miraculously, Christine's mother had escaped without a scratch and once the trembling in the ground had died away and the giant trees had become calmer, she had hurried to her hut. She had stared at the rubble, stunned, her thoughts as paralyzed as her body. Then suddenly she had heard a sound from the debris—a shout. She had realized with horror that it was her daughter calling for help. Instantly, she had begun to clear away the debris with her bare hands, and after digging for an agonizingly long time, she had finally reached Christine. Tears of joy in her eyes, she had pulled her daughter from a gap in the wreckage. The girl had been shocked but otherwise unharmed, having been protected by the bed under which she had taken cover.

Christine had been overjoyed to finally escape the cramped space of the hiding place that had saved her. She had cried and hugged her mother. Neither of them yet realized what had happened, so they had crouched for a long time in the dust in front of the ruins of what had been their home, clinging to each other.

Christine's feverishly racing mind had been fixed on one thought, however, as they sat there. Had her father, who was now a zombie and had been chasing her, also been buried under the rubble? Was he truly dead now?

Only reluctantly did she now think back to her father's gruesomely contorted face, his jaw hanging down and the blood staining his ragged shirt.

She had not dared to tell her mother about the zombie who had once been her father until two days after the quake. She had not been afraid that Cécile would disbelieve her or even laugh at her; no, her horror went too deep for that. Her mother had not laughed. She was a deeply devout woman and knew that her daughter had not merely invented the gruesome story. It was clear to her that her husband, Etienne Dadou, had been turned into a zombie by a bokor.

A shiver ran through Christine's body at the thought, settling on her arms like a second skin. She reached for the new gris-gris around her neck, looked again at the cross over her brother's grave, and wished there was another next to it . . . with the name Etienne Dadou written on it.

Hearing Christine's report, Cécile Dadou had immediately fetched the village mambo, who was very busy in the aftermath of the earthquake, because there were corpses everywhere, and they needed to be given a proper burial. After all, no one wanted any of their loved ones to return as the undead.

Christine's brother too had been laid to rest according to traditional custom. The liberation of his *ti bon ange*, his soul spirit, had taken several days and had cost her mother the last of her savings. First, Frédéric had been stripped and washed with an aromatic essence whose composition was known only to the mambo and which was supposed to ensure the body could not be used by a black magician. Then the priestess had plugged his nostrils and ears with absorbent cotton and fixed his mouth with a chin bandage so that he would not be able to hear any sorcerers' incantations and respond from the grave.

Christine had watched attentively as the mambo moved around, all the while speaking softly with the dead boy as if he were merely asleep. Like all those present, she had emptied her pockets before the ceremony and turned them inside out to prevent the dead boy from taking anything of hers with him to the underworld and thus gain power over her. Nevertheless, Christine was afraid that her brother would haunt her dreams, even if the mambo did everything she could to prevent it.

Frédéric was finally placed in the coffin—without shoes, to make it more difficult for him to return to his living relatives as a member of the stony undead. For the same reason, the dead were carried to the cemetery by very circuitous routes and their coffins turned once more just before they were lowered into their graves, in a final attempt to confuse them and prevent them from returning.

Only when the coffin was covered with earth and the pit had been filled to the brim had relief flooded into Christine's cramped limbs. Frédéric's body was in its grave and protected from the machinations of Baron Samedi and his confederates! He would certainly not return.

Christine's father, however, had not been given such a funeral. After his disappearance he had fallen victim to the power of a bokor. But it was not too late to save him. Together with the priestess,

Christine and Cécile had searched the ruins of the house for the body. But there was no trace of Etienne Dadou. He must have "survived" the quake and freed himself from the rubble, and be wandering around out there as a restless *zombi cadavre*.

Christine let her gaze wander over the violet shadows of the mountains. Somewhere up there among the bushes and rocks he was hiding . . . watching her.

CHAPTER 7

February 7, 2010
New Orleans, Louisiana
7:15 pm

The setting sun was bathing the French Quarter in candy-colored light as Ondragon checked into the Royal Sonesta Hotel on Bourbon Street; a four-star hotel with a dignified charm and timeless elegance, whose hefty prices largely kept the mass of hardcore party tourists at bay.

He took the elevator to the second floor and entered his room, which as expected more than lived up to his upscale standards. It faced the courtyard and had the perfect escape route through a French door leading to the large terrace that rose above the tropical plants and fountain adorning the atrium. The Spanish-style wrought-iron balconies on the exterior of the hotel would have done just as well, but would have been no protection against the noise of the parties in the street every evening.

Ondragon looked around the room: marbled bathroom, thick damask curtains at the windows, a bed fit for a king, very comfortable, the ideal place to catch up on the wreckage of the previous night's sleep. But his unease kept him from lying down on the soft mattress and simply closing his eyes. He would stay awake until Strangelove reported back. But that was not the only thing worrying him. He thought back to his conversation with Charlize about Bolič. His body couldn't simply not be in the room. He had seen him lying there with his own eyes, dead as a doornail. But Charlize's information was beginning to make him doubt his memory. Had he made a mistake? Had he missed something? Maybe Bolič had just been drugged or had taken too many sleeping pills.

Housekeeping, apparently, had not noticed anything unusual in the Bosnian's room. Charlize had sneaked in and had, to her great astonishment, found the bed empty. She had searched the room thoroughly and later described it to Ondragon. Obviously, Bolič's things were still where they had been. Everything would have looked as if the Bosnian had only left the room for a moment.

"*Paul-san*, are you really sure he was dead?" Charlize had asked the inevitable question, and without meaning to, Ondragon had faltered. He had been absolutely certain that the Bosnian was dead. No pulse and no pupillary reflex; what was there to misinterpret? He had heard, of course, that athletes could have a very low resting pulse rate, but a rate of zero was unheard-of, even for elite athletes. The person in question would suffocate or die of heart failure. But what had happened to the Bosnian? Could someone else have removed the body from the hotel? Perhaps it had been shifted to another room. Ondragon had no idea what the point of that might have been, but he asked his assistant to stay nearby to keep an eye on what was happening and, if necessary, try to get footage from the hotel's surveillance cameras. Hopefully, they would be able to clearly see what had happened outside room 506. Because one thing was undeniable: Something was wrong.

As so often, Ondragon thought of his brother, who was also dead but continued to haunt his thoughts. Was Bolič the Bosnian now haunting him too?

To distract himself from these painful memories, he dug out the floater's cell phone and laptop from his travel bag. He wiped his burning eyes and told himself it was only the long car ride and the interrupted night . . . not to mention the alcohol. By the way, who had said no alcohol was no solution?

Ondragon went over to the window, closed the curtains, and fished the open bottle of Talisker out of his pocket. He poured a generous three fingers' worth into a glass, took two ice cubes from the ice bucket, and dropped them into the golden-brown liquid. For a while, he watched the streaks form in the drink, then took a deep sip and let the whiskey circle slowly on his tongue, taking in the smoky aroma of eighteen years of oak barrel aging and salty ocean air. Feeling the comforting, relaxing warmth of the alcohol working its way through his veins, he set the glass on the nightstand and began to examine the content of the two digital devices.

The cell phone was password-protected. It locked after three attempts to open it, and Ondragon turned his attention to the laptop. But again, none of his combinations worked. Maybe Bolič had used Bosnian words. Shoot. If he wanted to get at the data, he would have to call in his computer specialist, Rudee. But he would need an internet connection. Ondragon had no energy left to call reception and activate the WiFi in his room, so he closed the laptop. Tomorrow was another day. At least he hoped so!

He put both devices away and filled his glass with whiskey again. The clink of the ice cubes and the tang of the drink calmed his mind, and after a few more sips he found himself in an agreeably don't-give-a-shit headspace. Just the frame of mind in which to await his execution!

He heard a noise and opened his eyes. Instantly, he was wide awake. He sat up calmly in bed and listened, feeling under the pillow for his gun. Was that someone at the balcony door?

A faint scraping sounded, as if someone was trying the door to see if it would open. Quietly, Ondragon got up and crept over to the window. He was using the barrel of his pistol to push the curtain aside slightly when his cell phone rang. He jumped, startled, and let the curtain slide back again. He quickly went over to the bedside table and felt a sudden nervousness rise in him as he answered the call.

"It's me, Strangelove!" the voice on the other end whispered.

Ondragon peered at the alarm clock's digital display. It was just before three in the morning. "Strangelove, that took a long fucking time! Goddamn it, what the hell was going on? Did an anthrax epidemic break out in the unit, or what?" He realized he hadn't let his chemist get a word in edgewise, so he lapsed into sullen silence. But when Strangelove said nothing, he roared, "Just give me the result at last, however bad it is!"

"Negative!"

"Shit, what does that mean?" Ondragon was confused; his head ached from the repeated doses of the high-proof Scotch whiskey. He stared at the bottle. It was empty.

"Negative means the sample was negative; no pathogens were identified in it, *nada, niente,* nothing! You are not infected, Mr. Ondragon! Is that clear enough?"

"Not infected!" repeated Ondragon incredulously, letting out a relieved and joyful shout. "Wow, man, it really is my second birthday now—one of many, by the way. Man, you did a great job! Thank you so much."

"You're welcome." Strangelove sounded nervous and groggy, and having taken his bad mood out on him, Ondragon now decided to cheer the fellow up. "Is an extra thousand enough to compensate for the stress you've been under?"

"Mr. Ondragon, that's very generous of you, but I cannot accept your offer. It took me far too long to get the result, and I kept you in the dark about the fee. You were in a tough spot, and after all, I have my philosophy too."

"And that would be?"

"Results and efficiency!"

"Then we're not so different from each other. Listen, I'll give you the thousand as research funding, and you promise to stay true to your philosophy next time, okay?" Ondragon felt the life and the good humor flowing back into him. He had overcome the shadow of death—again. But he'd had his ass kicked pretty good. *I'm getting old,* he thought. *I never used to mind being so close to death.*

"Okay, Mr. Ondragon." Strangelove took the deal in an audibly better mood.

"Why did it take so long this time?" Ondragon asked.

"The test itself only takes three minutes, but the machine at the university was broken!"

"Oh, so what did you use to test the sample?"

Strangelove explained that he had a friend who worked security at LAX. He had given him enough hush money to be allowed to use the Bioflash at the airport. Due to the anthrax attacks in recent years, every airport in the USA now had a machine.

"Interesting," Ondragon replied. "But what's in the sample if it wasn't anthrax? Were you able to figure that out?"

"The entire sample went for the scan. There's nothing left that I can use to check what kind of substance it was. But if you send me some more, I can examine it," Strangelove said with a newly ignited researcher's spirit.

Ondragon promised to send the young chemist some more of the stuff if he could get hold of it, and said goodbye. Freed from a mountain of worry, he sank back on his pillow, and the sleep that now followed was very restful.

The next morning, he relished his breakfast as if it were the last one for the rest of his life. While he ate, he planned his day; after all, he wasn't here for pleasure. He would have plenty of opportunity to indulge his celebratory mood tonight when he painted Bourbon Street red. But first of all, he was going to see Madame Tombeau in her store to show her the pictures of all the Voodoo stuff from Tyler Ellys's house. After that, he would hopefully be one piece of knowledge further and could use it to go to Chalmette and talk to Sylvester Stern, assuming he was home.

Ondragon dialed the mailman's number. This time the busy signal sounded. Well, that made a change, at least. He put the phone away, left a tip on the table for the waiter, and headed for the address he had gotten from Günther Ludewig. It was only a short walk along Bourbon Street, which was sleepy and full of delivery vehicles in the bright morning light. There was still no sign that the craziest carnival in the world would be celebrated here in a week's time. Thousands of revelers would flood the French Quarter for Mardi Gras and drown it in beer. But for now it was wonderfully peaceful. Ah, New Orleans!

Ondragon took a deep breath, inhaling the scent of the city: pregnant with moisture and with a slightly putrid aroma, which of course came from the fact that the entire neighborhood had been built on river mud. There was barely any trace of the damage done by Hurricane Katrina in 2005. The locals had painstakingly rebuilt N'awlins, as they called it, and helped it flourish once more. Ondragon thought again that if he hadn't made his home in Los Angeles, he surely would have chosen this musty cesspool overflowing with sin. The Big Easy and he would have been a good match for each other; a depraved beauty and her lover.

As Ondragon strolled along the sidewalk overhung by wrought iron balconies, he looked happily at the glittering, colorful displays in the tourist stores, and the bars, restaurants, and music joints for which the French Quarter was famed.

When he arrived at the store named Captain Zombie, he looked briefly at the shop window, which was crammed from top to bottom with Voodoo and mystic paraphernalia. A sweet, spicy smell was drifting from the open door. He gave an amused smile, entered, and was greeted by a completely alien universe. Half amazed, half entertained, he strode through the dimly lit rooms, playing the curious tourist and looking at the bursting shelves.

They had everything! Complete Voodoo shrines with offerings, statues of the Virgin Mary, images of saints, crucifixes of all designs from simple to opulent and set with semiprecious stones, tarot cards, lucky charms of all kinds, witches' brews, bottles with magical healing potions, artifacts that Ondragon could not place—soaked in a yellowish liquid, crystals, love amulets, cigars, teeth, hair, bones, incense, hand-dipped candles, mojo bags, Voodoo dolls, and necklaces of dried seeds. From the ceiling hung bundles of herbs and animal parts, mainly alligator heads and claws. And all the stuff was giving off a pungent smell of flowery perfume and mummified animal skin, which made Ondragon feel faintly nauseated.

He looked around unobtrusively and counted two other customers in the store, female, one of whom actually seemed to be serious. At least, she was engaged in an enthusiastic conversation with the woman behind the counter, which was covered with items to do with witchcraft.

Ondragon looked closely at the dark-skinned and somewhat portly lady behind the counter. In her white blouse with ruffled collar, red headscarf, and large gold earrings, she looked like a typical

Creole Queen. She was taking labeled can after labeled can from the shelf behind her, filling paper bags with mysterious ingredients, weighing them, and handing them to the customer. Was that Madame Tombeau?

Ondragon positioned himself behind some shelving and peered over it at the cash register. He would have to wait until the customer had left; after all, he didn't want to embarrass himself if this address turned out to be wrong. He picked up a porcelain skull painted in the Mexican style and pretended to be interested in it. Over the rims of his sunglasses, he watched the Voodoo lady.

Once the customer had finally paid for her botanicals and left the store with a cheerful *au revoir*, Ondragon took the initiative and headed for the cash register with the lucky charm closest to hand.

"You are not from New Orleans, monsieur." The Voodoo lady smiled at him. Her voice was deep and pleasant.

"No, I'm just passing through. A few days' entertainment, you know the kind of thing," Ondragon replied amiably.

The Creole Queen pointed to the lucky charm he was holding, made of glass chili peppers. "This amulet is from Mexico and wards off bad luck. All the items here in the store have had the appropriate words said over them or been consecrated by a priestess. You will see, it will work its magic. Hang the amulet on the rearview mirror of your car and it will protect you from accidents. It's always useful if you drive an expensive car." She gave him a wink. "Can I help you with anything else?"

Ondragon wondered how the hell she knew he drove an expensive car. It was probably pure luck, especially since in his disguise as an ordinary tourist in a T-shirt and jeans he didn't look like money at all. "No, thanks." He pulled out his wallet and thrust a twenty into the lady's hand. As she passed him the receipt and the paper bag with the amulet in it, Ondragon leaned over the counter and asked in a whisper. "I'm here to see Madame Tombeau. Am I in the right place?"

"Who wants to know?" The smile was gone from her face, her tone suddenly harsh.

"Let's say I got your address from an esteemed academic colleague. I need the help of a Voodoo priestess on a, let's call it . . . confidential matter."

The Voodoo lady eyed him suspiciously. Then she clicked her tongue. "You don't look to me like you believe in the magic of Voodoo, monsieur! Why do you need the advice of a mambo?"

Ondragon felt little desire to explain until he knew if she was the person he was looking for. "As I said, it's confidential, and I can only discuss it with Madame Tombeau herself." He was beginning to feel ridiculous, standing here in flip-flops in this mumbo jumbo store. And on top of that, that name! Tombeau, *tombstone*, such a bad joke!

"Madame Tombeau is not here!"

"Please . . ."

"What is the reason for your consultation? Tell me. Otherwise, how can I know you're actually serious and not just a tourist after a sensational experience?"

The lady was starting to get on his nerves, so he pulled out his iPhone, opened the photo of the vèvè of Baron Samedi, and showed it to her.

The Creole Queen gave a sudden start as she looked at the picture. *"Bondieu!"* she gasped, "and you carry that around with you?" She crossed herself quickly and looked from the photo to his face.

With surprise, Ondragon saw pure fear in her dark eyes.

"Madame Tombeau is in her office. One moment please, I'll see if she has time." She pulled an old-fashioned telephone from under the counter, dialed a short number, and then spoke almost frantically and with such a strong Creole accent that he understood only the words *Samedi*, *maléfique*, and something like *cadavre*. Why was the lady so upset about the photo?

Her hands trembling, she hung up and said, "Madame Tombeau is expecting you, monsieur. Go through that door there and then down the hall. Her office is behind the last door on the right. Knock four times, and under no circumstances open any of the other doors!" She gave him a warning look and crossed herself one more time. "Go! *Allez!*"

Ondragon followed her instructions and opened the door at the back of the store, which was hung so densely with African masks and animal skulls that he hadn't noticed it before. It opened onto a dark corridor, on whose walls hung more objects of unfathomable origin, glaring at him. They too were giving off the same unpleasant odor, which grew more intense the farther he went down the hallway. He counted six doors, then stopped at the last one on the right. There was no name or any other label on it. He knocked four times. A voice called him in and he pushed the handle downward. Then he froze on the threshold, stunned.

He had expected to enter a candlelit room crammed with Voodoo paraphernalia and come face-to-face with another version of the Creole Queen from the front of the store, but what greeted him was anything but a cliché!

The woman who rose from behind a modern desk had a dark complexion, but was not clad in any kind of priestess garb. She wore a gray business jacket and knee-length skirt with a white blouse and black high-heeled shoes. Her hair was pulled back into a severe chignon, highlighting her exquisitely pretty Creole features. However, perched on her nose was a pair of distinctive black-rimmed glasses that made her look serious . . . *very* serious . . .

She approached him with a look that clearly indicated amusement at his agitation. "Were you expecting someone else, monsieur . . . ?"

Ondragon broke out of his stupor, pulled off his sunglasses, and remembered his manners. He smiled charmingly, shaking the hand she held out. "My name is Paul Eckbert Ondragon. I'm a consultant from LA." He looked for his business card but found he didn't have one with him, because he was wearing his ridiculous tourist outfit. Suddenly, he felt insecure and wished he had put on a suit and tie.

"How do you do, Monsieur Ondragon, I am Madame Tombeau." Her speech was very soft and tinged with a French Antilles accent. "Are you coming to see me about your two curses?"

Ondragon frowned. "My curses? Um, no . . . I . . ."

"But I see two curses attached to your aura. I could remove one if you wish, but not the other. I am afraid it is your destiny and stronger than my modest powers."

"But I'm not here for my curses." *This is completely absurd,* Ondragon thought, drawing himself up. "Forgive my casual appearance, madame, this is not my usual attire and may give the wrong impression. It is merely . . . a disguise."

She raised her narrow brows in interest. "Why do you need a disguise?"

"Well, normally I advise companies and private individuals on their problems, but at the moment I am acting on behalf of a friend, looking for one of his employees who might have come into contact with Voodoo magic in Haiti. I found at least some evidence of this at his house and took photographs. I came to you because you were recommended to me by an expert who said you could help me analyze the photos. Every little clue is vital. And to come back to the disguise: I like to use a cover for my detective work. Don't want people to see me coming from a mile away, you understand."

Madame Tombeau nodded, slightly amused. "Well then, you are welcome to use my store as cover. It's just a little sideline. The tourists like to shop here. I am primarily a trained and initiated mambo, a *Vodou prêtresse*, and I practice here in New Orleans, serving all the people in my community. These are not only men and women from my native Haiti; Americans and Europeans also believe in the power of Vodou and seek to consult with me. I not only mediate on their behalf with the high angels, the loas, I also solve everyday problems like illnesses or lovesickness. But do sit down, *s'il vous plaît*. May I offer you something to drink?"

"I'd like some water, if it's no trouble." Ondragon sat on the chair in front of her desk—which boasted a new MacBook—and watched his hostess surreptitiously as she retrieved a bottle of Perrier from a refrigerator and a glass from some wall-mounted shelves. She was maybe thirty-five years old, had flawless ebony skin, and great legs. And she moved with a grace that was the preserve of personalities who were very aware of their charisma. She set the drink down in front of him with a polite smile.

"Ice?"

"Non, merci." He poured himself a drink and took a refreshing sip. "You have a fine office here." He looked around the minimally furnished room, which was lit by neon lights. It gave not the slightest hint of her outlandish profession, and Ondragon wondered what kind of Voodoo Queen this was, who worked in a sterile office instead of a smoky altar full of idols. He would be happy to be further

surprised by this woman; her charms were working their effect on him. He generally preferred the Asian disposition, but it was never too late to refine his tastes.

Madame Tombeau settled into her chair and folded her hands on the glass desktop. "Natalie—one of my hunsi, my temple assistants, you met her out front in the store—said you were carrying a forbidden vèvè. Would you please show it to me?"

"But of course." He pulled out his cell phone, opened the photo of Ellys's porch, and passed it to Madame Tombeau. Without commenting, she also looked at the pictures of the other Voodoo paraphernalia. Her expression remained professionally cool, quite unlike her assistant in the store.

"Alors," she said after a while, handing the iPhone back to Ondragon. "Let us discuss the vèvè first. This one here is a forbidden image used only by black magicians. It combines the invocations of Baron Samedi, Lord of the Graveyards, and of Maître Carrefour, Master of the Crossroads. You only ask for his help if you want to summon a diab, a devil. This is a dangerous business, because a diab eventually demands payment for his help, in the form of a human sacrifice. If he does not get it, he will take the bokor himself. So you should be quite sure you can pay for the curse you want to cast, otherwise it will turn around and destroy you. The vèvè in your picture looks professional, but something bothers me about the way it was made. White paint has been used, mixed with something glittery. A bokor would use flour or bone powder instead. Also, the dead bird— you said it was black—makes me wonder, because for Master Carrefour, the bokor should have chosen a red one. Well, maybe he had his reasons. Now let's move on to the pendant. It is a small bag on a ribbon with a chicken foot and feathers. It's a gris-gris, a protective amulet—"

"What does it protect against?" interrupted Ondragon, who still didn't know whether to take this balderdash at face value. However, the seriousness of the Madame had aroused a certain curiosity in him. After all, he found people's beliefs interesting.

"If the amulet is related to the vèvè," Madame Tombeau replied matter-of-factly, "or if the wearer at least knew an evil spell was going to be cast against him, then it would protect him from the bokor's diabolical schemes."

"A curse deterrent, so to speak? Or more like Austin Powers's mojo?"

The Madame gave him a reproving look. "*Oui et non.* Yes, it is a kind of curse deterrent, but it is not a mojo bag. Mojo is a term from Hoodoo. It's a new-fangled variation of certain Vodou rituals, but for the most part it deals only in magical spells and talismans, and has nothing to do with genuine belief in the loas. In Vodou, on the other hand, there are many different amulets. Most of them are known as gris-gris, ouanga, or makandals." She paused and looked at Ondragon, as if studying him. "I am not talking nonsense, Mr. Ondragon. There are those who believe in the magic of Vodou, just as there are those who believe in God or in Allah."

Damn it, she had realized that he was secretly amused by her. "That may be so," he said placatingly, "but you must admit that your words sound a little fantastic."

"Mr. Ondragon, I saw right away that you are the kind of person who does not believe in anything. But that does not give you the right to judge what other people believe. After all, they do so of their own free will, and religiosity, of any kind, is not a bad thing. Since we are akin to colleagues—we both help people with their problems—I would ask you not to make fun of our faith!"

Ondragon shifted on the chair and forced himself to look less cynical; after all, he needed her help. He was about to apologize, but she beat him to it.

"If you don't open your mind a little to the subject, you will think the rest of what I have to tell you about your photos is humbug. That would be a grave mistake, because in reality it is deadly serious and you may be in danger."

He nodded and raised his hands guiltily. "*Je suis desolé.* Forgive me, madame, I did not mean to behave improperly. Please, continue."

She looked at him doubtfully. "*Eh bien*, but only so you cannot claim later that I did not warn you of the potential danger." She raised an index finger. "So let's come to the letter you photographed. It tells us clearly of the bokor's intentions."

"I found a strange powder in the envelope; I forgot to mention that," Ondragon interjected.

"I know." Her gaze took on an unsettling depth. "You say you can't find the person who received this letter, and that another person who touched it was dead in his hotel room and has now gone?"

"Oui, c'est ça!" An uneasy feeling rose in Ondragon . . . slowly and inexorably, like a balloon filled with gas.

"You too have touched the letter?"

Ondragon nodded.

"Do you feel anything? A numbness in your limbs, itching on your hands, or a headache?"

"I had a headache, but what's it all about?" The balloon of his discomfort had left the ionosphere behind and was heading wildly out into space.

The Madame leaned forward and looked at him anxiously. "It's like this: There was a *coup poudre* in the letter. A zombie powder!"

"Zombie what?" Had he heard that right? Zombie?

But the Madame was far from smiling at his reaction. To all appearances, she had not been making a joke. "The powder in the letter," she said gravely, "is a magic substance that black magicians use to turn a human into a zombie!"

CHAPTER 8

February 8, 2010
New Orleans
11:45 am

Ondragon stood outside the store, the sun shining on his face. He was irritated. Not only by his strange encounter with Madame Tombeau, but even more by his own feelings. The rational side of him didn't believe a single word the Voodoo Queen had said. Zombies! This was the height of ridiculousness! It was something you only found in bad B-movies. But there was also his instinct. And that kept reminding him of the dead Bolič and his mysterious disappearance. Had the Bosnian really been turned into a walking corpse by the powder in the letter? And if so, where had he gone?

Come off it!

Ondragon put on his sunglasses. It was all utter nonsense. When you were dead, you were dead—except perhaps if your name was Jesus. But, as was well known, it was God himself who had had a hand in that case and not a black magician. Which was of course not to say that Jesus was a zombie . . .

Ondragon shook his head vigorously. What an absurd train of thought he had let himself be carried away by! He had argued with Madame Tombeau for half an hour about whether zombies existed or not. She had even explained to him what the letter meant. *Son corps doit être comme une bouteille vide.* This apparently meant the recipient of the letter had been judged and would soon be turned into a zombie by a black magician. Through magic and the *coup poudre,* his body would be transformed into an empty vessel into which the bokor could subsequently implant his own will. After zombification, the victim would be a creature without a will, with greater physical strength but no mind; a slave who did as he was commanded. This, according to the Madame, was the most terrible fate that could befall a Haitian. But even this explanation had not convinced Ondragon of the existence of zombies. The whole thing was just *too* freaky.

But Madame Tombeau had not let up and had implored him to at least wear a small amulet she had put in his hand in the store, to counter the zombie magic! Ondragon snorted snidely. He himself was beginning to feel like an empty bottle—which she was trying to fill with her witch humbug.

With another shake of his head, he stuffed the bag-like amulet into the pocket of his pants and pulled out his cell phone. There had to be another explanation for the disappearance of Bolič's body. He dialed his assistant's number. Maybe she had something new.

But Charlize unfortunately did not, and Ondragon reminded her more harshly than he had intended about the video footage. After that, he hung up, sullenly stuck a piece of gum between his teeth, and went back to the hotel, where he changed his clothes. He wanted to take his Sig Sauer with him when he paid Sylvester Stern a visit and not just rely on the knife he had been carrying on his leg, hidden under his tourist togs. So he put on his holster, pulling a light windbreaker over it, and exchanged the flip-flops for his cowboy boots.

On the short drive to Chalmette, Ondragon tried once more to reach Sylvester Stern on the phone. Sadly, he was, as always, unsuccessful.

The navigation system on his iPhone guided him unerringly through the streets of the desolate New Orleans suburb. Chalmette had been completely destroyed by Katrina and so was not exactly one of the most upscale addresses these days. Nevertheless, there were a few quite sizeable, newly built houses in the center. Stern's was at the far end of a street bordering a canal and a levee. Beyond, there was nothing but miles of treacherous, mosquito-infested swampland.

Ondragon parked the car around the next corner in a larger, undeveloped area and walked back to Stern's residence, which was displaying a similar degree of neglect as Ellys's. It was obvious that

these bachelors did not take particularly good care of their properties; like Ellys's, Stern's front yard was more weed paradise than green
lawn.

He knocked on Stern's door and looked around. The neighboring houses looked deserted, or at least no one was home, and there
were no cars in the driveways. People were probably at work or at the
supermarket, as befitted decent Americans.

When no one answered his second knock, Ondragon decided to
enter the house via the back door. He slipped on his gloves and crept
through the garden, where he got through the door in only a few
moments. His gun drawn, he entered the house through the living
room and looked about him. A slightly sour smell reached his nose
and he was immediately reminded of the stale air in Bolič's room.
Quickly, he went through the house. First downstairs, then upstairs,
where the stench grew stronger. As he entered the bedroom and
looked at the bed, he was unsurprised.

Sylvester Stern lay face up on the mattress, his eyes closed, his
expression peaceful. The sheet was folded partway back, revealing
his pajamas. One arm was hanging out of the bed and Bugs Bunny
grinned up at him from the exposed skin of the man's beefy forearm.
No doubt about it, this was the blond mailman from Ellys's photo
gallery.

Ondragon moved to the bedside and checked his pulse and
breathing. Then, as a precaution, he stabbed his finger into the soft
spot behind Stern's ear, which would have been very painful if the
man had not breathed his last a long time ago. Ondragon straightened up, thinking. It was the same scenario as with Bolič. And it
certainly didn't look like Stern would be coming back from the dead
anytime soon to terrorize the area in zombie form.

He took several photos of the body and then searched the house
for Stern's cell phone and laptop. But he found nothing. He had disappeared, just like Ellys.

Next, he knocked on all the walls, searching for the mailman's
secret room. He soon found it behind a mirror in the guest room
next to Stern's bedroom. The mirror was the size of a man and opened
like a door. It had a handle on the inside so it could be pulled shut.

Ondragon noticed that the mirror was one-way. You could see out from the inside, and he suspected that the secret room was also a kind of refuge, where you could be safe and observe any intruders. As ingenious as it was simple.

Ondragon flicked on the bulb, and the yellowish light illuminated a narrow room like Tyler Ellys's: shelves on both walls, neatly stacked with weapons and special equipment in cases—but this time without a collection of unpleasant books. There was no hint of the kind of right-wing views Ellys had been cultivating. Ondragon flipped open the suitcases. Pistols, hand grenades, and ammunition, but no Voodoo stuff.

After taking a few photos, he left the room and returned to the dead man, who was still lying there in the same position.

What did you expect? Ondragon snorted contemptuously at the foolishness of his thoughts. He laid his weapon on the bed, close to hand, and laboriously began to undress the corpse. He had seen many dead bodies before; some had been harmless, but some had been distinctly unsavory. But over time he had gained some experience in the external examination of corpses, and this now helped him to interpret the signs and marks that might be found on a dead body.

Stern's skin was pale and cool and his body was limp, which meant that the time of death had to be either less than six hours or more than three days ago. Rigor mortis was known to be one of the so-called sure signs of death and was fully developed after six to twelve hours at room temperature. After three to four days, it disappeared again and the body went limp. Since Alejandro Green (assuming he was telling the truth) had told Ondragon he had spoken to Stern on the phone barely forty hours before, Stern must therefore have died or been murdered in the past six hours.

Ondragon examined the dead man's limbs. There were bloody welts on the hands and forearms, and he found particles of skin under Stern's fingernails. Either Stern had fought back or he had inflicted the scratches on himself. Why, however, was not clear to Ondragon. He held his breath and turned Stern over onto his stomach. The stench was overwhelming—sweetly musty, as if the corpse had been embalmed with perfume. He looked closely at the skin on the back. There were a few reddened spots, but they could not be lividity, since the corpse had not been lying there long enough for that. He also found no other abnormalities or indications of the cause of death. Ondragon rolled the corpse back to its original position, his weapon slipping off the mattress and falling to the floor with a thud. Cursing, he knelt down and reached under the bed. But instead of hard metal, his fingers hit something that rustled. Ondragon bent down and looked under the bed. There lay a crumpled sheet of paper. Even as he pulled it out, he suspected what it was. Hot waves of fear rolled through his stomach. Had he unknowingly put himself in danger again?

With bated breath and keeping the paper as far from him as possible, he smoothed it out. On the sheet was a single sentence, *Sylvester Stern, your body shall be an empty bottle!* Next to it, Ondragon recognized the same spidery drawing of a coffin as on Ellys's paper.

He noticed his own frantic heartbeat only after he had succeeded in looking away from the paper. He made an effort and tried to think things through.

It wasn't the letter that was dangerous, it was the powder.

He bent down. Where was the envelope?

It lay next to his weapon. Ondragon reached into his jacket pocket. As a matter of prudence, he had brought a number of ziplock bags with him. Carefully, he put the letter and envelope into a plastic bag, and this in turn into three more. Not a single nanoparticle of this substance should be able to leak out.

Then he left the house as quickly as possible. He had seen enough and would go straight to Madame Tombeau. He would take her with him and prove to her that Stern was a real dead man and not undead, even though he had received the zombie letter.

As he drove back to New Orleans, his heartbeat calmed agonizingly slowly. Against his will, the fear of the powder kept his pulse rate undesirably high.

This is all nonsense! He slapped his hand on the steering wheel. *You can't really believe in something as silly as zombies!* Ondragon fished his cell phone out of his pocket and dialed Alejandro Green's number. He had to warn the mailman. He was the last unharmed member of the crew. The whole story was beginning to look like someone was eliminating the CSAC one by one. But why? Had they seen something on one of their jobs that they were not supposed to see?

On the other end of the line, the voicemail answered. Shit! Ondragon quickly switched to Roderick DeForce's number. He needed information. The phone rang. If his friend didn't pick up soon, then . . .

"The person you are calling . . ." Ondragon hurled the cell phone at the dashboard. It bounced off with a crunch and landed on the passenger seat. Glancing sideways at it, he realized the screen was cracked. Suddenly, he felt completely calm.

Why are you getting so upset? Who gives a shit what happens? You can always get out of this stupid case. Obviously, Rod doesn't care much about what happened to his employees, otherwise he would have gotten in touch long ago. And Bolič and Stern are dead, you can't help them. So it's the lowest priority. And Rod is paying your expenses. Forget the zombie bullshit. You're in New Orleans. Go down to Bourbon Street and have a good time. Live it up!

Ondragon turned into the underground garage of the hotel and parked. It was 3:15 pm and high time he got something to eat. He went to the popular seafood restaurant The Bourbon House and ordered two dozen oysters with spicy Cajun sauce.

From the restaurant, he went directly to Madame Tombeau's Voodoo store. He wanted a second consultation. There were some more things he needed to know.

Natalie stood behind the checkout counter and greeted him with a knowing smile. "Monsieur Ondragon, there you are. Unfortunately, Madame Tombeau is not available. She has a *séance magique* with a client. But she knew you would be coming back and asked me to give you this." She held out a paper bag.

Ondragon concealed his surprise, took the bag, and looked inside. It contained dried herbs.

"They help combat the magic *méchante* of zombification. Madame said you had come into contact with it and might be craving them. Take them like a tea. Just brew them with hot water. They will turn away the eyes of the diab that the bokor has set upon you."

"But that's nonsense!" grumbled Ondragon. "Nobody has set anything on me, certainly not a diab or a devil. I don't believe in this baloney, all right? All I want is to speak to Madame Tombeau on an urgent matter. When will she be back?" He was thoroughly fed up with all these spirits, and with the Voodoo witch's smug, arrogant smile.

Natalie's smile became even more condescending. "Madame Tombeau will be engaged until late this evening. But she has invited you to her club, despite your *conduite mauvaise*, your bad behavior. She seems to think you are a particularly interesting case. Hence the invitation."

Bad behavior? Me? The composure he had so laboriously regained after his meal was gone. Ondragon was on the verge of putting the woman's headscarf around her neck and . . .

"The club is called Voodoo-Child and it's on Dumaine Street, number 34." She held up a key with a skull engraved on it. "This makes you a member, sir. Open the red door with it and show it to the man at the entrance. Madame Tombeau will find you."

Wordlessly, Ondragon took the key and the bag with the anti-zombie herbs and loped out of the store. This contrived secrecy was really starting to grate on his nerves. Voodoo, Hoodoo, schmoodoo! He felt like he was in an African old wives' tale.

To cool off, he went into an empty bar, sat down, and ordered a large beer. The jukebox fell silent and Ondragon enjoyed the quiet as the cool drink ran down his throat. A fan above his head was trying to cut through the sultry air, which smelled of rain and decay. Darkness fell abruptly outside as storm clouds passed over the afternoon sun. Soon the rain was pelting down on the hot street, submerging it within seconds.

Great, Ondragon thought, and ordered a second beer. The bartender passed it across the counter and then gave the jukebox a kick.

"Damn thing! It was working a minute ago!"

I actually prefer it like this, Ondragon thought, listening with half-closed eyes to the soothing sound of the rain, which was mixed with a rushing sound that rose and fell whenever a car passed by the open door. Bourbon Street was not yet closed to vehicles; that would not happen until after sunset.

Cooler air gradually entered the bar and Ondragon relaxed. Outside, tourists in summer clothing scurried along the sidewalk, which was only partially covered by the balconies. Water rushed through the holes in the guttering onto the street as if spouting from medieval gargoyles, giving anyone who didn't have their wits about them an involuntary shower. Ondragon grinned as a young couple, soaked from head to toe, sheltered in the bar entrance and kissed passionately. More and more passersby stopped there, waiting for the rain to end. The neon sign lit up their silhouettes in all the colors of the rainbow. Suddenly, there was a movement in the group by the door. A man pushed his way between the waiting people. He looked dead drunk, even this early in the afternoon, and was staggering awkwardly. His gaze fixed, he wobbled past the entrance and turned his head briefly. For a split second, he looked into the bar.

Ondragon jumped up, taken aback and blinking.

Was it possible?

He ran for the door, but the indignant bartender rushed after him and grabbed his sleeve.

"Hey, friend, pay before you go!"

Ondragon reached into his pocket, hastily thrust a twenty-dollar bill into the man's hand, and dove into the crowd outside the door. On tiptoe, he looked around over the heads of the people, but the tottering figure had disappeared.

Ondragon stepped out onto the open street into the rain to get a better view. Instantly, he was wet to the skin, water running into his mouth and eyes. The murky twilight of Bourbon Street was abruptly illuminated by a flash of lightning, but unfortunately even the glowing sky couldn't help him locate the enigmatic apparition he had been peering at just moments before. The guy had been wearing sunglasses, and not much else of him had been visible in the crowd . . .

It was impossible—and yet Ondragon had recognized the pale face.

The Bosnian.

The doorman at the Royal Sonesta Hotel looked pityingly at the guest who had clearly experienced the intimate, wet kiss of New Orleans, and confined himself to murmuring a restrained "Good evening, sir."

Ondragon stomped past him through the lobby without responding and went directly to his room, where he took a warm shower. He only calmed down when a little later, sitting on the bed in his bathrobe, he heard the voice of his assistant answering the phone.

"Boss, I was just about to call you. I've been watching the videotapes from the hotel! It wasn't especially hard to persuade the surveillance service guy."

Ondragon lifted the corners of his mouth, amused. She had always been good at talking people into things. He could vividly imagine the hotel clerk getting hopelessly distracted by her world-class cleavage. He might not even have realized what was going on. Ondragon almost envied him. "Very good, and what did you find out?"

"You won't believe what I saw; at first I could hardly believe it myself!"

"Out with it, Charlize. Don't keep me in suspense!"

"*Yossha*, Boss! First you enter the room and come out a little later with a briefcase in your hand. Then nothing happens for hours. Around one o'clock in the morning the door opens and Bolič comes out. But he looks very strange."

"Strange how?" asked Ondragon in alarm.

"He's as pale as a freshly whitewashed picket fence and swaying like he's three sheets to the wind! He can hardly stand up. He staggers to the elevator and goes down. And this is where the strange thing happens. I also watched the footage from the lobby. One camera was angled to allow you to see through the glass of the revolving door onto the hotel driveway. Bolič staggers from the elevator toward the door and gets caught there. He goes around the door several times like a maniac, beating the glass with his fists and screaming as if he doesn't understand how a revolving door works. All of this obviously goes unnoticed by the night guard at the front desk, because no one comes to help him. After going around at least a dozen times, he finally finds the exit and stops abruptly outside. And here it is: A dark figure appears out of nowhere outside the door. Unfortunately, you can't see him very well; his face is in shadow. But you can see one thing very clearly: He's wearing a black tailcoat and a top hat!"

Ondragon laughed in amazement. "A top hat? What's that all about? Was it a hotel guest coming in late from a wedding?"

"I don't think so, because Bolič bowed to him and then they left. They clearly went off together."

Ondragon's thoughts were racing. "Are Bolič's things still in his room? How long did he book it for anyway? Has his disappearance been noticed?"

"I checked on that too, Boss. His stuff is still there and the reservation is for a total of ten days. So he's due to leave the day after tomorrow. And that means the hotel isn't yet aware of his disappearance."

"Very weird," Ondragon muttered, trying to line up Charlize's observations with his own. A man he had thought was dead had gotten up hours later. Apparently, drunk off his ass, he had left his things in the room and met up with another man wearing a top hat. Both had disappeared. That was two days ago in Tucson. Today Bolič, or at least someone who looked damn like him, had shown up in New Orleans. He too seemed out of it. What did it all mean?

"Boss?"

"Yes?"

"What should I do now? There's nothing going on here."

"Get on the next plane to Miami and go see a guy named Alejandro Green. I'll send you his contact details. He's a member of the crew that Tyler Ellys and Sylvester Stern were part of. I found Stern dead in his house today. He looked just like Bolič, and I'm worried the same will happen to Green, if it's not already too late—I can't reach him. I'm afraid I'll be stuck here in New Orleans a little longer."

"Are you cheating on me, *Paul-san?*"

Ondragon smiled. "Jealous?"

"Not in the least. A city in a swamp can't hold a candle to a California beauty queen!"

"When you're right, you're very right, Charlize," he said, becoming serious. "Please be careful in Miami. Someone is playing a very nasty game here."

"Hai, Paul-san."

He hung up and ran a hand through his wet hair. An appraising glance in the mirror confirmed the worry lines in the form of the San

Andreas fault distorting his forehead. Otherwise, he looked all right. His dark hairline had hardly any gray sprinkles despite the dawn of his fourth decade, and the skin on his face was—apart from the worry lines on his forehead, of course—pretty smooth. The California tan highlighted his green eyes and gave him a certain boyish charm that he liked to deploy when sweet-talking members of the opposite sex. All in all, it was an attractive presentation that was eminently suitable for a nice evening in The Big Easy. Of course, he planned to accept the Madame's invitation to the club, because one of his most outstanding qualities remained, after all, his undying, almost feline curiosity. He secretly hoped the rest of his traits could be described the same way; in his job, he could use seven lives.

He picked up *USA Today* from the floor, which he had kicked into the room as he entered earlier. It wouldn't hurt to browse through world affairs a little before he got dressed to kill. He opened the paper and froze. Sudden machine-gun fire began to pound in his chest and his fingers were seized by the violent tremor he thought he had long overcome. Trembling, he dropped the newspaper and with it the thing that had been hidden inside.

A doll made of rags.

His face had been cut out from a photograph and pasted onto the doll's head. A long pin was stuck through the right eye of the hideous rag man . . . and the head of the pin was a slippery, impaled eyeball.

In the same instant, stabbing pains shot through the right side of his brain. Ondragon clapped his hands to his temples and managed to stumble to the john just in time to gift his oysters and beer to the Mississippi.

CHAPTER 9

February 8, 2010
New Orleans
9:39 pm

Ondragon came to as if waking from a deep sleep and found himself curled up on the bath mat. Groaning, he rose. The pain and nausea had subsided, but were still resonating dully through every fiber of his body like a bad memory.

Having rinsed his mouth and splashed cold water on his face, he felt strong enough to return to the room and look at the disgusting Voodoo thing a little more soberly. But first he went over to the porch door and opened it to let fresh air into the room. Then he turned his attention to the doll.

Using a cotton swab, he turned the hand-sized, misshapen object back and forth on the newsprint. It was made of coarse brown linen, wrapped around with black yarn and soaked in a fetid liquid. Ondragon wrinkled his nose. It smelled almost like the mixture in Captain Zombie. Also, the doll clearly had his face. It had been carefully cut out from a poorly taken photo, probably taken from a great distance with a cell phone camera, and sewn onto the doll's head with thread. Protruding from its right eye was the finger-length steel needle on the end of which a bloody eyeball had been impaled. The organ was nowhere near the size of a human's and probably came from an animal—at least that's what Ondragon hoped as he wrapped the puppet thing firmly in the newspaper. As he stood up to close the porch door, his eyes fell on a small object hanging on the knob outside. He stepped closer, but had long guessed what it was.

"Another of these joke items," he growled, taking the little gray pouch off the knob and dangling it from his index finger. It looked like Tyler Ellys's amulet. A black feather was stuck in the string that held the pouch closed, and a shard of mirror that had been glued to the coarse fabric was ominously reflecting the light from the bedside lamp. Ondragon snorted in annoyance and stuffed the thing into the newspaper package along with the doll. He would take both and shove them under Madame Tombeau's nose. By now he had some idea of what this mumbo jumbo was supposed to do.

Since he wanted to show off his breeding and fashion awareness at this second meeting with the Madame (he was, after all, a diplomat's son), he put on his cream-colored suit with a white shirt and burgundy tie, light brown leather shoes, and an expensive but discreet wristwatch.

He arrived on Bourbon Street half an hour late, which he considered very respectable. It was not a long walk to Dumaine. The rain had cleared, leaving the night sticky and muggy. Under the feet of the countless partying tourists, both local and foreign, the wet asphalt reflected the colorful neon signs. Music was spilling out from all the bars and clubs, and from an illuminated balcony someone was throwing handfuls of the famous glittering plastic bead necklaces, which the enthusiastic passersby picked up and hung around their necks. The mood on the street was joyous and informal. You didn't often find that in the US, and nowhere in this country did you see scantily clad girls standing next to battle-scarred country rockers in leather vests, wisecracking and tempting the public into stores . . . except in New Orleans.

Ondragon would have liked to enjoy the unique atmosphere on Bourbon, but the packet of newsprint in his left hand and the fact that someone was trying to get him thoroughly tangled up in the case had completely wrecked his mood.

On the quieter side street, he immediately located the red door with the number 34 and inserted the key into the lock. The door opened with a soft creak, revealing a dimly lit hallway adorned with ferns in hanging pots and leading to another door, in front of which an old man sat on a barstool. He was wrinkled as a raisin, but dressed in a fine double-breasted suit and a jaunty jazz hat. Above him glowed the red light of a surveillance camera. Ondragon avoided looking directly into it and showed the old man the key.

With a smile that revealed a row of healthy, white teeth, he said, *"Entrez, s'il vous plaît. Amusez-vous bien, monsieur."* He pulled open the door and Ondragon went in.

Dim light and a babble of voices greeted him. As did exotic drumming, which stopped abruptly as Ondragon made his way through the entrance area to the main room. A salon, relatively small but decorated in a tasteful mix of modern lounge and colonial styles, opened up in front of him. On the left was a bar with a colossal gilded baroque mirror on the wall and a large selection of alcoholic beverages. To the right were at least a dozen low tables with comfortable armchairs; a stage of sorts protruded into the front of the room. Above the purple velvet curtain, which was embroidered with white Voodoo symbols, *Voodoo-Child* was written in old-school neon letters. In front of it a dark-skinned, bare-chested beauty had just finished her performance and was retreating with a graceful bow. Ondragon looked surreptitiously at the patrons, trying to take the measure of the place. Was this a high-class whorehouse? Or just a typical New Orleans strip bar?

The fifty or so men and women who were sitting chatting at the tables or as they leaned against ornately carved wooden columns were of various ages and chicly dressed. Their applause for the dancer was appreciative and their genteel reserve spoke of understatement and money.

Ondragon tucked the newspaper packet under his arm and searched the faces for Madame Tombeau. But the Voodoo Queen was nowhere to be seen, although Natalie had said this establishment was her club. Very well then, he would wait. The oh-so-friendly store assistant had given him to understand that the Madame would find *him*, after all.

He sat down at the bar, where the mirror afforded him a good overview of the room and the clientele, and ordered himself a Zombie cocktail. After all the trouble of the last few hours, he felt an irrepressible desire to relish this irony to the max. He placed the repugnant packet on the counter and sipped the fruity rum drink.

Meanwhile, a range of paraphernalia was being positioned on the stage by two women dressed in white: a skull topped by a lit candle, a clay jug, a white chicken with its legs bound, and a bowl.

Was one of the women Natalie?

Ondragon tried to see more clearly, but the flickering light from the multi-arm candelabras on either side of the stage was too dim. The women in the white skirts seemed to be following a strictly defined ceremonial ritual; they moved in an emphatically solemn manner and each of the objects had to be positioned correctly. When they had finished, they drew a large image of a snake on the front part of the stage with some white powder and then retreated. A hush fell over the audience.

The guests looked expectantly at the curtain. A light drumbeat began, and the purple fabric slid aside. Out stepped a lithe, barefoot figure in a green frilly dress with a wide neckline.

The green gave Ondragon a sudden stab of memory. He had met a fascinating lady dressed in this color once before. A fateful and deadly experience! Kateri, his beautiful huntress . . .

As the woman onstage began to sway to the rhythm, his attention returned to the present. Her serpentine movements captivated the audience. The beat grew faster and faster, and like the rest, Ondragon watched her performance as if spellbound.

The dancer—there was no doubt it was Madame Tombeau—opened her lips slightly and, in ecstasy, rolled her eyes so far upward that only the whites were visible. Her hair was loose, and she threw her head back and performed an obscene dance, twitching over the podium.

Ondragon noticed that the audience was being worked up into a state of palpable sexual excitement. Even he himself was not immune. The dance of the snake woman became faster and wilder, and her assistants sprinkled her over and over again with a clear liquid from the clay jug. The pungent smell of alcohol assailed Ondragon's nostrils, as did a heady, exotic, musky scent. Convulsing almost spasmodically, the dancer was now throwing her hands alternately into the air and around her body, as if she longed for the touch of a lover, a lustful moan escaping her throat. Excited by the erotic performance, the audience swayed in their seats.

Ondragon watched as the priestess, in a trance and dancing, was handed the chicken. She took the bird's head between her teeth, her gaze focused on another dimension. Suddenly, the drum rhythm and her movements quietened, only to resume all the more violently a few seconds later. By the time Ondragon realized the priestess had bitten the chicken's head off with her teeth, the headless animal was already wriggling in the hands of an assistant who was draining its blood into the bowl.

Her face smeared with blood, Madame Tombeau danced on, picking up even more speed as she twisted and turned. The second assistant stepped up unobtrusively behind her, bent down, and pulled a wooden cover from a hidden opening in the stage floor. The square seemed to be filled with water: Ondragon could see the light of the candles reflected in its silvery surface.

The swirling drum rhythm reached its climax, and with a scream the priestess dropped into the pool. After the loud splash, a breathless silence filled the room, and it was two minutes before a soft rippling sound was heard and the head of the Voodoo priestess appeared over the edge of the pool. She pushed herself sinuously out of the water, slid like a snake across the stage floor and through the powder. The dress stuck to her slender, flour-dusted body. She rolled onto her back, the neckline of her dress slipping and revealing her breasts.

Ondragon felt an electrifying, tingling excitement rise inside him. Stealthily, he looked around. The audience seemed to feel the same way. A murmur went through the rows, and here and there a hand reached furtively under the table in search of bare skin. Gradually, the priestess's dance became slower and more ponderous. She rolled sluggishly from side to side, finally coming to rest quietly on her back. Her chest rose and fell after her exertions. After a while, the two assistants approached her and helped her to her feet. Madame Tombeau looked into the audience with a surprisingly clear, powerful, and penetrating gaze. She stroked her neck and chest in satisfaction. Goose bumps covered her dark skin, and the water was beading off it like tiny diamonds. Directing an ambiguous smile at Ondragon, she slipped her dress back up over her nakedness. And as he was trying to tear his eyes away from the ravishing sight of her, about twenty spectators lined up in front of the stage as if to receive communion.

Madame Tombeau took the bowl of chicken blood and drew a bloody cross on the forehead of each disciple. As she did so, she murmured in French, "The energy of life from the guardian of cosmic treasure, Damballah!"

Sitting next to Ondragon at the bar half an hour later, she was hardly recognizable. She wore her business outfit, including the impossible glasses, and was acting cool.

"So you came, monsieur," she noted with a mocking undertone. "And, what strikes me even more, I can sense that your attitude has changed. Have you been taking the herbs?"

"Oh, I forgot about those. I'll make up for it later, I promise," he lied nonchalantly, deliberately trying to distract from any discussion of his frame of mind. He felt little desire to talk about it. Perhaps because he was feeling manipulated. "Tell me, are you really the owner of this illustrious club?"

"Yes, the club belongs to me. This is where I hold my rituals. It's a low-key meeting place for my community."

"If the authorities got wind of you beheading defenseless animals here and splashing blood around, they'd shut you down real quick . . ."

"I did not invite you here to threaten me, monsieur!"

"Nor am I, madame. I found your show exceptionally enjoyable; perhaps I'll come again . . . if I get to keep the key." Ondragon smiled his "charming" smile and drank his cocktail.

"It was not a show. This was, if you will, a church service!"

"Be that as it may. I'm here on another matter." He pointed to the newsprint package lying on the counter. "And I must say I'm not very amused by it!"

The Voodoo priestess raised her eyebrows questioningly, and Ondragon motioned her to open the packet. Warily, she flipped the paper aside and peered into it. Shaking her head, she looked up again. "This did not come from me. It's amateur hocus-pocus. I don't do that sort of thing."

"You sure? But I've seen Voodoo dolls at your store."

"The dolls are not real. Trinkets for tourists. Followers of Hoodoo may use something like that, but it's not real magic. Even in Haiti, we don't use dolls of that kind."

"Oh, that's news to me. You don't use dolls in Voodoo?"

"*Non!* The thing with dolls is nonsense, but unfortunately many people believe it. We have cheap fiction and third-rate horror movies to thank for that. But no one who is serious about Vodou would stick needles into dolls. That is absurd! And makes our religion seem archaic and violent. Which is not the case. Vodou is highly complex and not a tool for spreading fear and terror; on the contrary, it takes great care of its members. We priests offer help with problems, in times of need and illness. And the image of zombies as man-eating, semi-decaying undead is utter foolishness. But why am I talking to you about this? You don't believe any of it anyway." Madame Tombeau shrugged.

"And what about the little bag? Is that just lazy magic too?" Ondragon pointed to the package of newspaper.

Impatiently, Madame Tombeau pushed the paper aside again and looked at the item next to the doll. The next second, the color drained from her face and her hand flew up to her chest. She made the sign of the cross. "*Bondieu!* It's an ouanga!"

"But that's a good thing, isn't it? At least that's how you explained it to me this morning. An ouanga is a protective spell."

"No, I never said that. An ouanga is an *amulet* and it can contain white or black magic!"

Ondragon inwardly rolled his eyes. "And how can you tell that this is an evil one? It looks like the other one, the one in the photo I showed you."

"You can't see it from the outside. You can only feel it. And I feel that there is an evil magic in there."

Of course! Black magic, white magic! Bad juju, good juju! Ondragon was tired of being taken for a ride by the Madame. He was about to make a scathing reply when he saw the priestess looking at him. Her eyes seemed almost to glow from within.

"Listen!" she said beseechingly in her dark voice. "I can see you don't believe me. But this ouanga was sent to you by a bokor! He wants you to feel the fear. He has turned the eye of the diab upon you. The mirror shard on the ouanga is to attract the devil. You are in danger!" Without warning, she grabbed the package and dragged him by the arm past the stage, where another Voodoo dance was being performed. This time by a muscular, almost naked youth who was using torches to scorch his skin without feeling any pain.

They reached the back of the salon, where a door led into a small private room. Madame Tombeau took a key and locked the door from the inside, telling Ondragon to sit on the comfortable sofa while she stuffed the package, including the doll and the ouanga, into a plastic bag and threw it under a small side table. Visibly agitated, she then filled two glasses with water from a carafe and offered one to Ondragon. When he declined, she drank her own glass in greedy draughts. In the hushed seclusion of the small room, her nervousness seemed surprisingly genuine, and Ondragon wondered if he was actually in danger.

"What's so bad about this amulet, if I don't believe in it? I always thought Voodoo only worked on people who firmly believe in it. But this whole curse nonsense is of very little concern to me," he said, trying to get the Madame to give a reasonable explanation for this performance.

"You don't have to believe in it! It works the same way. When the spirits are called, they will come, regardless of whether you believe in them or not. It's a law, as it were. Or rather, it's a primal force of nature. A cosmic truth."

"Truth?" repeated Ondragon cuttingly.

"*Oui c'est ça!*" She raised both hands in confirmation. "And one truth is that you are in grave danger!" She pulled open a drawer in a small black cabinet and took out various items. They looked very much like the accessories on the stage.

Ondragon pursed his lips skeptically. "What are you doing?"

"A counterspell! Now hold your tongue, at least for a few minutes. I will explain to you what I am doing. And maybe afterward we can finally have a sensible conversation!"

"Go ahead!" Indignantly, Ondragon watched the Madame go about her tasks. The erotic imprint her dance had left on him had long since faded.

Madame Tombeau spread a white cloth on the small table and on it arranged a raffia-wound stick with a chicken foot at the end, a tiny packet wrapped in cloth and holding a feather (not unlike the "evil" sachet, but this time undoubtedly charged with positive energy, Ondragon thought wryly, finding the confusing designation of the paraphernalia suspicious), a crucible containing a grease-like substance, a vial, and a white candle.

"This is my magic pointer," the Madame said, pointing to each of the items in turn, "that is a paquet that will later hold the evil curse, pig fat and protective oil. And this is a hand-dipped candle into which I will work an onyx and the name of the loa I invoke." She reached to the wall behind her and pressed an old-fashioned bell button. Then she took the candle and did what she had described. Meanwhile, there was a knock at the door.

"Would you please unlock the door?" she said, handing him the key.

Ondragon opened the door and Natalie entered the small room.

"What do you need, madame?" she asked in French.

"Five leaves of *concombre zombi* and *un petit peu* of the chicken blood."

Natalie nodded and disappeared. The hypnotic drum rhythms of the fire dance drifted in from outside.

Moments later, the Madame had finished the wax work on the candle, the door opened again, and Natalie handed her mistress the bowl of blood and five serrated leaves.

"This is fresh datura, white jimsonweed, a key ingredient in the recipe. I'm making a very great concession by telling you this, Monsieur Ondragon. I do so only because otherwise you and your eternal skepticism would not trust me," Madame Tombeau explained, taking out a stone mortar in which she crushed the leaves with a coarse pestle. She then mixed the mashed leaves with the lard to make a greenish paste.

"Right, undress please!"

Surprised, Ondragon widened his eyes. "Pardon me? Don't you think that's going too far?"

"Not in the least. *S'il vous plaît*, your shirt and pants."

His teeth clenched, Ondragon did as the Madame asked and soon he was standing before her in his underpants. This was completely humiliating! At least they were in a private room. He found it difficult to tolerate the undisguised interest with which the priestess looked at his well-honed body; her gaze briefly lingered on the dragon tattoo on his chest, and the scars. Then she looked at his back in the mirror on the wall.

"You are a Marassa! I knew it," she whispered in obvious awe.

"A what?"

"I'll explain later. Come." The Madame rose and began to coat his temples, the crooks of his arms, and the backs of his knees with the paste. "Don't worry, it won't kill you!" she said teasingly, as he flinched when she tried to draw a cross on his forehead with the blood.

So Ondragon endured this process as well and hoped fervently that no one would open the door to the room and see him like this. Paul Eckbert Ondragon at a Voodoo séance!

Once the Madame finished with the painting, she sat down at the table while Ondragon continued to stand in front of her. She took the vial, dripped a few drops of the substance within onto the candle, and lit the wick. A flowery fragrance rose into the air. "This is your spirit candle. I am now calling upon the loa to fill you with its energy. After that, you must burn the candle for an hour every day until it is finished. This will prevent the curse from being renewed." She took the strange wand in her hand and raised her voice: "Bondieu, I call upon you, destroy the mirror of dark power, turn away the evil spell. Give me strength and give Paul Ondragon new life. Madame Brigitte, free his soul from the eye of the diab." She touched first him with the wand in various places and then the paquet. She then repeated the chant twice more until Ondragon felt the words take on a life of their own in his mind, multiplying to a deafening crescendo. An almost painful tugging sensation spread through his chest as the priestess's voice echoed from the inside of his skull back to his inner ear. The room began to spin before his eyes. Faster, faster, and faster. He began to sway.

"Ah, your *ti bon ange*. He shows himself!" he heard the Madame whisper reverently through the fog of buzzing colors and sounds.

"The *ti bon ange* is now free, the diab is vanquished, and the curse is broken." She touched his forehead one last time with the wand. Then she blew out the candle. "Wake up!"

Ondragon came to himself, reeling. He groped for a firm hold with both hands, like a man who had jumped off a speeding merry-go-round. It felt as if he had taken a trip in his own centrifuge of thoughts!

Madame Tombeau took a cloth and wiped the paste and blood from his body. "You may dress again, monsieur. Ah, *un moment!*" She picked up the wand, blew on it three times, and plunged it into Ondragon's stomach.

"Ouch! Isn't there a less violent way to do that?"

The Madame murmured something and then said, "I just took away one of the two curses you entered my store with today. It wasn't a bad spell, not as dangerous as the zombie curse, but it's bad for my business."

"For you?" Ondragon slipped back into his clothes.

"It was a music block. Someone put a spell on you—when I can't say—but the spell causes any kind of music to stop immediately when you enter the room. Haven't you noticed?"

"Um, no."

The Madame laughed. "That's what happened when you entered the club earlier. I was watching you. You came in and the performance ended. You think it's coincidence, but it's not." She looked at him seriously. "I could never invite you to my club again if I hadn't broken the spell; you would have ruined all my performances!"

Ondragon scratched his head, which was still spinning slightly. There was probably something to it. He lifted his eyes and looked at the Madame steadily. "Can we talk?"

"And I was afraid I'd never get you to see reason." Smiling, she pointed to the armchair opposite her.

Once Ondragon sat down, mentally as well as physically, he was ready to show the Madame some respect for her profession. He began to tell her about the video footage from the Arizona Hotel in which Charlize Kaplan had witnessed Bolič's resurrection. He told of the doltish, brainless behavior of the Bosnian and the man in tails and a top hat. The Madame had a violent reaction to this description. Whereas before she had merely been nodding, this time she drew in a sharp breath and regarded him, her nostrils quivering. Tiny beads of sweat formed on her forehead.

"*Bondieu*, why didn't you say that before? That was Baron Samedi!"

Ondragon had heard the name many times. "The Lord of the Graveyards?"

"*Correctement.* He is the leader of all gèdè, the dark loa, the gods of the night. He can be recognized from his solemnly frivolous appearance. He likes to wear a tailcoat and top hat and sometimes sunglasses, carry a walking stick, and smoke cigars. His face is a skull, pale and haggard. He usually speaks in a nasal tone . . ."

"He speaks?"

"Yes, when the Baron rides someone, that is, when he takes possession of him in the trance, he speaks through the human mouth. The possessed person behaves like the Baron and sings the song of the gravedigger. In my homeland, Samedi is feared as a god, but besides the terrible power he has over the dead, he is also a wise loa. There is a test to determine if someone has actually been possessed by Baron Samedi. They must drink sugarcane liquor laced with corrosive herbs. No ordinary person with merely a normal *ti bon ange* inside him can survive this murderous drink without harm."

"By *ti bon ange*, you mean the soul of a human being?" Ondragon wanted to know.

"Not exactly. There is the *gros bon ange* and the *ti bon ange*, the big and the small angels. The big angel is the energy that keeps a person alive, and the small one is closest to what your enlightened Western world calls the soul, spirit, character, and conscience."

Ondragon nodded. That was interesting, he had to admit. But he still doubted it had been Baron Samedi who had received Bolič in front of the Arizona Hotel.

"That Samedi took this man from the hotel does not surprise me at all," Madame Tombeau continued, as if she had guessed what he was thinking. "The Baron commands the dead, so he also commands the zombies. Black magicians have to ask his permission if they want to take someone from the grave and turn them into a zombie. Wherever there is a zombie, Samedi is not far away."

"And the Baron can also appear without taking possession of someone and riding them?"

"*Oui.* He appears whenever he wants, with or without possessing someone."

Because he did not want to start an argument with the Madame about her faith, he left it at that, instead talking about his visit to Sylvester Stern and the condition in which he had found the mailman. He also mentioned the letter, of course.

"Did you bring it with you?" the priestess wanted to know.

"No. But it's safe."

"There is zombie powder in it; be careful with it. It could take you straight to your grave."

"Would you tell me what the powder is made up of?"

"Of course not; it's a secret recipe!"

"And you know what's in it?"

"*Bien sûr.*"

Ondragon looked at her seriously. "Madame Tombeau, can you make a zombie?"

The priestess regarded him for a long time. Then she nodded. "It is not illegal to make a zombie, if someone has received a warning."

"What kind of a warning?"

"A *coup l'aire* from the *Shanpwel.*"

Ondragon smiled. "You see? I find it hard to believe all this when you speak in riddles like that. That's why I'm taking a very rational approach to getting to the bottom of this spirit. I have sent the letter to my chemist. He will examine the sample and determine what kind of substance it is."

Madame Tombeau raised a finger admonishingly. "That is not a good idea. The *coup poudre* is dangerous! In the wrong hands it can do a lot of harm. You have seen for yourself!" Her hand swept through the air. "Tell me, where does he live, this star, the one you visited?"

"In Chalmette."

"Then we'll go there right away!" She reached across the table for his wrist and turned it so she could read the time on his watch.

"Maybe I can still save him. A man who has passed through the earth can be changed back, unless the bokor has completed his spell. In that case he will remain a *zombi cadavre*, a slave of the *malfacteur*! But we can't just let a zombie run around out there either. They are dangerous creatures with no spirit. They do whatever their master tells them." The Madame rose. "If he's beyond saving, we'll have to hunt him down!" She reached for the candle and passed it to him. "Light it every day, remember." Then she reached under the table, pulled out the plastic bag with the doll and the ouanga, tossed the paquet into it, and opened the door of the small room. Natalie was standing outside.

"Take this to the master of ceremonies and have him burn it!" The Madame handed the bag to her assistant, who bowed and hurried away through the salon, which was still full of people.

Ondragon watched her for a moment and then followed Madame Tombeau out of the club.

Outside on the street they were greeted by surprisingly cool air, and the sky above the roofs of the French Quarter was jet black and starry. From Bourbon Street, which was still bustling, music and laughter drifted over as if from a distant fairground. Ondragon nodded to the Madame and led her through the colorful neon light in the direction of his hotel.

Neither of them noticed that they were followed by a man in a top hat.

CHAPTER 10

February 9, 2010
Chalmette, Louisiana
1:57 am

More or less in silence, they drove through the New Orleans night. After thirty minutes, as they turned into the street where Stern's house stood, Ondragon was overcome with doubt. Would Madame Tombeau actually be able to cure the mailman?

Yeah, right, cure! It would be more accurate to ask whether she would raise him from the dead. That seemed pretty dubious to him, even completely absurd. Now that he was here in his car and the effect of the magical atmosphere of the ceremony had worn off, he found the Madame's alleged witchcraft even more amateurish than before. He gave his passenger a quick sideways glance.

Had she actually released him from a music spell? He laughed to himself. Probably not. He had more likely been taken in by the Madame's little magic show. And the only purpose of that had been to convince him of something that did not exist. His headache and dizziness were gone too. It was all just imagination, as was so often the case with mystical superstitions. It was a well-known fact that imagination had led many people into the most bizarre delusions. And with the right drugs, a pseudo-priest could transport his victim into all sorts of states where they would willingly and unreservedly believe in the most irrational things. Zombies, for example. He gave another silent laugh.

"You still think I'm hoodwinking you!"

Caught off guard, Ondragon blinked and was glad the Madame couldn't see him in the darkness of the car. "I'm not thinking anything!" he replied gruffly. "I just want to find out why someone is going after people and turning them into . . . the living dead."

"I can't help you with that, unfortunately. I can only tell you if it's a zombie or just someone who seems dead. And I might be able to cure them. You'll have to figure out the *why* for yourself." Her tone sounded haughty. Did she think she had convinced him? Well, she had misjudged him.

They reached the mailman's address, and Ondragon parked in the same undeveloped spot as before. Under cover of darkness, they crept into Stern's neglected garden and through the back door into the house. Only now did Ondragon flick on his little finger flashlight.

Madame Tombeau clicked her tongue. "You're well equipped!"

"It's my job to be well equipped," he replied dryly.

"Ah yes, I forgot."

Was that sarcasm?

Ondragon did not dwell on it. If he did not take her completely seriously, she had a perfect right not to take him seriously. He couldn't hold that against her.

With the Madame in tow, he climbed the stairs and stopped by the closed door to Stern's bedroom. The stench was still suffocating. He jerked his thumb toward the door. "He's in there, but don't be alarmed. He's not exactly looking his best."

"Thank you for your concern, but I've seen one or two dead bodies in my time."

"And zombies too?"

The Madame snorted contemptuously. She had of course heard his skepticism.

Unable to hold back a sardonic grin, Ondragon was about to push the door open when his phone rang. They both jumped.

Cursing softly, Ondragon took it out and looked at the display. It was Rod! Now, of all times. He answered it. "Hey, Rod. It's very inconvenient just now. I'll call you right back, okay?"

"Are you banging a hot chick or what?"

"I wish. See you later." He hung up.

"Your boss?" the Madame asked snarkily.

"No, my mother!" Ondragon put the phone away and punched the door. It swung open. It was no longer possible to disturb the dead man's peace anyway. He aimed the flashlight beam at the bed.

"He's gone," the Madame stated.

Ondragon quickly slid the light over the room. Unfortunately, Stern had not rolled out of bed onto the floor either. How could he have, he was dead! But then why wasn't he here? The *centrifuge* in his head began to spin alarmingly fast. Was he falling victim to a major con here? A hoax that Rod had concocted? For the sake of the good old days? He took the phone from his pocket and pressed recall.

"All done?" Rod said, amused, picking up.

"Rod, you tell me right now what's going on! I'm starting to think this isn't funny anymore. Besides, I really don't like it when people waste my time!"

"What are you talking about, Ecks?"

"The tasteless joke you're playing here. Tell your people they can come out now and stop laughing!"

"I still don't understand. What happened?"

"You"—Ondragon tried to contain his anger—"you didn't make up this nonsense about the zombies?"

"Zombies?" Peals of laughter rang out from the phone. *"Holy shit!* What in the world are you talking about?"

Ondragon stared at the wall. So Rod had no idea . . .

He heard a racket coming from the first floor. Immediately, Ondragon ended the conversation. Rod would have to wait. He looked at the Madame and she nodded. Then he turned off the flashlight, drew his gun, and went ahead down the stairs. Before he reached the landing, a long-drawn-out groan came from the living room, and Ondragon paused, his back pressed against the wall. Pistol at the ready, he listened to the stranger's ponderous steps shuffling across the carpet. Ondragon felt a tug on the sleeve of his jacket and turned his head. The Madame looked up at him, the whites of her eyes glowing eerily in the darkness, and her mouth formed one word: *ZOMBIE!*

Another sound came from the living room, and without warning Ondragon sprinted off. It was the back door banging. When he reached it and tried to get through, he came to an abrupt stop.

"Fuck!" He rubbed his aching shoulder angrily. "Son of a bitch locked it!" He took out his lock pick set, and after what seemed like an eternity, the door was open again. Almost relieved, they stepped out and listened to the moonless night. From the street came the sound of soft footsteps.

Crouching, Ondragon ran around the house and peered at the sparsely lit street. A shadow was stumbling away from them on the sidewalk, making muffled roaring sounds, as if it had a lung disease. Ondragon cautiously took up the pursuit, working his way from front yard to front yard. The Madame followed him determinedly. She was amazingly skillful, moving as silently as a snake despite her high-heeled shoes.

After a few hundred yards, they came to a crossroads and paused, concealed by a bush. Where had the man—or whatever it was— gone? Had he turned right or left?

"There!" said the Madame at his side, pointing down the street to the left.

In the distance, Ondragon spotted a shadowy figure and was surprised it could move so fast, although it was staggering like a shot bear. How could you achieve that kind of speed with such an uncontrolled gait?

They quickly followed the staggering shadow, ducking behind garbage cans and fences, never taking their eyes off it. The presumed undead marched on with determined purpose.

Where was it going? Was its master calling it?

They kept at it until the figure reached a row of cars parked on the side of the road. It was only two more blocks from the main street, which was busy at night.

It's now or never, Ondragon thought, and set off at a sprint without regard for the Madame. Whatever this guy was, zombie or not, he would hunt him down now!

As if the zombie had heard something, it turned its head jerkily and looked in his direction. Ondragon didn't have time to take cover in the open street, so he decided to go all out. Still running, he raised his pistol and shouted, "Freeze!"

Amazingly, the zombie did as it was told and froze mid-grotesque shuffle. Its arms hanging, it stood there like a big doll whose batteries had suddenly failed. Ondragon strained to see in the darkness, but he couldn't even tell if the guy's hair was light or dark.

When he was only an estimated fifteen steps from the guy, he slowed down. The other guy seemed to be unarmed, but he preferred to be Mr. Play-It-Safe than Mr. Autopsy. That had always been his motto.

Before Ondragon could react, the figure sprang with tremendous agility. But not toward him, as he had expected, but into the gap between a van and a pickup truck. Cursing, Ondragon followed it, pointing his gun at the gap.

But there was nothing there!

"Shit!" He dropped to all fours and aimed the Sig Sauer under both cars.

Hell!

He couldn't see anything there either.

He jumped back up and circled the vehicles. Where could the guy have gone? It was impossible.

Ondragon lowered his weapon. Only now did he remember Madame Tombeau and turned around. But the street behind him was empty. He stared intensely into the darkness lined with sleeping houses. Had Madame Tombeau gotten stuck somewhere with her high-heeled shoes? Or maybe she had gotten scared after all and was hiding.

"Madame?" he called softly, spinning around. "Where are you? Come on out. The guy's gone." No answer. Was she playing a trick on him?

She didn't do that kind of thing.

Ondragon had just reached this realization when Bugs Bunny and his toothy grin appeared before his eyes, just as the arm wrapped around his neck and squeezed.

Was he lying in his bed? Was he dreaming?

What else could this strange state be called, if not a dream?

Ondragon was familiar with this kind of nightmare, where you lay in bed and saw images that scared you to death. It was like that now too. He felt that he was lying on a mattress with sheets. The room was dark except for a sliver of bright light that fell through a slightly open door. He heard unidentifiable snatches of speech. A laugh. Then it went quiet again. Ondragon breathed evenly. *Don't get agitated.* Experience told him such dreams would pass. But the voices came again and suddenly the crack in the door widened, and the light got brighter and brighter as it fell into the room onto his bed. Onto him!

A shadow appeared in the doorway. A small, dwarfish shadow.

Ondragon turned his head; he wanted to see who it was.

The dwarf came slowly toward him, stretched out a hand, and croaked in a strange toneless voice . . . and in Swedish, "Paul, you are to blame. You are to blame for my death!"

Oh my God, it was Per!

His brother! Now that he was standing next to the bed, Ondragon could see his pale features too. A deep cleft gaped in his forehead. Blood and something else was oozing from it in thick threads and running down the boy's face like black tears.

Ondragon wanted to open his mouth to mollify Per, to apologize, but he could not. His mouth was suddenly full of the viscous black mass; the more he tried to spit it out the more of it there was. Desperately, he used his hands to pull the disgusting stuff out of his mouth. But the tar-like mush stuck to them too; it was going to suffocate him . . .

Like Per under the books!

Pleadingly, Ondragon raised his hands to his brother. Per stared back uncomprehendingly.

After a terribly long moment when he thought Per would simply leave him to die, Per very tentatively raised a hand. Ondragon reached out to touch it, to accept his help. He was about to sink to his knees and thank his brother for his forgiveness, but just before their fingertips touched, the ten-year-old jerked his hand back. His mouth opened and a horrible laugh escaped from it. At first gurgling and inarticulate, then full-bodied and contemptuous. He laughed and laughed until blood began to gush from the wound on his forehead. It pulsed forth in a rich, hot stream, sullying the bed, their clothes, and Ondragon's face. He quickly closed his lips, but it was too late. His brother's warm lifeblood mixed with the black mass in his mouth, forming a sweet mush that made him gag. Filled with revulsion, he turned away and spat. Again and again.

When he turned back a little later, Per had disappeared and finally the stuff was gone from his mouth. Instead, a new shadow stood in the brightly lit doorway. This time a very large one, because it reached right up to the lintel. The shadow was carrying a long, thin object and had a strangely misshapen head, long and angular.

The terrible laughter rang out again. This time it changed into a shrill and hysterical staccato. Ondragon tried to wake up from the nightmare and open his eyes, but his eyelids were partially glued shut. He sat in fear as the shadow moved slowly toward him and began to sing a French song.

Ondragon tossed and turned feverishly. Even if he couldn't fully open his eyes, he wanted at least to get up from his sleeping place and face his attacker, ready to fight. He tried to force himself free of the paralyzing grip of sleep, but it kept him strapped to his bed like a patient in a mental institution. The shadow had now arrived at the bed and was leaning over him. A skull face floated toward him. Only now did Ondragon realize that the shadowy figure was wearing a top hat on its head.

Baron Samedi!

Had he come to turn him into a zombie? A member of the walking dead, like his brother, Per?

Ondragon went to scream, but a hand was placed on his mouth. The skull grinned. "Sleep, human, go to sleep!" it whispered, blowing a powder into his face. Ondragon felt an itch in his nose and an urge to sneeze; an appeal to his body shot through his head, urging it to fight the hell back, but in the same instant the image of the skull swam before his eyes, and a dark swirl of damp earth and crushed bones took its place. Slowly but inexorably, this grinding maelstrom dragged him back into the oppressive darkness of his nightmare. Then there was nothing. Only the silence of the grave.

* * *

The next time he felt anything like the breath of reality, he was no longer in his bed. He was also no longer in a room. But he couldn't have said where he was either. He was lying on his back, that much at least was clear, but his vision was so blurred it was as if someone had put glasses on him that were far too strong. No matter how many times he blinked, all he could see were green shadows that changed from light to dark and back again. Likewise, his other senses didn't seem to be fully intact. His nose and tongue were numb and his hearing was acting like it had been right next to the jukebox throughout a night of disco. Only muffled sounds reached the nerve cells in his inner ear—a buzzing and something like a ringing.

He turned his head on the soft ground. Could he feel moisture on his skin? Immediately, he was gripped by excitement. What if he was injured and it was his own blood he was feeling? Making a great effort, he tried to move his arms but only succeeded after he realized that they had gone to sleep. How long had he been lying on them and cutting off his circulation?

Tingling painfully, first his fingers came to life and then his forearms and upper arms. When he could trust his limbs to obey him, he carefully rolled onto his side. But even this slightest movement caused sudden nausea. Ondragon paused until the acid surges in his stomach had subsided. Meanwhile, he dug his fingers into the damp ground and felt and groped . . .

What the hell was that?

It was not cold, but it was not particularly warm either. Was it blood or just water? His clothes were soaked in it too. He raised a hand to his head. Small chunks were hanging in his hair. They felt kind of slimy.

After a moment of puzzling unsuccessfully over what they might be, Ondragon continued with the reanimation of his body. Inch by inch, he rose from the damp ground as his mind tried to recall what had happened to him. But the knowledge would not come. All that was flickering in his mind's eye was a grinning Bugs Bunny. Absurd. Instead, the dull ringing in his ear gradually became clearer. Unfortunately, it still sounded suspiciously like tinnitus.

He sat for quite a while, staring and listening like a blind man for the slightest change in the green soundscape that surrounded him. Soon he noticed that the shadows before his clouded vision were taking on darker hues, and the light green was giving way to a muted pine green. The skin of his face also told him that the temperature around him was dropping. And as if a DJ had put on a record that better matched the changing mood, a little later the concert in his inner ear gained a new octave. A bright warbling sound.

Ondragon held his nose and blew air against the pressure in his eardrums. When he lowered his hand again, his sense of smell and taste kicked in and suddenly he knew not only what had happened, but also where he was!

"Shit! Shit!" He jumped jerkily to his feet, causing his eyes to black out briefly as his circulation failed to keep up. Immediately, his feet became wet in his shoes, and the ground began to suck at them. It was so soft that Ondragon sank in up to his ankles. Horrified by the wet reality, he stood motionless.

In the middle of the swamp!

And what was worse, the sun was just setting.

Exactly the time the alligators woke up!

CHAPTER 11

He was in the marshlands. Precisely where he was made no difference at all, because New Orleans was surrounded on all sides by mud. The Mississippi Delta was one huge, wet yard in front of hell! Several hundred square miles of nothing but swamp. Louisiana was the only state with an unmappable border to the south, for the Mississippi River dumped vast amounts of new silt and sediment into the swamps every year, constantly changing the coastline. Louisiana grew farther out into the sea every day.

And this was where he was stuck. Great!

He searched his pockets, sighing. Unfortunately, he found neither his cell phone, nor the knife, nor the Sig Sauer. The holster was dangling empty beneath his armpit. They hadn't even left him his wristwatch or gum. Well, that was just perfect! He was stuck here in the wilderness with nothing that could help him in any way. The only difference from the situation back in Minnesota was that this time he wasn't surrounded by fucking forest.

He was surrounded by a fucking forest in the water!

Ondragon almost wished he had stayed in the desert; then at least he would have dry feet right now.

He raised his head and tried to make out more. The dark green before his clouded eyes gradually changed to shadowy blue and finally to black. Nightfall at least made his poor vision irrelevant. Black was black. Now he would have to focus solely on his hearing. Ondragon had long since discovered that his ears were not as badly affected as he had previously assumed. The buzzing, ringing, and warbling were not the effects of hearing loss, they were the sound of birds, cicadas, and frogs raising their voices together in their evening swamp concert. How lovely!

Listening carefully all around him, swaying with his arms stretched out ahead of him, Ondragon put one foot in front of the other, feeling with his toes with each step to check whether the ground would hold him. He had to get up higher, and preferably find a tree he could climb. Only then would he make it through the night without drowning in the silt or being eaten by alligators and other silent swamp creatures like poisonous snakes and spiders. It didn't matter which direction he moved in.

After a few steps, his outstretched fingers bumped against something hard. He felt the obstacle and recognized a tree with expansive roots. Probably a bald cypress. With water all around. Well, wasn't that just peachy! This tree was no good as a hiding place. Ondragon pushed off the trunk and continued his laborious walk through the sucking ground. The water quickly became deeper and deeper, and when it reached above his waist, he stopped. He had probably reached a bayou, one of the countless small rivers that ran through the swampland. Briefly, he wondered if he should wade through. It would be better to swim, his instincts told him; at least that way he wouldn't get stuck in the mud at the bottom. But what if he swam and didn't reach a shore on the other side? Then he might never find his way back to the shallows, let alone his starting point. And then the only thing left for him to do would be to tread water . . . until he ran out of strength. Besides, swimming would turn him into perfect alligator food.

So wading after all, then. If only he had a stick to test how deep the mud was and keep the critters at bay.

The water became even deeper and quickly reached his chest. Ondragon paused and asked himself: *Turn back or continue?* He bit his lip, listening for sounds. Sure enough, he heard a splash. Right behind him!

Go on! If one of those hungry giant lizards is lurking there, your only escape is to keep moving forward!

He paddled with his arms in the water; this made his progress a little easier, but caused a lot of noise. He would definitely attract the predators doing that.

Suddenly, the ground disappeared from beneath his feet and he went under. He resurfaced, snorting, and kicked his legs frantically in the dark water, but found no bottom. Panic gripped him as he looked around in the liquid blackness. There was no chance of spotting even a muskrat tail, no prospect of hitting any solid ground that would save him! Ondragon knew there was nothing left for him to do now. He took a breath, leaned forward, and began to swim. After ten strokes, he still felt nothing. Even after twenty, he could only feel open water around him. It sloshed into his mouth and tasted slightly salty. Brackish water, on the one hand, was a comfort because, along with the lack of swell, it was a sure indication that he was not yet swimming out to the open sea. On the other hand, he couldn't drink it without experiencing Montezuma's revenge. And as if this thought had reminded his dry throat of the lack of liquid, he suddenly felt terribly thirsty.

How ironic! You are surrounded by water, but you can't drink it. Suddenly, another thought occurred to him. *What if you are in the middle of the Mississippi River?* He stopped moving his arms and legs and checked whether he felt a current. But the water was still as a millpond.

Keep swimming!

After a few dozen strokes, Ondragon felt something brush against his leg. He tried to stay calm, telling himself it was a piece of driftwood or seaweed, not a reptile with two rows of sharp teeth in its mouth. He quickened his pace until his muscles were burning and his lungs ached. If he got out of here alive, he would need to work on his swimming urgently.

His breath caught as his fingers bumped painfully against an obstacle. He quickly pulled them back and then felt his way forward again a little more carefully. He gave a relieved laugh. It was a root! And the root belonged to a dense network of many more roots, which in turn led up to a tree trunk as thick as his thigh. A mangrove! With trembling arms, Ondragon pulled himself up into the mesh, where he found a place where he could sit and lean back, slightly above the waterline. There he remained—hanging in the branches like a wet garment—until dawn.

* * *

With a jolt, he awoke from a brief, fitful sleep. He was tormented by blinding light, itchy skin, and numb bruises on his butt, and his clothes reeked of decay. Even as Ondragon registered all these things, he realized his vision was clear again. He looked around right away, checking his surroundings in the light of the rising sun.

In front of him lay the arm of water he must have crossed last night, around 80 yards wide, and beyond it the muddy shore lined with trees whose root balls sat directly in the water. These were massive water oaks, plumes of gray moss hanging down from their gnarled branches like the hair of aging witches. He turned around. Behind him stretched an almost impenetrable thicket of mangroves and other swamp plants, covered by a shady canopy of leaves. Not particularly inviting, but at least they offered a way of moving around without getting wet. Besides, he now knew which way was east. To his left, the sun was shooting its first rays through the branches, sprinkling the surface of the water with golden points of light. A pretty sight . . . but right now he was in no mood to be delighted by the contemplation of nature.

He looked down and hurriedly pulled in his dangling legs. Only a few feet beneath him, an alligator was lurking patiently in the water among the roots. It wasn't quite 6 feet long, but its wide mouth might easily engulf a basketball. And that would be enough to tear vicious wounds.

Ondragon stood up on the swaying branches, his limbs stiff, and made his way to the next root ball, away from the beast. He had little desire to find out if the reptile's big brother was waiting somewhere out there in the open water. An involuntary shiver gripped him at the memory of crossing the bayou in complete darkness. He had once heard that Mississippi alligators could grow to a length of twenty feet. They could swallow a human in moments without leaving a hair behind.

Ondragon suppressed the thought and tried to focus on his present situation. He looked down at himself. Another suit ruined!

A mosquito tried to settle on his cheek and he swatted it away. That scourge with wings was all he needed! He brushed the sweat from his forehead. In the sun, the temperature had risen rapidly and he was now sweating uncomfortably. Ondragon knew that this was due to 100 percent humidity, and a temperature of around 80 degrees Fahrenheit. You needed to drink at least half a gallon of water a day—and that was without physical activity and at moderate outside temperatures. With dehydration of around 3 percent, you began to feel thirsty. At 10 percent, it became critical. Ondragon quickly calculated how long he would last without water in these conditions.

The result was devastating.

He had less than thirty-eight hours. And he didn't know where he was. The swamp area he was in could go on for miles and miles, and he would be wandering around in it almost haphazardly until the first symptoms of dehydration set in: problems with speech, headache, general confusion. His blood would thicken and his heartbeat would slow before he would be felled by general circulatory collapse.

A wonderful prospect!

So it was all the more urgent to think calmly about how to get out. He leaned against a mangrove trunk and thought back to what he had learned from DeForce so long ago. If you were in the shit, the first basic rule was: Always gather the facts first, then look for a solution!

Well, he could always panic later. He looked around again and recapped what he could see in front of him and what he knew about it. After all, he wasn't stuck in the middle of nowhere, even if it felt that way. He was in Louisiana (or so he hoped), which was a state in the US. Gradually, his faithful *centrifuge* got going and retrieved everything he had stored in his visual memory vault about the Pelican State. First of all, he knew that Louisiana, at more than 50,000 square miles and with a population of nearly 4.5 million, had the largest wetlands in the United States. It could be deduced from this that the state had a population density of 105 people per square mile, who certainly did not dwell in the swamps! Most of the inhabitants were, of course, concentrated in the major cities and the less muddy northern half of the country. In addition to the state's well-developed network of back roads (which again, unfortunately, did not cover the swamps), four major transport arteries ran through it: the Mississippi River, a navigable waterway, Interstate 20 in the north of the state, Interstate 49, running diagonally through it, and Interstate 10, which ran through New Orleans to the north of where he was now, built on stilts and connecting The Big Easy with Baton Rouge to the west and Gulfport, Mississippi. to the east.

South of New Orleans was the Mississippi Delta, consisting mainly of swamps and bayous and with a few scattered settlements and roads, but no major city. All that was left was the fact that the highest elevation in Louisiana, Driskill Mountain, which had notable views, rose to all of 535 feet, and was located—where, of course?—in the north.

But that's the magic word, Ondragon thought. *Views!*

He tilted his head back. The mangroves around him were not especially tall. He looked across the bayou to the far bank. If he could manage to climb one of the water oaks or cypress trees over there and get an overview of the area, he would be halfway to civilization. Too bad those kinds of trees apparently only grew on the other side of the wide channel of water. Ondragon thought it through. Should he climb through the mangrove thicket and hope to come across taller trees there? Or even find help?

But heading off without knowing his rough location was pure suicide.

And so is racing an alligator across the bayou!

Ondragon was not certain about the decision. Should he wander through the swamp without a map or swim back through the bayou? If he listened to his irrational fear, he would choose the first option. But he was not a man who let himself be guided by mere emotions. Most of the time, at least. He remembered thinking he was infected with anthrax and his panicked reaction. Well, nobody was perfect. But at least he could claim that the larger half of his brain was rational and strategic. After all, he was an ex-mailman too! And an ex-mailman did not allow his mind to be unbalanced by a few unknown factors. On the contrary, he flourished in situations like these! All things considered, his meticulous mind had already saved his life on countless occasions. And it would do the same now.

Ondragon could literally feel his brain calculating the odds with mechanical precision. The result was that he had a greater chance of success crossing the bayou than hiking through the mangroves toward an uncertain destination. Hey, three cheers for probability calculus!

With fresh confidence, he climbed back to the edge of the water and peered down into the murk. The alligator had disappeared. It had probably realized that its peanut-sized brain was hopelessly inferior to the highly evolved intelligence of the being on two legs, and made off.

In preparation for the crossing, Ondragon removed one of his good leather shoes and put it over his right hand. He would shove it between the gator's teeth if it attacked him. And as long as it didn't attack from below . . .

He wrapped his jacket around his waist and loosened his ruined tie. You never knew. In all other respects, his fine city suit was somewhat unsuited to a survival march in the wilderness. But those were the facts.

Ondragon gazed out at the glassy bayou, looking for the small ripples that indicated movement in the water. But the surface of the river was motionless. He sucked in air sharply, feeling a slight twinge of fear. That unwelcome companion of all fraidy-cats had crept into the cooler compartment of his emotions and was now rummaging unhindered, looking for sustenance. There was no way he was going to let that happen. He shot down the intruder with his hard, direct, incorruptible logic.

Either you swim or you die! It's that simple.

Making a rapid decision, he stretched his arms forward and went down on his knees. Then he pushed off and dove headlong into the murky water. Before he broke the surface, he began to swim in long strokes, and when he emerged he moved into a powerful crawl. His movements echoed loudly in his ears, deafening him to other sounds. But he had no other choice. Crawl was the fastest.

Swimming steadily, he tried to increase his speed even more, looking over the water every time he took a breath. Everything was still, smooth, and calm. The opposite shore was getting closer. Yard by yard. When he was two-thirds of the way across, a handful of startled herons rose out of the reeds ahead of him, and he spotted something elongated pushing off the shore into the water. But rather than pausing, Ondragon changed his direction by a few degrees and increased his stroke rate. Once more, the burning pain ignited in his limbs and settled paralyzingly in his red muscle fiber, which was responsible for endurance. Ondragon felt a certain amount of anger at his inadequacy. He hadn't been in such bad shape in a long time. His captors had likely pumped him full of drugs, which were still slowing down his bodily functions.

To his great horror, a sharp V-line suddenly cut through the smooth surface on his right. Two bumps the size of Ping-Pong balls peeked out of the water. The eyes of an alligator. Whether it was the same one that had been keeping him company that morning or a much larger specimen, he could not tell. He quickly cast a searching glance ahead to the shore. He estimated that he was 20 yards from the narrow strip of reeds, which was also under water. No solid ground, then. Would that protect him?

There was no other way. He had to go there. In open water, he was lost. Desperately throwing his arms forward with increasingly powerless movements, he risked a sideways glance. The V-line was there and it had come closer; although the reptile was setting a leisurely pace, it was catching up effortlessly. Ondragon mobilized all his remaining energy and plowed his arms through the water.

Don't think about what's behind you, think about what's in front of you! Or better, don't think at all! Swim! Swim for your fucking life! One, two, breathe, one, two, breathe. Faster! You can do it.

He felt a huge blow to his right leg and a sudden stab of pain shot up his spine. Surprised, Ondragon cried out and rolled on his side in the water. He flailed his arms wildly, kicking his feet out at the bottomless depths like the hooves of a mule. Hastily, he turned his head in all directions, his hand raised with his shoe. Where was the brute? Of course, the V-line had disappeared from the surface: The alligator had dived so its victim could not see its next attack coming. Treacherous beast!

Something brushed against his calf again, and in shock, Ondragon inhaled brackish water into his lungs. Coughing, he strove to stay afloat and keep his eyes on the shore. There were only 5 yards to go, three measly body lengths! *Come on, keep swimming! Giving up is for amateurs!*

Despite his aching leg and unmistakable signs of fatigue, he threw himself forward into the waters, doing the crawl, not looking back. His whole world was brown, murky water rushing into his mouth and ears, the foaming roar of his movement. Like a channel swimmer, he struggled onward . . . until his feet finally hit the bottom. With a cry of victory, he heaved himself out of the river and was about to dash to the shore when the alligator's head emerged from the water beside him. Silently, its mouth shot forward, revealing a pink tongue and irregular rows of conical teeth. Ondragon reacted instinctively, stuffed the shoe deep into the reptile's throat, and quickly withdrew his hand.

The alligator, sensing that it had hit something solid, dove under with a gurgle and spun around several times. Ondragon used the death roll programmed into the animal and with his last ounce of strength wriggled his way to the shoreline, where he hastily fled to the nearest large tree. He managed to grab a low-hanging branch and swing his legs up.

About as elegant as a sloth, but safe from the alligator, he finally hung there until he could catch his breath and pull himself onto the branch. After that, it took a very long time for his heartbeat to return to normal.

At some point, exhausted, Ondragon lifted his head from the rough bark of the branch and looked down. The damn beast was still crouched in the shallows, waiting. Luckily it was his old friend, because if it had been one of its larger colleagues, he might now have a messily amputated lower leg instead of a cut. Ondragon dangled his arms and gave the reptile the middle finger.

"We'll talk later, you handbag with teeth!" At least he had regained his sense of humor; otherwise this crappy situation would be unbearable. He sat up slowly, checking every muscle. Except for a dull ache in his limbs and the burning of the wound on his leg, everything seemed okay.

Good, now we'll move on to the next project, he thought cynically. The crossing of the Amazon will be followed by the ascent of Mount Everest. The Jungle Olympics covered all disciplines!

He looked up into the crown of the mighty water oak in which he had taken refuge. The route up looked doable. Since he had no time to waste, he got right to it.

Branch by branch he worked his way up, and after an agonizing eternity he finally broke through the dense canopy of leaves.

The view that presented itself was . . . sobering.

The tree towered over its neighbors, but there was nothing for miles but the green carpet of swamp crisscrossed here and there by the silvery vein of a bayou. No evidence of human presence, no telephone poles or mobile phone masts and no roofs.

Disappointed, Ondragon pinched the bridge of his nose. What should he do now? Did he have any chance at all, or was he struggling in vain? Was he putting all his hope into a completely pointless illusion?

He slid listlessly back into the shade of the leafy canopy. Not even up here was there a breeze to refresh him. Streams of sweat ran down his irritated skin, accelerating the inevitable dehydration. Slumping, he hung in the fork of the branch and considered his situation once more. He didn't know what worried him more—the fact that he had no tools at his disposal, or his lack of provisions. He desperately needed water, that was for sure! He could last a little longer without food. The limiting factor was definitely the lack of hydration. Immediately, an image entered his mind: silvery puddles. He had seen drinkable water . . . here on the tree! Ondragon laughed at the sluggishness of his neural pathways, which had taken until now to relay the image to his gray matter. On the way up, he had passed several forks of branches in which water had collected.

Ondragon descended to the first water-filled fork. After some hesitation, he ditched his reservations about its palatability and scooped the clear water into his mouth with one hand. It tasted mossy, but otherwise seemed perfectly wholesome. He drank the fork empty and the next one too, until he felt his saliva production starting up again and his tongue no longer sticking to the roof of his mouth. Seeing there was no way to take the water with him, he emptied the third reservoir as well, just in case.

Arriving at the lowest branch, he was greeted by the slender silhouette of the alligator in the water, while in his ear Sir Elton John was softly singing "Crocodile Rock." How on earth was he going to get rid of the beast? An alligator like that could hold out for days, if not weeks. He was probably calmly digesting the shoe.

If I had a knife, friend, I'd turn you into crocodile sushi! Ondragon let his eyes wander from the reptile into the distance. First of all, he should think about which direction to go. North, he guessed, hoping to find the I-10. He would be able to use Polaris to maintain that direction at night, at least. He would not swim the bayou again, in any case.

For half an eternity, he pondered how he might get rid of the floating Gucci bag, but an adequate solution failed to materialize. Disgruntled, Ondragon registered that the sun was already lower in the sky again. One or two o'clock, he estimated. His gaze lingered on his feet, one in a shoe, the other shoeless. A single shoe was not much use to him.

Finally, the longed-for flash of inspiration came. He quickly unwound his tie from his neck and took off his holster. Knotting them and his belt into a long line, he attached the shoe by its laces. Let's see if we can't mess with Mr. Caiman a little. Maybe he would vamoose if he became too stressed.

Let's dance! Ondragon lowered the shoe and let it smack into the alligator's back. The predator dove and was lost from view. So much for the reptile stress test.

Ondragon was about to pull the shoe back up when the alligator's head appeared with a splash, its mouth open, and snatched at the bait. Quickly, Ondragon pulled on the makeshift line and just about succeeded in saving the shoe. In his head, he heard Roy Scheider's voice in *Jaws*: *"I think we're gonna need a bigger boat!"*

Once again, he let down the shoe and baited the lurking animal, which immediately went onto the attack. Again, it snapped at thin air and splashed back into the brown swill. This continued for a while, until the alligator seemed to lose interest in the game. It withdrew from the tree almost huffily and eyed it from a distance.

Satisfied, Ondragon reeled in the line. He would break the beast—if not with weapons, then with psychological torment.

Suddenly, a second head emerged from the water. And then a third, much larger one. The hoo-ha had attracted other alligators from the surrounding area. Ondragon turned pale. What a fine mess! His strategy had thoroughly backfired. Now he was stuck here for good!

CHAPTER 12

Conscientiously, the mambo packed all the things she needed into her woven straw shoulder bag. Christine watched her. The priestess's face was serious, as was that of her mother, who was also standing next to her, watching.

Not everyone was happy about the preparations for the expedition. But it was a matter of urgency. Etienne Dadou, Christine's father, was wandering around somewhere up there in the mountains, under a zombie curse from a bokor!

Christine's mother had begged the mambo to save Etienne, if it was at all possible. It was far more likely, the priestess had explained, that he had been in that state for too long and that his mind was irretrievably broken. But even then, Cécile Dadou wished to find her husband and . . . release him. And it would be best if they could also track down the black magician who had done this to Etienne Dadou. The mambo had already put a wasting curse on the guy, and she promised she would find him and deal with him.

The priestess had now finished packing. One of her hunsi passed her a bowl containing the blood of a chicken that had been sacrificed in a ceremony earlier, and she painted an isosceles cross on the forehead of each member of the expedition. As she did so, she said solemnly, "Saint Expeditus, patron saint of all expeditions, I beg you, find out for us where Etienne Dadou is hiding so that we can break the evil curse that the perfidious bokor has placed on him. Holy Saint Expeditus, raise all the dead from their graves and send them out against the bokor, so that his body may be consumed from within and take itself to the grave."

Christine knew that the mambo had also sought the approval of the dark gèdès. The priestess had gone to the cemetery the night before and had struck her machete three times against a stone cross, the sign of Baron Samedi. Making an offering of two black chickens, she had asked the Lord of the Graveyards to consent to her expedition and had returned to the temple with a handful of graveyard soil. This she now kept in a small pouch that dangled from her belt. She would stuff the earth into the mouth of the black magician to silence his evil tongue once and for all.

Christine wanted the bokor to be punished for his malevolent deeds, but even more she wanted her father to be saved. She had very little hope, however, because after all she was the only one who had seen with her own eyes how the zombie who had been her father had dislocated its own jaw so terribly. A zombie could survive such a thing, but a human being . . . ?

The priestess shouldered the bag, said goodbye to her master of ceremonies and the hunsi, and told the small group, which included two young men from the village, to follow her. They left the village, passed the cemetery, and began the climb into the mountains. One or two trees lined the steep path up into the limestone formations, providing a little shade. Not a cloud was in the sky, and soon the expedition members' faces were shining with exertion. In single file, they climbed the ever-narrowing path, whose switchbacks seemed to cling to the barren, dusty mountainside. No one spoke; everyone kept their fear to themself. The bokor might be lurking behind a rock, after all, and could bewitch any one of them from afar.

The climb to the ridge took an hour and a half. Behind it, the view over the barren canyon of the Ti Rivière de Jacmel opened up; the watercourse flowed eastward toward the sea and was almost empty in the dry season. The jagged peaks of the mountain range shimmered blue in the distance. The individual summits were not especially high, but some were very craggy. Somewhere out there the bokor was hiding, using his spell to control the zombie that had once been Etienne Dadou.

The priestess pointed north along the ridge. Christine knew that there, well hidden in a hollow beyond, was the camp of the *blancs*. No one had been there since the quake. No one knew what the terrain looked like now.

The mambo guessed that not only would they find the zombie there, they would also find the black magician. She had long suspected that the *blancs* were working with a bokor, probably to scare away the curious or even casual passersby from their territory. But even she did not know what the strangers were doing there in the mountains. The camp was heavily secured with high electric fences and cameras.

The priestess set off, following a barely discernible path below the ridge. Christine, her mother, and the two young men went after her reluctantly. They all hoped the mambo had enough power to protect them from the black magician and his slave.

Shortly before nightfall, they reached the tree-lined hollow with the camp of the Whites. Everything seemed quiet. Nothing was moving behind the fence. Protected by the bushes where Christine had lain and watched the White men, the group cautiously approached the close-meshed steel, which was about 3 yards high and topped with barbed wire. They looked around, but could not see a gate or anything similar. How did you get in? And how did the *blancs* get out? Could the White men fly like the evil owl spirit Marinette Bras Chech?

With growing unease, they crept around the sealed-off area and came upon a hole that someone had obviously cut in it. The priestess crossed herself and, without hesitation, entered the camp. Christine and the others waited, but no alarm sounded, no men with guns came running. It seemed as if the earthquake had driven away the strange whites.

The mambo beckoned to her companions, who, after some hesitation, followed her through the breach in the fence. Warily and sticking close together, they looked around; the area was no larger than a hundred by a hundred paces. The cool evening shadows were already gathering under the tall trees, making it hard to see.

The group discovered strange things during their search. Several white metal houses with flat roofs. A large circle in a clearing with an

H on it, a tall steel pole bent over like a straw, a collapsed cottage containing a machine and with a large tank at the back. The final thing they saw was a pile of rubble that had once been a white building, probably single-story. The mambo thought she remembered that this had once been the entrance to the mine. But apparently the concrete blocks from the ruined house had completely buried the shaft. As in the village below, the earthquake had done a great job. But there was one strange thing. Unlike in their village, there were no people to be seen anywhere, not even dead people. No corpses. Where had the *blancs* gone?

The mambo shook her head. It was not surprising to her, for the Whites had enlisted the help of a black magician. They were long gone. The priestess instructed the group to unload their equipment and camp here in the sheltered area for the night. By the light of a large fire, they would wait for Etienne Dadou to appear.

Accompanied by the singing of cicadas, the night settled over the five zombie hunters. They had lit a large fire and sat close together in the protective aura of the bright flames. Christine had grasped her mother's hands and was squeezing them in nervous anticipation. She flinched fearfully at every sound, be it only the crackling of logs in the fire or the cry of an owl. Was Marinette Bras Chech lying in wait for them out there with the bokor? So many people whose flesh the evil loa could devour; they would certainly come in very handy for her.

Shuddering, Christine snuggled closer to her mother, who was trembling just as violently at the sounds of the night. The girl looked into the faces of their male companions, who were clinging tightly to their machetes. She could clearly see that they would have preferred to be elsewhere. Their eyes were wide, and their dark cheeks were flushed with fear. The mambo had chosen the two young men because they had lost their families in the quake and were now destitute. She offered them a place under her roof and food twice a day. In return, she required obedience and handyman help around the temple: The village *humfò* had also been badly damaged by the earthquake. Despite the catastrophe, the priestess was still a wealthy and influential woman. She lived off the offerings of the community, whose members were seeking her advice and spiritual assistance more than ever.

A crunching sound came from beyond the fence.

Christine quickly exchanged glances with the others and listened fearfully to the blackness surrounding the small circle of fire. Suddenly, the priestess jumped up and pointed one arm toward the fence. She looked like a petrified fisherman who had caught sight of a sea monster from his boat.

Christine lowered her head, but fear grabbed the back of her unprotected neck and shook her violently between its fangs like helpless prey. Pressing her lips together, she looked out into the night. Footsteps could clearly be heard.

Ungainly, staggering footsteps.

CHAPTER 13

In the swamp—night two

The sun set without any change in the situation. Their stomachs growling mightily, both sides eyed each other.

Deep in clouds of black thought, Ondragon sat on his branch, staring at the impressive gathering of the National Alligator Association beneath the tree. He counted close to seven members as the last glimmer of evening gradually faded and night reclaimed the swamp, punctuated once more by a deafening chorus from the United Union of Frogs. Why couldn't the crocs feed on their amphibious compatriots and leave him alone?

Frustrated, Ondragon shimmied himself into a fork that seemed reasonably comfortable and tied himself to the tree with his belt and holster to keep him from falling out in his sleep. Once again, impenetrable darkness swallowed him, and he spent his second night in the swamp having moved pretty much nowhere. How was he supposed to get out of here at this snail's pace? His chances of rescue diminished with every unused hour that passed. But Ondragon also knew he needed sleep, because only if he got some rest would he be able to cover any appreciable distance. Assuming the Alligator Convention shifted to a different venue tomorrow.

Resting his head against the rough trunk of the water oak, he closed his eyes and listened to the croaking and chirping. There were better lullabies, but there were also worse ones. His exertions and the hardships he had been through had tired his body, which was already hanging limply in the fork; all that was missing was for his mind to realize he needed rest. The *centrifuge*, however, continued to rotate blithely, presenting him with endless repetitions of images of the day's events, into which his brother increasingly wormed his way. Couldn't his little tormentor give him a break now? He was in desperate need of sleep!

But Per didn't care. He sat next to Ondragon in a nearby fork and grinned mockingly at him. His piercing gaze said it all: "You must be in deep shit, eh, oh great Paul?" And every time Ondragon's eyes closed, he felt a nasty prod from his brother's pointy little index finger. Each time he would start awake in confusion, hearing Per's derisive laughter.

Groaning, Ondragon squirmed in his safety harness. His eyelids flickered, but his optic nerves registered no difference between the darkness of the night in *front* of his eyelids and the shadows *behind* them. It was impossible to tell whether he was awake or dreaming. His brain was running at full speed, but his limbs hung slack in the branches. What was imagination and what was reality?

He got an answer to this almost philosophical question when a scream shot through his auditory canal, making him tear open his eyes. Crystal clear, all of his senses took in every sound, no matter how small: the soft chirping of the crickets, the slight swaying and creaking of the branches, the rustling of the leaves and . . . the scream that came back again! Suddenly, the hairs on Ondragon's arms stood on end. The sound had come from down there, and it had sounded terribly desperate. What had it been? A human?

Ondragon bent over to find out, but the blackness prevented him from seeing farther than his feet. Suddenly, there was a loud roaring. Splashing and slapping and the scream again, this time panicked. Ondragon was now sure it was an animal. Perhaps a deer running for its life . . . because seven alligators were after it?

Ondragon listened, enthralled. The rhythmic splashing, presumably the deer's leaping, moved away, but came to an abrupt stop with the sound of an explosion. A final scream rang out and then there was only the deadly rush of water as the silent hunters fought over their prey, tearing and devouring it in the death roll. Ondragon could hear the snapping of jaws and the gnashing of teeth. A shiver ran down his spine. That's how he would end up, as nibbles.

He raised his eyes and jumped, terrified.

Right in front of him, grinning, sat Per.

CHAPTER 14

In the mountains north of Nan Margot, South Haiti

The shuffling footsteps came closer, and the two young men jumped up and brandished their machetes threateningly at the darkness by the fence. Christine ducked into her mother's shadow and waited for the priestess to do something. But she only muttered something that sounded like an incantation and stood rooted to the spot.

A low, barely audible moan floated over to them on the cool night air.

Christine stared with wide eyes in the direction from which the sound had come. *Is that my father out there?* The thought frightened her, breathed its cold sepulchral air into her face. She didn't want to face Etienne Dadou again, didn't want to have to look at him again—not like this, not as a zombie. She remembered with horror the mutilation he had inflicted on himself as he furiously tried to pull the gris-gris from his mouth. She heard the cracking of his jaw and the inarticulate gurgling from his throat, saw the almost-black blood.

Suddenly, the mambo stirred. She reached into her pocket, took out what looked like a dagger, and shouted to the two young men to follow her. Then she disappeared into the darkness. The two assistants looked at each other hesitantly.

"Allez, dare-dare!" rang out imperiously from the shadows, and finally the young men hurried after the priestess at a run.

Christine was left behind with her mother, who comforted her daughter while reaching for the machete at her feet. Christine clung to her arm. Conflict raged inside her. She knew her mother was the only one among them who still believed her husband could be saved.

Neither the mambo nor her two assistants had been convinced of that. Christine had also suspected from the beginning that the mambo would have to kill her father to free him from the curse. There was no other way, for she had seen him, had felt his tremendous power and the destruction of his spirit for all time. Etienne Dadou was long lost.

The bitter taste of fear rose in Christine's throat. What if the mambo was not powerful enough? Not strong enough to defeat the zombie? She glanced covertly at her mother. She had to tell her. But how? How could she explain that Etienne Dadou was nothing more than a brutal, disfigured monster? Christine squirmed as if she was in pain.

Sounds were coming from beyond the fence. There was a loud rustling and crackling in the undergrowth, and shouts rang out suggesting the priestess and her two companions had started the hunt. In confirmation, an indignant yelp echoed from the trees—the voice of the zombie. The shouts of the hunters grew more excited. Christine heard someone calling, "Look out!" then a horrified scream. After that, silence fell again. Although she was shaking all over, she jumped to her feet.

"The mambo will do it, Christine. I'm sure she's the one; only she can save Etienne. Come here, nothing will happen to you." Her mother tried to pull her close, but Christine didn't move. She bit her lip. She wanted so much to believe her mother's words, but she could not. She had stood face-to-face with the zombie, had witnessed its wild supernatural power. Dark premonitions forced themselves upon her. And suddenly, she could feel the certainty driving like a nail into her flesh: The mambo, as respectable and influential as she might be, had no power over this being. The diabs that the bokor had invoked were too powerful; they would kill the priestess.

Suddenly, the yelling by the fence began again. It sounded as if the hunters had cornered their victim, because the howling had also become more aggressive. Like an animal in distress, the zombie roared at its pursuers.

Abruptly, Christine turned to her mother and looked at her urgently. "Mama, I saw him! Papa . . . he's not himself anymore . . . and he's going to kill her!" She saw that her mother did not believe her. She grabbed her by the arm and shook her. "Mama, I beg you! Let's get out of here!" Behind her, the shouting increased to the wild howls of battle. The commotion sounded terrifying.

The devils are tearing each other apart, Christine thought, pulling her mother after her. They had to get out of there, or they would be trapped inside the fence. But Cécile Dadou was too scared to move. Christine took the machete from her hand and pulled her along by the arm.

A few heartbeats later, they reached the hole in the fence and slipped through. The battle cries took on an unbearable intensity. One person screeched in incomprehensible panic. It sounded like a pig having its throat slit. She urged her mother to run faster, away from the terrible sounds of the carnage whose outcome she had long suspected. Then the screaming stopped abruptly, and several muffled thuds echoed through the night behind Christine and her mother. The blood froze in her veins. *That sounded like . . . like a machete chopping flesh*, she thought, at the same moment realizing with horror that she no longer knew where they were. The trees, stones, and bushes all looked the same in the dark, and Christine had no idea where to find the path back to the ridge or the village.

In her headlong flight, she had made the mistake of simply running off without paying attention to where she was going. Tears came to her eyes. Tears of anger at herself! Because she had not managed to tell her mother everything. Because she had been too cowardly to explain that Etienne Dadou was long dead! It was her fault people were dying—right now, being torn apart and dismembered by a zombie. It was her fault. Weeping, she pulled at her paralyzed mother, who could not know what was after them.

As she walked, Christine felt the ground gradually drop away beneath her feet. So they were on the path down to the village after all. She tugged on her mother's hand. "Come on, Mama, we'll make it. We'll be home soon."

She did not realize the seriousness of her mistake was until too late. The terrain became rockier, and they scraped their knuckles on the sharp-edged boulders. Christine fell several times on the rough slope, bumping her bare skin on the rocks. Her mother stumbled too and unfortunately hit her shoulder against a boulder, where she collapsed, groaning in pain. Christine suddenly heard footsteps coming toward them in the darkness. The zombie was following them! She tried to pull her mother up. "Come on! We must keep moving. He's coming after us! I hear him."

"Christine! I . . . I can't. I think my arm is broken." Cécile palpated her mother's upper arm.

"But, Mama, we have to keep going, or—"

"Leave me here," her mother responded.

"No!" Christine tugged at the flagging figure. "Please! He's coming!"

"Let him come, I—"

Her mother did not finish her sentence, for a large shadow fell down onto them from the mountainside above. With ice-cold horror, Christine recognized her father's misshapen face. But before she could utter any warning, the zombie grabbed her mother brutally by the hair and dragged her forcefully toward it.

Cécile Dadou gave a piercing scream and desperately tried to free herself. Christine threw herself fearlessly at the nightmarish monster, her machete raised to strike. She had to help her mother. Cécile was the only family she had left!

But the zombie saw her coming. With one jerk of its fist, it broke Cécile Dadou's neck and raised the other to defend itself. Christine heard first the cracking of her mother's vertebrae and then the crunching of her own cheekbone as the zombie that had been her father smashed its fist into her face. Pain exploded like a firework of glaring needles into the sudden silence of her thoughts. Dazed, Christine rebounded from the fist and tumbled backward into the void. After falling for what seemed like an eternity, she slammed into the ground hard and lost consciousness.

CHAPTER 15

In the swamp – day two

Ondragon opened his eyes, blinking in the orange light falling through the canopy of the water oak. The process of awakening brought hellish pain. His back felt like it was fused to the bark of the tree, and his butt was numb from the hardness of the wood. He had to crunch his bones to release the two body parts from their cramped positions.

Ondragon let out a groan. Whoever had done this to him, he would pay them back threefold! His head was throbbing infernally and his neck was stiff. It took time for his muscles and joints to become supple enough for him to move without falling. Only then did he unfasten his seat belt. Clinging to the trunk, he straightened up and ventured a look down. He expected to see seven dark silhouettes and was somewhat surprised to find this was not the case. He quickly climbed farther down and scanned the area around the tree. The water was glassy and calm. Not an alligator to be seen. But appearances could be deceiving, he knew. The beasts might be lurking beneath the surface. He put together the fishing line from the day before and splashed it into the dirty water several times.

As he did so, he recalled the events of the previous night. The alligator gang had received a visitor—probably a deer, or some similar mammal. And the hungry reptiles had welcomed it in the friendliest way they knew how: They had first shown the deer their smiles and then tore it apart alive.

Ondragon checked the surface once more. There was nothing to indicate the massacre that had taken place there a few hours ago. No carcass segments, or any other residue from the feast, were floating in the water. There was no blood anywhere. There was also zero response to the shoe fishing rod. The alligators were either full or had gone. Chance had gifted him a gap in the attention of his besiegers. In his mind, Ondragon thanked the deer for its sacrifice and swung himself unceremoniously out of the tree. He had to make the most of this opportunity.

After another unsuccessful day of trekking through mud and water varying in depth from ankle-deep to waist-deep, Ondragon leaned exhausted against a tree trunk to catch his breath. He was dizzy with hunger and thirst, and the heat and mosquitoes were wearing him down. He had broken off a solid branch from a dead plant and was using it as crutch, plumb line, and club.

He looked up at the sky, trying to set his course from the sun's position. Unfortunately, there was a huge difference between the modern man's sense of direction in an urban context (his functioned perfectly) and the primitive environmental instinct that had been integral to *Homo erectus* on the first rung of the evolutionary ladder thousands of years ago. Cro-Magnon man would certainly have known exactly what time it was and which direction was north. But it was the year 2010 and Ondragon man was as good as helpless without technical devices.

As good as.

He still had rudimentary scraps of memory of his ancestors' struggle to survive though—an instinctive gut feeling, so to speak. Unfortunately, this was located in his appendix. And this told him there was something floating on the water in front of him that did not belong there.

Ondragon bent down and fished the object out of the water. It was a plastic bottle. Dr. Pepper! Empty, unfortunately.

"At least I have a container to collect water in," he mused aloud, tying the bottle to his belt with his tie. Suddenly, a smile lit up his tired features. "You've always been resilient and confident, Paul Eckbert!" he said, chuckling. "Don't let it get you down. That's the motto. Even if you're only around twelve hours from dying of thirst."

Continuing to giggle hysterically, he walked on as the sun sank lower and the shadows of twilight engulfed the swamp. The obligatory frog concert began again. *That might be the last thing you hear*, Ondragon thought, but he pulled himself together. What had he just told himself? *Don't let it get you down!*

He waded through a shallow channel of water and came across a second plastic bottle in the weeds overgrowing the shore, and then a little later a third. Garbage that tourists had thrown away, or the typical single-use mentality of the American underclass. Just toss it—out of sight, out of mind!

He paused, thinking. Alongside the PET bottles, beer cans, and empty plastic chip bags , a package of barbecue meat was bobbing in the dirty water. Barbecue meat?

Ondragon felt a surge of energy pulse through his veins. He looked at the package. Porterhouse steak. This meant there must have been a barbecue somewhere around here, which in turn meant there must be a larger area of dry land. Or had someone had a barbecue on a boat?

Ondragon looked around and followed the trail of garbage, finding further evidence of an extravagant barbecue. His stomach, which had been on a forced diet for almost three days, growled at the sight. Ondragon pivoted around and peered searchingly at his surroundings. The silhouette of a dark structure stood out against a bush to his left like a condensation of shadows. He walked toward the shadow, and it took shape, becoming angular. A wave of joy flooded through Ondragon.

It was a hut! Hidden in the reeds, it stood in the shade of some tall bald cypress trees. A footbridge extended from the wooden porch into the open water of the bayou. The place looked deserted, but hey, it was shelter!

"See? Never let it get you down!" whispered Ondragon triumphantly, stomping over to it with a big grin.

CHAPTER 16

In the last of the twilight, Ondragon searched the hut, where no one had been for a long time. The thick layer of dust and cobwebs on the sparse furnishings, which consisted of two rickety chairs, a table, a rotting mattress, and several beer crates, told him as much. On a lopsided shelf, Ondragon found more trash, tattered porn magazines, a box of fishing lures, dirty tin plates and cutlery, a bucket, a landing net full of holes, an oil lamp, matches, and tin cans, all empty except for one. Ondragon resisted the initial impulse to pounce on the can and continued looking around.

On the opposite wall, hanging from nails, were a faded baseball cap and a sweatshirt of indeterminate color. He also found a knife stuck into the lintel beam. Unfortunately, it was blunt. End of inventory.

He returned to the shelf and took out the lamp and the matches. There wasn't much oil left in the small container, but he still managed to get the short wick to burn. In the yellowish light, the inside of the hut looked even dingier. But when he looked down at himself, he didn't exactly make a good impression either. And after all, he should be happy he didn't have to spend the night in a tree, even if he intended to give the moldy mattress a wide berth.

Lantern in hand, he closed the door to keep out the mosquitoes and set about examining the last can of food. The label had fallen off, but he found it among the other empty containers. It featured a yellowed image by pop art icon Andy Warhol: Peach Halves by Del Monte. Peaches in their own juice!

Best before 04/22/2007, almost three years ago. Whatever. Since Ondragon had no energy for fishing, this can had to be his salvation. But how could he open it?

He searched the hut one more time, but found no can opener. He looked at the blunt knife. He wouldn't be able to get the lid open with that alone; he needed something heavy to drive the blade into the metal. Without further ado, he smashed one of the chairs in two and used one of the legs as a hammer. Like early man, he went to work on the can. The blade slipped several times and almost injured him, but he kept trying, cursing and sweating, until the tip of the knife finally punched a small hole in the lid. Hastily, he punched a second opening in the metal, lifted the can to his mouth, and drank greedily without first testing to see whether the contents were even edible. The juice tasted metallic and sweet as hell, but it was pure energy! Ondragon sucked the last drop out of the hole and ran his tongue over his lips in satisfaction. That had been the hors d'oeuvre; now came the main course. He placed the can on the floor, set the knife against the side wall, and drove it deep into the belly of the can. Again and again, he struck it with the leg of the chair until he could pry the container far enough open to reach the slippery contents. Sighing, he devoured the sugary fruit with his bare hands and felt life returning to his drained body. Pop art had never tasted so good! Now if only he had Campbell's Tomato Soup by the same artist . . . but alas, the feast was over. Oh well.

Temporarily sated, he licked his sticky fingers and looked around for a corner where he could settle down to sleep without immediately being eaten by bugs. As he finally stretched out with his crumpled jacket for a pillow and stared happily up at the ceiling beams, he was filled with bliss for the second time that day. Soon he noticed his eyelids getting heavy, and he put out the lamp. In the safety of the hut, sleep came quickly and bore him away to the realm of cotton-soft stupor.

In the morning, his digestive tract was rumbling violently, whether because of the unaccustomed food or because of its somewhat less than optimal palatability; whatever the reason, Ondragon had to hurry out of the hut to the jetty.

Once the cramps had subsided, he washed in the water of the bayou and returned to the hut on shaky legs, where he gathered together the few useful items the ramshackle dwelling had to offer. Using fishhooks and string, he sewed the bottom of the dusty sweatshirt shut, tucked the meager gear through the neckline into the resulting bag, and slung the knotted sleeves over his shoulder. This way he at least had his hands free when walking.

He left the hut at sunrise and continued along the water course, hoping an airboat would finally come by, pick him up, and take him back to the cool, clean surroundings of a hotel room. But nothing happened; no boat came and neither did any anglers. Instead, he soon found himself in intense sunlight suffering even more intense thirst.

Ondragon dragged himself along. His left shoeless foot hurt; he kept stepping on sharp branches and bumping his toes against rocks. It was worse than alligator teeth! He blinked away the sweat pouring into his eyes, trying not to take his eyes off the expanse of water in the bayou. How many more miles would he have to walk—would he be *able* to walk?

The heat became more and more unbearable, dragging physically at every square inch of his emaciated body. As if on autopilot, he worked his way through the lukewarm swamp water. Step by step. Mosquitoes attacked him from the air, threatening to suck the last drop of fluid from his bloodstream, and he was seized more and more frequently by a violent dizziness, which reached into his wobbly legs and forced him to lean on his stick until he regained his strength.

"You're just not cut out for the wilderness, Paul. You're such a milksop, you big-city nerd!"

Startled, Ondragon raised his eyes. Who had said that? He saw a small figure appear in the reeds to his right.

It was Per.

His deceased brother folded his arms and stared at him in amusement. He was hovering over the water like a second resurrected Jesus. But his face was pale as an alligator's belly and his lips were reptilian gray. Ondragon thought he could even see small pointed teeth flashing between them.

"Have you come here to annoy me?" he snapped at the apparition.

Per shook his head serenely. "You're pathetic, Paul Eckbert. Look at yourself! What has become of you? Are you so desperate not to be like our father? What did he do to you to make you hate him so much? He only wanted what was best for us!" Even his tongue was alligator sharp! The words hit their target.

Ondragon narrowed his eyes to slits. "Don't ask what Father did to me, ask instead what he did to US!"

"YOU knocked over the bookshelf! YOU did!" yelled Per, his mouth a black cavity.

"ME? But that's . . . not true! Father locked us in the library!"

"You knocked over the bookshelf because you were jealous of me, because Father favored me!" This point also hit home. In point of fact, Ondragon had always felt his father allowed Per greater freedom and treated him more lovingly. Suddenly, he felt himself being pulled back in time. He saw the hated door to his father's library in Cairo, saw it open, saw the tons of dusty books grinning at him and sniggering maliciously. Evil little predators, smelling his fear and salivating over it. No, that wasn't quite right. His fear of the blasted books had come on only *after* the accident! This fear was different. Somehow more foreboding, more instinctive. It too had been with him a very long time. But the harder he tried to pin down the feeling that was overpowering him, the faster it slipped away, and before he knew it, he felt a hard hand pushing him into the library. The door slammed shut behind him, and he was alone with all that printed paper! And with Per!

But what had actually happened? He could still remember that, out of anger against his father, he had hurled a small Egyptian figurine at the row of book spines, causing the shelf to sway . . . and finally collapse. An avalanche of rock-hard books had poured over them and buried them. Paul had almost suffocated and Per's skull had been crushed! In this respect, he was indeed to blame for what had happened, to blame for the death of his brother. But could a small figurine, barely the size of a pocketknife, tip over a bookcase the height of two men?

Ondragon clapped his hands to his face. Something was wrong with his memory. The images in his head were blurred, and he had the impression that they were misleading him with untruths. His hands moved down to his chest, and he folded them. He looked at his brother, who was waiting patiently in the swamp beside him. "Per, I'm sorry! Please, you have to believe me, I didn't do it on purpose. Sure, I was jealous of you, but I never meant to cause you any harm. I loved you, you know. You are like me, you are my twin!" He looked pleadingly at Per. If his brother could not forgive him in person, perhaps this translucent projection of his eternally guilty conscience could. "I beg you, Per, accept my apology."

"So you can forget about me? Pah, it's far from being over. First you need to reconcile with Father!" Per Gustav's boyish face was frowning sternly.

Ondragon stood there with his mouth open. What his brother was asking of him was impossible. He could not reconcile with his father. Their differences were, as the saying went, irreconcilable. He had felt that again last year, when he had flown to Berlin after the events in Minnesota, to see his parents after all that time, yes, and to make another attempt to get closer to his father. But all the old sourpuss had done was demonstrate that he had no desire to settle the old quarrel. In spite of everything, Ondragon had tried to communicate with him, and his mother had tried to mediate between them, but their efforts had been in vain, just like the whole trip!

After only three days, Ondragon had left Berlin again. Disappointed, disillusioned, and deprived of any hope. But the worst thing was that the old hatred had flared up again and was hollowing him out inside. Now it would be decades before he would have it under sufficient control to at least ignore it.

Although . . . the trip had not been completely in vain, because after all he had also gone to Berlin to discover whether there was any truth in the suspicion that his mother had been a spy, as an inmate of the clinic in Minnesota had implied back then. That unpleasant associate had unearthed an alleged source who claimed Ava Birgitta Ondragon was a Swedish agent and had spied for her government in the guise of a wife of a German diplomat. Ondragon had always suspected this was a lie that had merely been intended to unsettle him, but still he wanted to play it safe. He had waited for a quiet moment and without warning, had confronted his mother. In response, Ava Birgitta had merely smiled. And what she then told him about her marriage to Siegfried Ondragon, her time in the Swedish military, and her regular trips to her Scandinavian homeland had given him deep new insights into the complexities of life by the side of a diplomat.

Ava Ondragon had overcome all these difficulties. She had willingly followed her husband to another foreign city every three years, had attended official events as a faithful wife and mother, and had earned a reputation as someone who was culturally literate. Mentally and emotionally, however, she had had to cope first with the death of one of her sons, which had cast a shadow over her spirit for many years, and then with the departure of her second child from the family. But even then her loyalties had been clear. Though the loss of both sons pained her, she had always stood by her husband. She had remained steadfastly at his side until his retirement in Berlin. However—and this weighed more heavily on Ondragon's heart than he would have liked—his mother was no longer as steadfast today as she had once been, because she knew she had made a mistake. The mistake of letting him, Paul Eckbert Ondragon, go so easily.

Ondragon emerged only slowly from his recollections.

"I can't reconcile with Father, do you understand?" he said, raising a hand at his brother's pale ghost. Per stared back, his lips pressed together. "It's over with Father, forever! I tried, but . . . I couldn't do it."

"You didn't really try, Paul!" The spirit's voice sounded harsh.

"Oh yes I did, damn it! The man who calls himself our father is a stubborn old goat! An ossified bastard whose only pleasure was humiliating me." Ondragon waved his hands agitatedly. "Get that into your head and leave me alone!" He was tired of the taunts. With a final wave, he set off again, leaving Per behind.

Ondragon waded dully on, mile after mile. But his will remained unbroken. Like an ailing battery, it drove him on. It might be ailing, but it was still functional.

At least Per was leaving him in peace now!

He put one foot mechanically in front of the other to stop himself from thinking about the hopelessness of his situation, but his feet got increasingly caught in the mud, throwing him off balance, and when his strength finally left him, he stumbled and fell onto his knees in the water.

Goddamn fucking swamp! You should be drained. Natural paradise? My ass!

He would have liked to shout out loud and beat the surface of the water with his walking pole, but he lacked the energy to do so.

For a while, he stayed on all fours, his head drooping, his breathing shallow. His heart was performing crazy cardiological somersaults, as uncontrolled as the spikes on a seismograph. Everything kept going black and he needed to swallow, but his larynx was like a lump of cement, dry and bulky and as big as a house. He gasped helplessly, short of breath, and the spasms in his abdomen struck him relentlessly, like the fists of a boxer. Was this it? Was this the end?

No, it wasn't!

With a final huge effort of will, Ondragon pushed himself to his feet and walked on, his arms dangling and his spine limp. Splash, splash, splash—the sound of his footsteps in the water, that was all there was. Only hopelessness . . .

Suddenly, his right foot sank into the void, and Ondragon submerged. He resurfaced, snorting, and looked around, blinking. He had fallen into the bayou!

Paddling like a drowning dog, he dragged himself to the nearest shore and lay on his stomach, struggling for breath. The sun beat hotly down on his wet back.

Clack, clack!

Its rays sounded mechanical, as if a robotic celestial body was sending them out.

Clack, clack! Whips lashing as if they were automated. Clack, clack!

"Turn over!"

It was Per. His tormentor was back! He whispered directly into Ondragon's ear, "Turn around!"

"Oh, let me be!" defended Ondragon. "I can't take it anymore."

"Turn the fuck over, you yellowbelly!"

Clack, clack!

"Shit, Per, you just can't give it a rest, can you?" Ondragon turned laboriously onto his back, his eyes closed against the sun's lashing rays. "Are you satisfied now? Is this a better way to die, on my back?"

"No! Open your eyes! Do it!"

Clack, clack!

Ondragon sighed. All right, then, I'll open my eyes. It doesn't matter now if I scorch my retinas, anyway. He lifted his swollen eyelids, but at first he couldn't figure out what he was seeing. A black band cut across his field of vision, blocking out the sun.

Clack, clack!

Those sounds were coming from the ribbon of shadow. Clack, clack!

Abruptly, Ondragon raised his upper body. Could this really be happening? Or was his withered mind playing tricks on him? He rubbed his eyes and looked at the black band more closely.

Clack, clack!

It was the I-10!

Unbelievable. He was saved!

Leaning on the stick, he got to his feet and tilted his head back. The highway rose before him almost majestically . . .

On concrete piers 60 feet high!

The knowledge broke upon him slowly, but its impact was like a hammer to his skull. Shaken, Ondragon looked at the structure. The promise, the salvation, the route to civilization. He was so near . . . and yet so far.

Dejectedly, Ondragon slumped his shoulders. How was he supposed to climb this crappy concrete viaduct? The pillars looked slippery and inaccessible; not even the free climbing world champion would have been able to get up there.

He put his hands to his mouth and began to shout. His voice echoed back hoarsely from the underside of the bridge under the steady clacking noise of the moving cars. There was a lot of traffic up there, apparently, people driving by without having the least idea he was there. And they couldn't hear him either. He gave up calling and thought. The *centrifuge* had long since stopped working and refused to turn. He gave it an imaginary kick. Sputtering, it began to move, but immediately stopped again. Damn it! Turn, you son of a bitch! Another kick and the *centrifuge* finally began to circle. Wobbling and creaking in protest, it delivered a few suggestions:

"Examine pier—STOP—must be a maintenance ladder—STOP—find ladder and climb up—STOP—stop car—STOP—ask for help—STOP—kick yourself in the ass to get yourself going—STOP—love, Per—STOP!"

All right, you pain in the ass. Let's do it, he thought with a waspish grin. He began his inspection, walking through the waist-deep water, the upbeat Indiana Jones theme running through his head. He circled each concrete pier, searching for recessed iron rungs.

At pillar number seven, his eyes went black again, and it was a while before he could continue. Instead of a rumbling in his intestines, he now had a rumbling in his mind. Of course, it might also be Per, playing one last evil trick on him. An ironic twist of fate, so to speak. He had lured him here to the highway so that he could die looking at it. A final kick in the ass! Per's revenge.

Ondragon raised his head. "If this was what you wanted, you've succeeded. Are you satisfied now?" he shouted loudly at the bridge.

Clack, clack!

"Okay, you win." He closed his eyes, but before the comforting blackness enveloped him, he saw something else. A series of horizontal strokes. He snapped his eyes open again and realized he hadn't been mistaken. There embedded in the opposite pillar were iron rungs. They led straight upward.

Hastily, Ondragon waded to the ladder and began to climb. He had to catch his breath more often than he would have liked, because his arms could hardly hold him. He hung onto the rungs like a limp monkey, not daring to look down. Instead, he fixed his gaze on the underside of the highway.

Just a few more yards. You can do it!

He gritted his teeth and pulled himself up. Shortly before he reached the concrete balustrade, his dwindling strength forced him to take another breath. Just one body length separated him from the highway. The roar of the traffic spilled down to him. Making a huge effort, he reached for the next rung and almost slipped. But he managed to cling to the rusty metal with two fingers and save himself from falling to his death. The longed-for adrenaline shot hotly through his neural pathways, jolting him awake. Ondragon stretched out an arm and pushed himself up, his legs trembling with exertion.

Finally, he reached the upper ledge of the concrete parapet and heaved himself over it, groaning. He fell like a wet sack onto the hot asphalt.

A pickup truck roared past him, honking.

Dazed, Ondragon struggled to his feet and waved to passing cars for help. Shuffling and drooling like a zombie without a will.

But no one stopped.

That was not surprising. He was a filthy figure, staggering across the highway with only one shoe, in the middle of nowhere. The Americans' willingness to help was not in doubt, but not even Ondragon would have stopped in this situation.

He looked resignedly along the roadway, which stretched seemingly endlessly in both directions into the flat, deserted horizon of the marshland. With a sigh, he gave in. If fate wanted him to walk, he would walk.

Sluggishly, he set off and only a few moments later was moving at a stoic trudge. His senses shut down, and the clacking of the bridge beams became more and more muffled.

Clack, clack! Clack, clack! Clack, clack!

Suddenly, he heard a harsh honking, and shortly afterward, a police car with blue lights pulled up next to him. The passenger side window rolled down and a police officer stuck his head out. "Do you need any help, sir?"

Oh no.

"Sir, can you hear me?"

It took Ondragon an incredible effort to break out of his trudge and turn to face the officer. His mouth opened and at the same time he was overcome by the worry his voice might fail him. But his fear was completely unfounded, because he heard himself say, loud and clear:

"There you are at last, you slackers!"

CHAPTER 17

Ondragon had a patrol car drive him to the Royal Sonesta Hotel. He had spent the night in the hospital on a drip and had discharged himself early that morning, although his digestive tract had not yet fully settled down and his face was blazing with some nasty sunburn. He also still felt very shaky on his feet, but the case was waiting, and besides, he hated hospitals. Before they had let him go, however, they had given him new clothes, which came from donations. So now he was sporting a three-day beard combined with baggy Houston Rockets track pants, a plaid short-sleeved shirt, and flip-flops. A dream. For the past hour, he had also been sitting on his butt at the police station, since he hadn't been able to prove his identity the day before. His wallet had been taken by his kidnappers, which was no big deal, because he had more fake papers back at the hotel. Only the loss of his lucky charm, the keychain from Berlin that had once saved his life, caused him any distress. He would have to find out where his car was in any case. But right now, he just wanted to be alone in his room. He needed to think. After the episode in the swamp, he was on the verge of throwing in the towel. It wasn't usually his style, but somehow the case was turning into a disaster like what had happened in Minnesota. And he had very little desire for that kind of thing.

The patrol car stopped in front of the hotel entrance. One of the policemen got out with him, which didn't please Ondragon, but he couldn't do anything about it.

When they reached the entrance, the doorman looked first at his clothes and his red face, then at the cop. The guy hesitated, but finally welcomed them, making an effort to be friendly, and opened the door. It was all too obvious what he was thinking. *Another one of those outrageously dressed Mardi Gras tourists!*

Ondragon ignored him and headed through the foyer straight for the reception desk.

"Good morning, Mr. *On Draegn*!" the young woman behind the counter trilled. At least she recognized him, although she had mispronounced his name again. Her eyes fell on the officer behind him.

Ondragon cleared his throat. "Ms."—he glanced at her name tag—"Myers, would you be so kind as to confirm for the gentleman from the police department here that I had a room with you." He spoke in the past tense because he did not expect his room to still be available, having booked it for only two nights.

"But of course, sir," she said, glaring at the cop. "Mr. *On Draegn* has been a guest here for several days." She showed the cop the registration without being asked.

"Okay, ma'am, that's all in order, then. Mr. *On Draegn*." The cop tipped his peaked cap and left.

Ondragon glanced after him briefly, then turned back to the receptionist. "I apologize for the inconvenience, I was . . . indisposed for a few days and had no way of notifying you. You will surely have given my room away in the meantime." He forced himself to smile. "Might I be able to get another room?"

"But we haven't given your room away. It's still available. Number 218."

Ondragon raised his brows in amazement.

Ms. Myers registered his puzzled look and smiled. "The booking has been extended, and it's all paid for."

"By whom, may I ask?"

"Unfortunately, I can't tell from the documents. And the booking was taken by a colleague." Ms. Myers smiled apologetically.

"Was the bill paid by credit card?" echoed Ondragon. "Then there should be a name."

"No, payment was made in cash."

Ondragon was speechless. Who had done this? Charlize? Of the two phone calls he had made from the police department, one had been to his bank about his stolen credit card, and the other had been to his assistant, who had not answered.

"How long has the room been paid for?" he asked.

"Three more nights. You'll enjoy Mardi Gras, sir!"

Ondragon remembered that it was not long until the carnival on Fat Tuesday. That meant he had been in the swamp for a full four days. "Thank you so much, Ms. Myers. Oh yes, do you happen to have a new keycard for me? I lost my old one." He shrugged his shoulders apologetically.

"But of course, sir." The receptionist coded a new card and slid it across the counter. Ondragon took it, wished her a good day, and headed for the elevators.

Up on the second floor, he opened the door to his room. It was dark, and Ondragon flicked on the light. As he took a long, hard look around the room, he recoiled abruptly. His hand reached instinctively for his Sig Sauer but couldn't even find the holster.

Dammit, now I'm screwed! The though shot through his head. He surrendered, raising his hands above his head and narrowing his eyes in an attempt to see who was lying under the bedspread and holding the revolver whose muzzle was pointing at him.

"Boss?"

The revolver was lowered.

"Charlize!" He let out a surprised laugh. "Oh my goodness. And here I thought my last hour had come." Relieved, he moved toward the bed.

Charlize peeled herself out of the covers. "*Paul-san*, there you are at last! I was worried—I hadn't been able to reach you for four days. Wow, did you switch places with a lobster in a cooking pot? And look at this haute couture!"

Ondragon sat down on the edge of the bed without comment and tried not to notice Charlize's dove-gray negligee, the strap of which had slipped down over her shoulder. She looked sexy as hell.

"A lot has happened," he began, and then gave a sober account of his involuntary swamp expedition and the events at Stern's house. When he had finished, he asked Charlize to tell him what she had found out in Miami.

"Well, Mr. Alejandro Green, known to be the last member of the Central and South America Crew, was nowhere to be found. I surveilled his house for two days."

"Did you search it too?"

Charlize looked at him.

Of course she had. Ondragon made a placatory gesture, indicating that she should continue.

"*Hai*, I went into the house at night. But except for this letter, like the ones you found at Ellys's and Stern's, and Green's secret armory, I could find anything out of the ordinary."

Ondragon remembered he had to call Dr. Strangelove. He sighed. There were so many urgent things to do. "Did you bring the letter?" he asked.

Charlize nodded. "Sealed in plastic. It was like that when I found it though. The envelope was unopened. Isn't that strange?"

"No, because that means Green at least took my advice. The fact that he has now disappeared does not surprise me. It fits the pattern of this crappy case. And . . ." Without finishing his sentence, he jumped up and yanked open the door of the room safe in the closet. It was empty. "Fuck! I'm a fucking moron!"

"The safe was open when I arrived at your room two days ago, Boss. I thought you'd left it open because there was nothing in it."

"There was something in it though. Someone's broken into the safe without leaving any marks, but the stuff I put in there is gone. Fucking hell!"

"Do you think it was the guys who kidnapped you?"

"For sure."

"And what might they want with those things?" Charlize was thinking analytically, as usual.

"I don't know. Maybe they were covering their tracks. Actually, the only things in the safe were my notepad, computer, and the floater Bolič's cell phone. What a drag, I should have gotten Rudee onto it right away!" Ondragon slammed his fist into the closet door, frustrated by his own stupidity in not having hooked the computer up to the net right then and there. He went to his travel bag, which still lay beside the bed, and looked to see what else his captors had taken. But except for the spare magazine for his Sig Sauer, it was all there. Ondragon looked around, thinking. The notepad wasn't that important. It had very little information in it so far anyway. But he would need a new weapon.

"Paul-san?"

"Yes?"

"I have one more piece of good news." Charlize tapped the bed beside her.

Ondragon complied with her request and sat down.

"Your baby is down in the underground garage."

"The Mustang? And how did it get here?" While his memory of the evening at Stern's house and the hunt for the would-be zombie was hazy, he had been pretty sure his car was still out in Chalmette.

"A certain Madame Tombeau brought the car here and contacted me. She was the one who paid for your room before I got to New Orleans."

"Oh yeah? And how did she drive the car without the keys? And anyway, where was she when I was kidnapped? She suddenly disappeared."

Charlize nodded. "She told me about your visit to Stern's house and that you were following someone. Mari-Jeanne . . ."

"Mari-Jeanne?"

"Yes, Madame Tombeau."

Ondragon pursed his lips. So his assistant and the Voodoo Queen were already on first name terms.

"Well, anyway, she said you were going too fast and she couldn't keep up because she was wearing high heels, and then out of nowhere someone hit her over the head. When she came to, you were gone. She looked for you but couldn't find you. Then she went back to the car and found it was open. She waited for you there until dawn. When you didn't show up, she hot-wired the car and drove it to the hotel's underground garage. She had someone ask for you at the front desk almost every hour and she extended your room booking when they told her the reservation was about to expire. She got seriously concerned and finally called me."

"And how did she get your number?" Ondragon didn't know what to make of this. Somehow, he was suspicious of the Voodoo priestess. Maybe she had set all this up to convince him her hocus-pocus was real.

"You gave her one of your business cards that night, one of the ones with my number on it."

"Oh, did I?"

Charlize nodded, flipped back the covers, and got out of bed.

Ondragon couldn't help but notice that the hem of her negligee reached just below her shapely bottom. He averted his eyes and looked at the replica art on the wall while Charlize rummaged in her purse. When she found what she was looking for, she stood in front of him and held the item under his nose. It was an iPhone.

"I bought it from the Apple Store the day before yesterday. New SIM card, old number. You just have to set it up again."

"How did you know . . . ?"

She made a dismissive gesture. "I had a feeling."

Smiling, Ondragon took the phone. Charlize was sometimes even one step ahead of him. What would he do without her? He turned on the phone, logged onto the internet, and using a secure connection downloaded all the data, numbers, and everything else that had been on the old phone to the new one in encrypted form. Then all he had to do was enter a password and the files were installed. Easy as pie and foolproof. Rudee, his Thai computer genius, had set up a cloud for him on a protected server where all his sensitive data was stored. If he lost his cell phone or laptop, all he needed was a new device, and with one click he had everything back again. In addition, Rudee had programmed the software so that no one could hack into the phone. All content was automatically deleted if the password was entered incorrectly just twice. So it was virtually impossible for an unauthorized person to read his data.

The iPhone beeped and the familiar icons appeared on the display. Ondragon opened the app for detecting bugs—a special gimmick of Rudee's—and marched around the room for a while, looking at the display. Meanwhile, Charlize took the opportunity to use the bathroom. Ondragon heard the shower and preferred not to imagine what his assistant might look like under her negligee.

Having been unable to detect any hidden listening devices, he completed the scan and quickly checked his emails and missed calls. He saw Roderick DeForce's number and pressed recall. It was time to talk straight.

"Hi, Ecks. Boy, am I glad to hear from you! Your assistant called me two days ago and told me you had disappeared," Rod explained, the relief clearly audible in his voice.

"I've been in deep shit, Rod." Ondragon made his voice sound deliberately reproachful. "But I got off easy. Pulled myself out of the swamp by the pigtail, so to speak, like Munchausen."

"Like who?"

"Oh, forget it." Apparently, Rod wasn't familiar with the legend of the German Baron of Lies. "Did Charlize tell you Bolič and Sylvester Stern are dead and that Alejandro Green has also disappeared?"

"Yes, she told me everything. Is there anything new?"

Ondragon reflected. For some inexplicable reason, he suddenly felt as if Rod knew more than he was letting on. "No, nothing. But why don't *you* tell me something new for a change?"

"What do you mean?"

Was Rod that ignorant, or was he just pretending to be?

"Well, what kind of stinking infernal trip did you send me on!" replied Ondragon irritably. "Listen, you should remember it's not like it used to be! I'm not your mailman anymore, I don't do whatever you tell me to do. These days, I can just ditch the whole shebang if I feel like it. And I'm about to! So, out with whatever it is you've been keeping from me until now!"

The silence on the other end lasted just long enough for Ondragon to confirm he was right. Rod hadn't told him everything. Eager not to freak out, he waited impatiently for an answer.

His old friend cleared his throat. "Ecks, please forgive my lack of transparency. It has nothing to do with a lack of trust in you. I know you are the right man for the job. I just didn't want to give you all the information right away because I was afraid I might compromise your objectivity. I wanted you to form your own opinion, regardless of my preconceptions. I could have been wrong and you could have come to a completely different conclusion. It—"

"We're friends, for crying out loud! You should have told me," Ondragon interrupted him caustically, "but I accept your apology. However, my patience is at an end and so is my will to expose myself to dangerous situations that I might have been able to foresee if I had gotten a little more information from you. So stop beating around the bush, please. You're insulting my intelligence. Tell me what you've been holding back, and I may decide to move ahead with the case!"

A sigh came from the other end of the phone. "Mea culpa, Ecks. I'm really sorry if I offended you. I hope you know that it would never occur to me to underestimate you. So . . ." Rod paused, "it's like this: I don't have any proof yet, but I have a suspicion that there were irregularities in one of the CSAC contracts. The reports from those involved were wildly divergent. That made me wonder."

Since Ondragon was privy to DeForce's internal procedures, he knew that after a job, two mailmen had to deliver independent reports on the way the mission went down. This was one of DeForce's control mechanisms, which were supposed to guarantee the loyalty of its employees.

"Let me guess, Rod. This is about the Haiti mission?"

"That's right." His friend did not sound surprised.

"I have to admit that I wondered about the nature of the assignment. I always thought DeForce didn't do private army, only transports. The fact that you guys are now 'delivering' bombs and competing with the Foreign Legion is news to me. Are you looking to expand your operations?"

Rod cleared his throat. "No, not exactly. DeForce is and always will be a logistics specialist. But the job was very lucrative. I mean, *very* lucrative! But that wasn't the only reason I accepted it. I was hoping to access new customers via the client, who is a very big player on the market. Unfortunately, I had a bad feeling about it from the start. I should have listened to my gut."

"That's all right, Rod. Even an old hand like you takes a wrong turn sometimes. I'm not blaming you for that. Only for not telling me enough upfront. A little more information would have kept me from blundering into the trap like an amateur. I'll spare you the details. And now I need more information before I decide whether to proceed with the case. For example: Who wrote the reports?"

"Green, the Head, and Stern as the Body."

Ondragon had thought so, because it was customary for reports to be written by the crew leader and the lowest-ranking member of the team. He fished the small pad from the nightstand that the hotel provided for its guests and noted down the details. "And who is the client?"

"I knew right away I shouldn't have gotten involved." Roderick De Force sighed. "What the hell, it's too late now anyway. Actually, I can't disclose the client to a third party at any price, but you'd throw the case out instantly if I didn't, right?"

"Correct."

"Well then, I guess I have no choice. The *sponsor* is a large, publicly traded biotech company called Darwin Inc., headquartered in Portland, Oregon. Its main businesses are crop research and the production of herbicides, fertilizers, and seeds. In addition, it trades in these products worldwide. However, it owns other major subsidiaries such as specialty chemicals and materials factories and a pharmaceutical company."

"Darwin Inc., huh? Never heard of them, even though they're a global player?"

"They're not that into publicity."

"I see; skeletons in the closet probably." *But what big corporation didn't have those*, Ondragon thought, and asked, "What was that Darwin Inc. lab in Haiti and why the secret location?"

"As far as I know, it was a small, high-tech genetic engineering research facility. And the lab was secret because Darwin Inc. feared industrial espionage from competitors. So it's nothing to be alarmed about. It's not a super virus lab or anything like that."

"That's a comfort," Ondragon said sarcastically. He still wondered what it was about genetic engineering that required so much protection from espionage that they chose such a remote location. "Who's the contact at Darwin Inc.?"

"With the best will in the world, I can't give you that information. And you are not to show up there under any circumstances and make inquiries, do you hear me, Ecks? That would ruin DeForce's reputation! Everything I tell you must remain confidential!"

"Don't worry, Rod. I'll only come back to it if there's an unmistakable lead to Darwin Inc. Agreed?"

"This whole thing worries me, Ecks. If our customers get wind that there are any irregularities concerning us, DeForce will be toast. No one would let us transport even a crate of bananas. So I'm begging you to be careful!" Rod was almost pleading.

Ondragon was surprised. He'd never heard his friend speak like that. Spider was usually the one who lured his foes into the web and ate them without blinking an eye!

His internal sniffer dog began to bark. Tentatively at first, and then louder and louder. If Rod was showing something like fear, then things were more dangerous than he had suspected. And more dangerous meant more of a challenge. Ondragon felt his ambition stirring. "All right, Rod, I'll stay on the case. And I won't do anything that is in any way detrimental to DeForce. But I do have one request. Send me the reports from Green and Stern and have the equipment ready. I may be making a trip to Haiti soon."

"Ecks, is that necessary?"

"That'll be my decision. Make sure I can contact you, will you? And send over another floater. Someone you trust a hundred percent. I need another man here. Our operating base will be New Orleans. Mardi Gras will be great cover."

"Sure. I'll get someone on a plane today."

Ondragon said goodbye to his friend and hung up. Just then, Charlize came out of the bathroom. She was fully dressed, wearing jeans and a black shirt with a V-neck and rolled-up sleeves. She had tied her long, dark hair into a ponytail and applied only subtle makeup to her bronze skin. She noticed his gaze.

"I thought something inconspicuous would be appropriate here in the French Quarter. Add a camera and you've got a tourist outfit." She slipped into black sandals. Her toenails were painted dark red.

Ondragon smiled. Charlize had the camouflage thing down pat.

"Here, Boss! Catch!" His assistant tossed him a tube of aloe vera gel and a see-through bag. "You can use this to cool your sunburn; I found the other thing behind the curtain." She winked at him.

"Thank you." Ondragon opened the bag he himself had secured with a safety pin in the folds of the curtain by the window. It contained his second set of papers: driver's license, fake US passport, credit card, and a couple hundred bucks. The bozos hadn't found them.

"Do you mind if I go down for breakfast?" asked Charlize.

"No, you go ahead. It's going to take me a little while to get up to speed. We'll talk about everything later. I got some new information from Roderick."

"*Hai*; see you in a minute, then." She shouldered her bag, in which she had stowed her rather large revolver, and left the room, humming happily.

While Ondragon took off his clothes from the hospital and got into the shower, he thought about how to proceed. After all, he had a new lead to follow: Darwin Inc.

CHAPTER 18

Later, over breakfast, Ondragon told his assistant of his plans. Charlize, looking sympathetically at his sunburned face, immediately offered to make inquiries about Darwin Inc.

"Good. I would have put you onto that anyway," Ondragon said, sipping his espresso. "Fly direct to Portland and do some sniffing around. Interview employees, workers, and maintenance staff. But please be discreet. Rod asked me to be careful, and I don't want anything to rebound on DeForce."

"You got it. And what are you going to do?" asked Charlize, eating the last spoonful of her fruit salad.

"First, we'll both go and see Madame Tombeau to reconstruct the events of the night I was kidnapped. Perhaps that'll give us a clue to my kidnappers and their motive. Second, I'll arrange to travel to Haiti."

"You really want to go there?"

"I'm afraid there's no way around it. I'll only be able to visualize this sinister laboratory if I'm on the spot. I suspect there's a connection between their research, the disappearance of Tyler Ellys, and all the zombie stuff with Bolič and the others."

"But do you want to go there all by yourself? You need support. I can come with you if you like," Charlize offered.

"No, I need you on the trail of Darwin Inc. Hunt them like a shark and don't stop until you get a useful bite! I'll find someone for

Haiti. I'll call our French secret weapon; maybe he can come over from Africa."

"Achille is in Mauritania right now looking for the missing TV crew. He may be stuck in the middle of the desert."

"I'll get him on the horn somehow." Ondragon thought about his employee. Achille Mercier lived in Marrakech and had worked for Ondragon Consulting for seven years. Ondragon mostly used him for the less complicated Standard- and Sherlock-level problems in the African region. Achille was extremely reliable and this left Ondragon himself more time to focus on the highest-level Magnum problems, his favorites.

"Let's move on to the next item on the agenda," he said to Charlize. "I need a new gun."

"You can have mine and I'll get a new one."

"Thanks, Charlize, but your gun is way too bulky for me. I need something lighter. And I already know where to get it." Ondragon rose and motioned for his assistant to follow him. They left the breakfast room and made their way to the underground garage, where they found the Mustang in one of the back corners. With its matte-black paint, it absorbed all the light like some dark tank. *Well, there's probably no need to pick up the keys from valet parking*, Ondragon thought, and opened the trunk with his lock pick. Charlize, meanwhile, stood guard.

"Just as I thought!" he groaned angrily.

"What is it?" asked Charlize.

"They took my precision rifle. The case I had it stowed in is gone." He slammed the lid of the trunk shut, walked around to the passenger door, and opened it. He crawled into the footwell, where he lifted the carpet to uncover a secret compartment. A gun in his hand, he reappeared. It was the gun he had taken from Bolič's hotel room, a Walther P99. A bit bigger and heavier than his Sig Sauer, but it would do for now. All he needed was an additional magazine and ammunition. He would get the other equipment he wanted under cover of night from the well-stocked secret room in the Stern house.

Ondragon tucked the pistol into the back of his jeans and hid it under his windbreaker. His eyes fell on the back seat, where Madame

Tombeau's Voodoo candle lay. He fished it out of the car and put it into his jacket pocket. Then he closed the doors, singing softly, *"Ooh, ooh, sha la la, I was dancing with the Queen of New Orleans, ooh, ooh, sha la la, dancing cheek to cheek on Bourbon Street."* He turned to Charlize. *"I was a deer in the lights of a speeding car—*on to Madame Tombeau! We can have a quiet word in her office."

"Oh yes," his assistant said meaningfully, "I've been to her office!"

"Uh-huh, and what do you make of the Madame?" Ondragon asked. He moved toward the elevator that would take them up to the lobby of the hotel.

"Well, I've spoken to her several times," Charlize replied, "and she seems professional. At least, it seems like she takes what she does very seriously."

"That Voodoo baloney," Ondragon said disparagingly. They entered the elevator.

"Well, I wouldn't necessarily call it baloney. There are people who believe in it. And everyone has the right to believe whatever they want, don't they? Whether it's in Voodoo, Jesus, or your smartphone. The fact is, people need something like religion; they need to believe in a higher power."

Ondragon sighed. Now Charlize was stepping into the breach for the Madame. "The main thing is that you don't convert to Voodoo!" he replied mockingly.

"No, Boss. I won't, don't worry. But you must admit, Mari-Jeanne is a very fascinating woman."

He couldn't argue with *that.* The elevator door opened and they went through the lobby toward the large exit.

"But can we trust her?" asked Ondragon, waving at the receptionist, who nodded back, smiling.

"You think she might have something to do with your kidnapping?" Charlize looked pensive. Her brows furrowed over her beautiful Asian eyes.

Ondragon avoided the gaze of the doorman holding the door open for them, and as they stepped outside into the bright sunlit street, he said, "I don't think so. Why would she have paid for my hotel room for days and then contacted you? It wouldn't make sense."

Charlize nodded. "Besides, her concern for you sounded genuine, Boss. I don't think she was in on it."

They walked down Bourbon Street and entered the Captain Zombie store just a few moments later. By now, the musty sweet smell was familiar to Ondragon, as was the suspicious face of Natalie, who reluctantly let them through to the back, and the Madame's office.

Mari-Jeanne Tombeau seemed surprised. She looked up from her sterile desk and gave a relieved smile when she saw Ondragon. She rose and came toward them.

"Monsieur Ondragon, I see you are well. I am very pleased. I was afraid for you. And, Charlize, *ma petite chérie*, come and sit down. It is good to see you." She took Charlize by the hand and led her to one of the chairs. Ondragon watched jealously, suspicious of the intimacy between the two women. He lowered himself gloomily into the second chair and accepted the Madame's offer of water. He waited until the priestess, who was wearing a gray business suit and red shoes today, had finally sat down and then spoke.

"Madame Tombeau, first of all, I would like to express my gratitude to you for taking care of my interests during my absence and notifying my assistant. You didn't need to do that." He saw Charlize give him a reproachful look and then look apologetically at the Madame. So the two women were already in cahoots. He cleared his throat. "I mean, that was very kind of you, and I would like to reimburse you for any expenses you incurred on my behalf." He pulled out his credit card.

Madame Tombeau raised a dismissive hand. "I'm not exactly starving, monsieur. Take my help as a favor that I was happy to do you. Perhaps you will be able to return it someday. However, if you are not comfortable being in my debt, I will gladly accept your money in the form of a donation to my temple." She looked him straight in the eye, without any apparent irony.

Ondragon realized she had a pretty good idea of who he was. But it was also possible that Charlize had blabbed a little too much. He put on his business smile, from the "I'll take the deal" category, and put his credit card away. He guessed he would offend the Madame if he insisted on paying the debt with money. That would be too easy. Besides, you couldn't just buy your way out of a favor. A favor was something much weightier than mere dollars. It was the Madame's way of showing she trusted him. And he had to respect that, whether it suited him to be in hock to the Voodoo Queen or not. He gave her a friendly look and an imperceptible nod. Then he told the Madame about the events of the past four days.

"Hmm, sounds like someone has it in for you, monsieur. But who could it be?"

"Well, I think," Ondragon continued, "there were at least two people, if not three. They punched my lights out—and yours too, madame—and took me out of Chalmette in a car or van. They were obviously less interested in you, so they left you unconscious. They searched my car, but not thoroughly enough, and took almost all of my belongings. Then they held me for a while in some unknown location and probably pumped me full of drugs. I only have very confused memories of this, like images from a nightmare—which supports my theory about the drugs. After that, the guys dumped me in the swamp. There are two possible reasons they might have done that. First, they wanted me to croak very slowly, which indicates how extremely sadistic these bastards are and is highly unprofessional in my line of work. Plus, my body would never have been found. The second reason could have been—and I tend to this interpretation—that they wanted to test me! In that case we would be dealing with a highly professional and far more sophisticated enemy than a sadist, because these kinds of people demonstrate a certain potential for ingenuity and planning. Also—and I'm not saying this to scare you—we can assume they are watching us all right now. Why?" Ondragon shrugged. "Perhaps they wanted to know what kind of opponent they were dealing with without having to kill me right away. That leads me to conclude that they either respect me or intend to play some kind of cat-and-mouse game. It's also possible it was a warning."

"A rather risky warning, if you ask me," Madame Tombeau interjected. "You could have died, or I could have recognized one of them. Unfortunately, other than the zombie that fled from us, I didn't see much that could help us. One thing is for sure, a zombie would not have been able to plan something like that by itself. It could never engineer even one step of this plot."

"What if it wasn't a zombie?" asked Ondragon.

The Madame looked at him. "You are of course free to believe or not, monsieur. But from experience I would say the man might well have been a zombie! You saw for yourself how it moved. That is typical. This staggering and shuffling, seemingly disoriented, but at an incredibly fast pace. Zombies have more strength than normal people. Their bodies are the only things that still function, so their whole being is focused on the physical. Besides, it was you, monsieur, who said you had found the man dead in the house. There is only one explanation. The bokor turned him into a zombie!"

Ondragon made a face. He still refused to believe in these spirits, although he was finding one thing extremely puzzling. He pressed his lips together and looked around. Finally, he said hesitantly, "I noticed something else before I passed out. The arm that choked me had a Bugs Bunny tattoo, the one that all DeForce mailmen have."

"So that's our proof," Charlize exclaimed. "Stern is the zombie. And he's working for the kidnappers. *That's* possible, isn't it?" She looked at the Madame, who nodded.

"A zombie does what its master tells it to do," the priestess confirmed. "It may well be that it is being used by these people."

Ondragon shook his head. "It could have been anyone who has that tattoo. Any mailman. Bolič too, in theory, I've seen Bugs on him too."

"But Bolič is in Tucson," Charlize pointed out. "How would he have gotten here? As a zombie?"

"The man in the top hat took him to New Orleans. Baron Samedi!" Ondragon joked in an eerie voice.

"That could be it, of course," Charlize considered seriously.

Ondragon looked at his assistant reproachfully. "Give me a break! You don't really believe this humbug, do you?"

"Mari-Jeanne explained it to me. It's a powder made of different ingredients that can be used to turn people into mindless slaves. A poison."

"A poison that doesn't kill, but just makes you seem dead?" he interjected sharply.

"The *coup poudre* can bring illness or death! And after death, you need magic to wake up the dead," the Madame explained matter-of-factly.

Ondragon put his hands to his head. "I can't believe I'm discussing this!"

"But the powder was in all those letters," Charlize continued, unperturbed. "That's for sure. So why wouldn't that work? Someone is giving the mailmen poison to turn them into zombies and then using them. Why they're doing it is for us to figure out. But it might also be that Stern and the missing people, Ellys and Green, saw something they should not have seen on the Haiti job. And Bolič is collateral damage. He stuck his nose in too deep and got too close to the people involved, so they got him out of the way. Maybe it was people from that Oregon company."

"And why didn't I become a zombie as well? I got too close to them too, *and* I had contact with the powder," Ondragon interjected.

"You were lucky!" the priestess interfered.

Ondragon raised his index finger. "This is all pure speculation!"

"But, Boss, wasn't it you who said there might be more things between heaven and earth than a human being is capable of comprehending? Soon after your encounter with the—what was it called again—ah yes, the Wendigo! If you believe in that forest monster, why not zombies?"

"Zombies *do* exist!" the Madame warned.

Ondragon rolled his eyes. The two women were taunting him. But he wasn't going to get involved with that. "Can we get back to the facts?" He clasped his hands in his lap. "Thank you. I think we can agree that something very strange happened to Bolič and Stern, which made them seem dead afterward. Maybe they are actually victims of a larger conspiracy and people are just using them as tools. The aim of the conspiracy remains to be seen, but these people are serious. I've heard their threat. And we're agreed it has something to do with the job in Haiti."

Charlize and Madame Tombeau nodded.

Good. That's something, at least, Ondragon thought. He went on. "So we should turn our attention to the question of what exactly happened in Haiti and what kind of laboratory it was. I'm also certain we will be partway to the solution to this mystery once we know what is in the zombie powder. Unfortunately, my chemist doesn't have a result yet. You wouldn't want to tell me what it contains, would you?"

"Sometimes it's better not to know." Madame Tombeau glowered at him. Apparently, she didn't like her magic getting too close to science.

"Save your mysterious warnings. You're barking up the wrong tree. I always want to know everything!" said Ondragon with a mocking smile. "So, now that we've dealt with motive and perpetrators, I'd like to ask you a few more questions about Haiti, madame." He glanced at the priestess; he was keen to tap into her knowledge of the stricken Caribbean nation. "My client has given me the exact location of the operation. It's a village called Nan Margot, west of the port of Jacmel on the southern coast of the island. The lab is supposed to be up in the mountains, hidden in a mine shaft. Does that mean anything to you?"

The Voodoo priestess's features brightened a shade. "I know Jacmel. It's a beautiful city. At least it was before the earthquake. I've heard there was a lot of destruction there. But I spent my childhood in Cap-Haïtien, which is to the north. I traveled a lot, with my father; he was a respected houngan."

"Well, I need my information to be as precise as possible for my planning. Maybe you can describe what it looks like there and tell me what to expect."

"I can do even better than that, monsieur!" The Madame smiled enigmatically.

"How?"

The priestess's smile widened. "I will go with you!"

Ondragon leaned back in surprise. For a moment, no one said anything.

"But that's the solution, Boss!" said Charlize finally. "Mari-Jeanne knows her way around very well there, and you wouldn't be traveling alone. Besides, she speaks Creole, and without that you're screwed in Haiti, I've been told."

Ondragon thought for a while. Should he really travel to Haiti with this woman? Admittedly, he'd have nothing against it on purely visual grounds, but he feared she'd try to convert him again and that she might hinder his movements. On the other hand, the Madame's knowledge of the country's language and culture would bring valuable benefits.

"I lost track of you once, monsieur, I will not do it a second time!" said Madame Tombeau firmly. "Haiti is not a package tour destination. Traveling there means being constantly on your guard. Even more so after the earthquake. Anarchy and violence hold sway in my homeland—unfortunately," she added sadly.

Ondragon looked up. "If I were to take you with me, madame, I would be in your debt twice over!"

"Monsieur Ondragon, this is not a favor!" The Madame looked at him seriously. "I too wish to discover who gave me this bump." She stroked the back of her head. "And besides, we need to find out who is daring to mess around with the *coup poudre.* If it's the same person, I will catch them!"

"You mean the black magician?" Ondragon asked.

The Madame nodded.

"But the bokor is here in the States. According to you, he is controlling Bolič and Stern at close range. So why do you want to come with me to Haiti, of all places, now that it's so dangerous there, as you say?"

The Madame took off her glasses and looked directly at him. "I know the enemy is lying in wait for you here, in my city! That is why I feel responsible for you. A bokor is after you. And only a person who has been initiated into the practices of magic can protect you from his spells. He will follow you, perhaps to Haiti, but I will be with you and will help you defeat him! The bokor needs to be put out of business, because he is dragging the honor of our profession through the dirt! I cannot allow that to happen. Do you understand?"

Ondragon still didn't know if he should burden his mission with this woman. It could be risky. On the other hand, she had proven that she had an alert mind and could be gratifyingly pragmatic when the situation required. She knew how to hotwire a car, at least. Not every woman knew that.

"Can you handle a gun?" he asked her.

"Bien sûr!" She looked at him confidently. "We live in America, don't we?"

Ondragon overlooked the hint of mockery and weighed up her usefulness. Finally, he leaned forward. As a woman, she would provide him with good cover, and if things got dicey, he could always be selfish and save his own skin. "All right, madame! I'll take you," he said, holding out his hand. "But on two conditions: You talk as little as possible about Voodoo, *and* you leave your high heels at home!"

With a grim smile, the Madame took his hand, but she froze abruptly when her hand touched his. She sat motionless for several heartbeats, looking at him. No, not directly at him. Her gaze was dim and rapt, as if she were looking over his shoulder into another world.

An eerie silence descended, and suddenly all the masks and fetishes from the store seemed to be present with them in the room that until recently had been a soberly furnished office.

"What is it?" asked Charlize anxiously from Ondragon's side. She slid uneasily back and forth on the chair.

But Ondragon didn't know; moreover, he couldn't move.

All at once the Madame blinked and murmured, "Your Marassa was here. He has shown himself! It's your twin, Paul."

Ondragon recoiled in amazement, letting go of the priestess's hand. Immediately, the tingling sensation on his palm faded, and instead an electric crackle filled the air. What the hell . . . ? How did the Madame know he had a brother? His head snapped around to Charlize.

"Did you tell her about my brother?" he asked angrily.

Charlize licked her lips nervously.

"She did not!" the Madame intervened. "He revealed himself to me. There in the mirror behind you, on the wall. Just as he has shown himself to you many times before, hasn't he, Paul? Out in the swamp. He helped you . . . this time."

"What is this? Is this another of your games?" Ondragon snapped at the priestess.

"It's no game. The power of the spirits! I have the ability to see into their world. The Marassa are the divine twins. In our faith, there are always two aspects. Day and night, man and woman, good and evil. The twins embody this completeness, and anyone born a twin is deeply revered by his family and community. Yet there is something strange about you . . ." She frowned, as if she were still looking into the afterlife. "Your Marassa has a strange aura, not that of a loa, nor that of a spirit from the realm of the dead. He seems more alive. How . . . is that possible?" The Madame raised her eyebrows. "There can be only one explanation for this: The reunion is not complete. Your brother is—"

"If you don't stop with this bullshit right now, I'm going to change my mind and not take you with me!" Ondragon had risen from the chair and was glaring angrily at the priestess. "I don't want to talk about my brother. Understand? He's been dead for over thirty years and that's that!"

Madame Tombeau and Charlize looked at him mutely.

Had he spoken that loudly?

He let his shoulders droop. This thing with Per Gustav was getting to him. Since the psychotherapy at Cedar Creek Lodge, his brother's death had weighed on his conscience, as heavy as a coffin lid. He ran his hand over the irritated skin of his face. There was a rational explanation for the appearance of his brother in the swamp. He had been delirious from dehydration and had imagined him, nothing more. What the Madame was saying, however, evoked much more oppressive feelings. How could she know about Per? Ondragon felt a paralyzing heaviness in his limbs. The hardships of his trip through the wilderness were still very much in his bones. Tiredly, he gestured to Charlize that they should leave.

His assistant and Madame Tombeau both rose. "So what do we do now?" they both asked at the same time.

Ondragon was dizzy with exhaustion. He pointed at the priestess. "You stand by. I want to leave for Haiti as soon as possible. Be prepared for at least five days of difficult travel. And leave your passport at home. I'll take care of the rest of the planning." He lowered his voice. "And I don't want to hear any more about my brother, understand?"

"Understood, monsieur. Forgive me."

"That's all right. It's what you do, after all. We're not so different from each other." He turned to Charlize. "And now we're going to the mall. I need some new clothes for the trip."

Long after the two guests had left her office, Madame Tombeau stared at the closed door, ignoring the look Paul Eckbert Ondragon's Marassa was giving her from the mirror.

CHAPTER 19

Haiti

Christine awoke with a jolt from semiconscious sleep. She had had a bad dream about her father. He had followed her secretly and had watched her in her sleep. Then he had reached out his hand, to . . .

Dazed, Christine shook her head and looked up at the bright square that continued to stare down at her, like a quadrilateral sun.

How long had she been asleep? The last time she had looked up, the walls of the shaft, the sky up there had still been black. Then there was the question of how long she had been stuck down here. A day, two days, a week? No, it couldn't be a week; she would have been dead long ago.

Groaning, she sat up, very carefully, making sure not to move her injured leg. She had broken it when she fell down the concealed shaft. At least, she thought she had, because her lower leg was very swollen and black.

She gave a soft cry of pain as she dragged herself on her hands and her one sound leg to the rough wall of the shaft that had been carved into the rock, and leaned her back against it. The sound was muffled and unnatural and was immediately swallowed by the mass of stone around her. Christine felt tears welling up in her eyes. But not only from pain. She kept thinking of the night when the power of the priestess had failed and her terrified flight over the mountain had led to her fate.

The night her mother died.

In her mind's eye, Christine saw the zombie breaking her mother's neck. Just like that, as if it were crushing a piece of rotten wood.

She saw the zombie's gruesome face. The disfigured features of her father.

Christine was seized by a fit of crying and she closed her eyes.

She knew she was going to die down here.

For no one from their village could have guessed what had happened to them.

CHAPTER 20

February 13, 2010
New Orleans
12:30 pm

Ondragon went through the checklist for the trip in his mind. Functional clothing and light camping gear had been procured. They would get weapons, ammunition, and special equipment at Stern's and buy food at the supermarket. The small private plane he planned to travel on had already been booked, fuel included. And all within a few hours. Not without some complacency, Ondragon congratulated himself for his organizational talent, raised his glass of mineral water, and toasted himself. He was sitting in the far corner of an elegant Bourbon Street restaurant, eating a light lunch and keeping a constant eye on the door. He was alone. He had sent his assistant to sort out a few things he needed for the trip to Haiti. Of course, he had not let her go without first impressing upon her that she should be on her guard. Even in the mall they had shopped in, they had been extremely careful. The forthcoming Mardi Gras meant everywhere had been very crowded, like the rest of the city, and Ondragon had constantly felt someone was following them. But when Charlize had dropped back and followed him at a distance, she hadn't spotted anyone suspicious. They had finished their errands quickly and returned to the French Quarter in Charlize's inconspicuous rental car.

Ondragon ate a forkful of shrimp and rice, chewing on it thoughtfully to help his screwed-up stomach with some of the work. Meanwhile, his *centrifuge* was spinning, keeping him on the alert. He looked out the windows at the street. Even if he couldn't catch sight of his adversaries, he knew they were out there, watching him through unseen eyes—though that gave him only the smallest pause for thought.

He swallowed the shrimp and rice and stabbed a cocktail tomato with his fork; it burst open and bled its contents onto the plate. Obviously, those guys had made a mistake. The stunt in the swamp had turned this into a personal matter. And having Ondragon as your enemy was worse than running into the four horsemen of the apocalypse.

Ondragon smiled pensively and ate the tomato. Then he dabbed his lips with his napkin and waved the waitress over. After settling his bill, he got up from the table and went to the men's room, where he first made sure he was alone and then locked himself in one of the stalls. He took out his cell phone and dialed a number from his own company register.

The other end rang. But when someone picked up, there was only a hissing sound at first, followed by multiple clicks, as if the operator hadn't switched the jacks yet. After half an eternity, he finally heard his employee's voice. It came in staccato bursts and there was a long delay on the line.

"Mercier here. Hello, Chief, what's up? Th— bad reception———— middle of the—— sert!"

"Achille, I need your help." Ondragon tried not to shout. He cupped his hand over his mouth and continued speaking, "You need to come over here at once. To New Orleans!"

"— no good! —— damn far — way. At lea —— two days by Jeep to — nearest oasis. No helicopter, no plane!"

"Any other options?"

"—— no way, Chief! But the Tuareg might take me there by camel. Hihi —— hi."

Ondragon contorted his face in annoyance. The guy had some nerve! He said goodbye and hung up with a quiet curse. In his head he had already calculated that Achille Mercier would need at least four days to get to New Orleans. Far too long. So that option was ruled out.

He went through the other possible candidates.

Dietmar Hegenbarth was his Middle East specialist. Previously a sales engineer for a major German defense contractor and an ex-intelligence consultant, he had taken tea with the Taliban in his younger days. But at sixty-six he was a little too old for this job.

Then there was Jorge Hidalgo Contreras, a former bounty hunter from Colombia who had earned his spurs in the drug war in the eighties, sometimes with Uncle Sam, but sometimes working under very different flags. Now he was a dirty-war expert with Ondragon Consulting. Unfortunately, Contreras was currently tied up with an undercover assignment on an illegal casino ship off the coast of Florida. One of the few jobs Ondragon had accepted from the US government. It was something he was extremely reluctant to do, generally, but had made an exception in this case; it could sometimes pay to have people who owed you one at the highest echelons of politics.

The last so-called freelancer Ondragon employed was a Swedish hitman who called himself Järnkors, meaning "iron cross." But he used his services only very occasionally. For reasons of caution, he had never met the man in person. It was said in the relevant circles that he was completely insane and a cold-blooded reincarnation of the San Francisco Zodiac Killer. However, he was also pretty good at what he did.

Ondragon sighed. Those were all the people he could consider for the job in Haiti. So was there nothing for it but to travel just with the Madame? The thought did not appeal to him. Only two of them, and he would be working with an amateur. It was just too much of a risk, and somehow he urgently needed another comrade with weapons experience for this operation. Someone, moreover, who knew how to keep their eyes open. He was not a team player himself and always found it difficult to work with anyone else, but this case might be—though he was reluctant to admit it—too big for him alone. He thought about the new floater from DeForce. If Rod had full confidence in the man, he could have too. Ondragon dialed Rod's number to ask if the floater was in the air yet. But all he got was a busy signal. He hung up, waited, and dialed again a little later. When the familiar female voice told him that the person on the other end was not available and asked him to please leave a voicemail message, Ondragon angrily ended the call. Had he been talking Chinese? He had told Rod to be sure he could reach him!

What a goddamn mess. Maybe he should drop the case after all.

At that moment, he heard the door to the men's room open. He waited calmly for the guy to do his business and leave. But nothing happened. All there had been was the sound of the door. Alarmed, Ondragon put the cell phone away and carefully climbed onto the rim of the toilet.

The silence continued.

Had he imagined the squeaking of the hinge? Or was one of his enemies standing right outside the cubicle door taking aim at him? Dammit, why had he wasted so much time in this restroom?

The thought had scarcely crossed his mind when a long, drawn-out groan came from the cubicle to his right. It certainly didn't sound like someone with digestive problems. No, it didn't even sound human!

Ondragon felt the adrenaline shoot through his limbs and reached for the gun in his waistband. The groan was not repeated. Instead, he heard a scraping sound and, shortly afterward, shuffling footsteps.

He aimed the gun at the closed door where the footsteps had halted and held his breath. Should he just pull the trigger? No, he'd be in a whole heap of trouble. A shootout in a restaurant would be suboptimal. He focused on the door. If it was indeed a zombie, then he would be able to overpower it easily. At least, that's what he believed. He tensed his muscles, ready to pounce. He would simply rip the stall door off its hinges and slam it in the zombie's face!

Suddenly, Ondragon jumped off the toilet rim and charged his shoulder into the door. Its hinges burst open. Less than a second later, he was crouching outside the stalls.

But there was no one there!

No zombie, and no surprised fellow citizen rubbing his nose.

Ondragon quickly checked the other stalls, but they too were empty. He put the gun away and, his senses on high alert, left the restaurant rapidly before anyone had time to notice the damage he had done.

* * *

Because he feared he might be followed, he did extensive counter-reconnaissance. He strolled through the French Quarter's checkerboard network of streets, stopping here and there by a shop window and pretending to be interested in the art on display, when in fact he was using the glass as a mirror to keep an eye on the other side of the street. Fortunately, the side alleys weren't particularly busy, even though the world-famous Mardi Gras was just around the corner. It was probably still too early for the big party.

Ondragon sat down for fifteen minutes in a small French café whose green terrace had tables looking onto the street and drank an adequate café au lait. Even before he left the establishment, he put in his earphones and pretended to listen to music on his iPhone. Shortly afterward, he continued on his way, strolling through the streets. This was one of his best tricks. A cheap one, he had to admit, but it always worked, because although he was nodding his head slightly to the beat, there was nothing coming through the earphones. To anyone tailing him, this gave the impression that he was distracted by the music and couldn't hear anything. It tempted most of them into carelessness; they became inattentive and sooner or later gave themselves away.

Ondragon noticed a young blond guy in decidedly nondescript clothing following him some distance away, and stopped. He pretended to turn up the volume, watching the reflection of the street in a car window as the guy also stopped, seemingly interested in the guitars in a music store window. Ondragon put his phone away again and carried on walking. He crossed the street and turned the next corner onto Royal Street. He would wait here until his pursuer appeared.

But no one came.

After five minutes, Ondragon risked a look around the corner. The street was empty, except for a few tourists who came toward him wearing Mardi Gras bead necklaces and silly hats, singing loudly. The blond guy had disappeared.

Either he had just been an uninterested passerby, or he knew what he was doing. Shrugging his shoulders, Ondragon stepped back onto Chartres Street and marched toward the cathedral in Jackson Square.

After another half hour and another four blocks, he was finally sure no one was following him and returned to the hotel via Dumaine and Bourbon Streets.

Charlize was already waiting for him in his room; she had placed two newly purchased black duffel bags on the bed and was in the process of checking their contents.

"I got everything, Boss: two radio units, two Kevlar vests, binoculars with residual light amplifiers, two headlamps, batteries, three rolls of armor tape, a climbing rope with carabiners and harness, black, climbing gloves, black. An envelope with small denomination banknotes, the patches with the military insignia—they weren't so easy to get hold of, by the way—light blue and white spray paint and two waterproof diving watches. Oh yes, and chewing gum. All that's missing now are the weapons, ammunition, provisions, and a few other odds and ends."

"Good. Did you make sure no one was following you?"

"Sure." Charlize straightened up and stretched her back.

"Because I just had a strange encounter, if that's what it's called, out there." He told his assistant about the creepy experience in the men's room.

Charlize looked at him. "Something like that happened to me too. I was walking across the sidewalk to the store where I got the equipment, when I though I saw floater Bolič's face reflected in the shop window for a moment. But when I turned around, there was no one there. I did an extra lap around the block as counter-reconnaissance and waited to see if he came back. Nothing." She gestured with her hands like a magician making a rabbit disappear. "Maybe I was wrong, or maybe there was someone there."

"I think our nerves are a little overwrought; we're seeing zombies on every street corner. We should see to it we keep a cool head."

"I do, Boss! Don't get the idea I suddenly believe in zombies!"

"But didn't you say as much to Madame Tombeau this morning?" teased Ondragon.

"I didn't say I believed in zombies or the undead," she said, putting her hands on her hips, "I merely suggested there might actually be some kind of drug or poison that takes away people's will and turns them into an instrument others can use. Which is no less creepy, if you ask me."

"We're yet to find out what's really behind it. Real magic or just smoke and mirrors." He gave a conciliatory smile. "What time is your flight?"

"Four."

He looked at his wristwatch. "That's soon. Are your things packed?"

"Of course. I've returned the rental car too."

Ondragon nodded appreciatively. Charlize was really the only woman he knew who could be ready to leave faster than him. He allowed a warm, affectionate feeling to flow through him. A luxury he rarely permitted himself.

"Oh, Boss, before I forget. I've emailed you the results of my initial research into Darwin Inc. It's just a rough compilation of a quick internet search. But it's enough to give you a foretaste of who we're dealing with here. And I've contacted Rudee and told him to be ready to do a little hacking into Darwin Inc. if we need it."

"Good job, Charlize."

"*Domo arigato gozaimashita.*" She gave a small bow in the style of her ancestors, making Ondragon want to kiss her adorable little nose. But at the last second, he resisted such foolishness and reached for his sunglasses.

"Well, let's get you to the airport. I can get the provisions on the way back and I'll take Madame Tombeau with me when I collect the weapons from Stern's place tonight; that'll give her a chance to show what she's made of right away."

Charlize walked over to the chair where her travel bag was sitting. "And when do you plan to leave for Haiti?"

"Probably tomorrow at noon. The plane has to be loaded first. I've already calculated the route. I estimate we'll be on our way in around twenty-four hours."

Charlize heaved a theatrical sigh. "What I wouldn't give to be going to the Caribbean. Beach, cocktails, good-looking boys . . . but instead my boss is sending me to Portland, Oregon. Great! Rain, bad-tempered people, and that dreadful clam chowder." She pulled a face. "But at least I'm in civilization, not Caribbean chaos like you guys." She gave him a humorous wink and shouldered her bag. "I'm ready."

"Okey-dokey, Miss Moneypenny!" Grinning, Ondragon opened the door for her.

When Ondragon returned to the hotel from the airport having bought the provisions, he checked his room again for bugs, because someone could have gotten in during his absence. Fortunately, everything was clean.

Reassured, Ondragon sat down on the bed and used his iPhone to look at the information Charlize had put together about Darwin Inc. She had already given him the key data in the car, but the fine print made it clear that this new player was not to be underestimated.

Darwin Incorporated—a multinational corporate colossus. Founded in the fifties, it had become a real heavyweight over the years, and not only in American industry. It seemed all the stranger that Ondragon had not heard of it before, but as he read on, he quickly uncovered the reason for that. Darwin Inc. was just the name of the relatively small agricultural technology division, which was also the main arm of the corporation. All the other corporate off-shoots and subsidiaries were other big names, including well-known chemical companies, petroleum refineries, semiconductor technology plants, a pharmaceutical giant, and countless automotive, aircraft construction, and energy industry suppliers—to name just the most important sectors; one stock exchange journal said the conglomerate was made up of more than fifty independent companies and just as many partners. *What a death star of a corporation*, Ondragon thought cynically.

What was particularly striking about the corporation's history was that most of Darwin Inc.'s acquisitions of other companies had only taken place in the last ten years, and had been done on the quiet, behind the public's back. Darwin Inc. had its fingers in almost every sector of American industry, and with its seventy-three overseas locations, it had a gigantic foot in the door to the world. However, hardly anyone knew that the empire was headed up by the company with the harmless-sounding name.

They certainly wanted it that way, suspected Ondragon, having found an advertising brochure in Charlize's provisional portfolio with the pithy slogan *We don't make Evolution, we ARE Evolution!* Unfortunately, there was nothing about the involvement of Darwin Inc. in the production of chemical or biological weapons. Which didn't mean much, because the corporation could certainly keep this branch secret, especially if it was working with the government. But, Ondragon thought grimly, he would likely find out very soon. Because Rudee, his highly gifted computer worm, had drilled into every file so far!

What really impressed him about Darwin Inc. was not its sheer size, but that it already controlled 90 percent of the world's genetically modified crops. And it gradually dawned on Ondragon what the company's long-term goal was. His suspicions were confirmed in the statements of critics Charlize had fished off the net:

"Darwin Inc. is looking to bring global agriculture under its control!" (*Greenpeace*)

"Darwin Inc. is deploying aggressive tactics in the takeover of other companies in the seeds and genomics sector, and has purchased sole dominance in the production of genetically modified seeds." (*Financial Times*)

"Darwin Inc. has command of our food and controls who goes hungry in the world and who doesn't! We will soon have to bow down before this new monarch if we want our plates to be full." (*New York Times* commentary)

Those were clear words.

Ondragon scrolled to the end of the document, where Charlize had listed the biggest competitors of Darwin Inc., kraken in the field of genetic crop research.

All formidable companies.

And a charming crowd of righteous champions for genetic engineering, Ondragon thought. *And I haven't even gotten to the scandals yet.*

He lay back on the pillow, folded his arms behind his head, and let the *centrifuge* spin.

It was possible that Darwin Inc. had something to do with the disappearance of the mailmen. That kind of firm had a lot of influence and would have no qualms about making three people disappear. First you used their services and then you got rid of the menials because they had seen too much. Just like the pharaohs of ancient Egypt. Those who had built the secret burial chambers were buried at the same time, to silence them forever.

But what made the whole thing even more sordid was that Darwin Inc. (if the corporation was indeed behind it) had not only taken out Tyler Ellys and Alejandro Green, it had also turned Sylvester Stern and Kaplan Bolič into some kind of mindless slaves with fried brains in order to make use of them. Presumably to create a false trail. This whole scenario was obviously meant to make it look as if a Voodoo curse from the Caribbean island had carried off the CSAC men.

So was Darwin Inc. the bokor?

But why had they taken Bolič? He knew absolutely nothing about the job in Haiti; Rod had confirmed that to Ondragon. Besides, there was no apparent connection, either internal or external, between the Bosnian and CSAC, except that he had done some research on Ellys. Was Bolič collateral damage, as Charlize suspected? Had he actually found something that might pose a danger to Darwin Inc. and that he had concealed from Ondragon?

He closed his eyes.

Questions on top of questions that all needed answers.

He felt fatigue dragging at his limbs. For a brief moment he resisted, but then he gave in to temptation. After all, he had a lot of catching up to do . . . and a night shift ahead of him.

CHAPTER 21

February 14, 2010
New Orleans
1:45 am

Tired and bad-tempered, Ondragon steered the Mustang through the streets of Chalmette. Tired because he was still short of sleep after the three shitty nights in the swamp. Bad-tempered because Rod was still refusing to answer the phone, and because Madame Tombeau just wouldn't shut up. She had immediately agreed to come with him to organize the weapons. Apparently, she was not afraid of getting stuck in. She had even put on a highly appropriate outfit—black jeans, black hoodie, and Doc Martens (he had to admit, it looked damn good on her)—but she didn't seem to remember her promise not to breathe a word about this damn zombie nonsense.

Testily ignoring her lengthy sermon about what to do if they encountered the zombie again, Ondragon kept glancing in the rearview mirror. But no one was following them, even if the late hour meant some of the motorists were literally driving like zombies.

They reached Stern's neighborhood, and Ondragon took another lap around the block by way of precautionary reconnaissance. He then coasted with the engine and lights turned off onto the driveway of the house. Before getting out of the car, he turned to the Madame and meaningfully put a finger to his lips. She stopped talking instantly and nodded to show she understood. Good girl.

Treading softly, they left the car and once again entered the house through the back door. They paused for a moment on the first floor, listening, to make sure that they were indeed alone in the building.

Then they crept upstairs to the guest room, where Ondragon swung aside the large mirror that covered the entrance to the secret room. He stepped into the narrow space beyond and pulled the light bulb string. The light spilled over the shelves and the stacked contents. Madame Tombeau whistled softly through her teeth as she examined the suitcases and boxes.

"You could equip an entire terrorist unit with that," she finally whispered. "What are we taking?" She looked up at him.

Ondragon opened the case with the pistols, took out a Desert Eagle, and pressed it into the Madame's hand. "Get used to this; it will be your guardian angel!"

The Madame took the gun, weighed it expertly in her hand, and tentatively took aim at the wall. Somewhat relieved, Ondragon remembered that this was not the first time she had held a firearm.

"Isn't there anything lighter?" she asked finally. Indeed, in her slender hands the pistol looked like a clunky Stone Age device.

Ondragon opened another suitcase and shrugged. "No." He took a silencer from the first case, plus four magazines and a holster, and put them all in the empty duffel bag he had brought with him. "Sorry, you'll have to make do, madame." He walked over to the wall racks where several rifles lay horizontally. After a moment's consideration, he grabbed not the Browning precision model, as had been his first instinct, but the assault rifle also used by the US Marine Corps. For the mission in Haiti, they needed something rugged that would match their camouflage. After all, he planned to enter the country disguised as a UN soldier.

Rifle and ammunition also disappeared into the bag, as did four hand grenades, ten sticks of dynamite, and two US Navy diving knives with matte-black blades. Watched by the silent Madame, Ondragon filled the bag like a customer on a shopping spree at a bad boys' department store. A smile flitted across his lips as he picked up some brass knuckles with a keychain dangling from them in the form of Bugs Bunny nibbling on a carrot. The smile vanished abruptly, however, as he thought of the tattoo of the sworn community of mailmen and the dead Bolič rose in his mind's eye like a ghost. Or rather, like a seemingly dead ghost?

Ondragon exhaled peevishly and threw the brass knuckles back on the shelf. He no longer knew what to believe and what not to believe. Into the bag he stuffed another small bag of tools, an olive-green combat helmet, and magnesium flares, and zipped it up. They could not take too much gear with them; the Cessna Stationair he had rented was not big enough, and they had to fly with a full tank of fuel.

"That's it. Come on." He flicked off the light and left the secret room. The Madame followed him, stashing the Desert Eagle in the pouch of her hoodie.

They left the house, got into the Mustang unnoticed, and drove back to New Orleans. Without being pestered by any zombies, they reached the hotel's underground parking garage, where Ondragon released the Voodoo priestess, telling her to stay on the alert and to come to the Sonesta the next morning with her luggage. Shortly afterward, they parted ways.

As he entered his room on the second floor, he saw that a notification form from the front desk had been slipped under the door. He unfolded the paper boasting the hotel's gold initials and read the two words written on it in curved handwriting, possibly by the delightful Mrs. Myers.

Coca-Cola.

Ondragon knew what it meant. He looked at the alarm clock on the nightstand. 3:20 am. Maybe the floater had arrived. He called Rod—who answered the phone after the third ring.

"Ecks! Everything all right?" he asked in a rough voice that sounded as if he had been sleeping.

"Yes. Has the floater arrived?"

"You could say that."

Was he mistaken, or could he hear his friend grinning down the phone? His patience was wearing thin. "Rod, I'm not in the mood for jokes right now. I have to get up early tomorrow morning, I still have the shit from the swamp in my bones, and on top of that I have the prospect of a trip in a tiny plane that I'll have to fly myself. So cut the bullshit and tell me: Is. The. Floater. Here?"

"It's all right, Ecks, calm down. The floater is there. Knock on door number 5222."

"Isn't that one of the suites on the fifth floor?"

"That's right. Because of Mardi Gras, nothing else was free."

Okay, then. Ondragon said goodbye and hung up. Then he would just prepare the floater for his task before he could get a well-deserved full night's sleep. The guy might have a pilot's license too and be able to assist him on that damn flight. His mood lifted at the prospect.

After checking the hallway was clear in both directions, he left his room, took the elevator to the fifth floor, and among the few doors that existed up here, looked for the one numbered 5222. When he found it, he raised his hand and knocked.

Of course, there was no reply. The floater was probably sound asleep in his soft bed.

Ondragon looked around and knocked again. Harder this time. The sound echoed loudly through the hallway, and he hoped it wouldn't wake any of the other guests.

Finally, he heard footsteps.

The door opened, and at that very moment he felt his face fall.

But before he could instruct his tongue to say anything, the man pulled him into the room. Shortly after that, he clapped him on the shoulder.

"Ecks! You're amazed, aren't you? I never thought I could still surprise you, you old fox! Heh heh heh! Sit down and have a strong drink before you do anything else. You look like shit, to say the least. Were you in the solarium too long?"

Paul Eckbert Ondragon regained the power of speech only after emptying the glass of whiskey Roderick DeForce thrust into his hand.

"What the heck are *you* doing here?" he snapped at his old friend.

Rod frowned, offended. "Boy, are you glad to see me!"

"Where's the floater?" Ondragon looked rapidly around the luxurious suite.

"Haven't you caught up yet?" A big grin appeared on Rod's tanned face and he pointed both his thumbs at his chest. "*I'm* the floater!"

As he had done many times before, Ondragon realized how little he knew of British humor. He adopted a grim expression. "Rod, that's a really great joke, but unfortunately I don't get it, because I'm pretty pooped, you know? So cut it out and let's treat this with the seriousness it deserves."

"But that's what I'm doing. I was completely serious when I said I was the floater!"

Ondragon looked at Roderick DeForce, stunned.

"I've been thinking about what you said, Ecks," the elder man explained calmly. "You said I should send someone I could trust absolutely. Well, I quickly came to the conclusion that that person could only be myself. Savvy?"

Ondragon remained silent.

"There is too much at stake in this matter. One wrong step and DeForce Deliveries is on the fast track to hell. That's not where I want to be, all right? In hell, I mean. Besides, I feel bad about letting you walk into that trap. So it's only fair to risk my own neck now."

Ondragon blinked as Rod's words finally landed with him. "Are you even fit enough for this kind of trip?" Only now was he able to take a good look at his friend. Rod had gotten older since the last time they had seen each other face-to-face. That had been three years ago. But he still looked like the mirror image of Peter Graves, alias Jim Phelps in the *Mission Impossible* TV series. His hair was now completely white but still enviably thick, and there were a few more wrinkles around his mouth and eyes, but these and his ice-blue eyes reflected the ongoing lust for life and determination that had always set his friend apart. His sinewy body too, which had barely gained an ounce of fat, seemed to be bursting with energy, despite the fact that he already had fifty-eight years under his belt. Rod was tall, almost as tall as he was, with a bolt upright posture and a broad back. He owed both to the sport of swimming, in which he had been highly successful in his youth—Roderick DeForce had been an Olympic athlete. Although he hadn't managed to win a medal as Ondragon's mother had done in the 10,000-meter cross-country race in Innsbruck in 1976, he had taken English sportsmanship to a new mental dimension.

"You know, I have a personal coach who keeps me on my toes," Rod affirmed, rubbing his hands.

Giving an amused smirk, Ondragon couldn't help but think of a suntanned surfer dude with gelled hair, getting puny silicone-pumped weaklings to do a few ridiculous rope jumps on the Santa Monica beachfront.

"Not the kind you know from Hollywood," Rod said, breaking into Ondragon's mental picture, and pointing to a small group of cocktail chairs in a corner of the living room. "Why don't you sit down," he said, dropping into one of the chairs himself. Ondragon took a seat across from him.

"My trainer," Rod continued, "is an ex-drill sergeant from the British Army. And he's under orders not to go easy on me. I do all the drills with him, including the martial arts sessions."

Immediately, a new image came into Ondragon's mind: the congenial Cato, lying in wait for Inspector Clouseau in his own apartment. He smiled pensively and felt himself slowly relax. Pouring himself another glass of whiskey from the crystal decanter, he stretched his legs out and, after raising his glass in his friend's direction, let the smoky liquid trickle down his throat. He relished it as it made its warm, burning way to his stomach. Then he put the glass on the table and looked at Rod.

"All right, Rod. You're hired! You will accompany me to Haiti," he said ceremoniously, then he immediately became serious again. "But I'm in charge! I will accept nothing less. If you have a problem with that, you'd better say so now."

Rod raised both hands. "No problem, you're the head of the operation!"

"Good." Ondragon was relieved and briefly explained his plans to Rod.

"Jolly good! But if you think I'm going to travel a single inch on that flying death trap you've rented, you're as lopsided as an Australian bedspring!" protested the older man.

"The Cessna is the best aircraft for this trip. A small seaplane is the only way we can transport our arsenal of weapons to Haiti unnoticed by customs and the security services."

"Well, I think I have a better suggestion." Rod looked meaningfully at Ondragon. "Out at the airport in Houma is my private plane, the one I came here in. A Gulfstream G650, the fastest plane in civil aviation. She'll get us from here to the Antilles in less than three hours, plus, there's a bar on board." He winked at Ondragon. And we don't even have to fly this baby ourselves. My pilots are part of the deal. What do you say?"

Ondragon gave his friend an appreciative look. "Great. How many passengers can your Lady of the Skies take?"

"In addition to cargo, she's licensed for six passengers and two cabin crew members. I've done without those though. I can still manage to make my own whiskey on the rocks."

"Good, then there'll be plenty of room for my personal adviser on local customs." Ondragon reached for his glass and took another sip of scotch.

"Your adviser? You mean your assistant?"

"No, I mean a very special authority in autochthonous superstition." He described to the Briton the woman whom—more or less of his own free will—he intended to take with him on the trip.

"A Voodoo priestess?" repeated Rod in amazement. "That sounds pretty strange. And I always thought you were joking when you talked about zombies in our earlier phone calls. Are you sure you can trust this . . . Madame Tombeau?"

Ondragon thought about it. The question was justified—and not easy to answer.

"It may sound strange," he finally said, "but I have not yet fully figured out the Madame myself. She's something of a mystery to me. I keep wondering why a highly intelligent woman—which she undoubtedly is—has devoted herself to this pseudo-religion. How does she manage to suppress her intellect to such an extent that she actually thinks she believes in all these . . . crazy things? It's completely illogical."

"I don't think so. Science and faith are not necessarily mutually exclusive. From my point of view, an intelligent person in today's world can certainly believe wholeheartedly in God."

"But Voodoo is not the same as God!" interjected Ondragon.
"Really?"

Ondragon hesitated, then waved off the question. "Back to the Madame. You wanted to know if I thought she was trustworthy. Yes,

I do in a very particular way. For example, I believe her reasons for helping me are sincere. Although she's a bit *coco loco* up top, she is very astute and eloquent, and she would never use her skills for malicious purposes. That is forbidden by her code of honor as a Voodoo priestess, which she takes very seriously. Madame Tombeau is truly an unusual woman, and even though I don't often agree with her, I feel she can still be very useful to us."

"Very well. I hope she's not a risk."

"I hope so too. But you'll meet her yourself tomorrow, and then you can make up your own mind. She's a feast for the eyes in any case."

"And what about that adorable assistant of yours?"

"Charlize is on the road doing research. I need her here in the States, as a kind of capcom. She'll stay in constant contact." For the time being, he did not tell his friend she had long since been in Portland putting Darwin Inc. through a thorough inspection. He didn't want to get into any unnecessary discussion. Besides, he needed to maintain confidentiality with regard to any covert operations on his part.

"That's too bad," Rod said. "And I thought I would finally meet her in person. She sounds very charming on the phone."

"Not just on the phone," Ondragon replied with a wink, and they both laughed.

Then he rose. "So, after that shock, I need a good night's sleep. I'll see you tomorrow. Eight o'clock?"

"Eight o'clock!" confirmed Rod, rising likewise and escorting his guest to the door, as befitted an English gentleman of the old school.

CHAPTER 22

February 14, 2010
Houma, Louisiana
10:45 am

Ondragon drove the Mustang across the tarmac toward the white lights of DeForce Deliveries' twin-engine private jet. En route to Houma, which was located in the swamps 57 miles southwest of New Orleans, he had made sure they were not followed in any way. To his relief, the side roads he had taken had remained empty behind them. He found this a little strange, since he had firmly expected his adversaries to be watching him, and to keep on watching him. Even a scan of their luggage for signal transmitters had revealed nothing. Was he so mistaken about the people who had kidnapped him and left him in the swamps?

He turned his head. The Madame was sitting in the passenger seat in full travel gear (the pants and hoodie from last night), and looking expectantly through the windshield at the plane. Rod had left the hotel long before they did, without having met the Madame, and had taken a cab to the airport.

Ondragon saw him waiting for them by the plane and, as he brought the Mustang to a halt at the foot of the gangway, Rod opened the door for the Voodoo priestess.

"Madame," he said gallantly. "My name is Roderick DeForce."

"Mari-Jeanne Tombeau." She extended her hand to him.

Aha, so she was telling his friend her first name right away. Interesting, Ondragon thought, almost jealously.

"Pleased to meet you, madame." Rod gave a slight bow. The old charmer.

Having completed the introductions, the three of them carried the equipment bags from the trunk to the plane.

Inside, Ondragon whistled softly through his teeth at the cabin's luxurious interior. "Fantastic decor!" He took a closer look at the quality of the leather on the upholstered seats. "Nice. Perfect for another nice nap during the flight." He took the bags to the back of the plane, where several boxes were already stacked in a small baggage compartment.

"I took the liberty of bringing a little equipment," Rod said behind him, with typical British understatement.

"A little?" Ondragon looked at his friend. "I see." He tossed the bag onto the pile, which made his efforts to get the gear together the previous night seem laughable. "There are only three of us; you know that, right?"

His friend shrugged apologetically and looked around at the Madame, who had already settled herself in one of the seats in the cabin. Although she couldn't hear them, Rod lowered his voice and continued, "This was only for two of us. If I had known this charming lady would be accompanying us, I would have packed even more, but you seem to have brought something for the plane."

Ondragon elbowed Rod amicably in the ribs, and they both giggled like ten-year-olds who'd had too much sherbet; then they pulled themselves together and returned to the cabin. Rod offered the Madame a drink, while Ondragon left the aircraft once more to drive his car to the hangar.

When he returned to the Gulfstream cabin a little later, Rod was up front with the pilots, giving final instructions. Ondragon sat down opposite the Madame in the quartet of seats, which had a fold-down table between them. He scrutinized the Voodoo priestess, who gazed serenely back at him through the lenses of her glasses. She didn't seem at all nervous, which surprised him: They weren't setting out on some laid-back Caribbean vacation. He wondered what she was thinking, but came to no conclusion. This woman and her behavior were not easy to interpret. Her facade was perfect, he had to give her that. But what she was hiding behind it remained a mystery to him.

"So, we'll be taking off in a few minutes," Rod said, sitting down next to Ondragon. "We got a good slot, even though we put in our request at such short notice. I also took the liberty—and I hope you'll forgive my forwardness, Ecks—of telling our contact on the ground our estimated time of arrival."

"That sounds good." Ondragon felt the plane start to move. It taxied to the runway, and took off shortly afterward. The landscape below them grew smaller and smaller, its marshy surfaces reflecting the silvery light of the sun.

After the plane had reached cruising altitude and set its course for the Gulf of Mexico, Ondragon fished a shoulder bag out from under the seat, folded down the table, and began the briefing by booting up a brand-new laptop and showing the two members of his crew a topographical map of Hispaniola, where the two nations of Haiti and the Dominican Republic shared a border that ran lengthwise through the island. He zoomed in on Haiti and pointed to a spot on the southern coast.

"This is Jacmel, a small port. And here"—he shifted his finger a millimeter to the west—"is the village of Nan Margot. Our deployment site is in the mountains to the north of there at twenty-six hundred feet and is apparently hidden in an old mine. So much for the coordinates. Rod will link up with another satellite in a moment and give us a detailed picture of the terrain around the village and the mine. But first, I want to brief you about the schedule. If all goes according to plan, we will land at the airfield in Jamaica, right on the coast, just before four o'clock local time. We're landing in Jamaica because all airports in Haiti are currently controlled by the American military. A Jeep will take us to the beach, where the speedboat the CSAC men used for the Haiti mission will be waiting. The crossing is two hundred sixty-nine nautical miles and by my calculation it'll take us eleven hours at a speed of twenty-five knots. The weather forecast for the next three days is for hardly any rain and calm seas. So we can expect to make good progress and arrive off the coast of Haiti in the early hours of the morning. At daybreak we'll land at this small headland in one of the uninhabited bays and go ashore with our gear, which will be light enough for us to carry." He pointed to a ravine that led away from the beach to the west. "We'll hike about four miles inland through this narrow river valley, and then work our way two miles due north cross-country into the mountains, to the village and Route 208. We'll collect information in the village as quickly as possible and then continue north into the mountains, over the ridge with the Darwin facility behind it. We'll set up a small base camp there and conduct reconnaissance. I've planned one or two days at the most for that, depending on whether we manage to get into the laboratory—as we know, the entrance to the shaft has been blown up. After that, we'll head back to the coast along the CSAC mission team's route, to see if we can discover something to tell us what might have happened to the mailmen." He paused for a moment, opening a text file.

"Let's move on to the current situation in the country, which, as we know, is very tense, and not only in the capital, Port-au-Prince. The quake, measuring 7.0 on the Richter scale, occurred exactly one month ago and caused severe damage throughout the south. Victims are still missing. An estimated three hundred thousand people have been killed and as many more injured, and more than a million and a half are homeless. The country is in a state of near–civil war and there is a risk of epidemics; hospitals and morgues are bursting at the seams. Food and water are scarce, and looting and violence are the order of the day—they could easily fuel an uprising. Although our mission is in the mountains, it is no less dangerous here. So I want you to be aware of the lion's den we are walking into. Be constantly on your guard and do not hesitate to make use of your weapons." He looked sharply at the Madame. She returned his gaze, giving a barely perceptible nod. "When we explain to the village who we are and what we want, we will cause quite a stir. The key is to remain absolutely calm," he continued speaking. "Our camouflage doesn't have to be perfect, but it does have to be convincing. As I mentioned earlier, we will be posing as UN soldiers, Blue Helmets, tasked with searching the research facility in the mountains for any hazardous substances that may have been released by the quake. And—"

"Will I also be a Blue Helmet?" asked the Madame.

"Yes, you will." Ondragon looked at her sternly because she had interrupted him.

"But, as a woman *and* a Haitian, don't I stand out? Wouldn't doctors be a better cover?"

"I don't think so. Imagine if we arrived in the village and they asked us to treat the injured."

"I could do that. I know how to cure wounds and diseases the traditional way."

"That's nice, but it would take too much time."

The Madame pursed her lips. "I submit, Monsieur Ondragon, that the people of my country are very suspicious, particularly of White people. To treat some of them would inspire confidence and loosen their tongues. And besides—"the Madame now pulled out her bag from under the seat, took out a white coat, and put it on—"I look pretty good in this outfit." With a precise gesture, she adjusted her glasses on her nose and threw him a mischievous smile.

Ondragon raised his eyebrows as he read the little tag pinned to the coat above her left breast. DR. MARI TOMBEAU—MÉDECINS SANS FRONTIÈRES.

"This is—"

"That's brilliant, madame!" exclaimed Rod, delighted. "We'll probably actually get more out of the villagers this way."

"And how is she supposed to wear her bulletproof vest with that?" objected Ondragon.

"Well, under the sweater and the coat. It's not a problem."

Ondragon thought about it. The Madame's idea was actually not bad, it just annoyed him that he hadn't had it himself. "All right, since you've obviously prepared so well for your role already." He cleared his throat to make it clear he didn't want any further interruptions, and continued.

"On the ground, our job is to gather every last clue and find out what the purpose of this secret lab was and how it's related to the disappearance, or death, of the mailmen—"

"Maybe we should plan on spending a whole night in the village," the Madame interrupted again.

Ondragon took a deep breath, trying not to shout. On the one hand, he had to address the Madame's questions because she had never taken part in a paramilitary action before; on the other hand, he wanted to get through the briefing as quickly as possible so that he could get some sleep before things got serious. He saw Rod and the Madame looking at him expectantly.

"We'll see how things go. Every schedule is just a guideline and can flex and be modified. In fact, it *has* to be, because operations rarely go as planned." He glanced briefly at Rod. "So, now a few things about procedure." He demonstrated to the Madame some hand signals for nonverbal communication, and explained how to use the radio telephone and a dozen or so abbreviations for operational missions, using the more common terms instead of the DeForce formulas. He then asked Rod to connect to the satellite, feed it coordinates, and provide an image of the operations site.

The first image they saw was far too rough, and Rod entered the command to zoom in closer. The image became clearer, and mountainous terrain emerged from the mottled browns, speckled in places with varying density of tree cover that appeared as irregular patches of green. After making a few adjustments, they located the site of the Darwin Inc. facility and mine. They could clearly see the H of the heliport, the ruined building, and the buried mine shaft. Even the fence was visible, a perfect square enclosing the tree-covered area.

"If only we had more information about the mine, for instance if there might be other entrances. Unfortunately, you can't see anything like that on the satellite image," Rod murmured thoughtfully.

"Madame Tombeau will find that out for us. I'm pinning all my hopes on a second entrance, because if your men have done as good a job as I think they have, Rod, the main shaft will be impassable. At least for us with our little apparatus."

"But if Darwin Inc. knew about a second entrance, wouldn't they have had us seal that one too?" asked Rod.

"That's right. I'm hoping we'll be able to blast our way into the main shaft or the underground labs from the second shaft."

Rod nodded, and Ondragon shut down the computer. "Good, then we've covered everything for now. There'll be another briefing on the boat. I'm going to take a little nap now, if you don't mind." He moved to the row of seats behind them and settled down by the window. His thoughts circled for a while around the upcoming operation, then he fell asleep.

He woke up because he had the feeling someone was staring at him. He jerked open his eyes, but there was no one but Rod and the Madame in the seats in front of him, and they seemed to be engaged in an animated conversation. Ondragon could hear their murmuring voices well, despite the noise of the turbine. That was one of his special abilities, that and the *centrifuge*. He could filter different sounds so that he only heard what he was focusing on. Probably came from the hated cello lessons his father had insisted on when he was young. But because of that, he was now able to block out the howl of the turbine and let the voices of his two companions come through as clearly as if he were sitting right next to them. They were talking about Haiti and the Madame's childhood, when she had attended a private school in Cap-Haïtien. Nothing especially exciting.

Ondragon yawned and looked at his watch. Another hour. He could safely sleep a little longer. He crossed his arms in front of his chest and closed his eyes.

Shortly before he dropped back into the world of dreams, he heard Rod ask the Madame why she had moved from Haiti to the States of all places to work as a Voodoo priestess. That aroused Ondragon's curiosity and he listened to the conversation with half an ear.

The Madame laughed, he wasn't sure why, then replied, "I attended Harvard Business School when I was twenty and got my MBA there."

The Madame had been to Harvard? Now Ondragon pricked up his ears and he gave the conversation his full attention. He was surprised, not only because she had studied at an elite university, but also because studying there was damn expensive. As a poor Haitian child, how had she been able to afford it?

"After that, I worked for a consulting firm," the Madame continued, "but only for two years. My father became very ill, and I had promised to follow in his footsteps. So I flew to Haiti and underwent several years of training to become a priestess. I am deeply attached to the traditions of my country, you must know that, but I knew then that I would not be able to live there any longer. I was, as they say, spoiled. Nevertheless, I wanted to make my father's wish come true; and it makes me very proud to be able to do so. My father was a very influential and very wealthy man in our town; he was not only a houngan, a priest, he was also the head of the Shanpwel."

"Ah, I've heard of those," Ondragon heard Rod say. "They're secret societies, most comparable to Masonic lodges. They exist beneath the surface of the Haitian state apparatus, dispensing justice in their own community, independent of state jurisdiction. They are feared, but they also take care of their members when they are in need."

"That's right, Mr. DeForce. You're well informed." The Madame's voice sounded appreciative. "I can't tell you any more about it though; I'm bound by an oath."

"Of course. And why did you come back to the US?"

"After my initiation as a mambo, my father died. I did not want to take over his *humfó*, his temple, and I could not. My cousin had claimed it. But I wasn't sad about that; I left my home and looked for a place where I could start a new community."

"And you chose New Orleans."

"Yes, New Orleans has a long tradition of the Vodou faith. I found fertile ground there. The city has three different sanpwel. One of them is mine."

Astonished, Ondragon realized the Madame was now speaking without any accent and without any francophone terminology. He was also surprised at how candidly she was telling her life story to his friend. He felt a twinge of envy. Why hadn't she told him about it? And why had she pretended that she spoke only accented English?

Because you're an ignorant ass, that's why!

Ondragon pressed his lips together and clenched his teeth, realizing that the Madame had used the same tricks on him as he himself used to fool people. Unfortunately, he had let his prejudices run away with him and he had fallen for it. A beginner's mistake!

He continued to listen, his expression peevish.

Meanwhile, Rod asked, "What's it like being a Voodoo priestess, if you don't mind me asking?"

"It's a mixture of different professions. The closest thing you can compare it to is the life of a counselor, life coach, entertainer, and"—she laughed softly—"pop star. Vodou priests, in fact, enjoy a high degree of celebrity. Not only in Haiti, but in all the exclaves of the Vodou cult. We are like celebrities with a spiritual aura."

"You say that as if you're not completely serious."

"Oh, I'm completely serious about all this. But in Vodou, we aren't as deadly serious as Catholicism, for example. We are a very undogmatic and elastic religion. Our ritual always follows a certain sequence, but it can diverge, even from priest to priest, because everyone has their own master god, their loa mèt-tèt. It is the same with our gods, who reveal themselves through a typical habitus, when they swing themselves into the saddle of a human 'horse' and displace his soul angel, his *gros bon ange*, for a moment; but here too there is no strict rule. We are a living faith that directly involves humans. And humans themselves are unpredictable, we know that. There's a Haitian saying: To church you go to talk to God, you go to the temple to be a god."

"Because in the trance, the gods take possession of people and speak through them?"

"Not quite. It would be closer to say they *live* through them. They charge people with their energy. It's not necessarily always positive energy. We also have a whole dynasty of gods who belong to the shadow side."

"Demons and devils."

Again, the Madame laughed. "That's what you would call it with your, forgive me, Western black-and-white upbringing. Good and evil. Angels and devils. That's also a principle we're familiar with, except that a loa who belongs to the shadow side can also bring about good. They are very experienced gods who are therefore often called upon for advice. But they also like to play tricks. So you see, our universe is far more complicated."

"And what is it like to be 'ridden' by a loa?"

"It's the total loss of control. For a westernized person, a total nightmare. For an adherent of Vodou though it's a sacred moment.

The energy of the loa hits you like lightning, striking the body simultaneously from heaven and earth. It unites the world of humans with the world of the Mystères, the spirits. Everything is one. The one permeates the other."

"That's truly fascinating. But how do you make a living from it? I mean, don't you ever want to go back to the 'normal' world? You have a university degree and could make any amount of money as an executive."

The Madame made an amused noise. "I am sufficiently provided for by my profession, if that reassures you. And if money were important to me, I would also have taken a position in this world that is ruled by money. However, I am glad not to be subject to the heteronomy, the external control, of the pursuit of money. And I have never regretted taking this step. I feel I am doing the right thing, *being* the right thing! It's like what you have told me about yourself, Mr. DeForce. You don't live in the 'ordinary' world in that sense either. You live by and for the extraordinary challenge and do the job primarily because you are passionate about it, not because it makes you rich. Just like Mr. Ondragon. He seems to me to be strongly driven by something that cannot be described in mere words. In any case, it is not money. He loves mystery, doesn't he?"

"You have seen that very clearly, madame. Paul is a truly special person, and I am lucky to have him as a friend. There aren't many of his extraordinary ilk in the world."

"He used to work for you, Mr. DeForce?"

"Oh please, call me Rod, I don't like formality, it reminds me of my boarding school days in England."

"Sure, Rod. I'm Mari."

Ondragon guessed they were shaking hands and clenched his teeth even harder.

"By the way, something else interests me," Rod said. "Is Tombeau your real name?"

"Yes. Believe it or not. Our family name dates back to a gravedigger. To my great-great-great-grandfather. He was a notorious magician."

"Uh-huh."

"But we were just talking about Mr. Ondragon," the Madame reminded him.

"Yes, that's right. Well, Paul used to work for me, but that was a long time ago," Rod said in a wistful tone.

"And why is he your boss now?" asked the Madame.

"I'm the client, but it's his operation, so his rules apply. I have no problem with that. Paul is damn good at what he does! He was the best mailman I ever had, and I was very sorry to see him go at the time. But he really wanted to start his own business. For him, having his own business was the only thing that worked. He's a loner, a solitary hunter—always looking for the thrill and the trickiest puzzle in the galaxy. Always on the move. I can't believe the energy that drives this guy. Incidentally, his education was very similar to yours, Mari. A Harvard degree in politics and an MBA. He also started at a big consulting firm, in Germany, I think. But he was very unhappy with the job. From what he says, his unorthodox ideas rubbed people up the wrong way and the sector quickly began to view him as a freak. Finally, he met me on a business trip in Egypt. And then he quit. I took him under my wing and taught him everything a mailman needs to be able to do. That suited him fine and for a while he was the best worker at DeForce, but then his ambition, as you might call it, took hold and he left. Unfortunately. But Paul is just unstoppable. And he has developed at an incredible speed. But he also has a very particular nature, as I think you've noticed."

Ondragon heard the Madame make an approving sound and Rod continued in amusement. "Today he rampages all over the world doing these tricky jobs without it seeming to bother him. I don't think he even gets jet lag; he's always on top form. And he's not afraid of anything!"

Ondragon was flattered to hear all this from his friend, of course. But his mood dropped abruptly as he heard the Madame's next remark.

"Mr. Ondragon is very particular indeed. His manner's a bit stiff too, I'm afraid. And he is not quite so fearless as you describe him."

"No?"

"No, he definitely has fears that slow him down!"

Rod seemed to hesitate before asking, "What do you mean, Mari?"

"His fears are his Achilles's heel. They lead him to dark frontiers, which he prefers to avoid rather than face. That is his mistake: He goes to the threshold, but no further."

That's not true, Ondragon thought indignantly.

"He knows he should face them," the Madame continued, "but he's too afraid of the consequences, so he backs off and ignores his fears."

"What fears are those? I had always thought Paul was fearless."

"I'd prefer to keep that to myself. It's not my place to talk about his problems, especially since he hasn't confided in me personally either."

"Then how do you know about them?"

"I can feel them. I saw something unusual in his aura."

"Oh-ho."

From the row of seats behind them, Ondragon could clearly sense that it was now Rod's turn to cast doubt on Voodoo magic and all the strange powers it supposedly conferred on the Madame. He heard the priestess lean forward in her seat and ask Rod in a hushed voice, "There is one thing I would like to know though. Did you know Mr. Ondragon's twin brother and do you know what happened to him?"

"He had a brother?" replied Rod in amazement. "I'm sorry, Mari, I don't know anything about that. It's strange that he never told me about it."

Sorry, my friend, thought Ondragon.

"Well," continued the Madame, "Mr. Ondragon claims his brother has been dead for over thirty years. But I have a feeling he's not telling the truth."

The conversation had taken a decidedly undesirable turn. And while Roderick DeForce remained uncomfortably silent on the subject, Ondragon decided to bring things to an end. It was time they prepared for landing anyway. The bright stripe of the Jamaican coast was already coming into view below them. So, giving a loud and audible yawn, he rose from his seat and stretched his limbs.

CHAPTER 23

Haiti
In the shaft

With a startled cry, Christine sat up. Someone was above. Very briefly, she had seen the shadow of a head peeking over the edge of the shaft. Now it was gone again.

Christine wondered if she should call for help. Perhaps someone in the village had organized a search for her and the others in the group. She balanced herself on her healthy leg, threw back her head, and shouted as loudly as she could. Her voice sounded rough and desperate. But the bright square continued to stare down at her, unblinking. No outline of a head appeared. She called out a few more times until she was shaking with exertion and had to sit down again. Her injured leg throbbed as if the thin skin stretched over the painful swelling were the skin of a drum being beaten in a devilish rhythm by one of the temple servants. Bad blood pumped through her lower leg to the same relentless beat and back into the rest of her body. She could literally feel the evil in it. Soon she would be sick and bloated.

Christine pressed her lips together. She didn't want to think about the agony of death; she just tried to imagine what it would be like to see her brother and mother again in the realm of the spirits. Her family would finally be together again. No, not quite. Her father was missing. He was still wandering through the world of the living, doomed to be a zombie. Restless, helpless, without will. Forever, or until the bokor had mercy on him and released him. Christine rested her head against the rock wall, as if it were too weak to bear this terrible thought.

Would she ever see her father again? Would he manage to enter the world of spirits? Christine was worried. Now that everyone else in the group was dead, who would complete the work of the priestess?

"You should prepare yourself not to see your father until you get to the spirit realm!" That was what the mambo had told her in the silence before organizing the expedition. "He will not be able to return to the world of the living. That's the way of the sanpwel law; they have judged him, do you understand?"

Christine had not understood, of course, why the sanpwel wanted her father to remain a zombie. Hadn't he been bewitched by the bokor of the *blancs*? That evil wizard had nothing to do with the secret society of her village. Or did he? She had asked the priestess the same question, but the priestess had only laughed scornfully and said she should not be as foolish as her mother, who actually believed Etienne Dadou could be saved. "The only thing I can do for your father is to kill him," the mambo had said in an ominous voice, and then simply left Christine to prepare the ceremony in her *humfó*.

Christine winced at this painful memory. She hugged her lean chest for warmth. It was much colder down here in the shaft than at the surface. And moisture trickled constantly down the walls—lifegiving water that she kept licking from the stone so that at least she had something in her hollow stomach. Christine felt the drops falling on the crown of her head.

But were they even drops? She ran her hand over her hair. It was as dry as dust. Again, she felt something trickling down onto her. She caught it in her open hand. It was sand. She jerked her chin upward. The sand fell into her eyes and clouded her vision, but she was sure.

Someone was up there and had kicked the sand loose.

Suddenly, a dark, round silhouette appeared over the edge. Someone was looking down at her.

Too weak to get up, Christine threw her arms into the air and screamed. Tears ran down her face, leaving dark streaks in the dirt on her cheeks. Her crying turned to sobs. Desperately, Christine screamed at the bright square . . .

But the head did not move.

Was it even a head?

Christine rubbed the dust from her eyes and tried to make out more. Then a sound reached her ears. The trickling of stones and . . .

Her heart stopped and fear breathed cold against her neck, as if it were sitting right behind her. As if the fear had been cowering there in the shadows between the rocks all this time, just waiting to pounce on her.

Unable to move, Christine continued to look up.

It was her father up there.

The *zombi cadavre*!

Now he was even stretching his arms out toward her. Gurgling sounds escaped from his throat, as if he were trying to speak. Saliva dripped from above onto Christine's face, but all she could do was sit and stare. The eerie sounds coming from the zombie echoed off the walls, multiplied, and soon it was as if a whole horde of the hideous undead were squatting up there.

Up at the opening, the zombie that had been Etienne Dadou began to flail its arms more and more violently, its hoarse shouts becoming louder and somehow more desperate. Christine wanted to cover her ears, but she was paralyzed.

The next moment, the zombie was gone and silence descended on the shaft. Dazed, Christine blinked at the square of light—the only movement she was capable of.

Where had the zombie gone? And what was it up to?

What was certain was that it had not tired of pursuing them.

But if I can't get up the shaft, the zombie can't get down it either, Christine thought bitterly. How strangely fate sometimes played out. With relief, she felt the fear leave her and retreat into the shadows. At the same time though, Christine knew that from its hiding place, fear had its beady little yellow eyes fixed on her, ready to strike at a moment's notice.

If only death would finally come, Christine thought, exhausted.

She had no strength left to fight the fear. She would not conquer it anyway.

Quietly, she began to call to Baron Samedi and ask him to finally take her.

Into the world of the dead.

The road there could not be too long.

After all, she was already underground.

CHAPTER 24

February 14, 2010
The coast of Jamaica,
7.6 miles west of Port Antonio
3:35 pm local time

Once the plane landed on the asphalt runway and slowly come to a stop in front of the hangar—which looked more like a flat corrugated iron hut—a rickety gangway was pushed up to the plane by two employees of the private airfield, and the door to the cabin opened. Out stepped three figures. Two white men in dark combat fatigues with sunglasses on their noses, and a dark-skinned woman in glasses and a doctor's coat. The insignia of the American military and the United Nations peacekeeping force were clearly visible on the soldiers' clothing, and the female doctor appeared to belong to a well-known aid organization. It was obvious they were going to Haiti on a relief mission.

Lugging heavy bags, the three new arrivals walked over to a waiting Jeep and got in. Wordlessly, the driver started the engine and drove to the end of the runway, where he passed through a gate in the chain-link fence. Following a barely discernible path, the Jeep bumped between pink-flowering shore bindweed and low sea grape trees directly to the beach, where a speedboat with a covered stern was waiting for them.

The group disembarked and, balancing their bags on their shoulders, waded through the shallow turquoise water to the boat, which had a small cabin at the front that was already loaded with eight huge gas canisters. Their return ticket.

The man who had been guarding the boat saluted the leader of the group and jumped off the boat into the water. As he reached the beach, the three outboard engines, each with 300 horsepower, roared into life and the bow of the boat lifted out of the foaming water. The craft moved swiftly away from the shore in an elegant arc, setting an eastward course.

No one had asked any questions.

Holding the rudder firmly in one hand, Ondragon checked the course. The boat was a joy. It had tremendous power, and raced across the calm waters. The sea was glistening in the Caribbean sun, and the hull lifted off briefly with every wave they crossed, only to touch down hard again immediately, as if it were hitting concrete and not water. The constant shocks to the intervertebral discs were exhausting, and the engines were crazy loud and set the whole ship vibrating. But the power behind it was irresistible. Ondragon grinned in the airstream. A real man's toy!

He looked around at his two companions, who, having sorted and lashed down the equipment, were now sitting in their padded seats, each looking out to sea, where pelicans glided low over the water, as if hoping that flying fish, fleeing the spray from the machine monster, would jump right into their beaks.

Ondragon caught Rod's eye; Rod winked at him companionably, and immediately a pleasant feeling spread through him. He was glad to have the Briton by his side for this mission, although he usually preferred to work alone. But there could be no better partner. With the father of all mailmen as his brother-in-arms, he felt invincible.

He looked over briefly at the Madame, who was sitting across from Rod. She seemed pale and more withdrawn than usual. Was she seasick? Or was she worried about going back to her homeland? Ondragon felt the old distrust rising. What if she wasn't quite kosher despite everything? After all, in her conversation with Rod on the plane, she had unknowingly revealed her little game of pretense. Ondragon resolved to keep a closer eye on her. This gorgeous moth was not what it claimed to be.

* * *

Two hours later, the sun was setting, a luminous protagonist in a spectacular play. The sky took on a brief, violent glow, as if someone had detonated an atomic bomb, and then was quickly doused with blackness. In tropical latitudes, the nights fell quickly and without ceremony.

Ondragon pressed the memory button on his dive watch, storing the current time, and looked up at the first stars. The wind on his skin still felt warm, and although it was early evening, he felt the continued grasp of his old friend, fatigue. *If I want to be fit for the mission, I'd better get a couple hours of sleep now*, he thought, and asked Rod to take the first watch at the wheel.

His friend now sat there, talking to the Madame in subdued tones while enjoying a Havana. The smoke from the cigar drifted aft on the breeze, to where Ondragon lay on a sleeping bag, trying to ignore the constant vibration and the pitching of the boat. The aromatic smell and Roderick's distant laughter brought back pleasant memories. His eyes closed, Ondragon saw himself sitting with his buddies on the beach in Mombasa, in his favorite bar, where all the mailmen always met and partied. There was good reason for this after every successful job—you were still alive.

Ondragon had been twenty-five when he was hired by Roderick DeForce and through him entered a completely new and exciting world. A world beyond the dry theory of optimization concepts for corporate structures and controlling departments, a world behind the scenes of politics and business, shady and fascinating. His father had been against it, of course, but Ondragon had grown tired of dancing to his tune. He had tried long enough. It had been time to finally follow his own path. The move from New York to Cairo to join DeForce Deliveries put the final seal on the fracture in his relationship with his parents. In no way did it make him sad; instead, it lifted him up, gave him a triumphant feeling, as if he had won a hundred-year battle. Ondragon had fond memories of the nearly six years he spent at DeForce. The job had been like hatching from an egg, the rebirth of his long-suppressed abilities. Skills he could finally put to use in the service of someone who appreciated them and didn't treat him like a crazed freak. Roderick DeForce had found him and molded him, had laid the foundations of who he was today. Sure, the job at DeForce had been tough and the missions risky, but Ondragon had never felt more alive.

The characters he had to deal with had also been tough. His comrades were rough fellows, but very reliable. Always ready to walk through fire for each other. Roderick DeForce had set great store by this when selecting his people. For two years, Cairo had been Ondragon's home and operational base; most of the missions had taken them to the Middle East and Afghanistan. Then DeForce's main office moved to Mombasa, taking two-thirds of the mailmen with it. A man without a homeland, Ondragon didn't care where he lived, and he was happy to be in the Kenyan port city, where he shared an apartment with a colleague just yards from the beach and their regular bar. He could literally feel the exotic atmosphere that tingled through the city back then, and enjoyed the multilingual buzz of voices from inhabitants from all over the world mixing in with African music, and the feel of the iced glass of beer in his hand.

Ondragon sighed and allowed himself to be enveloped by the memory like a welcome guest, gently stalling the rotation of his *centrifuge.* Before it had completed its final rotation, he was asleep.

Roderick woke him at the stroke of midnight. Drowsy, Ondragon sat up and took a few seconds to realize where he was. Had he slept that deeply? That was truly amazing, considering the boat was bouncing over the waves like a bucking bronco at a rodeo.

Gratefully, he took his friend's hand and let himself be pulled to his feet. Shouting through the noise of the engine, Rod made his report. According to the GPS device, they had passed the westernmost tip of Haiti two hours before and were now about 75 nautical miles from their destination. The wind had picked up a bit, causing a higher swell, but otherwise the weather was steady and conditions were calm.

"Whew! You call that calm?" Ondragon held his overtaxed back. "The boat's kicking like a mule! What about the Madame?"

"She's trying to get some sleep in the cabin."

"By the gas canisters? How cozy."

"I tried to talk her out of it, but she preferred to keep to herself."

Ondragon understood. The Madame had not wanted to bed down next to him. There wasn't much room on the small ship, and the only place that remained was the cabin. He patted his friend on the shoulder. "Off you go, Rod. I'll wake you when we reach PO."

PO stood for Point One. This referred to the starting point of any operation and it frequently also marked the end point. If the mission ended elsewhere, that location was called PT, Point Two. PC, Point of Contact, denoted the point of contact with dangerous or enemy territory (in this case, the coast). RT, Reach Target, denoted the target, which could be either a moving object to be transported or fixed coordinates to be reached. And MC was the signal to all crew members that the mission had been accomplished. Mission Complete!

Roderick DeForce knew these and many other terms in his sleep, and he nodded, leaving Ondragon to keep watch and curling up on the sleeping bag.

Bucking, the boat sailed through the starry night. Far enough from the coast not to be noticed, but still within the 12-mile zone. So far, no Coast Guard vessel or aircraft had noticed them.

They probably have other things to do, Ondragon thought. And hopefully things would stay that way. He put one hand on the wheel, felt the engines vibrating, and let it flow through his arm into his body. He became one with the power of the boat, enjoying the feeling of flying through the blackness of the night as if on wings.

At 3:14 am, he killed the engines and let the boat glide slowly toward the coast, an uneven black band against the dark blue night sky.

They had reached PO!

In about three hours, the sun would rise. But if everything went to plan, they would have long since gone ashore by then.

CHAPTER 25

February 15, 2010
The coast of Haiti
5:47 am

But unfortunately nothing went to plan!

Soon after they had landed and hiked a few yards up the river cut, they had to take cover, as a military helicopter suddenly flew close over the ridge in the still, gray morning sky. Hastily, Ondragon, Rod, and Madame Tombeau threw themselves into a sparse collection of bushes and waited until the aircraft was out of sight.

"That was close," Rod said, helping the Madame to her feet. Fortunately, she was no longer wearing her coat; she had on the dark hoodie over the Kevlar vest. Ondragon had insisted on it. The white doctor's outfit was far too risky, too obvious in the field. She should only put it back on shortly before they reached the village; that was when it would be useful to them.

He gave the Madame an appraising look.

She had hooked her fingers into the straps of her backpack and was looking up the shady river valley. Her hair was tied into a braid and she had exchanged her glasses for contact lenses. Ondragon noticed that her face showed no sign of strain yet, while under his own outfit he had begun to sweat as if he was at the Scandinavian sauna championships. Let's see how she did with all that baggage. His gaze lingered on the bulge in the pouch of her sweater. A grin stole furtively over his lips. The Madame was keeping the Desert Eagle handy.

He nodded to Rod, who, like himself, was kitted out with a helmet, backpack, and an M16 rifle, and they continued their march west.

A little later, the sun rose above the horizon at their backs, bathing the valley in orange light. Its rays crept over the dusty ground and caught up with the small group just as they turned north and began climbing up the slope. Suddenly, the clatter of rotors echoed across the valley again. Hurriedly, Ondragon looked around. There was not a tree or bush to be seen anywhere. Darn, they were perched here as if they were on show.

"There!" shouted Rod, pointing to an overhang of loose rock.

If they hurried, they would reach the shadows just in time to take cover.

"Go!" Ondragon urged his companions, and they ran stumbling through the loose scree of the alluvial fan. He reached the overhang, threw himself into the shadows, and beckoned the others to hurry while he scanned the sky for the helicopter, whose roar was growing louder.

A few steps before the overhang, the Madame stumbled. Ondragon saw her tumbling face-first toward the rocks, but Rod grabbed her by the arm, got her to safety with a great sweeping push, and himself dove into the shadows, where he landed heavily on his belly beside her. At that moment, the helicopter appeared over the southern shoulder of the ravine.

From the safety of the shadows, Ondragon tracked its flight across the valley, and gradually his breathing calmed. The pilots had not seen them.

"It's the same one as before. Probably a patrol," Rod said, sitting up and checking to see if his weapon had sustained any damage in the stunt.

"Looks like it," Ondragon confirmed. "Let's hope they don't patrol around here more often. There are hardly any hiding places up there on the slope. Not until we get to the road." He turned to the Madame, who was wiping dust from her face. "It's about three miles to the village—can you make it?"

"Is this my fricking country or yours?" she snapped back. "*Merde!* Of course I can make it!"

Aha, so they were back to the Francophone expletives, Ondragon thought. For a while he listened down to the valley, and when everything remained silent, he gave the signal to march on.

* * *

The helicopter did not appear again, and so an hour later they arrived at Route 208 unscathed. After a short break for a drink in the shade of a tree, they continued on their way, following a narrow trail that led through a patch of tropical forest at some distance from the road. Here at least they were protected from prying eyes and the occasional passing cars.

As the terrain got steeper, Ondragon stopped once more and issued final instructions. "We'll soon reach the village. I want us to question the people as quickly as possible and be at our destination in the mountains by tonight. In the village, we should stay together at all times and behave in a calm and professional manner. And always keep our eyes open." He looked at the Madame, who had been surprisingly adept at climbing despite her baggage. A thin film of sweat covered her face and made her cheekbones shine. She looked damn good.

"You can put on your coat now, Doctor," he said, giving her a wink to lighten the tension.

But the Madame merely clicked her tongue, pulled her sweater over her head, took the white coat out of her backpack, and slipped her arms into the sleeves. Then she stowed the Desert Eagle in its holster and gave a nod to indicate that she was ready.

Ondragon put on his helmet, which was sprayed with blue lacquer and the white UN letters, and led the group to the village, the M16 held loosely in his arms. Followed by the Madame and Rod, he stepped out of the forest and looked out across the plateau, which was covered with small plots of land and only sparsely populated with trees. The village of Nan Margot was not really a village at all; it was more of a scattered collection of desolate dwellings made of corrugated iron, rough-hewn stone, and wood. Some of the huts had roofs made of dried palm fronds.

Ondragon looked around as he approached the first huts. It was quiet, and he could only see the occasional thin black body working in the fields. In a small, fenced-in lot was tethered a donkey with cropped ears, wearing a primitive straw saddle. It was a pitiful creature. So were the skinny chickens that ran back and forth between the dwellings. There was no one else to be seen. Many of the huts they passed had collapsed. Smoke from cooking fires billowed from others. There was a smell of garbage, chicken droppings, and the sweet scent of tropical flowering plants.

Ondragon was reminded of his missions in Africa.

Except that this Africa was right on the doorstep of the United States of America.

He stopped in front of one of the huts and asked the Madame where all the residents were. Before she could answer, a horde of children came running across the street toward them. They flowed around the three strangers like water around a rock, stretching out their thin arms, shouting loudly in confusion.

"What do they want?" cried Ondragon, who, despite his very good French, had no chance of understanding Creole.

"They want us to come with them!" replied the Madame.

"Where to?"

"They say one of the villagers has returned from the mountains."

"What do you mean?" Ondragon pushed away a small hand that had begun to rummage in his pockets. "Tell these squealers that anyone who takes us to someone who can tell us about the mine and the lab gets candy."

The Madame gave him a look that said she did not approve of this kind of conversation, but then turned back to the children.

Ondragon shook his head. What had she thought they were here for? Certainly not to give handouts.

Once the Madame had translated, however, the shouting of the children did not decrease. Everyone seemed to want to tell them something, and the crowd gradually became uncomfortable, and not only for Ondragon. He saw that Rod was also raising his rifle to make room for himself.

"Tell the kids to keep their distance! Otherwise they won't get anything at all. Now!" he shouted to the Madame over the heads of the clamoring children. But his request was lost in the noise.

There was only one way to create order. He raised his rifle and fired three shots into the air.

Suddenly, the horde of children fell silent and fled in all directions. Except for one small boy, who looked up at the Madame with wide eyes, speaking to her in a thin little voice.

"He says they need a doctor urgently, and since I am one, he wants me to come quickly."

Ondragon sighed and lowered his M16. Very well then, she would now play doctor. He gestured to the Madame and Rod to follow the little boy. He could at least hope that they might meet other people they could question in the place he was leading them to.

The child ran ahead, barefoot, leaving a thin trail of dust in the air for them to follow. He ran across fields of dry corn stalks and puny banana plants, past abandoned shacks, a rusted wreck of a car, and burning piles of garbage. They reached a flat wall framing a dusty field with hewn stones and wooden crosses jutting from it, and saw a large gathering of people standing in the blazing sun at the edge. Ondragon slowed his pace as the little boy ran over to the group, shouting loudly and pointing back at them.

"Approach slowly!" warned Ondragon to his two companions, taking the safety off the rifle again as a precaution.

Meanwhile, the people had turned around, and they were met with hostile and suspicious gazes. Absolute silence fell as they arrived at the group, which was hiding something in its midst. Ondragon stared at the faces. There was hatred in their eyes.

He asked the Madame to explain who they were, and the people listened in silence. Suddenly, an elderly man stepped forward and unleashed a wild torrent of words at the Madame. His gnarled fist kept pounding the air in front of her face.

Ready to intervene at any moment, Ondragon moved over to her, not taking his eyes off the guy. "What is he saying?" he asked in a whisper.

The Madame frowned and translated the strong dialect. "He says he is the deputy of the deceased village chief and he's ranting about how we haven't shown up for weeks and we should now go to hell! They'll take care of it themselves, he says. He's complaining about the poor organization of the relief forces after the earthquake. A dozen Jeeps drove through their village, but no one stopped to look after their wounded. Not a single *blanc* was interested in them. We are the first to show up here—and it's been a whole month. But the sick in the village are in desperate need of medicine. Seventeen people have died of infection resulting from their injuries, because they have no doctor. In Jacmel and the other towns, he says, the *blancs* were keen to help, distributing food and medicine. In the countryside, however, they have left the population to their fate!"

Oh man, thought Ondragon. This kind of conflict was all he needed. It would have been better if they had avoided the village and investigated the mine on their own. But it was too late for that now. "Tell the people you'll do preliminary examinations, and promise them we'll send more doctors."

"But that's not true!" the Madame objected indignantly.

"I know that, but we're not here to play the Good Samaritan. We have a specific mission! I hope you haven't forgotten that."

"Don't worry, I haven't." She turned to the old man and asked him something. Then she turned back to Ondragon. "He says then we can start the examinations right now!"

No sooner had the Madame spoken than the ring of people parted, revealing what they had been concealing until now.

Ondragon drew a sharp breath, and next to him Rod did the same when he saw what was lying there on the ground.

"Holy shit!" his friend whispered.

"Bondieu!" The Madame rushed to the center of the circle and knelt beside the bloodied figure on the ground. Ondragon hurried after her. His lips pressed together and his gun ready to fire, he looked down at the young man, as the Madame put a finger to his neck to feel for a pulse. His face was pitch-black, despite the blood loss he had suffered, and his eyes were closed. The clothes he wore were soaked with blood, most of which had dried, however, except for places where it looked as if he had been struck by an axe or machete. There, it shone moist, fresh and red.

Soberly, Ondragon counted four deep wounds on the boy's torso, smiling at him like open mouths. The left arm was nearly severed at the elbow and held only by a string of fibrous muscle and some skin. It lay folded up at an unnatural angle next to the upper arm.

"He's alive!" the Madame said excitedly, stroking the battered boy's cheek.

"What an appalling mess," Roderick said, raising his rifle and taking aim at the crowd. "Who did this to the boy?"

"The people are saying he came back from the mountains this morning like this. No one knows who did it. The boy is apparently a member of an expedition that left the village five days ago."

"What kind of expedition?"

"They don't want to say."

"Dammit, they're lying!" Ondragon turned to Rod, who was scanning the area in alarm. He knew the Brit had experience with these kinds of situations and was glad to have him along.

"Holy Loco," the Madame exclaimed. "He's moving his lips." She put her ear to the wounded boy's mouth and listened. It seemed a miracle that he was alive at all; the wounds looked as if they had been inflicted on the fellow at least a few days before, and besides, they were badly infected. The moisture on the slashed clothing was, Ondragon now realized, not just blood, but pus and secretions. What the hell had happened to the poor guy?

The Madame looked up again, with a sad expression. The boy's head was tilted to one side. Obviously, he had just succumbed to his severe injuries. Ondragon looked up at the rocks of the mountains. How had the fellow managed to drag himself all the way down here, mutilated as he was?

The Madame rose and walked toward the old man who had so eloquently insulted her earlier. She addressed him in a forbidding tone, and Ondragon saw the man flinch fearfully.

"What's wrong?" he asked, cursing inwardly at his inability to understand.

But the Madame did not answer; she continued to stare angrily at the man. Then she said something in Creole that sounded like an order, and shortly afterward the group dispersed, carrying the boy's body away. The old man, however, remained and bowed reluctantly. With a wave, he gestured for them to follow him. The Madame nodded to Ondragon, who agreed they should follow the old man back to the village.

"I told him I was a *Dokte Feuilles* and a mambo, and that I wanted to see the priest of Nan Margot," said the Madame quietly as they walked side by side. "The man says the mambo led the mysterious expedition. However, except for the poor boy, no one has returned so far. I have asked him to take us to the temple, which in the absence of the mambo is guarded by La Place, the Master of Ceremonies. We will confer there on how to proceed. *D'accord?*"

"*D'accord!*" agreed Ondragon grimly.

They arrived at a house that was larger than the others in the village and went around it. Behind it, they saw a colonnade, an altar room and the *kay-mystè*—the sanctuary of the *humfó*, as the Madame explained. The roof of the *kay-mystè* had collapsed, making the "hut of the spirit" inaccessible. The Madame looked at the damage and asked the old man to see to it that no one but La Place entered the grounds of the *humfó* while they were here. Then she looked at Ondragon. "I recommend that we set up camp there under the colonnade. I will treat some of the people and try to find out about the mine. I will no doubt find the means for treatment here in the temple. That's the only way the people will tell us anything. Is that to your liking?"

Ondragon nodded, but before the Madame could turn to her task, he held her back by the arm. "What happened to the boy? What did he say to you? I saw very clearly that it troubled you."

The Madame avoided his gaze, and at first it seemed as if she wasn't going to answer him. But then she looked directly at him and said, "You don't want to know, monsieur!"

"Oh, and how can you be sure of that?"

"Because this has nothing, absolutely nothing to do with our operation!"

"But I think it does have something to do with it. Because we're going to go up into those mountains soon, right where that unfortunate guy came from. And it seems like there's someone up there who is pretty good with a machete. And as long as there's even a hint of threat to us, what happened to that boy is very much my business. So, out with it!"

"Very well. Have it your way. The boy told me he was attacked by a zombie! And the expedition was a zombie expedition. Someone named Etienne Dadou has been turned into a zombie by a bokor and is hiding up there in the mountains. The priestess of the village agreed to do something about it, and now she has disappeared. Are you satisfied now, Mr. Ondragon?" She folded her arms defiantly over her chest.

"Of course, zombies! I should have guessed! Are you actually kidding me?" Ondragon had raised his voice. He was tired of this nonsense.

"I told you you didn't want to know, you ignorant ape!" the Madame barked back.

"Ignorant ape? *Fuck!* And what are you, then? An angel? Dammit! You're an idolater! A phony! Do you think I don't know you've been pulling the wool over my eyes all this time? Your French accent, all your Voodoo blah-blah, it's all just for show. You co—"

"Hey, folks, stop it. Let's all calm down," Rod said. He stepped between them and extended an arm. "This is an operation, not a talk show. Do you guys understand that? I want you to settle your differences and get along for the duration of our time on this miserable island, understand? After that, you can fight, or you can sleep with each other, I don't care. But I don't want to hear any more about it now. After all, we want to get out of this thing alive. And that'll only be possible if we work together!"

Ondragon looked at Rod in surprise, then raised a hand and gave in. His friend was right, of course. "I'm sorry," he said.

"Shake hands!" the Briton demanded.

Ondragon sighed and held out a hand to the angry, glinting Madame. She smacked it, turned away, and trudged over to the colonnade, where she set about preparing to treat the people.

"Stay cool," he heard Rod say beside him. "She's not going to wrest command of the *Bounty* away from you, Captain Bligh!"

Ondragon grinned despite his bad mood and took off his backpack. The stuff in it was heavy as hell. The sticks of dynamite, the rope, the provisions, and the ammunition. Rod and the Madame had the rest of it in their packs. Along with their gear and the Kevlar vests, they were lugging around quite a bit. Ondragon realized this part of the job, which had also been part of his role with DeForce, was not something he missed.

They set up a makeshift camp on the trodden-down clay floor of the colonnade, which was open on all sides, but at Madame's request kept a respectful distance from the wooden center post adorned with sacred symbols.

A little later, Ondragon was sitting next to the Voodoo priestess on a wobbly child-sized chair, watching her treat the people, who were standing in a well-ordered line. It was now noon and the sun was blazing unhindered onto the corrugated iron roof of the colonnade, which unfortunately offered only dubious protection against the heat; despite the open sides, it was blisteringly hot underneath.

With a calmness that was almost driving Ondragon mad, the Madame examined and questioned one supplicant after the next. He glanced irritably at the line of waiting people and counted about fifty-five patients. Was everyone in the village sick? This hole couldn't have that many inhabitants. Ondragon estimated that the people probably included individuals who were simply hoping for the spiritual assistance of a priestess. If that was the case, they'd be stuck here until doomsday. But he could not accept such a delay. Besides, there was the case of the boy, which was bothering him. He tapped the Madame on the shoulder.

"Yes?" she asked without turning her head.

"Do you see how many people are in the line there? The actual plan was for you to look at two or three to gain their trust, not half the village! I don't have time to wait for you to bless everyone. Tell them only those who are really sick will be treated. Let the rest go!"

Now she did turn her head and look at him. "Do you want information about the mine or not?"

"Of course, but preferably yesterday. I can't afford to waste a whole day here while you play at laying on hands. Besides, there's always the danger that our presence will be detected. Then we won't have just the authorities on our backs, we'll also have the US Army MP!" He clenched his jaw angrily. It had been a mistake to bring the

Madame. She was turning out to be a second Mother Theresa. He should have known. "I'll give you three hours, then tell people we have to move on." He rose and walked over to Rod, who was standing in the shadow of the main house leaning against the wall, looking at the line of waiting people with as much skepticism as himself.

"This is a fine mess!" grumbled Ondragon as he walked up to him.

"The woman is persistent, I'll give her that."

"We could just leave her here and go up to the mine without her. We could do what we came to do and pick her up later."

"We could do that . . ." Rod replied. He wiped the sweat from his neck and bared his strong teeth. "But I'd feel better if she could actually find out something about the mine and this boy. I don't want to be groping around up there like a blind man among bear traps. Besides, I'd still like to know what happened to my mailmen."

"That's why we're here!" Ondragon took a pack of gum from his pocket, offered one to Rod, and then popped one into his own mouth. Crossing his arms, he leaned next to his friend and watched the Madame's audiences.

"I keep wondering," Ondragon began a little later, "why it was so important to Darwin Inc. that the lab be sealed. Industrial espionage seems too thin a reason to me."

"Genetic engineering patents are worth a lot of money," Rod countered.

"That's what makes me wonder. If it's worth so much, why not get the material out of the lab before sealing it? Why was the entrance blown up and the facility not saved this time? What about the research results? A lot of money was spent on that too. Surely, Darwin Inc. must be interested in securing them."

"Maybe this was a different assignment for a different group."

"You mean someone got there before you guys and secured the materials from the lab and then you guys came and did the blasting?"

"Could be."

"Hmm, if I remember the report correctly, the CSAC had RT on January 16. That was only four days after the earthquake. Who could have gotten there earlier?"

"An operation by Darwin Inc. itself?"

"But then they might as well have blown it up. No, I think the CSAC was the only group up there."

"It was just a guess." Rod shrugged his shoulders.

"At any rate, no one—including your mailmen—was here in the village after the quake, so no other crew either," Ondragon stated. "Assuming the people here are telling the truth, that we're the first soldiers to show up."

"Hmm-hmm."

"I've been reading through Green's and Stern's reports."

"So, what do you think?"

"Green writes that they reached the mine at two in the afternoon, searched the area, found destroyed buildings and four dead. They removed the remains of the hut that stood over the shaft entrance and had collapsed like a house of cards during the quake, exposing the entrance, which had been secured with steel plates. A trapdoor with an electronic lock was embedded in the plates. Since there was no electricity or emergency power, they were able to open the lock quite easily and enter the shaft, where a steel staircase led down into the darkness. The crew was stopped halfway down, however, by a landslide that destroyed the stairs and made it impossible to continue. Green decided to leave it at that, and set the charges. As planned, setting the dynamite dragged on until late in the evening. When the mailmen were finished, they moved the dead bodies and other suspicious materials, including anything with company logos, down the shaft, or at least that was the order: Leave no trace on the surface!"

"Are you trying to blame me?" growled Rod.

"No, definitely not."

"Good!"

Ondragon gave Rod a critical sideways glance. Why was he suddenly so sensitive? Was he growing a conscience? Or was the thing with the boy troubling him? It was just as well that kind of thing didn't affect him. Compassion and conscience only got in the way in his line of work. Maybe his friend needed some anti-conscience training. And maybe they should leave the Madame to her own devices right here and now and go to the mine without her. Too much thoughtfulness was unhealthy, after all. He glanced over at the Madame, who had worked through a quarter of the line, and then at his watch. Two and a half hours to go. She was on time. Perhaps they would stay on schedule after all, despite the unforeseen disruptions.

He shrugged his shoulders and continued. "The shaft was scheduled to be blasted in the early hours of the morning. During the night, Green took first watch, then Ellys, and finally Stern. No incidents. The next morning the area was secured by Stern and Ellys, while Green rechecked the charges. At 6:15 am he left the shaft and at 6:30 am he detonated. The blast went according to plan and the shaft collapsed. A subsequent inspection confirmed that the entrance was completely sealed. The crew packed up and returned to the coast via the route they had come by, through the river valley, where they boarded the boat at 12:40 pm. PO and MC. Good clean work!" Ondragon snapped his fingers. "Stern's report is identical so far, except for the fact that he mentions only thirteen charges of dynamite, instead of fifteen, like Green."

"One of them just miscounted," Rod remarked wryly.

"I hardly think so," replied Ondragon. He narrowed his eyes thoughtfully and looked up at the sky above the mountains, where a flock of turkey vultures were flying their rounds. "Which of the two do you trust more?"

Rod glanced at him. In this heat, his blue eyes seemed even cooler. "Green, that's why he's the Head."

"Well, let's assume his report is correct, then what do we conclude from the difference in Stern's?"

"That the number of charges in the shaft was increased without Stern knowing about it. After all, Green was the last one in the shaft that evening and the only one to check the charges the next morning. Maybe he set two additional rods that Stern and Ellys didn't know about. Could be, couldn't it?"

"Could be. Ondragon took off his helmet and scratched his head. It made him extraordinarily nervous that he couldn't come up with a solution to this riddle. Of one thing he was certain. One of the two mailmen was trying to cover something up. That's what his gut told him.

"I hope we'll know more soon," he said, pushing himself off the wall. "I'll go and hear what the Madame has found out." He walked over to her and lowered himself onto the chair. The rifle between his knees, he eyed a young pretty woman who was just showing the Madame a nasty wound on her arm. Pus-filled blisters had formed under the scab, and the skin around the injury had a bluish tinge. The woman avoided his gaze shyly and bit her lower lip while the Madame spoke to her in Creole and began rummaging in a worn, old-fashioned suitcase.

"Where did you get that thing?" he asked.

"From the altar room; that's where all priests keep their ingredients for remedies and potions." She pulled the cork from a green wine bottle and poured a brown powder into the woman's cupped hand. Then she took a battered tin and added two spoonfuls of the dried herbs inside. "This should help with the infection. Her arm was torn open by a piece of corrugated metal that came off the roof during the quake. I hope she will survive. The wound looks gangrenous. She really needs antibiotics."

Modern medicine? From the mouth of this herb witch too! Ondragon did not look at the young woman. Her fate was not his problem. "And have you been able to find out anything about the mine or the boy?"

The Madame dismissed the woman and waved in the next candidate, whose potato-sized ulcer over his left eye was definitely not from the quake. "So far, not much. Give me some more time. People are just starting to get a little more talkative."

Ondragon looked at the clock. "Two more hours, then we leave! No matter what we know by then!"

"*Bien sûr, mon générale!*" said the Madame, asking the man before her a question in his impossible native language.

Ondragon remained seated for a moment, but quickly grew tired of the villagers' pleading looks and rejoined Rod, who had lit a Havana. "How can you smoke in this heat?" he asked the Brit, taking a sip from his water bottle.

Wordlessly, Rod held the cigar out to him. Ondragon took it and inhaled. The nutty aroma of the tobacco flowed over his tongue, and he was surprised to find that the smoke felt almost cool. At least it seemed that way at over 100 degrees Fahrenheit in the shade. He took another drag and handed the glowing stick back to his friend. "Good stuff!"

"Yep."

For a while there was an amicable silence between them. They gazed thoughtfully across the courtyard to the colonnade, where the Madame was busily mixing her herbal cures. But then Ondragon sensed that Rod wanted to say something, but obviously didn't quite dare.

He nudged his friend. "Out with it. What's on your mind?"

"The Madame and I, we talked on the plane while you were asleep. She told me something I thought was strange. And I don't know if I should believe her." Rod turned to face him, so he was just leaning against the wall with one shoulder. "Do you really have a brother? One who's been dead for over thirty years?"

It was understandable that Rod would ask about it, Ondragon realized. After all the years of their friendship, he now felt he'd been duped because he had never told him about it. He turned to his former mentor and looked him in the eye. "This is between us now. The Madame—or anyone else—can't know anything about this."

"I'm your friend, Ecks! Probably the only one in this world you can really trust!"

Rod was probably right about that. And because he was also the only one who knew his complete family history up to the quarrel with his father, Ondragon wanted to tell him about the thing with his brother. "It's true, I had a twin brother. Per Gustav. He died when we were ten years old. And I'm probably to blame for his death."

"You?"

Ondragon squirmed inwardly. But he had known that one day he would have to say it out loud. "We were grounded and my father locked us in his library. I thought it was unfair and kicked or threw something at a bookshelf—I don't remember exactly. Whatever, the shelf started to shake and fell on top of us. You should know that the shelves were filled to the ceiling with . . ." He hesitated because even the word was loathsome to him. "With . . . fucking *books!*" He spat it out like a disgusting black bug. "They buried me and my brother. I could barely breathe, but I managed to dig myself out of the mountain after a while. Or was it my parents who freed me? I can't say that for sure now either. It's strange, isn't it? I only remember how pale their faces were when they finally found Per Gustav. It was only later that they told me he had suffered severe brain trauma and had suffocated under the pile of paper." Ondragon felt sudden nausea rising in his throat and put a hand over his mouth. *Now, for the love of God, don't throw up,* he thought, trying hard to get his emotions under control. "I'm sorry, Rod," he forced out with difficulty, running his hand over his throat, which felt constricted. "It . . ." He cleared his throat. "It's hard for me to talk about it."

"It's okay, you don't have to . . ."

Ondragon raised a hand. "Yes, I do! I can't stop thinking about it, do you understand? Since I've known about it, I can't get my brother out of my mind. I repressed his death, indeed his whole existence, for decades. But he has a right to be remembered by me. It is my duty to remember him!"

"What about your parents?"

"What about them?!" responded Ondragon gruffly. "They've kept their mouths shut all these years. Pretended the whole thing never happened. Else how do you explain me just forgetting about Per?"

Rod shrugged his shoulders. "Is that really how it was? Maybe your psyche just did you a favor and pushed it far enough down for you to endure the pain."

"Now you're starting to sound like the psycho-doc I went to see last summer. No, it all sounds plausible, but I think there's something else behind it. It sometimes feels like my memory has been erased."

"You're imagining things, Ecks."

"That's the thing. I solve all these knotty problems for other people, but I can't get a handle on my own. The lousy irony of fate! Or is it something else? A mystery that's too hard for me to crack." Ondragon spread his arms. "The great problem solver Paul Eckbert Ondragon is foundering on his own past. It's such bullshit!"

"If it helps, I can get some research done."

"Thank you, my friend, but I've already done that. For the last six months, I've been going through all the documents and information I could get my hands on. From Per's birth certificate to his death certificate, from the medical report to the dubious claim that my mother was a spy for the Swedish government—it's laughable!" Incensed, he ran his hand through the air. "You see, a few fellows who thought they were pretty smart claimed to have found that out. Turned out to be wrong, of course. Those carrion crows were just trying to piss me off. Believe me, Rod, I have run every scrap of information through my *centrifuge.* There's nothing there! *Nada, niente!* But I can sense it's not all kosher."

"Have you ever thought your intuition might be leading you astray? Maybe there really isn't anything there and you're just getting carried away."

Ondragon waved a hand irritably. "I know there's something there! And if I have to dig away at it for another thirty years, I'll prise this secret from the devil's fingers too! Could I have another drag?" He pointed to the extinguished cigar between Rod's fingers.

His friend did not react immediately, but then took out his lighter, relit the Havana, and gave it to Ondragon, who began to smoke with fervor.

CHAPTER 26

Time was up, and Ondragon and Rod went over to the Madame, who had actually reached the last patient. An amazing achievement, he had to admit. All that remained was to see how many would survive the herbal treatment. Having shouldered his rifle, he stood next to her and had some fun tapping her on the shoulder in an admonitory manner.

"Yes, I'm nearly finished!" she hissed, stroking the hand of the patient, a sad-looking man with a square head, and speaking soothingly to him. When the man finally rose and left with a grateful nod, the Madame breathed a sigh of relief and rose too. Groaning, she stretched her back.

"I'm waiting!" warned Ondragon.

"Now, don't get all stressed out. I've got what you want." She walked a few laps around the painted center post of the colonnade. "That was exhausting, I need to stretch my legs a bit."

Ondragon drummed his fingers impatiently on his rifle butt, and the Madame raised her hands placatingly as she caught his eye. "All right, all right, I'm coming." She came over to Ondragon, spread her fingers, and, as if counting off a list, touched a finger to the index finger of her open hand. "Let's start with the mine. The young people don't know much about it; the old people had more to say. Their grandparents worked there when it was still in use. It has been closed for eighty years. Silver was mined there for twelve years, until the deposit was depleted. So the mine is not particularly large. There are two main shafts, a side shaft that runs horizontally into the mountain but collapsed years ago, and—according to different sources—five to eight tunnels that crisscross the mountain. They have never been mapped. The mining was undertaken on the basis of ancient methods using pure muscle power and without technological aids such as compressed air chisels, electric conveyor systems, or trolleys on rails. The men worked the rock with hammers and picks, then the ore was loaded by hand into baskets and these were brought aboveground by winches or donkeys. Just like in the Middle Ages. They weren't much concerned with humane working conditions back then, even under US occupation—though I have to admit it's not much better today." The Madame ran her hand pensively over her hair. "The ore was hauled down a narrow path to the village, where it was crushed in a mill and the silver extracted in large vats using what an older man called the *méthode l'amalgame.*"

"The amalgamation process. Pure poison. The mercury that is used to dissolve the silver is vaporized, leaving only the silver behind," Rod explained. "Something like this, by the way, is still the practice in the gold mines of South America. Ugly business and, of course, it's at the expense of the native population."

"Hmm, yummy. I guess we'd better avoid that part of the village." Ondragon motioned to the Madame to continue.

"Nevertheless, the mine did help the village achieve a certain prosperity. When it closed, things went downhill, and the people have lived only on the meager yields of farming ever since." She pointed to her middle finger. "Now let's move on to the unofficial reopening. Three years ago a group of Whites came and moved a lot of material up into the mountains, with helicopters and columns of porters. There is no other way to reach the area. But again, the accounts differ—some say it was the Americans, others say it was the French."

"Could have been Canadians."

"Possibly. I asked for the company name. No one remembers hearing or seeing anything. Looks like Darwin Inc. wanted to stay incognito."

"So it actually was a secret research facility," Ondragon said.

"But certainly backed by the Haitian government," interjected the Madame, "because they don't let foreign companies into the country without some kind of kickback. When the *blancs* come into the country, they cash in. That is general practice. *Blancs* are cash cows. If it weren't for the earthquake and the chaos it caused, I might be able to put in a few phone calls to find out if such an 'arrangement' had been made in advance. But as it is, it will be impossible to reach the person in charge by phone. I can still try, anyway, when we get back to the States."

Aha, thought Ondragon, *now, that's useful information!* The Madame had contacts within the Haitian authorities. So she was more than a Voodoo priestess. The daughter of a politician or other top brass; hence her influence.

"All right," he said finally. "Have the people from the village said anything about what went on in the lab?"

"No, because the area around the shaft was hermetically sealed. A very high electric fence and armed guards. It was forbidden to go there. And it was said that a bokor was working with the *blancs* and would punish any intruder who dared to go there. The villagers abided by the rules; they were afraid of the bokor."

"Could have been a very effective campaign by Darwin Inc," Rod opined.

The Madame nodded in agreement. "That's possible. It even got to the point that people kept on disappearing from the village. They say that the bokor of the *blancs* took them for himself and turned them into zombies. That brings us to recent events." The Madame gave Ondragon an intense look as her finger moved to her ring finger. "I know you don't want to hear any more of this, and in that case I'm just relaying what people have told me. Recently, a man named Etienne Dadou disappeared from the village. That was four months ago. However, his young daughter reported seeing him just before the earthquake, up there by the road. He was a zombie, she said; he had chased her to her house and was then driven away by the quake. Her mother, she said, notified the village mambo and asked her to find her husband and rescue him. Five days ago, an expedition left for the mountains to track down Etienne Dadou. Today one of the boys came back . . . and we know what happened to him." The Madame gave an almost pained grimace. She didn't seem as tough as she pretended to be.

Ondragon decided to give her another chance. "So that means the zombie is still walking around up there now, armed with a machete or an axe?"

"Yes, probably," replied the Madame.

"And the other members of the expedition? How many were there, did they find out?"

"Five: the mambo, Madame Dadou, her nine-year-old daughter, and two temple assistants, one of whom was the boy."

"Why the hell would you take kids along on that kind of trip?"

The Madame shrugged her shoulders.

Ondragon shook his head. Some customs were a mystery to him. "Well, fine. Let's assume, then, that the other members of that ill-advised 'research trip' are also dead and rotting away up there." He pointed to the vultures circling in the sky and then looked back at the Madame. "But in you, we have a highly trained zombie hunter on our side. You know what to do if we encounter a member of the undead. That's why you wanted to come, isn't it? You wanted to protect me from the evil spell of the bokor."

The Madame glared at him angrily without saying anything.

Ondragon didn't care if he had offended her. She would have to learn to deal with it. He pulled out his cell phone and looked at the screen. No message from Charlize. Which wasn't because roaming was bad in Haiti. They actually got great reception here. But apparently the cell towers had stopped functioning during the quake.

Just this morning, he had talked to his assistant on the phone, shortly before they had gone ashore, and asked her to speed up her research. He would feel much better if he could have more information on the lab and its possible aims before they headed up there.

"Will someone from the village take us to the second shaft?" he asked the Madame, putting the cell phone away.

"I don't think so."

"Then we need an accurate description, or better yet, a drawing. Can you arrange that?"

Capitulating, the Madame beckoned to the La Place, who had been sitting at some distance in the shade of a tree and eyeing them suspiciously. She spoke a few words to the gray-haired, somewhat stocky man, who nodded languidly and finally waddled away on his stubby legs.

"He'll get someone to give us directions." The Madame took off her doctor's coat, stuffed it into her backpack, and drank thirstily from her water bottle.

"Hopefully sometime today!" growled Ondragon, looking after the Master of Ceremonies as he shuffled away.

"Can the zombie from the mountains do us any harm?" asked Rod abruptly. He had moved over to stand next to the Madame, and his expression made his unease far too obvious, thought Ondragon.

The Madame gave a dry laugh and replied sarcastically, "About as much as he did that boy, I think."

Rod didn't seem satisfied. He put a pensive finger to his lower lip and asked, "But couldn't a . . . normal man have done that too?"

"Of course. *I'm* not saying it was a zombie, the boy whispered it to me before he died. He said he fought with the undead. But there's one strange thing."

"What?" Rod asked.

"I'm surprised that the mambo and the sanpwel, the members of the secret society that must also exist in this place, have accepted that a strange bokor is doing mischief here. Normally, such a person is driven away or even killed, unless he has been authorized by the sanpwel to practice black magic."

"Madame, you said yourself earlier that it was possible the bokor thing could have been a campaign by Darwin Inc.," Rod interjected. "Let's take it a step further. Maybe it wasn't an *outside* bokor at all. Couldn't the sorcerer have come from the secret society itself? Might he have been hired by Darwin Inc.?"

"Are you saying the priests here in the village might have worked with Darwin Inc. to spread the evil spell so people in the village wouldn't get curious and would stay away from the lab?" asked Ondragon.

"Could be." Rod shrugged his shoulders.

The Madame was silent for a while.

"Well, many a priest has played on both teams, the loas and the diabs, for money," she finally said mysteriously, without looking at either of them.

Ondragon looked sideways at her, keenly. What if *she* had played on both teams?

"I know what you're thinking, Monsieur Ondragon!" The Madame's dark eyes flashed at him. "But it is not true, I swear it on my father's *ti bon ange*. I do not serve the devils."

"But you could if you wanted to, right?"

Before she could answer, the La Place came shuffling across the backyard, accompanied by an athletically built young man with stained shorts and a bare torso. The Master of Ceremonies said something and then the fellow spoke. The Madame held out an imperious hand to Ondragon, and he wordlessly handed her his notepad and a pen.

Diligently, she began to take down the young man's instructions. His voice was a restrained singsong . . . and his eyes darted nervously back and forth like two hunted animals.

He was fear personified!

Even Ondragon's grandma would have seen that.

When the kid had finished, he quickly ran away, leaving behind a smell of sweat and dust.

"Do we know where to go now?" asked Ondragon impatiently.

"I think so." The Madame tapped the pen on the pad.

Ondragon threw both hands up to the sky theatrically. "Praise be to the Lord and all the deities of Voodoo—we can finally set out!"

After having a quick bite to eat, the three packed up and shouldered their backpacks. They left their helmets dangling from a strap at the back, because it was still far too hot to put them on. Instead, Ondragon wrapped an olive-green scarf around his head. He wasn't keen on a second bout of sunstroke.

They left the village in a northerly direction, passing the desolate graveyard and the corner of the wall where the boy had died, marked by dark bloodstains in the sand. Ondragon glanced up at the vultures hovering like black streaks over the ridge. The winged scavengers almost certainly knew the whereabouts of the expedition group.

He pushed his sunglasses onto the top of his head and took a close look at the increasingly steep terrain ahead of him. Between the dry bushes and the few puny trees, nothing but yellowish rocks rose from the sun-baked ground. Where half a century ago there had probably been lush green rainforest, now everything seemed parched and dead. Like in parts of Africa, the inhabitants had ruthlessly felled wood for their cooking fires, and the mountains had become deserts; dusty slopes where nothing grew anymore because they could no longer store rainwater. Only cacti thrived here.

Ondragon looked again at the well-trodden path stretching like a yellow snake up the mountain shoulder and carefully put one foot in front of the other. He led the group, his rifle in front of his body ready to fire; this didn't exactly make the climb any easier, and the damn Kevlar vest made him sweat like a beast too. But he wanted to be ready for any attack. The Madame walked behind him, carrying a heavy load and with the improvised map in her hand. She kept a lookout for the waymarks it described. Rod followed at the end, his M16 also to hand. But despite all his experience, the Briton also seemed more on the alert than usual. Ondragon heard him exhale several times and clear his throat. A clear sign of the tension his friend was feeling.

Yard by yard, they laboriously climbed the mountain in the heat. After half an hour, they took a short break to catch their breath and have a drink. The switchbacks continued up the mountainside to the right. They were already halfway to the ridge. Ondragon looked back at the village on the hazy plain below them. Somehow, he was glad they had left that desolate place, and he also felt little desire to ever go back. Fortunately, their return journey would take them farther east past the village to the coast.

They started moving again and half an hour later they reached the ridge. Here the path ended abruptly at a rock wall.

"Blast!" Rod said. "So where do we go from here?" He wiped the sweat from his face. "It's sweltering!"

Ondragon looked at the sun, which was already making its way toward the horizon.

It would set in just under an hour and a half, he thought. Hopefully, they would have reached the mine by then.

The Madame, meanwhile, was consulting the directions. "I think we have to go that way," she said, pointing to two almost identical round boulders.

"You think?" asked Ondragon irritably. He was very uneasy that only the Madame knew the way to the mine. Although *knowing* was also putting it a bit too optimistically.

She rolled her eyes. "The way you parse every single word! I meant, I am sure it's that way. The description said we have to go between the *Marassa Pierres*, and behind them there is a path that is difficult to see and leads north along the ridge. Those two rocks there look like stone twins, don't they?"

Ondragon nodded, his expression dark, and went ahead. Scouting carefully in all directions, he climbed between the two man-sized rocks and found himself looking into the abyss of a canyon on the other side. A narrow ledge led along the rock face. This was the path. Ondragon whistled for the others to follow him.

In an agonizingly slow single file, they shimmied along the dangerously narrow path—to their right the rock face and to their left the precipitous drop to the river valley. In the distance rose the blue-gray ridge of the jagged mountain range, which gradually began to turn purple in the twilight. They would have to get a move on if they didn't want to spend the night here on the ledge.

Exhausted, they reached the end of the mule track and looked down on a tree-covered hollow that opened up several hundred feet below. Ondragon looked up at the sky again. The vultures had disappeared. He reached for his binoculars and scanned the area. He made out the square construction of the high steel fence, a corrugated metal shack that presumably housed a generator, adjacent to it two large fuel tanks, a downed transmission tower, a clearing with a helipad, and farther to the right, the white metal boxes of accommodation containers shimmering between the trees. Next to them, Ondragon could see collapsed sections of buildings in the dense green of the forest. This had to be the blasted entrance to the mine. The fenced-in area looked deserted, but he still wanted to exercise the necessary caution when entering it.

He signaled to the others and began to descend the slope ahead of them. After a few yards, they reached the refreshing green vegetation of the hollow and it became noticeably cooler and darker. But this was not only due to the dense canopy of the forest . . . Ondragon looked at his watch. It was 6:12 pm. In a few minutes, the sun would disappear and the tropical night would literally fall upon them. He hurried to find a way through the undergrowth to the fence.

Suddenly, he stopped.

An unmistakable smell was drifting into his nose.

Something was decomposing nearby.

He told the others to fan out and look for the source of the stench.

The Madame finally found it and brought it to the attention of Ondragon and Rod with a choking sound. She stood there with one hand over her mouth and the other pointing to a bush. Tears were in her eyes as Ondragon arrived beside her and moved the branches of the bush aside.

"Well, here we have expedition member number two," he said dryly, bending down to the mutilated corpse, from which the vultures had long since removed all soft tissue with surgical precision. Empty eye sockets stared back at him, but the face and body were definitely female. "The mother or the priestess?"

The Madame ventured a quick glance. "From the clothes, the mambo!" she groaned behind her hand before quickly turning away again.

"Same wounds as the boy," Rod stated matter-of-factly.

It was true. Cuts littered the dead woman's arms, but it was the deep gap between her neck and shoulder that had probably been fatal.

"What a mess! Must have been a mighty blow. And the woman is missing half of her right hand. The blow must have come from the front and she tried to deflect it. My guess is machete; the cuts are too long for an axe."

Ondragon nodded. He knew all the kinds of injuries a machete could cause.

From Africa.

Long-forgotten images appeared in his mind's eye. A burned village, the hacked-up bodies of men and women who had refused to give up their children for the rebels' war. He had seen a lot of things working for DeForce. Some of it didn't bother him, some of it did. That was why he'd begun to put the rest of his feelings into the freezer.

"How long has she been lying there dead?" the Madame asked, breaking his chain of thought.

"Hmm." Rod leaned forward and nudged the body with the muzzle of his rifle. The body was long past stiff. "At least four days, I guess."

"So what do we do now?" The Madame's anxiety was clearly visible. Her dark facial skin had taken on a paleness.

"We'll go ahead as planned, find the fence, and then look around the site," Ondragon replied. "I want to get a first impression so we can put together a plan for tomorrow. Once everything is clear, we'll retreat to the hillside and set up camp in a spot that gives us a good view of the terrain. Now, let's go; we don't have much time before dark. I'll lead the way. And, Rod, you bring up the rear."

"Aye!"

They began to move, creeping on through the jungle-like forest. After only a few minutes, their path was blocked by a ten-foot steel structure.

"Now, that's a security fence!" said Rod in hushed tones. "But where's the hole my mailmen cut?"

"On the eastern side; that's what the report said," Ondragon whispered.

"All right. Let's go!"

Suddenly, there was a crack in the bushes behind them.

Ondragon and Rod wheeled around simultaneously, aiming their assault rifles at the impenetrable greenery. The Madame too listened spellbound, her nostrils flared, her hand on the Desert Eagle in her holster.

But the sound did not come again.

"Damn it!" growled Ondragon. "Whatever that was . . . let's walk quietly along the fence to the hole. Have your headlamps ready; it's about to get pitch dark."

He stalked along the fence to the next corner, where he paused and spied out the path. The shadows around them grew longer, licking at them with black tongues. But they were static shadows; none of them moved in the now rapidly fading daylight.

Crouching down, Ondragon crept on. He left his headlamp off and was relying entirely on his senses. His pupils dilated, allowing him to identify the different hues of the trees. He felt the temperature drop on his skin and smelled the earthy scents of the night rising from the ground. The cautious footsteps of his companions were the only sounds his hearing had to filter out of the density of darkness.

The hole in the fence was not very big, but it was easy to slip through.

"Lights on!" whispered Ondragon to his two companions on the other side.

Rod and the Madame nodded and turned their headlamps to the brightest setting. Like small searchlights, the bright beams crisscrossed the night. Within half an hour, they had searched the dark area and the containers, and it took Ondragon another fifteen minutes to take a closer look at the blasted entrance.

The mailmen had done a really great job. Earth and shattered pieces of concrete and steel had wedged themselves into a forbidding mass in the shaft. Without an excavator they had no chance. They would never get through the rubble to the lab here. They would actually have to use the second shaft. But they couldn't take a look at it until tomorrow.

Ondragon gave the signal to move off. They left the area through the hole and returned as quickly as prudence permitted to the vegetation-free shoulder of the slope, where after a while they discovered a sandy hollow that was almost level and offered a good view in all directions. Exhausted and their nerves frayed, they unloaded their packs. Rod and the Madame began preparing a small dinner, while Ondragon sat a little apart with his cell phone and notepad. He needed some quiet time to collect his thoughts, and the quiet conversation of the other two would only disturb him.

He turned on his cell phone and dialed Charlize's number.

"Boss? Are you all right?" the familiar voice of his assistant answered.

"So far yes; we've arrived at the mine, hopefully we'll get into the lab tomorrow, and then we'll make our way back, unless something comes up. So? Have you discovered anything yet?"

"So far, just a couple of nice scandals. I sent you the information by email. Other than that, I haven't made any progress yet. I'll try to contact the staff tomorrow. It won't be easy; the premises around the Darwin laboratories are heavily secured. I can't use my usual tricks to get in there. But I'll come up with something. Unless I freeze to death by then." She shivered. "It's terrible weather here. Temperatures close to freezing and fresh snow!"

"Well, it's no better here. Way too hot and not a pool in sight! But all kidding aside, did you notice anything suspicious? Did anyone follow you?" Ondragon was worried his captors might be nipping at Charlize's heels.

"No, no one has followed me yet, and yes, *Paul-san*, I will be careful. For now though save your battery. I'll send you a text message when I have anything new. *O-yasuminasai!*"

"Good night to you too, Charlize." He hung up, went to his inbox, and opened the file. He quickly skimmed the contents and turned the phone off again. The battery would last another day. He had to use it sparingly. With his headlamp on its lowest setting, he began transcribing what he had just read into his notepad.

There were four newspaper articles from the internet. One dealt with a scandal from the 1970s in which a subsidiary of Darwin Inc, a well-known chemical company, had disposed of its PCB-contaminated waste in a private clay pit in a small town in Oklahoma. The poison leaked into the drinking water and many of the residents became seriously ill or even died as a result. The injured families filed a class action lawsuit years later. The trial dragged on for two decades, but in the end, Darwin Inc. was found guilty. The company was proven to have known about the toxicity of PCBs for years, but to have continued to dump them in the convenient pit. Gritting its teeth, Darwin Inc. paid more than $300 million in damages to the victims. To this day, production facilities in Oklahoma were contaminated with PCBs.

Ondragon clicked his pen.

Well, the plots of land there must be cheaper by the dozen now, he thought ironically. Hard for the people who lived there, but every third or fourth major company had now had a PCB or dioxin scandal by now, so it was therefore hardly something out of the ordinary.

Click.

He summarized the second article, which was already somewhat more interesting and stated that in 2009, seven farmers from Germany had poisoned themselves with the well-known and globally available herbicide Weedsweep, made by Darwin Inc. The farmers had inhaled the pesticide, damaging their central nervous systems. All seven became disabled and went to court. Their joint counsel accused Darwin Inc. of systematically concealing the dangers of the herbicide, from which the corporation earned billions. He demanded that the product be taken off the market. A case that naturally caused a worldwide sensation, because it was the first to prove that Weedsweep made people ill. In the course of the trial, the constituent ingredients of the herbicide were tested and were indeed found to include solvents of concern. Since then, some countries had considered banning Weedsweep, which would have meant serious losses for Darwin Inc. So far, however, no link had been established between the ingredients of the Darwin product and the damage to the farmers' health.

Click.

No wonder, Ondragon thought cynically. It was obvious, somehow. And the experts were still providing opinions and counter-opinions, so the trial was still dragging on today. A clear delaying tactic no one could do anything about. In addition, a spokesman for the biotech giant announced that Darwin Inc. was considering filing a counter-claim for damage to reputation and loss of business.

Click.

Ondragon laughed bitterly. This was the usual saber-rattling the big boys indulged in and certainly the end of the proceedings, for ordinary citizens were powerless against the corporations' shrewd lawyers. The world was a tank full of shit, and all you had to know was how to keep your own boat afloat so you could sit back and watch the others drown in it.

Click.

Ondragon stroked his chin thoughtfully. Was this a first connection between genetic engineering and the laboratory in the mine? Weedsweep was Darwin Inc.'s number one seller, and the company had pulled off a brilliant coup by designing crops that were resistant to its proprietary pesticide. That meant farmers only had to sow Darwin Inc. seeds and then apply the associated herbicide to the crop. Weedsweep destroyed everything but plants made by Darwin Inc. It wasn't cheap for farmers, as Darwin Inc. charged a high price for its green technology, but it was still a good option for farming businesses, paying dividends when it came to their annual balance sheet. Of course, the herbicide-resistant crops and pesticide were patent-protected, and both provided Darwin Inc. with a steady stream of cash every year. It would not be surprising if the corporation fought tooth and nail to protect this revenue stream, Ondragon thought. He felt the *centrifuge* give a brief jerk.

Click.

Was it trying to tell him something?

Click.

A hunch that was slowly taking shape?

Click, click.

The next two articles dealt with one of the varieties of genetically modified plants produced by the Darwin laboratories, more precisely the maize variety DWIN 411. Darwin Inc. had made this maize not only resistant to Weedsweep, but also immune to any pest infestations. According to a euphoric company report in 2002, Darwin bioengineers had succeeded in inserting into the corn genome genes from a specific organism that killed all insect pests within a very short time. Darwin Inc. kept the identity of the organism under wraps, a trade secret, so as not to encourage competitors to copy it while the corn was still in the test phase, as it was called.

Click.

That would fit with what Rod had said, Ondragon thought, but that sounded a deliberately trivializing. Just like the other statements from the company: the newly designed product was definitely harmless to humans; it was only lethal in the digestive tract of the insect larvae, and it was a blessing for humans and the environment, because in addition to increasing yields, the corn also reduced the burden of pesticides on the environment, blah, blah, blah. The usual drivel. *Honi soit qui mal y pense*, shame on him who thinks evil of it.

Click.

In 2005, studies on the feeding of DWIN 411 to laboratory animals were completed and the variety was classified as safe by the US Department of Agriculture. It was approved in the States shortly thereafter. Mexico, Brazil, India, and the EU followed. So far, so good. DWIN 411 arrived in the fields, and the rubles would have rolled into the pockets of Darwin Inc. . . . had it not been for Germany again.

This was the subject of the final article. The population of Germany was not very tolerant of genetic engineering in general and, in particular, the food produced from it. In contrast to the US, where the area of genetically modified crops under cultivation was already a hair-raising 70.9 million hectares, there was no significant commercial production in Germany. No sooner did the wonder weapon DWIN 411 arrive on the market in 2005 than the German minister of agriculture banned the sale of the seed. The reason was that the corn allegedly killed not only harmful insects but also beneficial species such as bees, butterflies, and beetles—in other words, all other creepy-crawlies. Darwin Inc. appealed against the ban, of course, but surprisingly lost the case. Because in fact, it was demonstrated that there was a decline in general biodiversity and beneficial insects near DWIN 411 fields. Whether this was due to the corn or other parameters, however, was not entirely clear. In any case, this result was enough for the Germans, and in 2006 the Federal Republic of Germany renewed the ban on cultivating DWIN 411 on German farmland, much to the chagrin of Darwin Inc. The German example was soon followed by France, Denmark, and Austria—a dangerous trend for Darwin Inc., which was worried its latest invention would meet an early demise and was now working flat out to improve its product.

Click.

Ondragon chewed thoughtfully on the end of the pen. What had they been researching in the lab here in Haiti? Was it something highly contagious to humans or something dangerous to the environment? Why all the security measures? And what had been going on here that was so secret that even the mailmen had been eliminated? Had it been Darwin Inc. itself, or had the corporation merely commissioned the work, as it had previously commissioned DeForce?

His pen hovered indecisively over the pad, but there was nothing left to write down. Ondragon simply did not know. Nor did he feel able to share his suspicions with Rod. He feared the Brit might feel he had been personally attacked and possibly launch a rash counterattack—which would not end well for him, because from all that Ondragon had already found out about Darwin Inc. it was not advisable to mess with the biotech kraken.

Click, click.

He put the notepad away and returned to the other two, who had long since finished their meager meal of cold mashed potatoes, a bacon-flavored dry sausage, and a foil-wrapped egg waffle, and were now sitting on their sleeping bags, silent and wide-eyed.

"What is it? Why do you look like you've seen the ghost of Elvis?"

"Didn't you hear that?" whispered Rod.

"No. What?"

No sooner had he said this than he heard a long-drawn-out howl coming up from the hollow.

CHAPTER 27

February 15, 2010
Haiti, N 18° 13' 50.7", W 72° 34' 6.36"
8:32 pm

Holy shit! Do they have wolves here?" asked Rod in a muffled voice.

Ondragon, who had also felt the howl in his bones, raised a hand to silence his friend. He could not use scare tactics now. He extinguished his headlamp and listened to the night, hearing nothing except the metallic sawing of cicadas.

Then the sound came again.

It rose from the black thicket of the forest below and floated up the slope toward them on the warm air.

An eerie howl, drawn out and hoarse. The sound ended in a gasp and died away completely.

None of them dared move. But Ondragon could sense what the other two were thinking. Because it inevitably crept into his thoughts as well.

Zombie!

Dammit, he couldn't let himself be scared by something so absurd. There was bound to be a rational explanation for the howl. It might have been an animal or someone from the expedition group who was injured and calling desperately for help. If the latter was the case, they would not be able to help him; the schedule did not allow for that.

"We stay up here no matter what, and keep the slope in view," he ordered. "All lights stay out unless I give the order to turn them on! Clear?" He looked at the others. "I'll take the first watch and Rod the second. You, madame, can sleep. Don't worry, you'll be safe here.

Whatever was howling down there won't be able to harm us, because it can't get up to us unnoticed. And should it still try to approach us, we will give it an appropriate welcome." He tapped the M16 he had automatically reached for when he heard the howl. "Now, let's all settle down and focus on tomorrow!" He sat down decisively on a rock and began peering into the darkness.

Rod handed him the food. "It's not tasty, but before you turn to skin and bones . . ."

"Thanks." Ondragon took the aluminum bowl.

"So, what do you think that was?" whispered Rod so softly that the Madame couldn't hear. She had just laid back down on her sleeping bag behind them.

"Honestly, I have no idea. But if you think it was the machete zombie, forget it! There's no such thing! The Voodoo people may believe that kind of nonsense, but we mustn't let ourselves be influenced by such talk."

"I'm not being influenced, Ecks. I'm just of the opinion that you shouldn't completely ignore these things, no matter how fantastical they sound. Maybe zombies do exist."

Ondragon turned to his friend and hissed, "Rod! Do me a favor, please, and never mention the word *zombie* again, will you? Man, I thought you knew enough about the world to know when you're dealing with a superstition and when you're not!" He was disappointed. Why did Roderick DeForce suddenly believe in this nonsense too? He sighed. Was he the only normal person in the world?

Rod noticed his friend's irritable mood and retreated to his camp with an apology. Soon, Ondragon heard only the quiet breathing of his two companions.

The first half of the night passed uneventfully. Not another howl sounded, and no one tried to climb up to them. Only once did Ondragon hear the soft trickling of stones somewhere above him on the slope. He stood up and listened in that direction, but it remained quiet. It was probably just some rock that had come loose on its own. He sat down again and looked at the clock.

An hour later, he woke Rod and lay down himself. Exhausted, he closed his eyes and immediately fell asleep with one hand on the gun.

* * *

The next morning, Rod had nothing to report either, and Ondragon was glad. The zombie hysteria was beginning to get on his nerves. He glanced over at the Madame. She was sipping her water pensively and acting remarkably calm. The night on the mountain didn't seem to have bothered her much. He, on the other hand, could feel a twinge in his back. He already knew why he didn't like the wilderness. It always made you seem older than you were.

A little later, they packed up their things and shouldered their backpacks. But before they started the descent, Ondragon surveyed the terrain once more through his binoculars. Everything looked the same as the day before. He beckoned to the Madame.

"Where's the second shaft of the mine from here?"

She pulled out the crumpled notes and finally pointed west. "There, at the edge of the canyon. Where the forest ends."

"Perfect, then we can steer clear of the pesky brush and avoid any ambushes at the same time." He looked into Rod's ice-blue eyes. Today his friend also had a scarf wrapped around his head and looked like a white-haired version of Willem Dafoe in *Platoon*. Ondragon smiled to himself. Finally, Rod was back in combat mode. He liked him a lot better that way!

Imitating a broad Texas accent, the Brit said, "Sir, yes, sir!" And, grinning, tapped two fingers to his forehead.

"Okay then, Privates, follow me unobtrusively," Ondragon replied, going to the head of the small squad.

They left the wooded depression on the right and worked their way westward along the stony slope. The terrain here dropped steeply to the canyon that the Ti Rivière de Jacmel had eaten into the yellowish rock over the millennia.

When they finally arrived at the edge of the gorge, the sun was already threatening to burn them, though it was only 9:00 am. Ondragon instructed his companions to discipline themselves and drink as little as possible. Not even three days ago, he had almost died from lack of water, and he was reluctant to repeat that experience. Since they were traveling light, he had kept the water supply tight. Three gallons each for the three to four days of the operation. In case of need, they still had water purification tablets with them, so they could drink from a river or well without getting sick.

Grimly, he looked around. They were standing on a small, bare hump. To their right lay the green pool of the forest, and to their left a sheer rock face dropped into the dry river valley.

"Where's the shaft?" he said, more to himself than to the others.

An answer came, nonetheless.

"Back there. It looks like a spoil pile, doesn't it?" Rod pointed to several small knolls that seemed to be mounds of debris; in addition, the rock in the piles appeared somewhat lighter in color than the rock surrounding it.

"You could be right. Let's take a look. But be careful! I don't want that howler from last night taking us by surprise!"

They approached the knolls cautiously. When they reached them, a flock of vultures suddenly flew up and soared into the air, screeching. Startled, the small group paused and waited with bowed heads until the dark cloud of flapping wings and claws had moved away and only the distant cawing of the scavengers reached their ears. They sensed that nothing good awaited them.

And having peered between the scree cones, Rod finally confirmed what everyone had suspected. "Another body."

But Ondragon wanted to be sure and stepped over to the half-eaten cadaver, which lay face down in a hollow. Behind him, the Madame kept a careful distance so as not to have to inhale the sweet stench emanating from the dead woman—once again, it was a woman. Her cleavage was clearly visible, and she had been wearing a skirt that now hung raggedly around her skinny legs.

"Must be the mother. Expedition member number three." Ondragon gave an involuntary shudder. He did not want to imagine what the girl and the other boy might look like if they had shared this woman's fate and were rotting somewhere down there in the bushes. Despite the sickening sight, he squatted down and looked more closely at the carcass. It bore no cuts or other injuries. All gashes had been inflicted by the scavengers. Ondragon looked at the woman's head and involuntarily flinched again as he realized what had happened to her. You couldn't say a posture was natural when the back of the head was pointing toward the chest. Someone had used brutal force to literally twist her neck!

He quickly rose and wiped the sweat from his upper lip. What a slaughter.

"She broke her neck," Rod commented on the obvious. "A fall, or—"

"Not a fall!" Ondragon looked around. There was nothing to be seen on the gravel around the knolls. Only the edge of the forest was staring darkly at them from some distance. Was something watching them from there? He squinted, but couldn't make out anything suspicious. He was sure though that if they were attacked, it would be from the direction of the trees.

"Hey, guys! Come over here. I found the shaft!" Rod beckoned to them. He had climbed over a few more knolls and was now looking down a square, black hole. "Looks inviting, doesn't it?" He got down on his knees and peered over the edge. "You can't see the bottom." He picked up a rock and dropped it. Shortly afterward, they heard a dull thud. "Forty feet, I guess, maybe fifty."

"Our rope is long enough." Ondragon set down his backpack and took out the climbing gear. "But where do we tie it?" He looked around.

"I saw some old wooden beams, probably buttresses, back there," the Madame said.

They went back to the black weathered beams that were scattered around the edge of the gravel cone and examined the wood, which was as thick as his thigh. Most of the beams were rotten, but one seemed sturdy enough and long enough to place over the shaft. Together they carried it to the hole, slid it diagonally across a corner, and fixed it on either side with a few rocks they laboriously rolled against it.

"Good!" Ondragon patted the dust off his gloves. "Before we get to work, there's something I need to do. Get everything ready. Then I'll go down and check things out." He pulled out his cell phone and looked at the display. An unknown number had tried to call him. He briefly considered calling back, but then dialed his assistant's number. It rang. Three times, five times, then it went to voicemail. Ondragon hung up. Odd. He hoped Charlize wasn't in trouble. He saw that he had received an email from her an hour ago, opened it, and read:

Hey Boss,

Attached are two newspaper articles. They're very interesting! Found them this morning in the Portland newspaper archives after getting a tip-off. Otherwise, all okay here, haven't seen anyone following me yet. Please be careful when you go into the mine. I have a feeling they've been handling some dangerous stuff there.

Charlize

He looked at the battery indicator. Enough juice to look at the newspaper articles. He opened the attachment.

Deadly Fungus Spreads in Oregon
(10/04/2006, *The Oregonian*)

The spread of a highly infectious microorganism in Oregon is causing the public health authorities concern. US scientists have identified the pathogen as a variant of the yeast *Cryptococcus neoformans*, which previously only posed a risk to immunocompromised patients. However, this new variant is now capable of causing severe or fatal illnesses in healthy people as well.

Portland—Doctors in Oregon are at a loss after an increase in fungal infections, including in healthy people, since the summer. An unknown variant of a yeast fungus, which previously only posed a risk to patients who were immunocompromised due to HIV or after an organ transplant and in fact only grows in tropical and subtropical climates, is now also attacking healthy people. Researchers have now identified the culprit as a mutation of the known species, *Cryptococcus neoformans*. *Cryptococcus mattesii* is aggressive and is much more lethal. The team, led by Dr. Abel Brouwers of Boise State University in Idaho, warns that it is only a matter of time before the fungus spreads to Washington and the more densely populated California.

So far, seven of the thirty people who have fallen ill have died from the new, more aggressive form of the fungus, a mortality rate of almost 25 percent. The health authority is not alarmed by this and is warning the media not to stir up unnecessary worry. The numbers are too low and not sufficiently supported by studies to justify an interstate outbreak alert, they say.

Cryptococcus mattesii spores enter the human bloodstream via the lungs and, after an incubation period of a few days, trigger a series of symptoms, beginning with a severe cough and severe pain in the chest area. Sufferers have increased mucus production in the nose and throat and severe nerve pain. This is later joined by shortness of breath, febrile seizures, weight loss, and headaches. The pathogen also attacks nerve cells and lymph nodes, causing swelling and lumps, mostly in the head and neck area. In severe cases, it may give rise to meningitis. *Cryptococcus mattesii* is also known to infect domesticated animals such as dogs, cats, and sheep. However, the fungus is not thought to transmit from person to person. So-called *cryptococcosis* is difficult to diagnose, but can be treated with antifungals.

Where the new fungus, which reproduces by cell division, has come from is not yet clear. Dr. Brouwers suspects that one cause could be climate change. The fungus from the tropics may have genetically recombined with its harmless relatives from temperate latitudes so that it is now able to survive in colder climates. So far, all tests of soil and water samples and tissue samples from infected domestic animals have been unsuccessful. Dr. Brouwers is currently working on sequencing the gene of the new fungus, which he hopes will shed light on the origin of the variant.

Researchers are alarmed. Does the pathogen come from the laboratory?
(11/29/2006, *The Oregonian*)

Since the summer of 2006, a mysterious fungal infection has been spreading in Oregon and threatening to cross state lines into Washington and California. Will we soon see the yeast

fungus variant, *Cryptococcus mattesii*, threatening humans all over America?

Portland—Initially, Dr. Abel Brouwers's research group at Boise State University in Idaho suspected that the origin of the deadly pathogen *Cryptococcus mattesii* lay in its ability to genetically recombine with more harmless variants. Now, studies of the fungus's gene sequences indicate that the mutation could not have arisen naturally. Dr. Brouwers is vocal about his suspicions. He believes the aggressive variant of the yeast fungus may have escaped from a laboratory. Since only one company in Oregon deals in microbiology, suspicion initially focused on the Portland-based Darwin Inc. group.

However, Darwin Inc. denies all accusations. The company has ruled out the possibility that the pathogen originated in one of its laboratories. In addition, it says, no research is undertaken at the Portland site on any fungus from the *Filobasidiaceae* family, to which *Cryptococcus mattesii* belongs.

The US Department of Agriculture, with which Darwin Inc. works closely, has also confirmed that Portland laboratories operate to the highest safety standards and that all biotech employees are required to undergo biannual safety briefings and routine physicals.

"There is no possibility of germs or genetically modified material getting out of the lab," a Darwin Inc. spokesman reassured people in Portland who live near the research facilities, and who expressed concerns in an open letter in yesterday's Sunday edition of *The Oregonian*. "Nonetheless, we will reassess and strengthen all safety measures," the spokesman promised. Darwin Inc. is also concerned, he said. Especially since it is clear the pathogen is now threatening to spread to California and Washington. A special unit was set up last month and is now working with microbiologists at Portland State University to identify the pathogen and where it may have come from. Some say this is just a diversionary tactic by the company to cover up a laboratory accident.

The biotech company with offshoots worldwide is of course known not only for its extensive research in the seed and herbicide sectors, but also for its aggressive approach to critics and its tactic of systematically buying out rival companies. Darwin Inc. maintains a number of laboratories in Portland and the surrounding area that produce genetically modified crop seeds. Plants are grafted with genetic sequences from other plants or bacteria to make them resistant to insect infestation, drought stress, or soil salinization, which Darwin Inc. says will be of great benefit to the future population of the earth and could solve the problem of world hunger in just a few years, when the research is complete.

Whether this is evidence of noble intentions or greed for profit and carelessness remains an open question. But after a health department investigation also found no evidence that the pathogen, which scientists have since named *Cryptococcus mattesii lethaliensis*, originated in Darwin Inc. laboratories, the biotech giant appears to have been exonerated.

Ondragon quickly typed a text message to Charlize:

Find out more about this Dr. Brouwers. Try to get in touch with him. I'm off to the mine now; keep your fingers crossed. Thanks—Paul

Then he turned off the phone and thought for a moment. Was this a lead? A vague picture was forming in his mind. But unfortunately it was fuzzy, and he would need more building blocks to fully understand it. Oregon—Haiti. He could literally smell the connection but couldn't get a grip on it to drag it into the light. He bit his lower lip. There had to be something in this mine in Haiti that was dangerous. That could be the only reason Darwin Inc. had commissioned someone to seal it. They had wanted to prevent it from getting out into the open at all costs. Could it be the deadly fungus?

Ondragon remembered Rod had said something about corn. Research on corn and soy. The fungus couldn't have anything to do with that, could it? But what could be so risky about corn that it had to be moved to a mine, far from the official laboratories? Ondragon thought of the symptoms Bolič had had just before he . . . well, before he died. Cough, fever, aching limbs. So maybe it was the fungus after all? Had the floater been infected? He had not been in Haiti. But Stern had been. Had he come into contact with a dangerous pathogen here in the mine? The mailmen had brought the bodies into the shaft before they had blown it up. They had touched the dead. What had the Darwin Inc. employees died of anyway? Had they actually been killed by falling debris, as he had previously assumed? Or had they been killed by something else? Ondragon thought it through. There had been nothing in the reports about the possible cause of death. But if Stern had been carrying the pathogen—or whatever—he could not possibly have infected Bolič. The two men had never met. Dammit, this was just too convoluted!

Ondragon turned to his two companions, who had now prepared the equipment. However, one item was still missing. He went quickly to his backpack and pulled out the gas mask.

The others looked at him questioningly.

"What's the matter with you? You're all pale around the nose." Rod stood and moved toward Ondragon.

"I think the lab down there has been researching a dangerous pathogen. Hence the seal. I got the info from Charlize. I'm not going in without a respirator! I don't feel like catching anything."

"Are you sure?"

"No, but I don't want to take any chances. Better have yours ready too." He pointed to the mask. "Is everything set?"

Rod nodded and held out the climbing harness. Ondragon slipped into it but first removed his bulletproof vest. It would only hinder him down there. He took his empty backpack and filled it with the things he would need: armor tape, a second flashlight, batteries, a water bottle, the sticks of dynamite, and the fuse extension. Then he put on the comms equipment. Fortunately, he had had Charlize get them throat mics. They worked well with a gas mask. He checked the connection to Rod.

"I hear you clearly, Ecks." The latter confirmed the reception.

"Well, I may stay down longer, keeping in constant contact. Either I'll find an existing entrance to the lab—which I don't think I will—or I'll lay the dynamite charges and come back up. Then we'll blast and I'll go back down."

"Isn't it risky to blast in the mine?" asked the Madame. "I mean, the shaft and passages could collapse."

"Indeed they could. But it's the only way to get into the lab."

The Madame nodded with obvious unease.

Ondragon, however, was under no illusion that she was worried about him. Even if he liked the idea of it. He shouldered the backpack. "And keep your eyes open; the machete guy is sneaking around here."

"Just let him show up here and we'll kill him!" Rod spat on the dusty floor.

Ondragon took the end of the rope that Rod had attached to the wooden beam with a tubular webbing and two counter-rotating carabiners, dropped it down into the shaft, and then threaded it twice through the belay device on his harness. Then he stood at the edge and adjusted his headlamp. Caving had always been a hobby of his. Besides, he was glad to get out of the sun. He looked down the shaft, which yawned blackly at him. He checked his equipment one last time. His knife was strapped to his lower leg and his pistol was in its holster. Then he pulled the gas mask down over his face, raised a thumb, and lowered himself into the abyss like a diver. With a jerk, the rope gripped, and he slowly rappelled down, his right hand on the safety loop. Foot after foot, he sank into the silent darkness of the mountain. His headlamp illuminated the rough-hewn shaft wall, where moisture seeped from countless small cracks and crevices and ran down the rock. The air grew cool, but remained damp. Cold sweat settled on his arms like a thin film.

After about 25 feet, he paused and tried to look down. The bottom of the shaft was somewhere, but Ondragon couldn't see it yet. Was the damn hole deeper than they had estimated after all? He lowered himself farther down. Only the scraping of the rope through the carabiners and the groaning of the mask's air filter reached his ears. Finally, his feet touched the bottom and he came to a stop. Quickly detaching himself from the rope, he spoke softly into the microphone:

"I'm down."

"Roger!" replied Rod through the receiver in his ear. The reception was still quite good down here. It remained to be seen how it behaved deeper in the mountain.

"I'm going to look around now." Ondragon swept the light about. Fortunately, there was only one passage leading into the mountain from the shaft. He breathed a sigh of relief. But just as he was about to crouch down, he heard a noise. A soft scrape.

He stopped.

Was there someone else down here? Or was it just rats and other critters? He pulled his pistol out of its holster and shone the light into the passage. The beam of light passed over damp rock and ancient garbage on the floor. But stop! What had that been? A piece of wood with cloth?

Ondragon returned the beam to the strange object.

It was a leg.

More specifically, two legs sticking out into the passage from a dirty skirt, only one of them was twice as thick as the other.

Another dead body?

Ondragon braced himself for another terrible sight and approached the body, which sat with its back against the wall.

When he shone the light into the corpse's face, she opened her eyes.

With a surprised cry, Ondragon drew back.

The girl also let out a shrill sound. She raised both arms defensively.

CHAPTER 28

February 16, 2010
Haiti, in the mine
10:48 am

Hey, what's going on down there? Ecks?" Ondragon heard Rod's voice barking almost painfully in his ear. That brought him back to himself.

"It's all right. I came across a kid here. Probably the one from the expedition. She's hurt." He watched as the girl rolled onto her stomach and tried desperately to pull herself across the floor, arms first, whimpering and screaming as if the devil was after her. It occurred to Ondragon that in the gas mask, he must look like a creature from hell. And the swollen leg seemed to be causing her unspeakable pain. She had probably broken it when she fell down the shaft.

Feverishly, Ondragon thought about what to do. Then he grabbed the screaming child and carried her to the shaft.

"I'm going to put the rope on the little girl now and you pull her up. Take care of her. She's broken her leg."

"Okay, will do," Rod replied.

Ondragon wound the rope around the girl's narrow ribcage; she had now lost consciousness and hung limply in his arms. He made a loop with a knot that would not tighten. Then he jerked the rope three times. Slowly, the girl floated up to the square of light, her arms hanging down and her head tilted forward.

"We've got her!" said Rod, snorting with effort.

"Good, let the Madame take care of her. I still need you to guard the shaft, Rod. I'm going to follow the passage into the mountain now. It leads right toward the Darwin compound, if I'm not mistaken."

"Roger, Ecks!"

Ondragon saw the rope being lowered back down to him and made his way back to the passageway, which was silent at last. He took a deep breath to focus on his upcoming task and then started moving.

The tunnel was low and he had to keep being careful not to bang his head on the rocks. He walked, hunched over, in the deceptive safety of the support beams, hoping to feel a draft. But there was none. So the shaft through which he had rappelled was the only exit for the moment. Not exactly reassuring.

In some places the passage was partially blocked, and regardless of whether it was the result of the recent earthquake or some long-gone rock fall, Ondragon had to scramble awkwardly over mountains of rubble. He hailed Rod at regular intervals. The reception was still okay.

Sweating, he worked his way forward and, pushing his backpack ahead of him, squeezed through the passage, which was just two feet high. The damn gas mask impaired his vision. Crawling on his stomach, he could barely see, but he was afraid to take it off.

There can't be any access to the lab from this side, he thought. *So the air here should be clean except for the shit from the bats. You could take the mask off.* He shook his head. No, better safe than sorry. He would keep the mask on, even if it was annoying him. He could do without being haunted by that helpless fear he had felt when he thought he was infected with anthrax.

At last, he reached the other side of the pile of rubble, crawled down, and straightened up. Breathing heavily, he shone his lamp into the passage in front of him, hearing the eerie creaking of his gas mask.

Like the eye in the center of a black hole, the hallway stared back—there was no light at the end of the tunnel.

How long would it be before he came to a fork in the road? Would he even get to the lab? Maybe there was no connection at all. He looked at his watch. He had been in the mountain for half an hour. He wondered if he was close to the blast site at the entrance.

Ondragon looked up as if he could see through the rock to the surface. Where was he? He shrugged his shoulders. He was relaxed, still. After all, he hadn't had much chance to get lost yet.

He put the backpack on and kept walking. After a few yards, his surroundings finally changed. The passage widened on all sides into a small vault, with small worm passages branching off in all directions, seemingly at random. Hole followed hole. The rock was perforated like a rat's burrow. Ondragon shone the light around. Reddish and black veins ran through the stone, and yellowish crystals glittered at him like thousands of tiny eyes.

This must be where they mined the ore, he thought, searching the maze of openings with the lamp for anything that looked like an exit. Diagonally to the right, a larger hole opened up. He marked the adit he had come from with a strip of armor tape on the rocky floor and stepped into the next one. Here, the ceiling had barely any support beams to secure it and the entire passage was more of a round shape. He clambered with difficulty through the funnel, which was getting narrower and narrower. Or did it just seem that way?

"Are you all right?" asked Rod's voice in his ear.

"Yeah, sure."

"You're groaning."

"It's pretty darn tight in here."

"Where are you?"

"Very funny!"

"All right. Let me know if you come across anything interesting. Over."

"Over."

Stooping, Ondragon stumbled on. Again and again he had to squeeze past debris that had fallen from the crumbling walls into the corridor. Hopefully, it wouldn't cave in even more behind him.

Then the passage suddenly came to an end.

Ondragon paused, staring at the even concrete wall that had been constructed vertically into the rock. He placed a hand on the light gray surface, which was shot through from floor to ceiling by a deep crack.

"I found it!" he said into the microphone.

"The la—tory?" asked Rod. Unfortunately, the transmission had begun to hiss and crackle badly.

"Yes, this must be it. There's a wall that clearly doesn't belong here."

"Di— you say a —all? I ca— —ear you. Please re—eat."

"A wall of concrete!" said Ondragon loudly into the mask. "I'll set the charges and come back up. The fuse won't reach the top, so I'll extend it as far as I can, then light it and run quickly to the shaft. You guys have to pull me up! Got it?"

"Ro—er. You d— t. We'll wai— oh —wa— s—" The connection failed. It was amazing it had lasted as long as it had.

In the silence that now ensued, Ondragon opened his backpack and took out the sticks of dynamite. He stuffed four sticks into the crack, which had probably been caused by the quake and was ideal for a detonation. Calmly, he lined the rest up at the base of the wall, connected all the detonating cords to the main cord, and covered the dynamite at the bottom with large stones, which he brought from the passageway, sweating and cursing. This took a whole hour, during which he became thirstier and thirstier. Unfortunately, he couldn't drink anything with the mask on his face. So he had to hold out until he got back to the top.

When he had finished his work, he quickly stuffed the rest of the equipment into his backpack and began his retreat, unrolling the red fuse from a small reel as he went. Hopefully, the concrete barrier would not be too massive. He would be extremely reluctant to have to crawl in again and set a second blast. It was impossible to say what weaknesses the rock might already have, fissures caused by the earthquake, which could lead a wall to collapse at any second. And the detonation would shake it all up again, making it more and more dangerous down here. It was suicidal to go in again anyway, he thought. Not only because of the impending collapse, but also because of the unknown risks from the lab. He trudged morosely on.

"Rod? I'm coming back to the shaft. Stand by," he told his friend through the mic, but got no response. Obviously, the radio was still down, although it had worked just fine at this point before. Frowning, Ondragon passed through the potholed vault and turned into the large tunnel he had marked. The reel was already half empty. Hopefully, the line would at least reach beyond the narrow section.

Of course it didn't!

"Fuck, I knew it!" he grumbled loudly, taking off his backpack. There had been 75 yards of fuse on the roll. Not enough. But at least now he knew how far it was from here to the concrete wall. He put the end of the fuse under a rock and took out his storm lighter.

"Hello up there? Rod, if you can hear me, I'm lighting the fuse now!"

Silence.

Dammit, why wasn't anyone responding? Ondragon wondered if it would be better not to ignite until he made contact with his friend. But who knew how much time they would lose in the process. And the radio might not be working at all. He could go to the shaft and call up. But then he'd have to squeeze through that crappy passageway two more times. Did he feel like doing that? No!

He calculated the time there would be to the explosion based on the length of the fuse. It had been a while since he had worked with explosives of this type, but he thought he remembered that the red cord, which was the fast one—dammit, why had they brought the fast one?—burned at one second per inch; 75 yards was 2,700 inches, so he had 45 minutes to get from here to the shaft and up the rope. That was close, but doable.

Anxious, he breathed out and then tried Rod again. Again unsuccessfully. What the hell? He flicked on the lighter, pressed a button on his watch, and after a moment's hesitation, put the yellow flame to the fuse, which immediately began to burn like a sparkler.

No risk, no fun! Ondragon threw himself, backpack first, up the pile of rubble. Panting, he squeezed through the narrow gap between the ceiling and the rubble, which took him a full seven minutes. Arms bruised and knees battered, he leaped up at the other end and hurried on until he finally dove into the bright column of light from the shaft.

He took the rope and threaded it into the harness. Then he raised his head.

"Hey!" he shouted into the mic. "Get me out of here!"

He waited for an answer, but nothing came. Why the hell wasn't the radio working? Impatiently, he tore the gas mask off his face and yelled up at the top of his lungs.

"Rod? Mari-Jeanne? Helloooo! Get me the hell up! The charges are about to go off!"

A shadow appeared at the opening. Then the rope tightened and he was lifted up.

Once at the top, Rod helped him pull himself over the edge of the shaft. Panting, Ondragon rolled onto his back and looked at the stopwatch. Thirty-seven minutes! He dropped his arm and stared for a moment into the bright neon blue of the sky.

Only a few breaths later, he felt the vibrations of the explosion in the ground beneath his body. A rumble went through the mountain, as if it had digestive problems, and then it went quiet again. He had miscalculated by a few minutes after all!

"By Saint Barbara, that was close!" said Rod.

Ondragon sat up and looked over at the shaft, from which a yellowish cloud of dust was rising like smoke signals.

"What was going on with the radio?" inquired Rod.

Ondragon shrugged. "Bad reception. Must be too much rock down there blocking the radio waves. Where's the Madame?"

"She's with the little one behind that knoll." Rod pointed to a cone of rubble. "Mari-Jeanne gave her painkillers and antibiotics and splinted her leg. It looked nasty."

"What, you broke into our emergency kit?"

"Man, yeah! Should we just have left her like that?"

Ondragon made a dismissive gesture. "So, is it the girl from the expedition group?"

"Probably," Rod replied with a twinkle in his eye.

Ondragon squinted over at the fly-ridden corpse of the woman, which was fortunately far enough away for them not to detect the smell of decay. At some distance, however, the vultures were once again waiting with their characteristic patience for the pale-skinned troublemakers to finally leave them alone with their feast.

"Then that was her mother. Whoever broke her neck, the machete guy or—"

As if on cue, their conversation was suddenly interrupted by a distant howl.

Rod's head wheeled around as if he had been slapped in the face. His eyes probed the terrain like searchlights.

Ondragon jumped to his feet as if he had been fired from a catapult and was at his friend's side in the blink of an eye.

"What was that?" a voice called out behind them. The Madame's head popped up over the rubble cone, looking around equally worriedly.

"Same howler as last night, I guess," Rod replied in a tone full of foreboding, reaching for his pistol.

Another moan floated over to them. This time all three looked in the same direction: toward the edge of the forest, which rose like a living green wall not 50 yards away.

"There!" Rod pointed like a sailor sighting land. "Over there by that fallen log. A shadow. I saw it right there!" There was a flicker in his ice-blue eyes. Was it fear?

Ondragon shielded his eyes with one hand and stared at the place, where nothing was moving.

"I saw it too," whispered the Madame in an anxious voice. "It looked like a thin man."

"Our zombie friend." Rod looked from the edge of the forest to Ondragon, who let out an exasperated sigh.

"A zombie, of course!" he repeated sarcastically, looking at his watch. They didn't have time for this nonsense. He would go back to the mine now and do his job, no matter what was crawling through the bushes there!

"Keep an eye on the shadow. Rod, secure the rope, I'm going back in. Because I want to be out of this fucking country by tomorrow!" He paid no attention to the Madame's disapproving snort and turned back to the shaft, where he threaded the rope back into his harness.

"So what are we going to do without a radio?" wanted Rod to know.

Ondragon fumbled the transmitter out of his ear and tossed it away. "We can manage without it. I have a new schedule for you that works without a radio. Here's what we're going to do: I've got three hours to look around down there. If I'm not back here in three and a half at the latest, then you go back to the boat without me. Got it?"

"But—"

"Is that clear?" he interrupted. He didn't have the energy to argue. "Sure!" Rod said, a hard expression on his face, and ran his right hand through his white hair. A gesture of embarrassment; Ondragon had seen it before. "We'll go without you, Ecks."

Somehow, he didn't believe his friend, and that made him glad rather than unhappy. Despite everything, he did not want to put him in danger. So he insisted that Rod swore by the Russian bullet in his left shoulder blade that he wouldn't go looking for him.

"Man, Ecks! Leave off the Boy Scout nonsense. I'll do as you say, okay?"

"Good. Now can I have another drink?" Ondragon smiled wryly and accepted the water bottle Rod handed him. He took a long drink and handed it back to the Brit along with his pack of gum. "Just so you don't get bored up here. See ya!"

He lowered himself smoothly down the shaft and reached the floor, where he put on his gas mask again and switched on his head-lamp. The small delay caused by the howler had at least achieved one good thing, he thought; the dust from the explosion had largely settled.

A little more skillfully than before, he moved through the passage to the vault. Fresh boulders had fallen from the ceiling, and in front of the entrance to the vault there was now an enormous stone, almost the height of a man. Ondragon examined the passageway and found that although he could fit through the narrow gap, the walls were very unstable and might come down with any tremor, blocking the opening for good. So he was in danger of being trapped down here forever if he passed this point. He did not have much hope of find-ing another exit, even though he still had some dynamite he could use to blast his way out. But there was always the risk he would bury himself.

Despite all his misgivings, Ondragon eventually wormed his way past the boulder into the vault of holes and a short time later slipped into the tunnel-like passage to the lab. He squeezed carefully through the unsupported funnel, past fallen rocks, and soon came to the spot where, in place of the concrete wall, a large hole now yawned in the rock above a waist-high pile of rubble. Beyond, there was darkness.

Ondragon approached the hole and shone his light into it. Dust danced in the bright glow of his lamp, and as if he were looking into another world, a sterile-looking corridor opened up before him, with doors leading off to the left and right. The laboratory!

CHAPTER 29

February 16, 2010
Haiti, in the mine

The Darwin Inc. laboratory! The breeding ground of evil!

Ondragon checked the fit of his gas mask once more and crawled through the hole to the other side, where he could comfortably stand up in the corridor. Bracing himself for anything, but also with uncontrollably growing curiosity, Ondragon shone the beam of his lamp over the whitewashed hallway. He saw seven locked steel doors with small windows, four on the left, three on the right. An eighth lay at the end of the corridor.

Ondragon illuminated the signs next to the doors: OFFICE, ARCHIVE/STORAGE, KITCHEN/CANTEEN, LAB III, STAIRCASE/EXIT, LAB I, LAB II, GREENHOUSE.

When he reached the other end of the corridor, he first opened the entrance to the stairwell. It opened into another small room with an even more massive red steel door, with clear dents on the inside. He tried to open it. But he could only move it a tiny crack, because something heavy was blocking the way on the other side. Ondragon shone his light into the crack and saw dusty chunks of rock piled up to the ceiling. This must have been the shaft the mailmen had blown up and sealed. No chance of getting up there. Ondragon let go of the door and turned to the next one. Lab I. There were several warning signs under the viewing window, but no biohazard symbol.

He depressed the handle, went into the dark room behind the door, and looked around. It was the typical laboratory setup. Steel shelves full of glass containers, computer monitors, microscopes, and other technical equipment, tiled tables with aluminum foil–covered bowls and vials on them, cabinets with and without glass doors, containing petri dishes and more bottles made of brown and white glass, pipettes, tweezers, and other utensils. Except that everything seemed to have been mixed around by the earthquake. Some of the furniture had been shifted around and broken. Unidentifiable liquids had leaked from broken containers and had mixed together on the floor to form a pool, which, however, had long since dried up and glistened crystalline at the edges.

The walls of the lab were riddled with fresh cracks. Concrete dust had trickled out of them. Light boxes like those from an old-fashioned X-ray clinic hung askew next to whiteboards covered in formulae and hung with pictures of helix models and sequenced vertical bar codes. Ondragon took a closer look at the codes in the pictures. The uneven light and dark stripes were flanked by every conceivable combination of the letters A C G T, which, he remembered from biology class, stood for the four nucleobases of DNA. But that was as far as his modest knowledge of genetics went, and unfortunately he couldn't find anything that would help him understand what exactly they had been researching here. He couldn't decipher the cryptic notes on the whiteboard, and identifying an organism from its gene sequence was not part of his somewhat extensive repertoire of skills.

He shone his light into the beakers on one of the tables, into which someone had portioned out a yellowish powder. The label on a plastic spray bottle next to it read AQUA DEST.

Ondragon went back to one of the whiteboards, took some photos with a small camera he had brought with him, and then pulled one of the sequencing papers, titled DWIN 411-Crypt, from under a magnet. He folded up the paper and put it in one of the side pockets of his pants.

Then he left the uninstructive lab and stopped for a moment in front of the next door marked Lab II. Ominously, the yellow triangle with the biohazard symbol glowed in the light of his headlamp. He stared at it a long time until his gaze was drawn to an irregularity in the overall structure, a flaw in the picture. Five brownish stripes had been smeared on the inside of a warning sign above the small window, which was crisscrossed with security wire.

Blood, his instincts told him, and he pulled his gun from its holster, even though there was little chance anyone was still alive down here. The quake had been over a month ago, and even if the lab workers had supplies, they couldn't have lasted forever. How many people might have worked in the lab? The mailmen had brought four dead employees into the shaft.

Prepared for the worst, Ondragon opened the door with one hand. In an airlock beyond hung yellow hazmat suits with large face masks, which stared back at him like cyclops eyes. He snapped a few pictures and turned around. The rusty brown stripes ran down the inside of the door, from the window to the handle, where there were two handprints. Someone must have tried to open it. The only question was, where was that someone now? Still in Lab II, or somewhere else in this underground facility? Ondragon moved to the nearest door, which also had a viewing window, and peered through. His breath caught in his mask and his hand froze on the knob.

In a second airlock lay two bodies.

A man and a woman with disheveled dark hair. Two Caucasians. At least that's what he thought he made out in the glaring, reflective light of his lamp, because the dead people's skin was pale in color, like white sausage. Like bulging white sausage. Lumps the size of chickens' eggs were bulging out all over the heads and necks of the bloated corpses. They looked as if they had been caught in a swarm of killer hornets.

Gently, Ondragon withdrew his hand from the knob. He would not enter this room and the adjacent security area, no matter how much he was itching to; he was simply not equipped for it. He had already exposed himself to far too much risk. What if the pathogen that had obviously broken out here didn't just enter the human body via the respiratory tract?

Panic glowed at the back of his mind, as bright and hot as a signal rocket, but he quickly extinguished its ominous heat with the thick foam of reason and retreated out of the first airlock into the corridor. Having closed the door behind him, he turned to his right.

Stay calm! It is not yet clear what killed the Darwin Inc. people. It could have been something other than a deadly pathogen. To distract himself, he read the next sign: GREENHOUSE. What might lie behind this door? Ondragon took a deep breath under his mask and let the door swing open. Pointing the pistol in front of him, he submerged himself one step at a time in the sultry darkness, which immediately caused sweat to break out from his pores.

Again, he entered a kind of airlock, four times the size of the previous one. It was equipped with several large basins with faucets, a long yellow hose hanging carefully coiled on a wall bracket, and a large stainless steel table on which lay a stack of transparent plastic bags and something like a large sugar scoop next to a scale and a clipboard. On the opposite side, two silent refrigerators kept company with a behemoth of a steel cupboard that was almost certainly a drying cabinet. Ondragon had seen something like it in Dr. Strangelove's home lab.

First, he took a look inside the refrigeration units, which had been without power for a month. Plastic containers, carefully lined up and labeled with illegible abbreviations, containing dark, moldy lumps, peered out at him. Probably samples.

Only—samples of what?

He went over to the hefty drying cabinet and pulled the doors open. Tin trays stood neatly aligned on steel grates. In each of the trays were handfuls of yellow, brown, and reddish kernels. Corn, apparently.

Corn.

Ondragon remembered the article on Darwin Inc.'s genetic corn. DWIN 411! Not ten minutes ago he had put a reference to it in his pocket without noticing. He pulled out the paper and unfolded it. DWIN 411-Crypt. What kind of corn could this be? At any rate, it must be so secret that it was being researched here in a hermetically sealed high-security unit far away from the country. Secret or dangerous?

Probably both.

Ondragon put the picture with the gene sequence back in his pocket, took photos of the room, and moved over to the sliding door leading to another dark area; the glass had cracked into a spider's web of lines. He pushed open the door, which had no warning sign, and found himself in an underground forest.

A forest of corn plants.

Fascinated, he looked around. The room was huge. Not particularly high, but it extended an estimated 30 yards into the mountain. UV lamps and power lines hung at regular intervals from the rough-hewn rock ceiling, and an irrigation system of black hoses ran through the entire room like a net. The whole thing was an underground greenhouse with artificial sunlight and a sprinkler system. Ondragon was amazed. The old silver mine was more extensive than he would have thought, and Darwin Inc. had apparently spared no expense or effort in creating a high-tech research facility here. It all must have cost millions of dollars! Millions of dollars; an investment that must have been worth it from Darwin Inc.'s point of view, because otherwise they would never have gone to so much trouble.

The Madame had probably been right when she claimed a project of this size could not possibly go unnoticed by the leaders of this island nation. The Haitian authorities must have known about it, and he could vividly imagine that they had been only too happy to accept the suitcase of hush money from the American biotech company.

He continued his intensive search for clues, roaming the tall rows of corn that had been growing in individual tubs, and snapping pictures. Unfortunately, the perennials had now withered and looked like scrawny, bony skeletons. Their yellowed leaves drooped and rustled as he ran a hand over them. Only the ripe cobs were protruding from the plant stems, like admonishing forefingers. Ondragon broke one off and peeled away the carpels. The corn kernels curled around the cob, a haphazard mix of yellow and red.

Ondragon had seen them in Mexican restaurants, where they were often used as decoration.

But you've seen corn like that somewhere else too— just recently! Something flashed briefly across his memory. *Think hard. Where had that been?* He felt it pounding within him. He had come across this kind of colorful grain not too long ago. Only where, dammit? In Tucson at the Hotel Congress? They had decorated their entrance hall with all sorts of Mexican-Indian kitsch. Or had it been in the Madame's voodoo store?

The epiphany just wouldn't come, so Ondragon brushed aside the spasmodic twitching of his *centrifuge*. It probably had nothing to do with the Darwin Inc. case anyway. He tossed the corn cob into the flowerpot and took a closer look at some of the tags attached to the containers.

DWIN 411-CRYPT C034, DWIN 411-CRYPT C035, DWIN 411-CRYPT C036. They were obviously consecutive numbers. But what was DWIN 411-Crypt all about? What could this plant do? What made it so special that it was being cultivated here in secret?

He himself would probably never find an answer to these questions down here. Only a genetic engineering expert would be any good with these plants and the experiments linked to them. So he would have to collect some material and have it examined later.

Quickly, Ondragon left the greenhouse and headed for the door marked OFFICE, where he hoped to find better and more transportable evidence. A USB stick, for example. Or CDs. He entered the office, which had several desks with computers, an open file cabinet, and NO bookcase!

He breathed a sigh of relief and began to look through the drawers. Curiously, they were all open and had been rummaged through. On the floor in front of them was a jumble of notes and writing implements. He turned around. The filing cabinet did not contain any electronic storage media either. It was as if someone had systematically combed through everything in the room.

Ondragon pondered, staring at a crack in the ceiling. Removing the entire hard drive from the computer would take too long. Besides, there were over a dozen computers in the lab area, and he wasn't sure which one had the relevant data.

Going through the filing cabinet one more time, he found a folder with the company logo and the words *DWIN 411-Crypt/ C-Class/ Lab III/ Hum. Exprmt.* He flipped through it briefly, took off his backpack, and stuffed the folder and another one labeled *Weedsweep II* inside. Then he left the office and went to the archive room next door, the back wall of which was covered by a huge apothecary cabinet with countless drawers. Here, too, some of the drawers stood open. They seemed to be mocking him, sticking out their tongues and shouting, "You're late!"

Ondragon looked into the compartments. They were filled with small transparent bags. However, these were welded shut, had adhesive labels, and were arranged according to a system. Again, the DWIN 411-Crypt designation was everywhere. Ondragon fished out three of the bags and looked at them. Red and yellow corn kernels, always twelve in number, were loosely packed inside. He put the bags in his pocket and looked at his watch. He still had an hour and a half left. So he had enough time to examine the last two rooms.

Entering the canteen, he recoiled abruptly.

The room looked more like a slaughterhouse than a common room.

Along one wall was a sink, an overturned refrigerator, and several cabinets with china that had fallen out and broken, and in the center of the room was a row of tables and chairs. All around, the walls, linoleum floor, and furniture were adorned with grotesque patterns of dried blood. There were even splatters on the ceiling.

The cold light of the headlamp slid over the hulking forms of three bloated corpses scattered around the room. Ondragon grimaced in disgust, glad he could not smell anything through his mask. He turned to his right and looked at the first corpse, a woman with blonde hair, who was sitting right next to him with her eyes open and her back leaning against the wall, her legs stretched out in front of her. Strands of hair hung down her face, and her dried eyeballs gleamed yellow from beneath long, dark lashes. Her teeth were bared in an unnaturally wide grimace: an impression created only by the retraction of the withered lips far above the teeth.

Ondragon stepped closer to the woman and saw that her hands with their painted nails were clenched around an object sticking out of her chest. A delicate trickle of dried blood had seeped from under the hands, staining the fabric of her blouse red. A shiny scalpel handle flashed metallic between her fingers. The surgical instrument must have been rammed into her chest with such brutal force that she had died instantly, or more blood would have oozed from the wound.

Ondragon took two pictures. The flash bounced coldly off the woman's deathly stiff face.

Then he straightened up again and looked at the two other corpses, which were lying face down on the floor as if they had stumbled over each other in headlong flight. Large brown rosettes blossomed on their snow-white lab coats like coffee stains on a tablecloth at a cake buffet. The thick, whitish neck of the man lying on top was adorned with a black-rimmed wound. It almost looked as if someone had torn a piece of flesh from his neck. A large dark pool had formed under him on the other man. Presumably his carotid artery had been shredded.

Ondragon took a photo of the gruesome pair. The flash flickered once over their bodies. Twice. Suddenly, he froze. What was that?

In the light of the flash, he saw something he hadn't noticed before. He shone the lamp at it. Bare footprints led away from the large pool of blood.

Ondragon's hackles rose as he wheeled around, following the tracks with the lamp. They disappeared through the door he had just come through. He raised his gun. His breathing was rapid and the skin around his head had tightened into a cold shell. Everything about him was on high alert. His thoughts too were racing through the convolutions of his brain at the speed of sound, trying to reconstruct what had happened here.

Someone must have gone into a rage and killed all his colleagues. But which of the lab rats had done it? And why? Had he become hysterical after the quake and gone crazy because they were locked up down here? According to the mailmen's reports, the entrance to the lab had been clear of debris, but the stairs had collapsed. So the staff had been stuck here when the massacre happened. And what about the four Darwin Inc. employees on the surface? Had they been surprised and killed by the quake? And where had the dead even been when the mailmen had removed them?

"Holy shit!" Ondragon said under the mask. For the umpteenth time, he wished the reports had included more information about the dead on the surface. So he had no choice but to speculate. And he hated speculating. But there was not the slightest clue. Nor had there been anything out of the ordinary in the accommodation containers on the surface. No blood, no traces of a struggle. And there had been no signs of anything other than an earthquake at the site. He was literally in the dark!

And that made him furious.

It was as if a higher power was challenging him to a duel. The Queen of All Secrets was mocking him. He could not stand for that. He had to win this duel!

With a grim face and his weapon raised, he left the horrific scene in the canteen and followed the footsteps.

They led to the final door.

They went in, but not out.

He hadn't even noticed that earlier because he had been focusing on the signs. The killer must still be in Lab III.

Carefully, Ondragon turned the knob and pushed the door open in a wide arc. For a moment, he aimed the pistol into the room.

Nothing stirred in the white beam of his lamp.

His hearing attuned to the slightest sound, he entered the third lab, where chaos reigned. Shelves were overturned, and clear plastic boxes lay all over the floor, with light-colored litter trickling out of them. Among the boxes, Ondragon found empty water dispensers, food bowls filled with corn kernels, and numerous small, caved-in carcasses with white fur and long pink tails.

Lab rats.

Ondragon picked up a container and read the label. *RATTUS NOR-VEGICUS*/RTS44 - CRYPT-CLASS III. According to this, they had also been experimenting on animals down here. Rats had probably been fed the GM corn to see if it was suitable for human consumption. Nothing out of the ordinary. Except for the fact that some of the congealed bodies had dried blood on their mouths and fur. Others had their heads bent back so far in hellish agony that it looked as if they were trying to bite their own spines.

He documented the chaos with his camera and then made his way through the fallen boxes. Pointing his headlamp at the floor, he pushed aside a dead rat here and there with the tip of his foot and followed the increasingly faint footprints until he finally reached another room in which six large cages were lined up on the left side. In them lay lifeless gray balls of fur.

Rhesus monkeys, Ondragon thought. Their little withered hands had clung to the bars in unimaginable agony—dying of thirst and starvation in a deadly trap. Just as the lab staff had been trapped. What an ironic twist of fate!

Only with one difference.

Among the humans, there had been one who had gone insane and in a bestial frenzy had slaughtered all his fellow humans. Well, not all, because the two corpses in Lab II had almost certainly been killed by a malignant pathogen, which, Ondragon hoped, had at least only reached the airlock and not any farther.

He searched the floor for the bloody trail, which was faint but clearly led to one of three passageways sealed with what looked like prison doors, massive and with a locked viewing window at the top. To the left of each door frame was a small box with buttons and defunct indicator lights. Electronic locks, in other words. They had undoubtedly just popped open after the power failure triggered by the quake.

But what was behind them? What kind of laboratory animal had been fed the corn there?

A terrible foreboding was rising in Ondragon. He looked at the doors. Numbers one and two were only ajar. Number three, into which the bloody barefoot track disappeared, was locked. Ondragon felt his innermost being shying away from the foreboding that was pushing ever more strongly into his consciousness. This was . . .

His fingers gripped the cold metal of the sliding shield in front of the viewing window number three. He could hear his breath rattling and groaning in the mask. *The filter won't last too much longer,* he thought.

Besides, it's high time you got out of here if you don't want Rod and the Madame to leave without you. So hurry up!

With a quick jerk, he pulled the guard aside and let the beam of light from his lamp slant into the small room on the other side. It illuminated the interior of a cell that was perhaps four by four paces and painted a sterile white. On a cot across from him lay a man in a fetal position, his back to the door, the bare soles of his feet smeared with rust-red blood. He was clearly of dark complexion, though the ebony hue had turned a muddy gray. Stained and in some places torn clothing hung around his emaciated body. The figure lay there silently, and Ondragon could not tell whether it was a man or a woman.

Was it dead like everyone else down here?

He would have to go into the cell to find out. He sighed. Of course he would, because he still had to win his duel with the Queen of All Secrets!

Cautiously, he depressed the door handle. Without a sound, number three swung open, revealing a full view of the cell interior. A stainless steel sink and toilet in the front left corner completed the Spartan furnishings.

On silent feet and his nerves stretched to breaking point, Ondragon crept toward the figure, pistol at the ready. He expected the scrawny body to spring up and attack him at almost any moment.

But he did nothing of the sort. He lay there motionless like an oversized, mummified baby.

Ondragon finally prodded the figure's lean back with the barrel of his weapon. The backbone protruded from it like the spines of a primordial lizard.

Nothing happened.

He nudged the figure again, and when it still did not move, Ondragon turned it over. He was a little surprised to be looking into the emaciated face of a Haitian of indeterminate age. His broad cheekbones jutted out like shields, making the eye sockets appear even deeper. The man had closed his eyelids and twisted his lips into an almost beatific smile. Blood covered his chin and chest. And pale skin stretched around his skull, which, like his neck, was covered with bumps. It almost looked as if the bubonic plague had returned.

Ondragon took out the camera and snapped a few pictures.

The flashes bounced brightly off the walls, off the corpse, off the dried blood.

Without warning, Ondragon was seized by horror, and he staggered back. He had managed to suppress it up to this point, but now it leaped at him like a dervish, breaking his spell of self-control, and tore down all the walls. Nausea hit him in the stomach like a battering ram, and Ondragon let out a groan. Tingling, the disgust continued to rise up his throat and crawled over the roof of his mouth.

Don't throw up in the mask!

Pressing both hands to his stomach, he forced his out-of-control vegetative functions to calm down again. *Shh, quiet. Shh, shh.*

Gradually, his breathing slowed again. But he still had the feeling he was suffocating. *You're probably getting too little air under the mask and suffering from oxygen deprivation. That causes hallucinations.*

But the dead man on the cot in front of him was not a hallucination. He was real, as was the inhuman crime that had been committed down here. Ondragon overcame the nausea and quickly left the cell. He didn't even want to see what was in the other two dungeons.

His footsteps echoed loudly off the walls of the corridor as he ran to the hole in the rear of the facility. Fixing his thoughts on only one thing, he slipped through and stumbled down the narrow tunnel until he reached the rock vault with the holes. He stopped by the large boulder that had fallen from the ceiling and blocked most of the passage to the tunnel beyond.

He had to close off access to this laboratory of horror forever!

Groping around, he examined the rocks above the fresh demolition site. They were brittle, and small stones trickled out of the wide cracks at the slightest touch. Without hesitation, Ondragon snatched off his backpack and took out the remaining dynamite. There were three sticks left. Enough to seal the passage but too short a fuse. He would have to build himself a MacGyver gadget.

Ondragon glanced at the clock and cursed. Thirty more minutes until Rod and the Madame would be on their way! He rummaged hastily for the armor tape, tore a strip from the roll, and wrapped it around all three sticks of dynamite. Then he pulled the fuses from two of the sticks and connected them into one long string with the third. He squeezed the dynamite packet into a crack in the wall just below the crumbling blast site and pulled the cord into the passage as far as it would go. Once again, he rummaged in the backpack and unearthed a cardboard box from a side compartment. The Esbit sticks for the camp stove. He unwrapped them all and laid them on the floor like a row of toppled dominoes to extend the fuse up the passageway to one of the support beams. He looked back. Now he had three feet of fuse and about the same amount of Esbit. Still not enough! Ondragon reached for the armor tape again and twisted a piece into a rope several feet long. He threaded this between the gallery ceiling and the wooden beam lying across it, so that both ends hung down. To one end he attached his plastic water bottle and to the other a rock of about the same weight. He suspended both of them three finger widths above the ground. Then he flicked on his storm lighter and placed it at the end of the Esbit trail just below the hanging stone. He lowered it on a trial basis and realigned the lighter once again. Yes, that might work.

He quickly shoved everything back into the backpack and pulled out his knife. With the tip, he poked a small hole in the bottom of the bottle, and immediately small drops of water began to spill out of it. Drop by drop, the bottle would get lighter and lighter, and at a certain point it would no longer be able to hold the counterweight of the stone at the other end. The stone would descend and knock over the lighter. Right onto the Esbit trail. The fire would eat its way along the trail and reach the fuse. And then: BANG!

Hopefully.

Ondragon turned around and took to his heels. Holding his backpack tightly in his fist, he stumbled through the tunnel toward the rescue shaft. Hastily, he climbed up the pile of boulders to the passage and crawled into the crevice. Something tugged at his sweaty T-shirt. The fabric at the back must have gotten caught in a lug of rock on the ceiling. Trying to untie it, he tore his right forearm on a sharp-edged rock and gave a muffled curse under his mask. Hell, had the gap narrowed? Ondragon squirmed back and forth until the rock hook finally released him. Quickly, he crawled on. He was getting less and less air under the damned gas mask. He was already woozy. With all his might and despite his obscured vision, he pushed the backpack through the bottleneck. Headfirst, he slid down the pile of boulders and stood up. Crouching down, he continued his flight through the tunnel, sometimes on two legs, sometimes with his hands stretched out like a gorilla on speed. Time and again he was delayed by rubble and debris, losing precious seconds. The white glow of his headlamp danced ahead of him like a will-o'-the-wisp, as if taunting him. But then he finally saw a pale light at the end of the tunnel and soon he was looking up, dazzled, at the blessed opening.

He threaded the climbing rope through his harness, pulled his mask off his face, and roared as loudly as he could up to the glaring square, where a head instantly appeared.

"Hang on, Ecks! We'll pull you up!" shouted Rod from above.

Immediately, the rope tightened and bit by bit Ondragon was lifted into the air.

Thank God!

The explosive charge detonated as he hung halfway down the shaft. A tremor went through the air and a rumbling sound came from the rocks around him, as if the mountain was growling at him for daring to injure it again. Stones came loose from the shaft wall and fell down on him. Then a cloud of dust rose from below, enveloping him. Ondragon kept his eyes closed and clung to the rope.

"Pull!" he shouted through the mist and the taste of stone. "Keep pulling!"

When he finally got a grip on the lip of the shaft and heaved himself out, the tropical sultry air, thick as syrup in his dust-powdered nose, was the sweetest thing he had ever breathed.

CHAPTER 30

February 16, 2010
Haiti, at the surface
4:20 pm

Did you find anything useful?" asked Rod, helping Ondragon to his feet.

He had to get his whirring vision under control before he answered. He rubbed the dust from his eyes with his hand and nodded.

"So, now do you know why my mailmen disappeared?" Rod stuck to his guns.

Ondragon took a big gulp from a new water bottle and let out a satisfied sigh. He screwed the top back on the bottle and blinked at his friend. "I think I've gotten some idea of what's been going on down there. It doesn't have much to do with the disappearance of your men though, I'm afraid. That's another site."

Rod looked at him uncomprehendingly.

Ondragon put a hand on the Briton's shoulder. "Later, my friend, later. First, I need to think about it some more. Jumping to conclusions won't help." He pulled his cell phone out of his pocket and found that the screen was cracked. Hell, this was the second phone he'd smashed during this case. He turned it on. Unfortunately, no message from Charlize. Just the unknown caller who had tried to reach him three more times.

"So what do we do now? What does the schedule look like?" Rod wanted to know.

"We get out of here," Ondragon put the iPhone away and looked up at the sun. "There's still an hour until sunset. We can make it over the ridge by then. After that, another two to three hours' march to the coast and then"—he made a motion with the flat of his hand—"the fish swim free! Jamaica, put the cocktails on ice!"

Rod grinned and tossed Ondragon the gum; he popped a stick into his mouth. "Tell the Madame we're going. And clear out your packs. You can leave the excess gear here." Rod nodded and trudged over the rubble cone to the Madame while Ondragon repacked. Except for the folders, the bags of corn kernels, the camera, the ammunition, his water supply, and some food, he got rid of everything else. He lifted the backpack appraisingly. It was nowhere near as heavy as it had been on the way there.

Ondragon tipped his head back. Oh, how he longed for a shower and a cold beer! He strapped the luggage to his back and reached for his rifle. Three more hours, four at the most, and they'd be on the boat. And tomorrow morning they'd be on Rod's plane, heading for the Big Easy.

"Hey, Ecks! Can you come over here?" His friend's voice snapped him out of his glorious daydream of freshly made beds and iced drinks.

"What is it?" He climbed over the mound of rubble and looked down at Rod and the Madame, who were kneeling beside the parched body of the little girl.

Shit, he had forgotten all about her!

He jumped down the pile of rubble, preparing himself mentally for an argument. He knew what the Madame wanted. But he would not let that happen under any circumstances! This was his operation and he was in charge!

"I will not leave without this child!" the Madame flung at him determinedly as he reached them. As he had suspected, her opinion was already entrenched.

Ondragon jutted out his chin and said. "She stays here!"

"But you can't just leave the child like that!"

"She stays! And if you can't accept that, madame, then you stay too! We are not a charity."

The Madame jumped up with hate on her face. "What kind of a person are you? You refuse to help a child?"

He looked hard into her black eyes. "Indeed I do! I sacrifice this child's life so that she will not put ours in danger! Is that so hard to understand?"

"You sacrifice the child? *Sacré bleu*, I don't believe it! *You* were the one who saved her! Why did you bring her out of the shaft, if you're just going to let her die here?" The Madame had both hands on her hips. "You, Monsieur Ondragon, saved the girl, so she is your responsibility! And since you brought her up to us, that responsibility now rests with us as well. Do you understand?"

Ondragon looked at her furiously. She had actually managed to turn his argument into one with himself. That was very clever of her. And it was foolish of him to believe she could simply switch off her conscience like an old bedside lamp. Of course, the Madame was right. Again. And that annoyed him. Usually, he was the one who was right. He was absolutely not used to someone beating him to the punch when it came to logic. He clenched his teeth and tried to swallow his anger.

"Ecks, she's right."

Annoyed, Ondragon turned to his friend and hissed, "I know that!"

"We can just take the girl to the village. It's not much of a detour." Rod looked at the girl pityingly.

"But I don't want to take her to the village!" said the Madame.

"You don't? Oh, and where do you want to take her, then, may I ask? To a five-star resort?" Ondragon inquired ironically.

The Madame took a deep breath. "In the village, she will die. She doesn't have her parents now. Her father is a zombie and her mother is lying over there with a broken neck. She is an orphan in a desperately poor country and she is injured! She needs urgent medical care." Her pupils bored into his. "We'll take her with us to New Orleans. *I'll* take her!"

Ondragon let out an incredulous laugh. "And how do you imagine that will work?"

"I will adopt her, so to speak. And you, Monsieur Ondragon, will be her godfather. You will get her new papers showing that she's my biological daughter! You can do that. It's easy for you. And after that, you need have nothing more to do with it, I promise!"

Oh man! The woman was really good. Good, in the sense of damn convincing.

Without taking his eyes off her, he pursed his lips. His anger had faded, but he still couldn't bring himself to give in just like that. It wasn't in his nature. His nature as a *commander*. Although he had to admit the Madame had come up with a good plan. And she was right. It would indeed be no problem for him to procure a new identity for the girl. Nor would it be difficult to smuggle her into the US on Rod's private plane. Easiest thing in the world for him. Almost ridiculously easy. One question remained, however.

"And how do we get her to the coast in that condition?"

The Madame puffed out her chest confidently and crossed her arms. Her burning gaze did not leave his face for a moment. It was a staring context of the highest order.

The no-miracle realist against the Voodoo Queen!

He wondered who would win.

"It's simple. I'll carry her!" the Madame finally said.

She would? Ondragon continued to stare at her. His gaze did not leave her face either. He could very happily continue like that for hours.

But the Madame showed no sign of giving in. Effortlessly, she withstood his razor-sharp gaze. More than that. She returned his fire, shooting out blazing lances, and as she did so, she seemed inspired by a ghostly energy. Psychic energy. Voodoo magic.

After a while, it seemed to Ondragon that they were both holding each other in tractor beams. His stomach tingled hot, like liquid plasma. It contracted, pulsated out like rays, and re-formed again. As if something new was being created inside him, as if he were witnessing some kind of evolution that was taking place within him at that very moment. But what would he transform into?

The plasma began to glow.

Suddenly, something dark slid into his field of vision, completely filling it with the brightness of a supernova.

"No, no, guys. Calm down. I think I have a better idea!" Like the umbra of a planet, Rod slid into the bright beam of energy and severed the magical crackling connection of this duel.

The corona went out. The plasma cooled. And abruptly the warm tingling at the center of Ondragon's body departed. The Madame seemed disappointed too. Her Voodoo eyes had lost their electrifying glow and she was looking down at the ground, almost exhausted.

"Hey? Did you hear what I said? Are you dreaming?" Rod snapped his fingers in front of Ondragon's nose. "Ecks, I've got a great idea. *I'll* carry the little one. She weighs a bit more than a garment bag and is as thin as a twig. I'll cut two holes in the bottom of my pack and we'll sit her in it. That way I can carry her comfortably on my back. You two just have to take some of my equipment. So? What do you say?"

Ondragon turned his head, blinking, and looked at the shadow of his friend. He was the black cloth that had covered the magic trick before the magic could be revealed. He had prevented it.

What had he prevented?

The magic taking possession of him? The transformation he had been on the verge of? The feeling he had never had before?

"That's a good idea," he said wanly, and turned away. On legs of wet sand, he staggered up to the top of the rubble cone. And as he gazed numbly across at the dark, mystical forest, his senses very gradually began to return. He heard the birds chirping in the dense greenery, felt the humid weight of the tropical air in his lungs and the hard stones under his boots. His dazzled eyes also recovered and no longer saw the world as an overexposed photograph.

Magic . . .

He shook off the remnants of the feeling, which was alien and possessive, and turned to his companions, who had now loaded the girl into the backpack. The Madame helped Rod strap the child to his back. She was sleeping soundly under the anesthesia of painkillers, and her head, with its disheveled little braids, swayed back and forth feebly.

The Briton smiled. "Light as a feather." He hooked his thumbs under the straps and winked at Ondragon. "Can we go now?"

Ondragon nodded and took the lead as a matter of course. Although the forest on the plain to his right had a magical attraction for some inexplicable reason, he decided to hike back along the bare slope to the pass and over the ridge.

"By the way, did the howler pipe up again when I was down in the mine?" he inquired with a tongue that felt like a sponge and wouldn't quite obey him.

"He gave one hell of a roar, but he didn't show himself," Rod replied from behind him.

"Hmm. Although I hardly think he'll follow us here in open terrain, we should still be on our guard."

"Aye!" groaned Rod. It seemed his load was not quite as light as he had claimed.

Ondragon stifled an amused comment and continued to climb the stony slope. Above their heads, the sun sent its last rays over the ridge like a wistful farewell. Shortly afterward, blue shadows flowed down and spilled over them, far into the forested plain that was receding below them.

Sweating, Ondragon worked his way over the unstable scree. Step by step across a sea of yellow stones, in which he suddenly discovered something that did not belong there. He stopped by the object and picked it up.

"Hey, look! Our machete guy lost his accessory!" He waved the blood-stained machete above his head.

"But that also means he was here," Rod countered, panting as he paused and looked around. "We'd better keep our eyes open!"

"Yes, because otherwise the zombie will come for us! *Woooh!*" joked Ondragon. The Madame gave him a fierce look. Laughing, he turned and continued his ascent.

When they reached the narrow ledge below the ridge, darkness descended on them from the sky as if a cup were being placed over them.

"Shit!" cursed Rod softly, and Ondragon heard rocks rumbling into the depths behind him.

"You all right?" he inquired, but he didn't dare turn around. He had switched on his headlamp and was illuminating the narrow path in front of his toes, which scarcely deserved to be called a path. Painstakingly, he made his way along it, moving his left hand over the still-warm rock and waving his right in the air.

Meanwhile, above the Haitian mountains, the first stars were lighting up the dark sky. Bats flitted silently around their heads, catching the night insects attracted by the light of the lamps. The plain and the forest lay silent below them like a black lake.

After half an eternity of sideways shuffling, Ondragon finally saw the *Marassa Pierres* emerging from the rock face ahead.

"We're almost there," he called back over his shoulder. "There are the twin rocks. After them, it's all downhill!" Elated by this thought, Ondragon quickened his steps and soon reached the narrow passage between the rocks. He grabbed the stone and turned around.

"Go. Hup, hup!" he shouted, and slipped through the gap.

On the other side, a fresh wind was blowing up from the lowlands. The village lay in the shadows of the night beneath. Here and there a hearth fire was burning and the distant horizon to the west held a last glimmer of sunset. Ondragon could vaguely make out the bright ribbon of the path on the slope before his feet, its switchbacks zigzagging into the depths. He turned around.

At that moment, a violent blow hit him in the face and there was a loud, audible crack under his eye. Surprised, Ondragon cried out and raised his rifle. Eyes watering and feeling as if a chainsaw were stuck in his cheekbone, he searched his surroundings, systematically cutting through the darkness with his headlamp. But his attacker was nowhere to be seen.

Ondragon caught sight of Rod pushing through the gap between the rocks with his heavy load on his back. Something flashed over his right shoulder above the rock. Two pale, glowing eyes like those of a cat. Quickly, Ondragon slid the beam of his lamp to it.

It caught a figure crouched on the rock. About to spring.

"Watch out, Rod, behind you!" he warned his friend, aiming his rifle at the figure. But it responded with uncanny agility and lunged at Rod with a gasping sound.

The Briton went down on his knees under the additional weight. His hands fumbled with the holster of his pistol, but his attacker raked his fingers brutally across his face, leaving deep red welts. Rod reared back screaming, trying to shake off the shadow that was squatting on his shoulders like a bony imp and reaching for the girl in the backpack with a wet, gurgling grunt.

The zombie!

Ondragon felt as if he were trapped in a bad dream as he took aim over the barrel of his gun and moved toward the struggling figures. His cheek throbbed to the rhythm of his racing heart—as if it were an amplifier sending glowing needles into his right eye with each strike.

Rod was screaming and cursing and trying to shake the zombie off. But the zombie grabbed the child by the scruff of her neck, dragged her out of the carrier, and, letting out a triumphant howl, jumped off Rod's back with its prey. Its jaw hanging grotesquely open, it stood staring at Ondragon, holding the girl brutally by the neck, like a broken doll. Saliva poured from its torn mouth and dripped in shiny threads onto its bony chest, which was covered in holey rags. Gurgling sounds came from its throat, and the pink tongue rolled back and forth like a worm.

Ondragon kept his eyes on the hideous figure, ready to pull the trigger at any moment if it moved. But Rod was still too close behind her. Out of the corner of his eye, he saw the Madame appear in the gap between the rock twins and freeze. ZOMBIE, her lips seemed to form in horror, but she could not get a word out.

At the same moment, the zombie lifted the child in front of it with an outstretched arm, as if presenting a trophy, a satanic glint in its pale pupils. With horror, Ondragon realized that the girl had opened her eyes and was silently pleading with it.

He aimed at the zombie, which took a few steps toward him and moaned loudly, "Chrrineeee, chrineeee!"

"Yes, come here, you monster! You Satan from hell! Come on! Come!" he yelled back, squinting his aching eye. He saw the zombie staggering toward him, the girl in its hand. The creature took a step to the right and finally another. It was trying to sneak around him like a starving feline predator! But in doing so, it signed its own death warrant.

"Say goodbye, you bloody bastard!" whispered Ondragon, putting his finger on the trigger of the M16.

But then another shot whipped through the night, and Ondragon watched in amazement as the back of the zombie's head burst open in a spray of red. The grip of the bony hand around the girl's neck loosened, releasing her just before the scrawny body toppled over backward, hitting the stony ground with a dull thud.

Speechless, Ondragon looked at Rod. But he hadn't drawn his weapon.

Behind him stood the Madame, holding the rifle she had been carrying for Rod, which was pointed at the dead zombie.

Rod turned. "By the balls of Jesse James, what a good shot! I may be deaf in my right ear, but my compliments to you, Mari-Jeanne."

The addressee lowered the M16 without changing her expression. "Thank you," she said simply, and stepped out from behind Rod. She walked over to the zombie corpse with feather-light steps, knelt down, and took the girl gently in her arms.

Ondragon, still flabbergasted, watched her every cat-like movement.

"Jesus, you are a true Lady *Sureshot*! Where did you learn that?" Laughing, Rod crouched down beside the Madame and looked at the corpse.

"Look around. This is my country; I grew up here," Ondragon heard her reply. "It's always good to know how to defend yourself. *Aschhh, mon cher, aschht. Tout se byen!*" Lovingly, she stroked the head of the girl, who had begun to whimper weakly.

"*Se Papa. Se papa! Li fè move! Li zombie!*" the girl wailed over and over.

"She says that's her father," the Madame translated, "He's dangerous. He's a . . . zombie."

Ondragon shook off his stupor and joined his companions.

"*Li pa fè move! Li mò. Ma ti. Mwen regret sa.*" The Madame soothed the child with soft words.

She looked up at them with wide eyes and said, *"Mwen swaf anpil."*

"She is thirsty. I told her that her father is dead and she need not be afraid any longer." The Madame held the bottle to her mouth and the girl drank.

"Kouman ou rele?" she asked when the little girl had drunk enough.

"Me rele Christine. Christine Dadou." The child blinked shyly at them.

The Madame gave a meaningful look to Rod, who was muttering thoughtfully to himself.

Meanwhile, Ondragon stared over his friend's shoulder at the dead man. Could this really be happening? Had he been doing the Madame an injustice all this time? Was this a . . . zombie? He looked at the skinny figure's skull-like face, or what was left of it. The gray, cracked skin stretched across the skull like a dried-up fish. The mouth was wide open in a silent scream. The closed eyes lay deep in their sockets and even the nose looked as if it had withered in the heat and shriveled into a wrinkled remnant.

The skull is eating the skin, Ondragon thought, *sucking it into itself. Like someone who has been dead for a long time and is decomposing in the graveyard.*

Baron Samedi!

A shiver ran down his sweaty back.

The Lord of the Graveyards.

"Well, it sounds odd, but the undead is dead!" joked Rod, adjusting his lamp on his head.

Ondragon was literally wringing the barrel of the rifle he had been leaning on. He was torn. *Zombie!* The word burned his tongue like Tabasco, but the best thing to do was swallow it. He thought it was too silly to even consider. Besides, he had sworn to himself that he never wanted the word to pass his lips again!

It was absurd.

It was stupid.

But eventually his curiosity won out.

He cleared his throat and readied himself for the longest leap over his shadow he had ever made.

"Madame, is what the little girl saying true? Was he . . . was he actually turned into a zombie?"

The Madame directed the beam of her lamp at the dead body and looked expressionlessly at the emaciated figure for a moment; it seemed to slump before their eyes, as if the earth were already pulling at its limbs.

Then she pursed her lips and shook her head indecisively.

"What is it? Zombie, or not?" Rod wanted to know now too.

The Madame remained silent, deep in thought. Then she murmured something and touched her forehead and mouth once with her index finger.

"That's not a zombie!" she finally said with certainty.

"Not a zombie?" Rod looked at her incredulously. "Then please explain to me why he was acting like one. He jumped on my back and tried to turn me into haggis. And why did he slaughter the other people on the expedition?"

"I don't know. But one thing is for sure, he's not a zombie! He is . . . well, he doesn't look like a zombie! Look . . ."

"Oh yeah? Not like a zombie? Don't make me laugh. What does a real zombie look like, then, pray tell?" Rod was getting into the swing of things.

"Not like that, at least." Madame pointed at the man. "Those bumps all over, and the color of his skin. So gray. A *coup poudre* doesn't do that. No *zombi cadavre* looks like that!"

"But then what happened to him to make him slaughter men, women, and children as if in a mindless, bloodthirsty frenzy?" Rod raised both hands questioningly.

"I have no idea. In any case, a bokor was not at work here. I'd put my right hand in the coffin on that!"

Ondragon had long since stopped listening properly. His mind was focused on the bulging growths on the dead man's neck and head. In his admiration for the Madame, he had not noticed that the Queen of All Secrets had long since lifted her cloak. Thunderstruck, he stood there while the last cog clicked into place and the solution opened up before him.

CHAPTER 31

February 16, 2010
Haiti, Gulf of Jacmel
shortly before midnight

Calmly, Ondragon steered the boat south. They had to get past the Gulf of Jacmel before he could turn onto a westerly course. On the starboard side, Haiti's landmass passed by like a silhouette, the dark blue night sky motionless above.

The Madame had retired with the girl to the cabin containing the empty gasoline cans, and Rod sat aft, smoking a cigar. The boat glided at half power over the sea, which glittered in the starlight, and the cool airstream blew away his thoughts . . . but unfortunately only the fleeting thoughts, the ones that were like a puddle evaporating in the desert. The poisonous sediment remained, heavy and indigestible. Memories like lead . . . of this dark land and its all-destroying black aura.

It seemed unreal to Ondragon, like a dream, but he knew it was all true. As true as the throbbing pain in his swollen cheek. Everything he had seen in the mine, everything that had happened there. One of the most heinous crimes he had ever encountered in his work. A crime he wanted to tackle, but couldn't, because his opponent was a multinational corporation. And messing with something like that could get very ugly—for both sides. In disputes of this kind, there could only be losers. It was the opposite of a win-win situation, so to speak. And it was not in his nature to get involved in duels that left both parties bleeding on the floor. He definitely had to think about it in more detail. Lose-lose was out of the question.

He pulled out his cell phone and dialed a number.

"Hello, Boss," Charlize replied on the other end.

"*Mission Complete!* We're on our way back. If everything goes smoothly, we'll be in New Orleans by noon tomorrow. How are you?" He had to yell over the noise of the engines.

"I have something for you. Wait, I'll read it to you."

"Better email it, my battery's about to die."

"Okay, I guess I'd better call it a night. I'll come back to New Orleans as soon as I get the feeling I can't do any more here."

"You got it, Charlize, see you then."

"See you, Boss."

Ondragon hung up, and her email soon arrived. He opened it and read, one hand on the wheel of the boat:

Hey Boss,

It wasn't easy to find Dr. Brouwers because he was no longer resident in Boise. After some research, I found that he had died and therefore had been removed from the residents' register. However, he has a widow and two children, now adults, who moved to St. Louis after his death. I reached out to them as well. Unfortunately, Mrs. Brouwers would not tell me much about her husband and his research during our first conversation. I got the feeling that she was very scared of something. During our second conversation, she even became curt and told me to stay out of it and not to reopen old wounds. I then tried two other members of Brouwers's research group back then, which had been disbanded after his death, surprise, surprise. But here too I ran up against closed doors. Then I looked around for the cause of death and found a newspaper article. It's attached. If you ask me, this is the first clue to what might have happened to the DeForce mailmen!

Charlize

Tragic Accident in Rush Hour Traffic

(01/25/2007, *Idaho Statesman*)

Boise—A serious car accident occurred around 5:00 pm Tuesday afternoon on Broadway Avenue just before the on-ramp to Interstate

84. For reasons as yet unknown, a 55-year-old nationally renowned scientist from Boise drove his Mercedes into oncoming traffic and collided head-on with the Chevrolet of a 45-year-old woman. Both drivers died at the scene. Police suspect the cause of the accident was a heart attack suffered by the 55-year-old, which caused him to lose consciousness and control of his vehicle. Property damage is estimated at $54,000. The driver of the Chevrolet leaves behind a husband and three children.

Ondragon turned off his cell phone. He wanted to save the last of his juice. He tapped the device thoughtfully against his lips as the boat slid out of the Gulf of Jacmel and he changed course to the west.

This accident, in which Dr. Brouwers had died, could in no way be a coincidence! And it was clear who was behind the scientist's premature departure. Dr. Brouwers and his group must have gotten decidedly too close to a certain Oregon biotech company with their research into the new, deadly fungal infection. And then they had taken action . . .

Action here in Haiti.

Action in New Orleans.

In Tucson.

And Miami.

Charlize was right, they finally had a hot lead.

Deep in thought and with one of his "winner" smiles on his lips, Ondragon steered the boat out into the night of the Caribbean Sea, his hands only leaving the wheel when Rod came to relieve him.

At dawn, the gray, jagged band of the Jamaican coast loomed before them. The sky was covered with a feathery haze that soon turned to pink and then glowed orange as the orb of the sun rose above the sharp line of the horizon.

Ondragon awoke of his own accord on the sleeping bag he had spread at the stern of the boat and rose, blinking, with a protesting throb under his cheekbone. Fortunately, the swelling had not grown worse, leaving the eye free. With limp bones he stalked toward Rod at the helm; Rod had no time for the beauty of the sunrise at his back and was staring stubbornly straight ahead where the shores of Jamaica were coming closer and closer.

"Morning, Rod."

"Morning, Ecks. Oh boy, you look like you got Grandma's plum jam smeared all over your face."

"Doesn't taste so good though! Your face is also nicely decorated, by the way." He pointed to the scratches the "zombie's" fingernails had left on Rod.

His friend growled, "On the plane, we have ice. And whiskey."

"Perfect." Ondragon looked at the palm-fringed coastline ahead of them and was relieved he would be able to hang up his mercenary gear again soon. After all, he had had good reason for quitting his job as a mailman. Of course, it had also been because he was a loner and he was starting his own business. But there had been something else too. It was something he couldn't easily put into words. Over the years at DeForce, he had developed a certain reluctance. A distaste for the need to constantly expose himself to danger. That sounded ridiculous, because even today he wasn't exactly in a safe line of work. But it was the nature of the danger. Jobs at DeForce were dirty, raw, and direct. A relentless struggle for survival without much finesse or cleverness. And he had had enough of that. He hadn't been able to stand constantly digging around in society's muck and seeing the jadedness in people's eyes. That hopelessness and filth of those who were at the bottom. And the bottom was not somewhere he wanted to be, not even as a spectator.

At the end of the day, that's probably the difference between me and Rod, Ondragon thought. Rod liked to be where he felt superior; he liked to dig in the dirt.

"Hey, Ecks, when we get on the plane, will you finally tell me what you found out?" Rod finally snapped him out of his thoughts.

Ondragon looked at his friend. "Of course."

"Fine." Roderick DeForce nodded. "We'll be there soon."

An hour and a half later, as Rod slowed the engines and, with a bubbling sound, maneuvered the stern of the boat as close to the beach as possible, the Madame appeared on deck. She looked dewy-eyed, which almost made Ondragon jealous, because he himself must look like a squished blueberry muffin. How on earth was she able to get in such dazzling condition?

"We're here," he said dryly. "Get the little one up."

She nodded, disappeared into the cabin, and came out a few minutes later with the girl in her arms. Christine was awake, but didn't seem to take in much of her surroundings. Her eyes, glazed by the painkillers, stared raptly into space. The Madame placed her carefully on the sleeping bag at the stern and then helped the two men pack up the equipment.

A Jeep appeared on the beach. In it sat two tanned men, one of whom jumped onto the sand and waded into the shallow water. The guy grabbed the rope Rod threw him and pulled the boat closer to the beach. Then Ondragon and Rod swung into the water and got the gear into the Jeep. The last thing they did was carry Christine over and carefully lay her in the vehicle. The Madame sat down next to her and held her little hand.

In just five minutes, the Jeep pulled up to the bright white Gulfstream, where the pilots were already waiting.

"Cleared for takeoff in thirty minutes!" one of them shouted.

"Jolly good!" roared Rod against the idling of the turbines at the rear of the plane.

They quickly stowed the equipment in the plane and found Christine a comfortable berth across two seats. The aircraft door closed, and shortly afterward the Gulfstream taxied to the runway.

After takeoff, Ondragon briefly closed his eyes and took a deep breath of the cool cabin air. Rod, meanwhile, poured him a generous drink from the on-board bar, handed him the glass, and toasted him.

"Mission Complete! Well done, Ecks."

"Thank you. Cheers!"

Both took a big gulp.

"Ahhh, that feels good," Rod sighed, and laughed. "I never thought I'd be doing my boys' jobs again!"

"Well, now you know what it's like to put our asses on the line for you!" joked Ondragon, downing the rest of his drink. The whiskey flowed warmly through his bloodstream, dulling the throbbing pain in his cheek. He felt himself getting sleepy, but forced himself to stay awake, because after all, he had promised Rod he would finally enlighten him. He glanced at the Madame, whose care for the girl was almost touching; she didn't even seem to notice he was looking at her.

"Okay, Rod," he finally said, turning to his friend. "I'm going to tell you what I think about this whole thing, and then I'm finally going to take a shower!"

Rod grinned. "Go ahead, my jet is your jet!"

Ondragon leaned forward; he did not want the Madame to overhear. "What I'm about to tell you is all based on assumption."

"I realize that. But don't make such a secret of it!" Rod's *Blue Lagoon* eyes lit up inquisitively.

Ondragon moistened his lips and began, "So, Darwin Inc. has developed a kind of supercorn into whose genes components of another DNA have been inserted. The DNA is genetic material from a microfungus that can cause a deadly infection in humans. *Cryptococcus mattesii lethaliensis.* They were doing research on it in Portland, but the fungus somehow escaped from the lab and infected and killed people. Darwin Inc. came under pressure because the public became aware of it. They had no choice but to close the Portland lab and secretly move it to Haiti. To the press, of course, they claimed to have nothing to do with the fungus. And then at the new location, far from the authorities and any disruptive ethics, they merrily continued their research. This fits perfectly with the time periods Charlize investigated. In 2006, the fungus scandal came to light, and in 2007, the lab was built at the mine."

"What does Darwin Inc. want with this corn? What's so important about it?"

Ondragon raised a finger. "It was their intention to use the fungal DNA to design a new pest-resistant corn variety. They also wanted the variety to be immune to their new pesticide, Weedsweep II. Darwin Inc. is having problems with Weedsweep I. It's toxic and can cause damage if used in excess. It is poisonous to humans and can damage the central nervous system with frequent exposure. Several lawsuits have already been launched against Darwin worldwide because of this. Hence the research into a new product, which of course had to be tested."

"On people?"

"Yes."

"And where did they get the test subjects?"

"I'll get to that in a minute." Ondragon pulled the two folders out of his backpack. "This is from the lab, and I read it on the boat during the trip back. I'm not a biochemist, but I understand eighty percent of what's in there! The *Cryptococcus* fungus is dangerous to the human organism, but it also seems to have another special ability. It has a lethal effect on certain pest insects that consistently destroy entire corn crops in some regions of the world. Once brought to market, the supercorn, which incidentally is called DWIN 411-Crypt, was supposed to solve world hunger, according to the company's philosophy. But what Darwin Inc. really intends to do is use the corn and Weedsweep II to line its pockets. Clearly, however, there are still significant problems with the digestibility of this crop, which we know they have tested on more than just laboratory animals. I saw jail cells in the underground facility where they had the test subjects locked up. I saw what they did to these people. They exhibited exactly the symptoms found in the fungal infection: increased mucus production in the nose and throat, weight loss, and formation of bumps on the head and neck." Ondragon tapped the folder. "Clearly, Darwin Inc. has not yet gotten a handle on how to make the corn safe for humans as well. They ran systematic tests, fed the subjects corn mush, and watched what happened. All the subjects got sick and died from the worst effect of the fungal infection, meningitis! Up to that point thirteen people died, according to the report in this folder." He paused briefly to pour a little water into his whiskey glass. "Now let's move on to what happened in the lab after the quake. The earth tremors destroyed a number of things above and below the earth's surface. For one thing, the stairs in the shaft collapsed, effectively trapping the five employees down there. The fact that no one from the remaining employees at the surface came to their aid after the quake can only mean that they were also no longer alive. What happened to them remains unclear. There is no information about that in the reports of the mailmen who found the bodies. So it would be interesting to know what happened to them. Unfortunately, we can no longer question any of the mailmen about it." Ondragon put his palms together. "In addition to the stairs collapsing, down in the lab the power must have gone out with a thud. Apparently, there was no emergency power either, probably because the diesel generators on the surface were also damaged. However, some of the airlocks and doors in the three labs were electrically operated. In any case, one of them was the lock to the high-security area where the fungus was handled. It locked itself after the power failure and apparently could not be opened. The two employees who were locked in the lab eventually ran out of artificial air to breathe, forcing them to take off their protective suits. They must have known no one would come to save them, so all they could do was choose how to die. They instantly became infected with the fungus and died as a result. I could clearly see the bumps on their necks and heads through the airlock window. Another thing was the doors to the cells with the subjects. Unlike the airlock, they must have opened after the blackout and released the prisoners. Or rather, the one prisoner who was still inside at that time. He escaped from the laboratory and surprised the rest of the staff in the canteen, where they had retreated due to the quake. There he took brutal revenge on his tormentors. The sight was not pretty. I have some photos here." Ondragon handed Rod the camera.

The Briton grimaced in disgust as he clicked through the images. "Our guinea pig has been on quite a rampage."

"Indeed. After that, he dragged himself back to the cell and died there. I found him also covered with bumps on his cot."

"It's a Haitian," Rod said when he got to the pictures of the inside of the cell.

"Yes, and that brings us to the logistics of how the lab obtained its subjects." Ondragon looked at Rod. "They kidnapped them quite easily. Mostly people from the village of Nan Margot. Unfortunately, there is no solid proof of that yet. My guess, however, is that the priestess of the village was working for Darwin Inc. She supplied them with candidates for their experiments and then spread the rumor that the people who disappeared had been caught by a black magician. The story that they had been turned into zombies and sold arose of its own accord in that superstitious country!"

Ondragon heard the Madame clear her throat and looked over at her. She was sitting on the edge of her chair, hands folded in her lap, and judging from her expression, she had been listening for quite a while.

"I beg your pardon. Have I said anything that is not to your satisfaction?" he asked bitingly.

"Not directly. I have long been aware that you don't like my country. But I have something to add to your theory about the priestess of Nan Margot."

"Let's hear it, then," Ondragon prompted them.

"As you know, I was in the altar room of the village temple where I found the ingredients for the medicines."

"The rancid suitcase."

"Yes, among other things. There was also a hiding place. I didn't see that right away. An unusually large mirror hung above the altar. A beautiful and valuable piece with a heavy frame. The mirror symbolizes the gate to the spirit world and somehow it reminded me of the Stern house. The secret room behind the mirror. I moved it from the wall and discovered a compartment behind it. At first I thought it was where the priestess kept the *coup poudre* and the other magic powders, but there was money in it. Dollars. Counted out in bundles. That's not unusual as far as it goes, because priests often get a lot of money for their services, including American dollars. But it was far too large a sum for an insignificant *humfó* like Nan Margot's. Besides, there was something else in the hiding place. A small bottle with a rolled-up piece of paper. A list of names. A whole row of them. There was a check mark by sixteen of the names. One of them was Etienne Dadou. At that point I didn't think it was anything suspicious. Not even when I discovered the pencil the mambo had used to write the list. The sanpwel often have lists of persons under special observation. But the pencil was green and bore a scratched white symbol. A globe with two ears of corn around it." She pointed to the top folder, on which the same logo was emblazoned. Her gaze became bitter. "The priestess sold the people of her village to the bokor. And the bokor's name was Darwin Inc!" Her face contorted with hatred. "She sold those people to the lab, to the *blancs,* as if they were cattle. She abused her standing and spread lies about black magic. She is a disgrace to the priesthood. That the sanpwel permitted her machinations amazes me. But maybe the secret society that controls every village hadn't figured it out. In any case, the sanpwel would have convicted her if she had not long since received her punishment at the hands of one of her victims. Frankly, I'm glad this person is no longer alive and can't cause any more mischief!"

"Hmm. There's something else bothering me," Rod said. "And that is the man who attacked us on the mountain and killed all the other members of the expedition. Etienne Dadou. So he was on the priestess's list."

Ondragon nodded. "He must have been a test subject. How he escaped from the lab is a mystery to me though. But he was infected with the fungus and no longer lucid. He was probably already suffering from the effects of meningitis, which, when severe, also attacks the brain."

"Hence the frenzy and the slaughter of the expedition group," Rod mused, pouring himself more whiskey. "I need another one of those!" He downed the drink in a single swig and set it on the small folding table. "Well, we've cracked a few mysteries there. That just leaves one last one. And I'm curious to hear what you have to say about it, Ecks. What by all the Voodoo gods happened to my mailmen?"

Ondragon exhaled worriedly. "I'm afraid I only have guesses on this one too—you should know that. But Charlize has come up with something that I think is a bit of a breakthrough. I don't want you to freak out the minute I tell you though. Promise me you won't do anything rash!"

"What's it all about, Ecks? You know what I'm like. There's no such thing as a hasty response with me."

"I get it Rod, but I still need your word."

"Very well, you pain in the neck. Goodness gracious, out with it!"

"Okay. Remember I told you about the cover-up of the outbreak of the fungus from the Portland lab? The press, of course, were onto it like flies on shit. There was some newspaper coverage, and even the health department investigated Darwin Inc. but in the end they couldn't prove anything. A group of independent scientists from Boise State University also studied the fungus and wanted to find out if it had in fact come from Darwin laboratories. This group was on the verge of a breakthrough when the head of it all, a certain Dr. Brouwers, died unexpectedly in a car accident. Shortly thereafter, for some unknown reason, the research was halted. What does that look like?"

"Darwin Inc. got rid of the inconvenient doctor to keep him out of their hair. And fearing further reprisals or even deaths, his group stopped its research. Mission accomplished! They have silenced the people." Suddenly, Rod's eyes narrowed to slits, as if he were trying to use his lids to stop the icy flashes that began to shoot out of them uncontrollably. "Are you suggesting," he whispered menacingly, "that those dogs got rid of my mailmen too?"

"Gotcha! Darwin Inc. hired your people to seal the lab and got rid of them afterward because they were potential accomplices. Creative as they were, they disguised it as Voodoo magic, which I admit still irritates me a bit, but who knows what disposal people they work with."

"Those bastards! If I get my hands on them, they'll regret messing with me . . . Ecks, you know a good hitman, don't you?!"

"Calm down, Rod! That's exactly what I meant. Stay cool." It wasn't as if he didn't understand his friend. It would have offended his own professional honor to be taken advantage of and betrayed in such a way. But they had to keep cool heads now.

"Ecks, this pack has killed three of my best men, four if we include Bolič. They will pay for this!"

"I agree with you, we'll get those bastards." Ondragon tapped the folders on his lap. "All we need for that is an ingenious plan. And that takes time. Can you agree to give me that?"

Rod gritted his teeth, snarling. "All right, but only because I promised!"

"Well, I'm going to take a shower now. Three days in the same clothes! They're starting to get stale." He winked at his friend and rose.

Relieved to finally escape the ice lightning gaze, Ondragon went to the back of the aircraft cabin and opened the door to the fully equipped shower room.

CHAPTER 32

After landing in Houma, the three of them, along with the girl, who had since regained consciousness, drove in Ondragon's Mustang to the Madame's house on Ursulines Avenue in New Orleans, which was separate from her Voodoo store. She had kindly said the two men could use it for the next few days.

Ondragon parked the car on the street in front of the house. It was Ash Wednesday and deadly quiet in the French Quarter, as if a hurricane warning had caused the residents to flee. All that was missing were the boarded-up windows and doors.

Perfect timing, thought Ondragon, *they had missed Mardi Gras.* Fortunately, the clean-up operation had also long since left the alleys and removed the piles of Fat Tuesday garbage. He got out and looked around the empty street intently while Rod lifted little Christine out of the car and brought her quickly through an iron gate into a densely overgrown courtyard. At the back end of the narrow garden, they climbed up to the porch of a two-story house painted in white and old pink. Tall windows with bright green shutters and white columns adorned the facade. The Madame pulled out an old-fashioned key and opened the ornate double-leaf door, which gave admission to a large, dim entrance hall.

"Wow!" exclaimed Rod. "Now, that's a smart pad." He marveled at the open-air staircase that swung up from the parlor to a gallery. Walls covered with French Colonial–era wallpaper flanked the dark wood furniture, and ornate doors with inset stained glass windows led to the three downstairs rooms. Thick oriental rugs lay on the floor, muffling their footsteps. It all seemed as if time had stopped. And there was nothing to indicate that a Voodoo priestess lived in this grand American townhouse.

"I'm definitely in the wrong job!" joked Rod, whistling through his teeth as he caught sight of the expansive crystal chandelier hanging from the ceiling above him. The chandelier wasn't turned on, but its cut crystal prisms still glittered in the light streaming through the open upstairs doors.

Truly a magnificent home, Ondragon thought, having taken a look around the interior.

"Your rooms are upstairs," said the Madame, striding up the staircase like a Creole Queen. She had also freshened up on the plane and was once again wearing an elegant outfit à la *Sex in the City*.

Arriving at the first room, she pointed to the antique bed and said, "Rod, be so kind and put the girl in there. I'll take care of her right away. I know a good doctor who won't ask questions."

Rod did as he was told and laid Christine on the soft blankets. Then the Madame led the two men to their rooms. "The bathroom is opposite the stairs; you will find everything you need there, messieurs. And you'll find something to eat in the kitchen downstairs. My housekeeper, Camille, will come at four o'clock this afternoon and prepare you a meal. If you need anything else, please let Camille know. I will retire now and take care of the little one."

"Thank you, Mari-Jeanne," Rod said artfully. "We'll see you later."

"*À bientôt,*" the Madame replied with a smile, and left the gallery.

"Not bad, huh?" said Rod when they were alone, pointing to the open doors.

Ondragon shrugged his shoulders. He had noticed that the Madame had switched back to her Francophone mode. *Maybe it has something to do with this town and not me*, he thought, checking the view out the window. All that could be seen was the windowless brick wall of the neighboring building and a narrow path that led between the houses. Escape route: six minus. But what the hell. In the house of a Voodoo Queen, you should be able to feel safe from the intrusion of ill-disposed spirits.

"I think we'll take a little nap before we start thinking about where we go from here. I'm pretty beat."

"Okay." Rod yawned and stretched his arms above his head. "Wake me up in an hour, will you?"

Ondragon looked at his watch. "All right," he said, closing the door and pulling out his freshly charged cell phone. Before he lay down to rest, he really needed to let Charlize know.

His assistant picked up after the second ring.

"Boss?"

"Hey, Charlize, we're back in New Orleans, at Madame Tombeau's house."

"Oh, it's beautiful, isn't it?"

"How do you know that?" asked Ondragon, puzzled.

"She invited me to her place when you disappeared in the swamp."

"Ah, I see. Well, it's actually very nice. Charlize, I'm calling because I have important news! The lab at the mine was very revealing." He reported the results of the completed operation.

"*Kuso*, those bastards!" retorted Charlize after he finished. "Human trials; I'd never have believed it."

"Neither would I. But Darwin Inc. obviously uses all kinds of dirty tricks and, if need be, goes hardcore when it comes to corpses."

"So you think they got rid of the mailmen too?" asked Charlize.

"Yes. So please be careful. It seems Darwin Inc. is eliminating everyone who could pose a threat to them."

"Speaking of which, *Paul-san*. Since yesterday, some guys have been following me. They haven't threatened me yet though, they're just tailing me. Very conspicuously, as if they're trying to warn me. They're sitting in a car outside my hotel, waiting. I've been pretending that I haven't noticed them yet, which isn't so easy."

"Okay, the best thing to do is switch hotels today. And use your alias."

"I'm using that already, Boss."

"And do you have a disguise?"

"*Hai*, the lawyer-sleuth. Unobtrusive but practical clothing, a bit dowdy, glasses, dark circles under her eyes. After all, detective work makes you fat and tired."

"Perfect. When you get to the new hotel, lie low for now. Don't do any more research; stay in your room and watch TV or something until I contact you. It's too dangerous to provoke these guys. They killed three mailmen and a DeForce floater. And they weren't rookies who would have let themselves get ambushed!"

"You got it, Boss. I'll keep an eye out." Charlize sounded annoyed, as if he had insulted her professional honor. "So, what are you guys up to in New Orleans?"

"We're going to come up with a plan to get the pigs that killed Rod's mailmen. The material from the lab will help us do that. But the plan has to be damn good, because you don't mess with a corporation like this! You won't get far with clumsy blackmail; you need something more elaborate. Be ready. When the time comes, we may be in Portland. But until then, you keep your head down, you promise me?"

On the other end, Charlize let out a theatrical sigh. She always did that when she had to make a promise he knew she would have a hard time keeping. "All right, I promise!" she wailed with the expected dejection. "But I'll be bored to death!"

Ondragon smiled. "I hope not!" he said, saying goodbye and putting the cell phone in his pocket. Then he stretched out on the large bed with the wrought-iron frame, and no sooner had his head touched the wonderfully soft pillow than he was asleep.

The alarm on his cell phone woke him up. It was four thirty in the afternoon. His back stiff, Ondragon sat up and felt his cheekbone. It still hurt like hell. He might be able to find a painkiller somewhere. But first he wanted to make a few more calls. He pulled the cell phone out of his pocket again and dialed a number in Los Angeles.

"Yes?"

"Strangelove, glad to reach you. Do you have the results from the powder you analyzed from the envelopes?"

"Ah, yes. Hold on, Mr. Ondragon." There was a rustling on the other end, probably because the young chemist had jammed his cell phone between his ear and shoulder and was looking for the papers. "Here you go. Wasn't so easy, by the way. But your hint about toxins was quite helpful. It meant I didn't have to grope around in the dark for too long. That stuff is dangerous as hell, by the way. It works mainly via skin contact, but also via the mucous membranes and the lungs, if you inhale enough of it. It's quicker though via a little scratch on the finger, and wham, you've got a date with the Grim Reaper."

"So what was in it?"

"One ingredient was glass shards. More precisely, mirror shards, finely ground."

"Mirror shards?"

"Yes, I detected silver particles from the coating. The splinters probably help with the absorption of the poisonous mixture through the skin, because the glass irritates or injures the skin. Incidentally, the ingredient at the highest concentration in the powder was tetrodotoxin, the poison of the puffer fish. A neurotoxin five hundred times more potent than cyanide."

"I know that one. In Japan, they eat the puffer fish raw as sashimi. They call it fugu. It's a pure thrill to eat that, literally! Every year there are over a hundred deaths because of fugu." *And preparing it is an art*, Ondragon thought. It didn't always go well. Some gourmets wanted to push the limit of edibility higher and higher and ingest more and more poison. It was akin to Russian roulette. If you consumed too much poison, after a relatively short period of time, your extremities became numb, and the numbness quickly spread to the whole body. You also had problems that led to respiratory arrest. You became completely paralyzed and simply suffocated.

"I tried that stuff once," he said in response. "I was eighteen and looking for the ultimate thrill. In Japan, they say, 'He who eats fugu is stupid. But he who doesn't eat fugu is also stupid.' Fortunately, I knew a good fugu cook. All that happened to me was that my tongue tingled and the tip of my nose, lips, and fingers went numb. After that, I never touched the stuff again."

"Respect! And I always thought I was crazy. But I wouldn't have dared to do that. Because that stuff is not to be trifled with. There are reports of people with fugu poisoning whose whole bodies were paralyzed. Their heartbeat and breathing were so weak that they were pronounced dead. Only unfortunately, these people were still fully conscious, and they witnessed their relatives mourning them. Some were even in the coffin before they could communicate again. And no one knows what the dark figure is for those who were actually buried alive."

Tetrodotoxin, Ondragon thought, *paralyzed but fully conscious— clearly the precursor to a career as a zombie. That would explain the apparent death of Bolič and Stern.* "So, what else did you find?" he asked the chemist.

"Bufotenin, a hallucinogenic tryptamine alkaloid. Works in a similar way to the hallucinogen in magic mushrooms. You get visual delusions and states of confusion. Bufotenin is found in the skin secretion of the Aga toad, *Bufo marinus*, native to the Americas and the Antilles. I also found traces of serotonin, histamine, and acetylcholine. All neurotransmitters."

"Which are thought to speed up the uptake or the transfer of toxins in the body."

"You could say that."

"Anything else?"

"Any amount of organic material from plants and animals. But to decipher that would take weeks," Strangelove said apologetically.

"Hmm, okay." Ondragon mused. "And as a scientist, what do you think of this powder?"

"Well, if it does what I think it does, these ingredients were deliberately mixed together to serve a specific purpose. What, I can only speculate. At the beginning, when you sent me the sample, you said it was zombie poison and had a good laugh about it. Well, that got me curious. I've been digging through the information in the literature, and I found out—"

"There is primary literature on zombie venom?"

"Yes, of course. In the early seventies, an American ethnobotanist named Wade Davis looked into it and wrote a book that gives a plausible description of the zombie phenomenon and, of course, the poisons necessary to achieve the state. I can summarize it for you if you're interested."

Of course he was interested. "Go ahead," said Ondragon, concealing his impatience. At last, a rational explanation for this mystical mumbo jumbo! At last, some light to shed on the mystery of the walking dead!

"All right," Strangelove continued, "in his book *The Serpent and the Rainbow,* Wade Davis describes how zombie venom is used in Haiti to put people into a suspended coma-like state, but where they are fully conscious. This is part of a punishment imposed on the victim, as the zombified are primarily men and women who have broken the seven commandments in their village community; these are a lot like the Judeo-Christian Ten Commandments. The victim is sentenced by the secret society that exists in every village, the sanpwel."

Ah, wait a minute, thought Ondragon. He had heard that before, from the Madame's mouth. She had told Rod that she was a member of the sanpwel. So she had the power to judge people and turn them into zombies.

Strangelove continued: "The process of zombification is strict, almost ritualistic. The victim is given a warning beforehand, to terrify him. Then the poison is applied to him, mostly as a powder, which he absorbs through his skin. It is sprinkled on his doorstep. The glass fragments in the powder injure the soles of his feet and the poison is already in his body. From this point on, there is no escape. The victim feels himself slowly becoming unwell, his limbs begin to tremble and tingle. He goes into respiratory distress and finally falls into a paralysis that takes hold of his whole body. So he lies there, almost without a heartbeat and no perceptible breathing. His body temperature drops. In Haiti, even experienced doctors have declared victims of zombie powder dead. Of course, the mock dead person is then buried according to tradition, like all the deceased—but he is still fully conscious. He has to go through hell. Not only because he has been buried alive and the air in the coffin is getting scarce; no, he also knows that it will be his fate to be a zombie if he ever comes out of the grave again. If the book by Wade Davis is to be believed, this is a more terrible punishment than death for a superstitious Haitian. Being a slave without a will and being sold as a workhorse is their worst nightmare. And that nightmare, according to Davis, may well come true. Isn't that fascinating? So our victim lies in his grave, deeply frightened and completely out of his mind. Now the second party enters the field. The first were the sanpwel, who sentenced the victim. The second are the black magicians, the bo—"

"The bokors, who make common cause with Baron Samedi," Ondragon added.

"Exactly!" Strangelove sounded astonished. "The bokor and his assistants open the grave at night and take the victim out of the coffin. By that time, the poor fellow should be pretty much finished, mentally. But, to make sure his last sense of reality is really extinguished, they administer a second poison to him, containing mainly *datura stramonium*. The—"

"The zombie cucumber, *concombre zombi*, white datura." Ondragon again completed the young chemist's sentence, for he remembered well how the Madame had used this stuff on him during the Voodoo session at her club and how it had made him all woozy. That herb witch! She had tried out a part of the zombie recipe on him! What had she intended to do with him? Ondragon pushed that thought aside. He would deal with her later.

"Correct again," Strangelove said meanwhile. "You know everything already." He sounded disappointed.

"No, no, not everything, just some details. Please, go ahead."

Strangelove cleared his throat. He seemed to be really getting in the swing of it. He was obviously enjoying this conversation with his client. "Wade Davis claims that scopolamine, which is the poison found in the datura, and, by the way, has a very similar hallucinogenic effect to bufotonin, finishes off the victim's brain cells, so to speak. The victim falls into a delirium, a deep mental confusion in which he cannot even remember his name. He loses all memory of his previous life and any sense of space and time. He becomes willless. In this state, the bokor takes him away and sells him as labor to other unscrupulous people. This is what happens in the movie *White Zombie* from 1932. One of the earliest zombie movies. And the only one that portrays zombies roughly as they really are. As mindless slaves with no memory. Have you seen that one?"

"No." Ondragon frowned. What kind of movies was Strangelove watching?

"Well, I'm a fan of the old black-and-white flicks, so that's where I got this one. Worth watching."

"I see, but let's get back to reality now. So zombification happens more with the help of drugs than with hocus-pocus."

"Yes and no. Zombification certainly has that fatal effect on a Haitian because he believes all his life that there is such a thing as zombies. But a Japanese person who eats too much fugu doesn't automatically become a member of the walking undead just because he's taken the same poison. So it has a lot to do with superstition. The black magicians of Voodoo claim that a man only becomes a zombie because of their magic, not because of the potions they give him. What is certain, however, is that once you have passed through the earth, as they say in Haiti, you are never the same."

"What Voodoo mumbo jumbo!"

"Not mumbo jumbo. It's a punishment, a kind of social ostracism. As a zombie you are still alive, but for your relatives, for your village, you have died. It doesn't get more symbolic than that. Even the poison powder is anything but hocus-pocus. It is real and devilishly dangerous, at least as deadly as anthrax. Only a very experienced poison mixer could prepare this, because animal and plant products are always highly variable in terms of their concentration. They are difficult to dose, as the example of fugu shows."

"An experienced poisoner, then," Ondragon repeated thoughtfully. An experienced poisoner on the payroll of Darwin Inc.? Who could that be? Only a Voodoo priest . . . or priestess.

"Mr. Ondragon, are you still listening?" Strangelove's voice cut into his thoughts like an ice breaker.

"Uh, no. 'Scuse me. What was that you said again?"

"I wonder if you still want me to analyze the DNA for the other components of the powder."

"No. But thanks for the little zombie lesson. Very helpful!"

"You're welcome, Mr. Ondragon. You'll be in touch when you have another assignment for me?"

"Sure." Ondragon hung up and sat there for a while, deep in thought.

Then he dialed the number of Rudee, his Thai computer specialist from Bangkok.

"*Sabai dee mai*, Paul," he said in his ever-cheerful voice as he picked up.

"*Sabai dee*, Rudee. Do you have the information?"

"Not yet. Big chaos in Haiti right now. Not easy to find the right computer. But I'll stay on it. Don't worry, I'll get information! Me genius!" Ondragon heard the little Thai chuckle.

"Well, sure," he said with a grin, "if anyone's going to get it, it's you, Rudee!"

"I send you email when I have them."

"*Kap khun khrap*—thank you very much."

"You're welcome, Paul. Bye-bye!"

Ondragon hung up and looked at the cell phone. There was still this unknown number. Without further ado, he pressed the recall button. It rang, but no one answered, not even a voicemail.

Shrugging his shoulders, he put the phone away, rose from the bed, and left the room. As he stood by his friend's door, a loud laugh reached his ears from downstairs. It sounded like Rod and the Madame. So he was already awake, then. But why hadn't he woken him up?

Ondragon walked along the gallery, but stopped at the door to the girl's room and took a quick look inside. Christine was lying in bed under a thick layer of blankets, with transparent tubes snaked out to an IV stand with bags hanging on it, filled with a range of fluids. Obviously, the doctor had ordered this. In the shadows beside the bed, Ondragon spotted a woman sitting on a chair. She was looking at him. It was Nathalie. Her eyes shone brightly but her gaze was impossible to interpret. Ondragon nodded to her and closed the door again.

Unhurriedly, he descended the wide staircase, crossed the drawing room, and stepped through the door he thought was the entrance to the kitchen. In fact, it opened onto a large room with a high ceiling and furnished as it might have been a hundred years ago. A huge cast-iron stove stood in the center of the red-and-white tiled floor, and copper pans and other kitchen utensils hung above it like in a museum. And as if the Southern atmosphere wasn't enough, a plump Black woman in a white apron and headscarf stood at the stove, happily stirring a steaming pot.

Opposite the stove was a colossus of an oak table. Rod and the Madame were sitting at it, engaged in cheerful conversation, with unused plates in front of them. They looked up when he came in.

"Ah, Ecks. Come and sit with us. Camille, good soul, is whipping us up a Creole gumbo from her special recipe!" He rubbed his belly. "I'm starving already."

Ondragon accepted the invitation and sat down on one of the massive chairs. He could not resist the seductive power of the scent drifting from the stove, which was making his mouth water. He leaned back casually to create the impression that he was relaxed. As Camille rattled the pots behind him and hummed softly to herself, he secretly looked at the Madame.

The Voodoo Queen was increasingly a mystery to him, even though he should actually know her a little better by now. He had the feeling she was keeping a secret. A dark spot in her past, just like his own. He wondered who she really was and why she had so much influence. The fact that he still couldn't fully read her made him uneasy. Hopefully, Rudee would hurry.

Giving a mysterious smile, the Madame poured him iced lemonade from a carafe. She was wearing the same hot dress as she had at noon, but now her pretty face was disfigured by those impossible glasses with the thick black rim.

Inconspicuously, he sniffed the liquid in his glass and looked at the almost empty glasses of Rod and the Madame. Both seemed to have already drunk something. His gaze focused on Rod. He looked tired but not doped, and his blue eyes shone vividly above his cheeks, which were reddened by the kitchen haze.

Ondragon took a sip of the lemonade, and over the rim of the glass snapped his attention back to the Madame. He was sure it wasn't she who was working for Darwin Inc. That's what his instincts told him. But then what was she? Really just a Voodoo priestess?

The lemonade tasted refreshingly good and Ondragon emptied his glass. Soon, Camille came to the table, served up a large bowl of rice, and added a bottle of Cajun sauce. The pot of steaming gumbo followed, and everyone put a rustic helping on their plates. Ondragon saw shrimp and bits of fish in the red sauce and inhaled the aroma of the typical New Orleans stew. He took the spoon and waited until the Madame had eaten several bites. Rod also ate a spoonful with relish. Neither of them grimaced or grabbed their necks. Ondragon shook his head at his misgivings and began to eat as well. He would find out the secret of the Madame soon enough.

The gumbo was excellent and the pot was quickly empty.

"I learned some pretty interesting things earlier, by the way," Ondragon said after they had finished eating, wiping his mouth with his napkin.

Rod and the Madame looked at him expectantly.

"My chemist analyzed the zombie powder and figured out how it works. It is quite simple and not magic as you have always claimed, madame." He gave her a provocative look. "Puffer fish poison is not a magic ingredient, my dear! It is a powerful neurotoxin that can be absorbed through the skin. That's why mirror fragments had also been added to the powder. The aim is to injure the skin so that the poison can be absorbed more easily. After that, the entire body is seized by paralysis, and the candidate seems to be dead. Another poison, which is administered later, finally erases his memory, and there you have it, the will-less zombie!" He glanced at the Madame. She looked angry but remained silent. What was she thinking? That her pretty Voodoo magic had been debunked by the tools of science? Ondragon felt a certain satisfaction. At last, he was in control.

"Did you say mirror fragments?" the Madame asked suddenly. Her expression had brightened again.

Ondragon frowned. "Uh, yeah. My chemist actually found mirror shards in the powder."

The Madame looked at him with wide eyes. "I think I know who made it!"

"You know who mixed that devil's brew?" asked Rod, aghast. "But . . ."

"And what makes you think that now of all times?" Ondragon asked.

"The mirror fragments!" the Madame said firmly. "Show me the photographs you took in Tyler Ellys's house again."

Ondragon pulled out his phone and saw that the email from Rudee had finally arrived; but he couldn't open it now. Instead, he uploaded the pictures from his cloud and passed the phone to the Madame.

"There!" she said excitedly. "See?" She pointed to a photo.

Ondragon guessed which one she meant and braced himself inwardly.

The Madame nodded with mute satisfaction and finally turned the screen around so Ondragon could see it.

Although he had suspected it, he winced. It was the photo of Ellys's bookshelf in his secret room! Reluctantly, he looked at the picture more closely and read the individual book titles. Then he looked at the Madame.

The solution had been in that photo all along and he hadn't noticed it.

CHAPTER 33

February 17, 2010
New Orleans
5:55 pm

What? Are you saying Tyler Ellys mixed the zombie stuff?" asked Rod, aghast, looking at the picture of the books.

"No," said the Madame patiently, as if she were reprimanding a dense student. "Read the title and the author."

Ondragon had taken a step back and grabbed his hot forehead. Because his fear of books had kept him from looking more closely at the photo of the shelf, he had missed that little detail. Goddamn fucking phobia! He bit his own tongue in punishment for his sloppiness and let out an irritated sigh. The Madame had actually managed to show him up.

"'*Voodoo Magic, Practice and Theory* by Reverend Zombie!'" Rod now read.

The Madame smiled meaningfully, as if enjoying the moment.

Ondragon blinked at her.

"I sell this book in my store," she said, "and of course I've read it." Of course!

This blow also landed in the middle of his chest. Badly wounded, Ondragon's self-confidence dropped to its knees.

"Reverend Zombie is a houngan from New Orleans," Madame explained, without paying him any attention, "a professional colleague of mine. I know him and his congregation. He makes a secret of his real name. In his temple he holds completely exaggerated rituals and presents himself like a little king, or like a reverend, I should say; he always wears a black cassock. In my eyes, he is a charlatan who uses the clichés of Vodou to impress his followers. He even works with dolls!" She gave a contemptuous grimace. "No serious Vodou priest does that. And now I'm pretty sure the doll with the long needle in its eye that was planted on you was made by Reverend Zombie. And something else is now becoming quite obvious . . ." She called up another photo on the cell phone and showed it to Rod and Ondragon. "The vèvè on Ellys's porch is also by him! See the glitter in the white paint? Those are mirror shards. They attract the spirits' attention and catch their eye. You see, the Reverend is obsessed with mirrors. You should see his house; it's filled to the rafters with mirrors. He bathes in the attention of the spirits, that self-absorbed busybody! He uses mirrors whenever he can. They're practically his trademark."

"And why didn't you think of it earlier? We would have had a lead much sooner!" Ondragon said reproachfully.

The Madame put her hands on her hips. "Will you also allow me a little time to think about things and understand them? Not everyone is as bright as you! At that time, I was more focused on the meaning of the vèvès, not necessarily their creator. And besides, I had to be certain before accusing a colleague."

Ondragon raised both hands in defeat. "All right. But then why did you perform that ridiculous evil spell deliverance ceremony on me if the doll was made by a charlatan, as you claim?"

"Even if it seems ridiculous to you, Monsieur Ondragon, it was urgently necessary at the time. Do you remember the little bag with the mirror shard hanging on your balcony door? The evil spell was hidden in that, not in the doll. The doll was just for effect, so that a doubter like you would understand the message! Believe me, I have not fooled you at any time. My vocation is to interpret the messages of the loas and to direct the currents of magic. And I have done nothing else. I turned the dark magic away from you."

Ondragon gave an unwilling growl. It would take him a long time to recover from this low blow. He glanced at Rod, who returned it almost pityingly. His friend, of all people, had witnessed his unfortunate display of weaknesses.

Silence spread, weighing heavily on him like the cement of a Haitian tombstone.

It was Rod who finally broke it.

"Where did this Reverend Zombie find out about the zombie poison anyway? Is he Haitian too?"

"Yes, he's from Haiti, like me," the Madame explained. "He's also an initiate, having learned how to mix ingredients from several great magicians on the island."

"Like you?" asked Rod with an almost innocent expression.

"Like me," replied the Madame coolly. "But as I have assured you many times: I do not serve the diabs! I am not a bokor. A mambo must know about evil poisons in order to fight them. But she does not use them for dark purposes."

Rod nodded. "And if the Reverend is as honorable as you are, how does he come to be working for Darwin Inc.?"

"Money, vanity. There are many reasons why a priest becomes weak and works for the other side. And the Reverend is very vain!" Only now did the Madame look at Ondragon. "Have I finally been able to convince the gentleman?"

Ondragon didn't meet the eye of either of them. In his arrogance, he had run too far down a blind alley. And the fact that he hadn't noticed the book title gnawed especially hard at his pride. But there was one more question he wanted an answer to. Remorsefully, he looked at the Madame.

"Why did Tyler Ellys have the Voodoo book on his shelf?"

She raised a finger to her glasses. "Well, I guess he wanted to know about the signs on his porch and the little bag, the vèvè and the ouanga. They were warnings, even he understood that. Reverend Zombie's book is a standard work, it's easy to order on Amazon. However, the business with the vèvès does seem a bit strange. Why did Darwin Inc. bring the Vodou spell into play?"

"Maybe the idea was to convince Ellys and his colleagues, and anyone else who looked into the case, that a Voodoo curse had taken them away—like the curse of the pharaohs," Rod explained. "It's an authentic red herring because, after all, they were coming off a job in Haiti."

"Could be," the Madame agreed thoughtfully. She leaned back in her chair and stretched her back. Ondragon regarded her openly. She had delivered a brilliant deduction and kicked his ass mightily—but she had done it with such elegance that he almost admired her for it. A smile stole over his lips.

"Well then," he said, rising from his chair, "I suggest we pay this Reverend Zombie a little visit. Then we'll see if your supposition is in fact correct, madame!"

She rolled her eyes, sighing. "You really are a tough nut to crack, Monsieur Ondragon!"

"I know," he said unconcernedly, and grinned. Category: guilty lout.

Before they left, they waited another half hour, because they needed it to be dark outside for their venture. Ondragon used the time to read Rudee's email. He closed it again afterward feeling triumphant, almost bursting with anticipation. He couldn't wait to confront the Madame, but first they had to take care of this Reverend Zombie. He put the phone away and suppressed a victorious grin.

A little later, they made their way to Royal Street, at the corner of Dumaine, where Reverend Zombie's house was located. Although it was only two blocks away, they took a small detour, because Ondragon wanted to make sure no one followed them.

The streets were wet, and there was an underlying sense of depression after yesterday's Mardi Gras, but there were still enough tourists out in the approaching night to give them plenty of cover. By way of camouflage, each of them was adorned with Mardi Gras beads and held a colorful hurricane cocktail. Exuberantly, they strolled from one loud live music bar to the next until they reached Pikes, which was right across the street from their target. They left their drinks in the gutter and, joking with one another, entered the bar, where for a change there was no live band playing. They climbed up to the second floor, where they sat at a table by the window.

Ondragon was impressed as he glanced surreptitiously at the brick building where the Voodoo priest lived. It was a magnificent two-story corner building with ferns on its iron balconies and a modern art gallery in the basement. The tall, illuminated shop windows featured large paintings reminiscent of pop art. Apparently, you could earn pretty good money with the magicians' guild—or perhaps with the jobs you did on the side?

They ordered Blue Moon beer with orange and drank a toast. After taking a sip, Ondragon took a closer look at the house opposite, especially the upper floor, where the bokor lived, according to the Madame. The shutters were open, but the rooms behind the glass panes were all dark.

"Is he even there?" asked Rod. "He might be on the road."

"His *humfo* is over in Algiers on the other side of the Mississippi. But I don't think he's there now. He always holds his rituals on Saturdays, or sometimes on Tuesdays."

"Perhaps he's in one of his other establishments?" Ondragon looked at the Madame with raised eyebrows.

She shook her head. "No, he doesn't have a club like I do, he just has a temple. But the Reverend does own the showroom down there. It's quite profitable too. I guess we'll just have to wait a little while for him to come. I hear he likes to go to bed early on nights when he's not holding rituals. Needs his beauty sleep, I guess, the vain peacock."

"Well, well, do I hear a little antipathy there?" asked Rod jokingly.

"I never really liked him. He was always trying to steal members away from my community."

"So there is competition among the Voodoo priests in New Orleans after all?" Rod looked at the Madame with interest and sipped his Blue Moon.

"Normally, no. Actually, the three secret societies of New Orleans, which have divided all the temples among themselves, live peaceably alongside one another. Five years ago, however, the Reverend came to New Orleans and wanted to force his way into the Quarter with his *humfo*. Fortunately, we were able to prevent this by working together in the sanpwel and issuing a prohibition. The Reverend complied and built his temple outside the French Quarter, so he's over in Algiers. But the ban has not stopped him from setting up residence here. This, of course, is pure provocation, which for our part we punish with contempt. We consider the Reverend dishonest.

But he doesn't much care about his bad reputation; he has gathered many mystics and Hoodoo devotees around him, which also brings in a good income. He is not dependent on the true Vodou believers."

"So he's already persona non grata in your community, but he studiously ignores that," Rod stated.

"Yes. And I'd almost be glad if he is indeed involved in sinister dealings, because that would mean we could finally get rid of him!" The Madame stared grimly into her glass.

"And why didn't you dump him years ago if you didn't want him here?" inquired Ondragon in a mocking tone.

"Because everyone who is from Haiti is part of our family, part of our blood. And we stick together. Even if he's a black sheep, he's still family. But now he's crossed the line!"

"Aha . . . that's like in one of *The Godfather* movies. 'I have a stone in my shoe!'"

"Something like that . . ."

"Hey, shhh, something's happening," Rod quietly interrupted the conversation. He nodded inconspicuously in the direction of the now illuminated window on the other side.

Ondragon and the Madame glanced over from the corners of their eyes. Was the Reverend about to show up?

For quite a while, however, nothing happened in the room, except that the dim ceiling lamp was on. Slowly, they emptied their beer glasses, and the waitress came and went. Only when new drinks were on the table did the door in the dimly lit room across the way open and a man come staggering into it. Ondragon frowned. Only *one* man?

No, more like *three or four!*

Puzzled, he looked closer and was reassured when he realized the whole room was fitted with floor-to-ceiling mirrors, and in fact only *one* man had entered it, but he was reflected several times. And it was definitely not the Haitian, because the guy over there was White. His face was in shadow, but his blond, close-cropped hair was clearly visible. As was his muscular torso under his dirty sweater.

The man stopped indecisively in the middle of the room and turned to the right and then to the left as if he was drunk, as if he didn't know where he was. He wore a rope around his neck like a dog leash, and Ondragon noticed with surprise that the guy had a hump. In general, he looked like a zombie version of the Hunchback of Notre Dame.

The realization ran through Ondragon's whole body like a jolt of electricity.

But Rod spoke the name even before he did. The Brit seemed to be as surprised as he was.

"Sylvester Stern!"

Suddenly, a second shadow appeared behind the mailman. A tall figure in jet-black clothing. Ondragon's breath caught in his throat. The figure's face was a pale skull wearing a top hat on its parietal bone.

Baron Samedi!

With quick steps, the Lord of the Graveyards crossed the room. No, he literally glided to the window as if on bat wings, placed both hands on the glass, and stared out into the night with dark eye sockets.

Out at them.

Quickly, Ondragon and the other two turned their faces away and waited, their hearts pounding.

"Is that him?" snarled Rod through gritted teeth. "Is that the Reverend?"

"I can't tell. He's too heavily made up. As far as I know, his loa mèt-tèt is Erzilie and not gèdè or its incarnation, Baron Samedi. Hence all the mirrors. Saint Erzilie, Goddess of Love and Beauty, is the vainest of all loas," whispered the Madame reverently.

Ondragon ventured a glance over to the window. The curtains were now closed; only a thin sliver of light was cutting through the darkness on the balcony like a machete.

"I don't care who the guy is!" Rod growled angrily. "The pig has one of my mailmen in his power!"

Ondragon felt under his jacket for his gun. "All right! We're going over!" He stood up.

Down at the bar, they paid for their drinks and walked east on Royal Street. But only as far as the next corner, where they turned and crept back around the block until they finally arrived at the side of the Reverend's house that faced away from the bar. There, behind a crudely timbered garden gate, was the entrance to the upper floor. Cautiously, they waited in the tiny garden and listened while Ondragon looked up at the dark facade.

Everything seemed calm.

He took out his lock pick set and opened the door, which made a loud creak. Cursing silently, they waited to see if anything happened, then drew their weapons and entered the narrow stairwell. One by one, they climbed the narrow staircase that led directly up to the apartment door.

Once at the top, Ondragon listened again. He signaled Rod to cover the back and tinkered with the lock. Less than five seconds later, there was a soft click and the door swung open silently. They tiptoed into the Voodoo priest's apartment and were astonished to find themselves in a bizarre hall of mirrors. All the walls in the hallway were hung with reflective surfaces, mirrors of all sizes and shapes, round and square; there was even a triangular one. In heavy frames, flanked by real skulls and gruesome creatures of the underworld with horns and double tongues, adorned with rusty chains, mummified animal carcasses, and colorful sequins, painted with white snake signs and topped with withered wreaths of flowers. And above everything was that pervasively sweet smell of the grave that Ondragon already knew from the Madame's store. A shiver ran down his spine at the terrible beauty of those mirrors. He clutched his weapon tighter. No matter where he looked, he saw his reflection staring back at him with widened eyes and a strained face. A hundred times, a thousand times, multiplied to infinity!

Or was it his Marassa who was looking over at them from the gate to the underworld?

He heard a repeated, muffled sound somewhere, as if someone were banging his fist against a gate and demanding entry into the world of the living. Was it a demon? Ondragon suppressed this absurd thought and cast a reproachful glance at the Madame in one of the mirrors.

She looked back significantly. There was a mysterious glow in her eyes as she formed the words with her lips, "I . . . see . . . him."

Furious, Ondragon hissed at her, "My brother? Don't you dare do that! This is—"

Quickly, the Madame raised an index finger in front of her mouth. "I can see HIM," she whispered, barely audible. "Baron Samedi!" She pointed to a mirror that hung opposite the room they had looked into from outside.

Ondragon swallowed his cutting comment and leaned toward her. It was true, one of the Baron of the Dead's arms was visible from there. Cautiously, Ondragon leaned back again and signaled to Rod what he intended to do. Then he raised his weapon, took a deep breath, and stormed the room in three bounds.

But there was no one there. The Baron was gone.

Nervously, the three looked around them.

Suddenly, the light in the room darkened and little red lights flashed everywhere. The skulls on the mirror frames also let out hysterical laughter.

Ondragon whirled around and froze. What he saw made him suddenly expel the breath he had been holding. He felt Rod knock against his back and freeze in fear as well.

Behind them, standing tall, was the awe-inspiring figure of Baron Samedi. He had appeared out of nowhere and was reflected a hundredfold, distorted and shattered in the mirror walls like a kaleidoscope of black cloth and white bones.

Ondragon's eyes jumped back and forth, from the real Baron to his projection and back again. Mechanically, like a doll, the Baron's head began to spin while his gangly arms still dangled powerlessly beside his body. His dead eye sockets gawked at the intruders, half his face in the shadow of the brim of his hat. It wouldn't have taken much for Ondragon to think he was facing an automaton from a ghost train. But its yellowing rows of teeth suddenly opened like a bony zipper and gave a malicious grin.

And as if the Baron had long expected his guests, he raised both serpentine arms toward them and said in a low voice: *"Bienvenue, mesdames et messieurs! Entrez-vous!"*

Ondragon raised his weapon, which felt heavy as lead, and pointed it at the scrawny figure. Sweat beaded on his forehead and ran down his face as he struggled to keep a cool head. With burning eyes, he stared at the dead Baron, telling himself for the umpteenth time that this was only a Voodoo priest and not a ghost.

Suddenly, the Baron raised an index finger and let it twitch back and forth like the hand of a metronome. And only now did the dull, rhythmic beating Ondragon had heard before begin again. The sound was coming from the other side of the room.

Training the gun steadily on Baron Samedi, Ondragon risked a turn toward the sound. There stood the hunchbacked Sylvester Stern. His gaze lifeless, he was swaying back and forth, ramming his head repeatedly against one of the large mirrors.

Thummm, thummm, thummm.

Like a broken windup toy, the mailman ran into the glass, bounced off, and made another clumsy attempt to poke his head through the mirror, which already had a spider's web of cracks. But the gateway to the underworld remained closed to him. Blood dripped from his forehead onto the carpet and spread in streaks across the broken glass. It was an eerie spectacle; Stern was no longer master of his senses and obeyed only the silent commands of Baron Samedi, whose index finger still twitched in the same beat to which Stern staggered back and forth.

Thummm, thummm, thummm.

With each impact, the shards of glass in the mirror shifted, revealing a different shattered view of the room. Suddenly, Ondragon flinched.

Had he seen his brother's face there?

Confused, he blinked at the shattered mirror. There, in the moving web of shards, he had briefly appeared.

Per!

The face of a child.

Ondragon clenched his teeth so hard they crunched loudly. It couldn't be! It was quite impossible. Per was dead! Stone dead! Dead and buried in a cemetery.

And who rules over the cemetery?

Correct. Baron Samedi!

Do you still think I'm dead, Paul?

"Stop!" he yelled, shaking Per's ghostly childish voice out of his ear. "Stop it! Reverend Zombie, we've seen through your dirty game!" He took a threatening step toward the Baron, who paused his movements. Immediately, Stern also became a pillar of salt. The zombie gaped dully at the destroyed mirror in front of him.

"Rod! Mari!" shouted Ondragon over his shoulder to the rear. "You guys grab the Reverend and I'll take the zombie!"

"Aye!" he heard his friend reply behind him, and he dashed off.

But before he could lift even one of his feet from the ground—they felt as if they were made of concrete—the Baron made an imperious motion with his arm, and the zombie turned jerkily to face him. Like an electronic target, its clouded eyes locked onto Ondragon, and at another movement of the Baron's arm, the zombie began to stomp heavily, its bloodied face grotesquely distorted and its arms stretched out in front of it like something out of a bad horror movie.

With the small but subtle difference, however, that this was not a movie.

Ondragon kept his eyes fixed on the zombie and put his finger to the trigger of his gun. While he was still thinking about whether the Madame had ever told him how to kill zombies, the undead suddenly jumped at him with surprising agility, grabbing his neck in both hands. They squeezed mercilessly. Ondragon felt his larynx give way and his eyes bulge out of their sockets. Bright points of light danced in his increasingly narrow field of vision. If only he had listened before! But none of that mattered now.

He raised the gun, plunged it into the zombie's stomach, and pulled the trigger.

There was a dull bang.

Stern's eyes snapped open and he made a strangled sound. He staggered backward, hit his back against the cracked mirror, and slid down onto the floor. Mirror shards pelted his head as his chin sank to his chest and he closed his eyes.

The zombie was dead. So simple.

Ondragon quickly turned to rush to Rod's and the Madame's aid. He saw his friend standing in front of the Baron, seemingly paralyzed. He could just see the Lord of the Graveyards reach into his coat pocket fast as lightning and hurl something at Rod.

At the same moment, the Madame fired her gun. A dazzling flash filled the room, blinding them. Ondragon closed his eyes.

When he opened them again, a cloud of smoke hung from the ceiling, and the Baron had disappeared. In his place, Rod lay stretched out on his back. A glittering powder was trickling down on him. Instinctively, Ondragon put a hand over his mouth and nose and looked to the Madame for help. She was still pointing her gun at the spot where the Baron had been standing a moment before.

"I . . . I shot at him, but I didn't get him! *Putain de merde!*" she cursed. "I should have known what he was going to do!" She ran over to Rod, bent over him, her hand held out, and cursed again.

"Is he hit?" asked Ondragon anxiously, also wanting to settle down next to his friend, but the Madame pushed him back roughly. "Stay away from him! He is not hurt, but he has the *coup poudre*. The zombie poison. He's already paralyzed! You must not touch him."

Ondragon looked into Rod's bluish face. His eyes were fixed on the ceiling and his mouth was open, as if he was still surprised by the events.

"The poison works quickly. He needs help! Wait here, Monsieur Ondragon, I'll get the antidote! And I repeat, don't touch him, or I'll have to save you too!"

Before Ondragon could respond, the Madame left the room. Slowly, he stepped back from Rod and looked around.

Great!

Alone with a zombie corpse and a zombie in the making.

Helplessly, he looked again at his friend, who lay there unchanged. What could he do? Nothing! He had to wait. Hopefully, the Madame would make it in time. Ondragon cursed loudly. Once again, he was dependent on her help! His eyes fell on his reflection in the mirror opposite. Where had the Baron disappeared to? Could he walk through walls? Or had he escaped through the mirror into the underworld?

What nonsense. The Baron was none other than the Reverend, a

Voodoo priest, but still a human being. And people couldn't vanish into thin air, let alone walk through walls.

Out of the corner of his eye, he noticed a feeble movement and turned his head. But it was only another mirror and his reflection in it, nothing else. Ondragon looked scrutinizingly into his own face. Suddenly, it moved, seeming to turn away briefly, and then looked back at him again.

Was he going completely batty now?

Confused, he focused on the man in the mirror who looked like himself.

The reflection of Paul Eckbert Ondragon looked impassively back at him.

But nothing happened.

Ondragon exhaled tensely. It was stupid of him to think that was someone else in the mirror.

He was about to look away when he saw it again. The face in the mirror jerked to the side for a fraction of a second. Swiftly, Ondragon raised the pistol and walked toward his reflection.

If he could shoot a zombie, then surely he could also blow out his Marassa's lights once and for all! That would be practical; he'd finally be rid of him!

He stepped directly in front of the mirror, and his projection did the same in perfect synchronization. He aimed the gun at his twin's chest, and his twin aimed back. What if he pulled the trigger? Would he shoot himself?

It was an absurd thought—just like all the others that came to him. For example, what if he positioned the barrel of his pistol on the barrel of his opponent and pulled the trigger? Would the bullets meet in the middle? Would one bullet win, enter the other world, and obliterate the person there?

The Madame would certainly have been able to answer this question if she were here now. But as it was, he had to find out for himself.

Ondragon moved the barrel forward and there was a metallic clack as he placed it against the glass. His reflection moved at the same time and Ondragon pulled the trigger. The bullet pierced the mirror and the entire frame swung back a little.

Stunned, Ondragon paused and looked at the gap that had opened up between the massive frame and the wall. Then he realized, and felt like a complete fool.

It was all so simple.

The mirror was a door!

That was where Baron Samedi had escaped so gracefully.

But he had not closed the door properly again after his escape and it had swung back and forth slightly in the breeze, which was why his reflection had also moved.

Ondragon tapped the mirrored door with his gun and it swung open, silently, on oiled hinges. The Baron had tricked them. With the cheapest magic tricks in the world. He had exploded a small smoke bomb and slipped through the door into the next room.

Ondragon stepped into the adjoining room and looked around. But it was empty. Empty except for the countless mirrors, of course, from which his twin looked back unharmed.

At gunpoint, Ondragon walked through all the rooms in the apartment. Even in the bathroom and kitchen, everything was mirrored. There was no room in which you could feel unobserved. A thousand of your own faces stared back at you everywhere.

Ondragon lowered his gun. The Reverend had obviously run away. He was probably already squatting in his temple, playing with his next zombie. But they would track him down, even there. No one had yet had the last word. After all, the Reverend worked for Darwin Inc. and he had to be stopped. For once, he agreed with the Madame on this point. Damn it, where was she?

He looked at the clock. How long had she been gone? Worried, he returned to the room where the dead zombie and Rod both lay.

Ondragon went as close as possible to his friend so that he could see him. Strangelove had said that after being poisoned with the zombie powder, you were paralyzed but you could still see and hear.

He waved his hand in front of Rod's eyes and said, "Help is coming, my friend. The Madame is on her way. Don't worry."

Rod did not answer. Of course he didn't. He was paralyzed, after all. Ondragon bit his lips. Dammit, buddy, hang in there!

Behind him, he heard a sound like the tinkle of broken glass, and wheeled around. His eyes widened in disbelief. He went to raise his weapon, but was unable to move. Petrified, he watched as Stern, whom he had thought was dead, struggled up on stiff limbs and got slowly to his feet. The Stern zombie raised its blood-covered head and its dull eyes looked directly at Ondragon. A moment later, it stretched out an arm and groaned.

After a delay as long as an eternity, Ondragon finally managed to raise his gun. He fired. But the blast exploded not in the gun, but inside his own head. A glowing spike of pain bored through the back of his brain to his eyeballs, and a red haze settled over his vision like a matador's cape after the bull had received the death blow. His vision clouded and his limbs twitching uncontrollably, he watched the zombie walk toward him. A broad smile appeared on the zombie's chapped lips as it leaned down toward him . . . bringing the darkness with it.

CHAPTER 34

February 17, 2010
New Orleans
8:37 pm

The darkness gave way to a heavy gray that pressed against his eyelids from within. That was followed by a bright flash of light, and pain jerked through the gray cloud of his unconsciousness, leaving red dots of hot pain in its wake. The dots began to pulse, growing larger and smaller in time with a dull throbbing that seemed to come from inside his head. Swelling. Subsiding. The pain pressed into his consciousness like a floodlight that kept turning on and off. Light. Dark. Pain. Release. Pain. The red dots combined into a blotch and yellow dots appeared on it. A strange distorted croak reached his ears from a great distance. It came slowly closer. Became clearer. Another flash cut through his dogged awakening, and an involuntary groan escaped what must have been his throat. The pain jumped back and forth. Throat, head, face, throat. An unbearable fireworks of blinding white flashes. Then the pain suddenly stopped and flowed abruptly into his eyes as his lids finally lifted.

The red before his eyes dissolved in a yellow shower of sparks, and an image appeared. Blurred at first, like a thermal imaging camera, then with white-edged contours.

The croaking in his ears swelled to a roar. It sounded as if two thunder gods were at loggerheads, hurling words at each other in pandemonium. Only very slowly did the words take on meaning, and Ondragon understand what the thunder gods were shouting at each other.

"Told you so. It was a shit idea! Plus, these fucking contact lenses itch like shit! I wish we'd come up with something simpler than this zombie shit!"

"Don't be like that! You said you wanted to make fun of it!"

"Don't be like that? Have you ever taken a bullet in the bullet-proof vest at close range? Hurts like hell!"

"But it worked. He's here!"

"Aw shucks. You and your fucking mailmen code of honor! We should have gotten rid of him back then when we had him. It would have saved us all this shit here!"

"But he used to work for Spider too!"

"Who cares about that now? We have to finish him off either way! We could have done it much more easily."

"And what about Spider?"

"Oh, him. We shouldn't be worrying about him now! So much the better if he's rubbed out at the same time. Then there's one less person after us."

Ondragon blinked. He could see polished plank flooring . . . right in front of him, very close, and in the distance, the pink faces of two blurry figures looking down at him.

"Shit, he's awake!"

"Man, you can't even punch right! Just kill him already!"

One of the two figures lifted a black object. Probably a gun.

"Man, what are you waiting for?" The other figure grabbed the first one's hand and wrestled the gun away. "I'll do it, then!"

Ondragon looked directly down the dark barrel.

But nothing happened. No more pain that entered him and erased all other pain. No eternal darkness that received him full of grace. All he heard was a soft plop.

And then the figure with the gun tipped over to one side. It sounded like a sack of potatoes hitting the ground. The gun slipped out of his hand.

Ondragon blinked again.

With one figure motionless on the floor, the other figure very slowly lifted its hands above its head.

Ondragon raised his head. Immediately, the pain started shooting wildly back and forth again like a pinball. From his head through his neck and into his spine, where it raged aimlessly for a time. But Ondragon ignored the searing lightning bolts coursing through his body and sat up. His eyes went black. The pain returned to his head and raced there, trapped inside his cranial bone like a burning combine, around and around in circles.

When his vision finally returned, it was much clearer than before. Blinking, he surveyed the room. Not far from him and lying in a gradually spreading pool of blood was the zombie Sylvester Stern. Its face was turned toward him, but half of its head was gone, as if something very large had bitten it off. Blood gushed happily from the mangled arteries in its bisected brain. Unmoved, Ondragon raised his eyes and was unsurprised to see who was standing next to the ex-zombie. Tyler Ellys, the missing mailman!

He had raised his arms above his head and was staring at a point behind Ondragon. Ondragon took a breath and felt deep gratitude. The Madame had returned and blown Stern's head off. He turned and realized his mistake!

In the doorway stood not the Voodoo priestess, but a man whom he recognized only at second glance.

Alejandro Green.

Quick as a flash, Ondragon threw himself around and reached for Stern's gun, even though the combine in his head felt like it was going to explode. To keep from losing consciousness, he bit down hard on his tongue and pointed the barrel at Green. The taste of blood spread through his mouth as he put his finger on the trigger.

But the face of the other man did not take on the particular expression that Ondragon was familiar with from these kinds of moments, the one that said, it's you or me! On the contrary. Green's lips widened into an uncertain smile and he raised a careful hand.

"Hey, Mr. Ondragon. Don't shoot. I'm on your side!"

"And how do I know that's true?" snapped Ondragon, looking through one eye over the barrel at Green's chest.

"Because otherwise I would have shot you and not my comrade!

Besides, you could take a look at your cell phone. The number on it is mine. I've been trying to reach you all this time!"

Ondragon felt a puzzled expression come over his face even before he managed to control his expression again. "Your number? But that—"

"Hey, Ty! Stop right there!" Green suddenly yelled, pointing his gun at Tyler Ellys again.

The mailman froze in his attempt to get away and raised his hands again. His hatred was written all over his face. "Green, you little pissant!" he rapped out. "We should have killed you off long ago!"

"But you didn't get me! I rumbled you."

Ellys spat. "You really believe that?" He gave an evil smile.

"It's over, Ty. The game is up. Mr. O, would you be so kind?" Green tossed Ondragon a roll of duct tape. He caught it and, his skull throbbing, set about tying up Ellys while Green continued talking.

"After Mr. O called me, I still didn't realize what was going on. I initially thought our crew was in trouble because of the irregularities. That's why I kept my mouth shut, because I don't rat on comrades. But Mr. O had warned me, and when this strange Voodoo letter actually arrived later, I knew that it was about more than just irregularities. As a precaution, I took myself off to Mexico for the time being. I thought it all through there for a while and went through the reports on the Haiti job again. In the process, I finally realized what you were up to. An inside sellout! And I quickly realized I was in your way. But I needed proof of my suspicions so that I could report you to Spider with a clear conscience. That's why I've been shadowing you—for the last four days!"

"With a clear conscience? Ha! You've got to be kidding me. You and conscience?" hissed Ellys, who now sat bound like a mummy with his back against the mirror. "You're nothing but a cowardly ass. A bastard comrade. Go to hell, Green!"

"Me a bastard comrade pig? *You guys* were gonna kill *me*! Oh, man, how did you get so dumb, Ty?" Green laughed. But suddenly he froze.

Ondragon saw that someone had stepped up behind him and was holding a gun to his temple.

"Put the gun down, whoever you are, or your brain's going to get a little visitor!"

It was the Madame.

"Mari-Jeanne! He's with us!" shouted Ondragon to her. "Don't shoot."

The Madame hesitated, but then came up behind Green. "With us?" she asked, the Desert Eagle still pointed at the mailman.

"Yes, those are the bad boys over there!" Ondragon pointed at Stern and Ellys.

A wry smile appeared on her face. "Ah, I see you've already done right by the zombie."

"Stern wasn't a zombie," Ondragon said wanly. "He was just playing one. It was all for show."

"But why?" The Madame looked at him.

"That's what we're trying to figure out right now. But the very first thing we need to do is see to Rod!"

The Voodoo priestess nodded gravely, put a mouth guard over her face, and knelt down next to the motionless Briton. She pulled out a pair of scissors and cut the clothes from his body.

"Is there anything I can do to help?" asked Ondragon from a safe distance, for he was still aware of the poisonous powder.

"Yes, you can. Help me get him into the bathtub. But be careful and don't disturb the powder. The poison mainly enters through the skin, but if it gets into the lungs, it can also be dangerous. Especially if there are glass fragments in it. The slightest injury is all that's needed, and the poison will enter the body. The bokor threw the glass splinters into his face. They scratched the skin and allowed the *coup poudre* in. Take the mouth guard and apply this to your hands and arms." She handed him a sticky metal can with smelly, greasy contents. "This will protect your skin from the powder." She lifted her arms, and Ondragon saw that they were shining greasily. Her smell too was not quite as beguiling as usual.

He tied the mouthguard over his face, then dipped his hand in the paste and rubbed it liberally onto his forearms until he too smelled like a baboon's butt.

"Breathe as shallowly as you can," the Madame advised.

"No problem with this stuff!" He handed the can back to her with a wink.

Without comment, she dropped the greasy thing in her jacket pocket and resolutely grabbed Rod's bare feet. Ondragon grabbed his arms, and together they dragged the paralyzed Brit into the bathroom, where they hoisted him into the bathtub. The exertion caused the pain in Ondragon's head to surge again, and the combine engine began to howl. It drove off with a furious jerk, chopping his brain into little fragments. Ondragon had to brace himself against the wall and wait until the red haze before his eyes had disappeared.

Meanwhile, the Madame warmed the water and bathed Rod thoroughly. Then she took out a small ampoule from her jacket pocket and a disposable syringe in a packet.

"What?" asked Ondragon in amazement. "No Voodoo magic? No abracadabra?"

The Madame looked at him with a conspiratorial smile. "It is to you alone, Monsieur Ondragon, that I will now reveal my secret. I hope you will recognize this honor and promise me to keep it as silent as the grave."

Ondragon suppressed an amused laugh. "Um, yeah, of course. I promise." He raised two fingers and grimaced in pain. In his mind, his hand groped for the combine's ignition key, trying to stall the infernal machine's engine.

"Good." The Madame pushed the needle through the membrane of the ampoule and drew the clear liquid into the syringe. She flicked her finger against the chamber, pushed the air out, and injected the contents swiftly into Rod's thigh. She then threw the syringe away and looked at Ondragon.

"*Voilà*. Now all we have to do is wait. In the meantime, I'll explain my magic to you." She laughed softly. It was a warm sound; Ondragon liked it. "And you keep your ears open. You may need to know how to deal with a zombie again someday."

She began to wash the gunk off her arms under the faucet in the sink. "*Alors*, there are two antidotes for the *coup poudre* that, miraculously, are found in the same plant. Namely, *datura stramonium*. One of the two active ingredients is scopolamine, which can act as an antidote in small doses. However, if you administer too much, the affected person loses his mind and actually becomes a zombie. But if you take this"—she lifted the vial, and Ondragon read the label—"you can be sure the sufferer will regain consciousness and the paralysis will subside."

"Atropine?"

"Yes, it speeds up the heartbeat and dilates the bronchi. And in this extracted form, you can deliver a much more precise dose than when you work with plant preparations."

"I see," Ondragon said, sighing with relief. In his brain, the combine finally twitched its last, coughing, and soon after fell completely silent. "And where did you get the atropine? You certainly can't get it at the drugstore."

"You remember the doctor who doesn't ask questions?"

"Hmm, I see you are well equipped."

"That's my job!" She winked at him, and Ondragon grinned. Suddenly, she opened her mouth and exclaimed, "Oh, look at that, someone's awake!" She turned to Rod, who was lying stark naked in the tub, blinking excitedly, his pupils dilated. His mouth snapped shut, and very gradually the bluish tinge receded from his face. His fingers and toes began to move, and twitching uncontrollably, his arms and legs followed. Finally, a violent tremor seized his entire body and shook Rod vigorously, as if he were suddenly thawing out after a long period of being frozen.

The Madame took his hands between hers and rubbed them firmly. At the same time, she murmured some incantatory formulas in Creole.

It doesn't seem to work without magic, Ondragon thought, and he saw Rod's mouth open and his tongue try to form words. They looked at him, spellbound.

"W-w-where aaaare m-m-my cl-ooo-thes, goooddaaammmit?"

Ondragon grinned in amusement. "Hold on, old friend, I'll get you something."

He searched through the Reverend's apartment. In the mirrored bedroom he found a closet full of cassocks. He fished one off its hanger and took it to the bathroom. With the help of the Madame, he got Rod out of the bathtub and slipped the robe over his head.

The Brit stood there on wobbly legs and glared at her. "G-g-good-n-n-ness, th-that took a b-b-b-bloody l-l-long time! Do you know how b-b-bad it feels not to be able to move, but to be able to hear everything?"

"I can imagine," Ondragon said, only to correct himself immediately. "Sorry, I take it back, I don't think I can imagine. How are you feeling, Rod?"

"W-well, w-what a way to feel w-when you've risen from the undead!" He took a cautious step and when he saw that he could keep his balance, he took a few more right away.

Ondragon stopped him. "Wow, where are you going?"

"To rip that bastard of a mailman's head off!" With his chin resolutely thrust out, Rod escaped his supporting arm and stomped out of the bathroom, the other two trailing behind him with worried expressions.

As they entered the room, they saw Green staring fixedly down at the bound Ellys, holding him at gunpoint. The dark-haired CSAC Head turned, and a relieved expression replaced his scowl.

"Spider!" He cleared his throat. "I mean, Mr. DeForce. Glad to see you're okay."

"Green! First, I want to thank you for saving us from a worse fate, but I also have to reprimand you for not doing it sooner!" Rod went toward the mailman, who sheepishly shifted his weight from one leg to the other.

"Well, you know, the—"

"Yes, yes, the Mailmen Code of Honor! It's all right. After all, it's thanks to that we're all still alive, isn't it?" Rod gave Ondragon an enigmatic look. "And now for this little asshole here!" He looked back at Ellys, who avoided everyone's eyes. "You filthy traitorous pig! You and your buddy went behind my back and tried to pull a pretty little inside sellout. But not with me!" Rod lashed out with his bare foot, swinging it into Ellys' side.

The mailman squeezed his eyes shut and groaned.

"You scum, you bloody son of a bitch! Blast!" Rod kicked again. But this time at his face.

Ellys's head flew around and banged against the mirror. A fresh laceration opened up on his brow and began to bleed.

"I'm going to beat the shit out of you. You Judas, you miserable little fucker!" Again, his foot landed in twitching flesh.

"Hey, Rod," Ondragon finally intervened, "leave something behind. We want to hear how they planned the whole thing, don't we? We need a little entertainment! Besides, I've got some more questions for that punk."

Rod ran the back of his hand over his mouth. His white hair hung tangled over his face, and cold rage shot from his icy eyes. "All right," he growled, "make the bastard sing!"

Ondragon stood wide-legged in front of Ellys, who still did not look at him. Then he bent down, grabbed him by the hair, and forced him to look him in the eye.

"It's true what the mailmen at DeForce say about me. I'm a god-damn legend!" Ondragon's gaze burned into his counterpart's dilated pupils. "You know what I can do to you if you don't come clean. So the question is, which do you choose? Honesty, or the mirror shards I'm going to ram into your abdominal wall until shit spurts out of your mangled guts?"

Ondragon waited, but his little speech seemed to have had no effect.

The mailman blinked sluggishly, as if he were drugged.

In a sudden explosion, Ondragon kicked the mirror next to Ellys. The mirror rattled against its wall brackets and several shards fell out and landed with a clatter on the floorboards. He picked one up, held it in front of Ellys's eyes and then against the latter's lower abdomen. The glass pierced the fabric of his T-shirt with a ripping sound and slid into the top layer of skin. Blood shot from the wound, but the mailman didn't even flinch. There was complete indifference in his eyes . . . and something else.

Ondragon plunged the shard deeper into Ellys's belly and at the same time stared into the mailman's eyeballs until he literally felt it hit the back of Ellys's retinas. He felt the sweat in the other's hair, felt his heart beating far too fast.

Aha! So the indifference was only feigned. Inside, the mailman was at boiling point. But why? Was he afraid of death? Was he afraid of the pain?

Ondragon's mind sank into the cabinet in his head and riffled through his small torture archive. All his senses recalled the time eighteen years ago when Roderick DeForce had taken him under his wing and made him a mailman. Not everyone could read the signals sent out by a human body that had been manipulated both physically and psychologically. Ondragon smiled. He had been particularly good at that.

He looked into Ellys's pale face, registering every pore in his skin, every pulsating vein.

The guy was a DeForce mailman, he thought. And they were known to be forged of sterner steel than his usual clientele. He brought his nose close to the face and inhaled loudly. The sweat of the bound man smelled sweet, not sour. As if he were on endorphins, not adrenaline. He let go of Ellys's hair and once again examined his slack facial expression closely. And finally he knew what it was that he had read in Ellys's eyes.

Scorn!

The man was laughing at them. Despite his defeat, he was laughing at them. Dammit!

Ondragon turned to Rod. "Torture won't do anything. That's what he wants. He wants death. He'll keep quiet no matter what we do to him. I'm certain."

"Oh yes?" asked Rod, driving his bare heel abruptly into Elly's face.

The mailman struggled with the pain, spitting out blood and fragments of his incisors, but kept his composure. His next grin was riddled with black gaps.

"Blast, now I'll finish you!" Rod lunged in for a final assault, but the Madame held him back.

"Just a minute!" she exclaimed, "I think I could help the infamous Mr. O out a little."

Rod paused and looked at the Madame, his head bowed and his eyes bloodshot. In the Reverend's cassock he looked like a raging black bull, and for an anxious second Ondragon thought Rod would direct his wrath at the Voodoo Queen. But then a milder expression came over his red face, and the Briton suddenly spoke again like a well-bred English gentleman. "Mari-Jeanne, I would be extremely grateful if you would help us. Please, forgive my outburst. I have completely forgotten my manners."

The Madame gave a charming smile and put a hand into her mysterious jacket pocket, which seemed to contain a complete magic pharmacy. And when she pulled it out again, a small pouch decorated with feathers did indeed appear. "Just to be on the safe side, I also pocketed this. *Voilà.* Zombie cucumber! The original!" She dangled the Voodoo amulet in the air between her fingers. "Not only does it drive zombies crazy, you can also use it as a truth drug. You should know about that, Mr. O." She looked at him challengingly.

"Of course!" said Ondragon sarcastically. "Scopolamine. It's not just popular in the zombie industry. Until the more suitable drug thiopental came along, intelligence agencies around the world also used it to make prisoners talk. I never worked with anything like that. Wasn't my style. But here you go, try your luck." With an inviting gesture, he left the field to the Madame.

"Could someone please hold the offender's head?" she asked.

"With pleasure!" responded Rod, placing both hands on the struggling mailman's skull.

With an ostentatious gesture, the Madame opened the little bag and reached into it with two fingers. "In a moment you will have what you want, messieurs. And . . . *très vite.*" With quick movements she spread the dried plant powder behind both of Ellys's ears and on his temples, then straightened up again.

"Now we just have to wait a while," she said contentedly, and began chanting archaic incantations in a dark shaman's voice, just as she had done earlier when she rescued Rod. She took a small rattle from her pocket and struck it in front of Ellys's face in an ever-slowing beat. Until she paused.

"*Et bien*, your candidate is now ready for questioning!"

Ellys sat there. Beneath his half-lowered lids, his gaze was directed inward. Into the treasure chest of his memories, which they would now plunder.

Ondragon squatted in front of the mailman. "Let's start with the job in Haiti. What were you doing there behind Spider's back?"

Ellys's mouth flipped open like a tray into which coins are dropped, and his tongue rolled forward. At first only inarticulate sounds emerged, and Ondragon turned to the Madame. "Works like a charm, your magic!"

"Wait and see. His tongue needs a moment to become obedient. The powers of the spirits must first tame it."

"Ah yes, of course." Ondragon turned back to the mailman, whose stammering actually became clearer.

"Th-the mine. The entrance w-was collapsed, but we had to somehow . . . get in." Ellys was slurring horribly, but at least he was somewhat comprehensible now. "That night . . . we drugged Green after his watch . . . and used a stick of dynamite to blow open the entrance that had been buried by the earthquake. We went down . . . to the lab and took anything there that would be good to use as evidence. USB sticks and stuff like that. Then we went back up and used another load to seal the entrance again. Green didn't notice anything."

"But I did, you fuckers," Green hissed behind Ondragon. "Because I can count! And I checked again at the end of the operation and noticed that two charges were missing. At last, we have the explanation."

"And what were you going to use the evidence from the lab for?" Ondragon asked Ellys.

"We wanted to do an inside sellout, extort money from Darwin Inc. and retire. To Thailand. The girls are cheap there, everything's cheap. We would have had a nice life and lots and lots of money!" Ellys grinned moronically.

"And have you blackmailed Darwin Inc. yet? Does the corporation know you have the material from the lab?"

"No and no, hee-hee. We wanted to let the dust settle, we had to disappear first. Hey presto, the mailmen are gone. Spider had to be convinced we were dead so he would leave us in peace."

"How did you even know there was something in the lab you could use to blackmail Darwin Inc.? Usually, a mailman doesn't even know who the client is."

"It's simple. We got a tip."

"From whom?"

Ellys smiled, as if surprised he didn't know the answer. "From a mole, of course."

Now Rod also squatted down next to Ondragon. "What, a mole? In DeForce? Who is it? Damn it, out with it." He slapped Ellys impatiently on the cheek with the flat of his hand.

"Careful, Rod, you mustn't wake him up!" the Madame admonished him.

"Who is the traitor at DeForce?" Ondragon continued. "Who gave you the inside information?"

Ellys was silent. His head rolled from side to side and back again.

"Bugs Bunny!" he said a moment later.

"Who?"

"Bugs Bunny told us!" Ellys grunted in amusement. "The bunny!"

"Shit, we're not getting anywhere like this," Ondragon muttered pensively, trying to ask the question another way, "Who helped you?"

"Well, the Voodoo priest. I got him out of a book. He helped make everything look like we had been cursed. He's called Reverend Zombie; stupid isn't it?" Ellys giggled.

"So the Reverend doesn't work for Darwin Inc.?"

"No, he works for us. He mixed the powder and used it to turn us into zombies for a short time so that you could see us, Mr. O, and think we were actually cursed. Then the Reverend brought us back. He always wore the costume with the top hat. He thought he was a Baron. Hahaha. Baron! That sounds kind of European, doesn't it?" Ellys paused for a moment, as if remembering something. "Also, the powder in Green's letter was deadly. We had to eliminate him, even if he was a comrade. Sorry, Al!" He looked apologetically up at Green.

"The same way you used Bolič and got rid of him afterward?" Ondragon inquired.

"Yep! Bolič, the bunny! Hahaha! Hopalong, hopalong, bang and he's gone!" Ellys looked increasingly as if he was drunk. He seemed to be in a dazzling mood and chortled happily to himself.

"Does the Reverend know you were going to blackmail Darwin Inc.?"

"Nope. He just knows we want to go underground. But we would have gotten rid of him later. For safety's sake. Can't be too careful, you know."

"And why did you knock me down and leave me in the swamp instead of finishing me off right away? I was on your trail too," Ondragon wanted to know.

"Pfff, on our trail; Mr. O, don't make me laugh! You were miles away from having a lead on us. We weren't trying to kill you then. You were a mailman once. We were just testing you. It was a mistake, I know, but you made such a cute guinea pig. We filmed the whole thing. It was an entertaining show you put on. Really, hilarious!"

"So you watched me the whole time?"

"Of course! It was a lot of fun!"

Ondragon bit his lips. Those bastards! They had left him wandering around the swamps, making fun of him. "And where's the material that you took from the lab? Where did you hide it?"

Rod turned to him. "I really need this stuff. It's got to be destroyed. If Darwin Inc. gets wind of this whole thing, I'm toast!"

Ondragon nodded and turned to Ellys. "Out with it! Where's the material?"

"In the Queen!"

"In the Queen?"

"Street 545, haha! Queen Street."

"That's in Chalmette, not far from the house where the other guy lived, that star," the Madame exclaimed.

"Okay. And what will we find there?" Ondragon asked Ellys.

"Gold! Gems! The treasure of Captain Bugs! An inflatable crocodile and canned peaches! Hahahaha!"

"Now he's going completely crazy," Rod said, and stood up. "Can you do anything about it?" he asked the Madame.

She shook her head. "His tongue is free again; it say what it wants. The spirits no longer have power over it. If I give him more of the poison now, he will die."

"Well then . . ." Ondragon heard Rod say softly behind him. In the mirror, he saw the Brit raise a gun and pull the trigger.

With a start, Ondragon jumped back to his feet and rubbed his ringing ears. "Shit, Rod! Let me know next time. That was loud!"

"Hollow-point bullet!" the latter said with satisfaction, handing the Desert Eagle back to the Madame. "Makes pretty holes. Sorry, Ecks, I had to kill him. I can't take him to the police, after all!"

Annoyed, Ondragon wiped blood splatter from his face and stepped back from the bound mailman, whose head now had a fist-sized hole in the middle of the forehead; a shattered maw through which the gray mass of the brain could be seen. The mirror behind the skull was stained red and had shattered into hundreds of shards. As if in slow motion, Ellys's head slumped forward onto his chest. Blood poured from the hole in his forehead and gurgled onto the T-shirt with a sickening splash.

Ondragon looked at Rod in his cassock. "Now how do we find out who the mole is?"

"Oh, don't worry, I'll figure it out when I get back to Dubai. Then I'll really clean house!"

"I can send you one of my men if you want. Dietmar Hegenbarth is good at cleaning."

"By all means." Rod wiped his hands on the black fabric. "But right now I'd like to put on something a little more discreet, if that's possible."

"Let's go back to my house first," the Madame suggested. "And afterward we can go to Queen Street."

"What about the Reverend? And who's going to take care of this mess here?" Rod pointed to the two bodies and the pools of blood on the floorboards. "If someone hasn't heard the shots and called the cops anyway."

"Don't worry, I know someone who is good at cleaning up too," said the Madame. "He'll take care of it and leave no trace that could lead to us. You can leave the Reverend to me. After all, I know where he lives." She winked at Rod and turned around.

Ondragon stared at her. "I know who you are, madame!" he said suddenly. "That's why you can do all these things!"

Rod and the Madame looked at him in amazement.

"What kind of things?" she asked.

"Well, all this!" Ondragon made an all-encompassing gesture.

"Ecks, what are you doing?" interjected Rod. "We don't have time for this now!"

"Oh, we have time! There's always time for the truth. And I know the truth about you, Mari-Jeanne Tombeau—daughter of Michel Tombeau, granddaughter of Emile Tombeau, grandniece of François Duvalier!"

"Papa Doc?" Rod sounded aghast. "You mean to say she's related to the former dictator of Haiti?"

Ondragon nodded curtly. "Yep!" He kept his eyes on the Madame to see the impact of Rudee's research results.

But the voodoo priestess made no attempt to appear nervous in any way. Instead, her face widened into a pitying smile. "*Mon Dieu*, and you only just found this out now, Monsieur Ondragon? *Quel dommage*, I would have expected that from you much sooner. You are slipping, *mon ami*!" She clicked her tongue. "So, and now we should go."

With a smile, she walked past the surprised Ondragon and stopped at the door. "*Allez*," she waved at him, "before it gets any more unpleasant here."

Rod pulled Ondragon along by the arm and they hastily left the house. They crept back to Ursulines Avenue via empty side streets.

CHAPTER 35

They drove in the Mustang to Chalmette on Queen Street, which was indeed not far from Stern's abode. At a leisurely pace, they passed silent rows of houses, while the Madame sat in the passenger seat and made a quiet phone call to the cleaning crew that would take care of the Reverend's apartment. Ondragon listened grimly. She had set him a riddle, to test him, in her own way—and he hadn't solved it! It was unforgivable how long it had taken him! A pang of humility came over him and he looked ahead through the windshield.

In the darkness of the night, the lanterns along the street formed a steady string of pearls, islands of light. Only in one place was this rhythm interrupted, because apparently one of the lanterns had failed. Exactly outside number 545. Coincidence?

Hardly, Ondragon thought, brushing aside thoughts of the Madame. He drove the Mustang past the house, turned at the next corner, and parked the car in the dark gap between two streetlights. He, Rod, Green, and the Madame got out.

Cautiously, they approached the house, where no light was burning, ready to jump into a bush at any time if anyone appeared on the street. But the sober suburb remained quiet, and they reached the dark garage driveway of number 545 unhindered. As Ondragon looked at the house again from this perspective, it hit him like the kick of an elephant.

Of course he knew this place!

This was where he had been knocked down and dragged to after hunting the zombie! It was here, outside this house that Stern and Ellys had rented for their diabolical little game. *At last, piece after piece is falling into place*, he thought with satisfaction. And it would only take a few more moments for him to solve the case completely.

Under cover of darkness, he reached the front door and listened. Not a sound. He quickly took out a lock pick and opened the lock. Their guns drawn, the four entered the house, and Ondragon gave hand signals, instructing the others to secure the entire house first. It might be that someone else they knew nothing about was involved and slumbering peacefully in one of the bedrooms upstairs. Or Reverend Zombie might be hiding here because he was currently denied access to his own home.

But Ondragon's fears were not confirmed. The house was empty.

They gathered in the living room, which had a huge window overlooking the garden, and discussed what to do next.

"We'll sift through the whole shack again," Ondragon whispered, "but this time looking for the stuff from the lab. USB sticks, CDs, computers, folders, et cetera. Bring everything you can find. I'll take the living room, Mari-Jeanne the kitchen and bathroom, Rod and Green upstairs. And look for any secret rooms!"

"Aye," Rod and Green called simultaneously, and after they had fanned out, Ondragon directed his lamp at the living room furniture, shining light on each item. As he did so, he noticed that all the furniture was against the wall, leaving a larger space in the center of the room. Slowly, he walked across the carpet and approached a table on which various objects were lying. He heard the Madame rummaging in the kitchen. She was probably going through the cupboards.

He returned his focus to the table, which held a college notebook, pens, paper clips, a laptop, and a printer. He opened the notebook. The pages were blank, some had been torn out, nothing else. He flipped open the laptop and booted it up. Password protected. Damn it! He didn't even try to crack it, but continued searching the room. There was a shelf on the wall above the desk. On it he noticed a few bits of Voodoo paraphernalia, sachets with feathers and dolls, next to them were small glass vials with different contents. In one was a clear liquid and in another dark lumps and powders. He read the hand-written labels: *Concombre Zombie, Atropin, Bufo marinus, crapaud de mer/poison de poisson-ballon, Calaba, os humains*—a small voodoo poison cabinet, in other words.

Ondragon continued to move the beam of his lamp along the shelf. The light passed over medical supplies such as syringes, a pack of rubber gloves, and disinfectant until it caught on a familiar object dangling from a nail.

I LOVE BERLIN written on the belly of the bear.

It was his car key ring! Ondragon took it, glad to have his lucky charm back at last, and stuffed it into his pants pocket. He kept going, but his Sig Sauer was nowhere to be seen. Bummer. When this show was over, he'd probably have to get a new one. Or he'd keep Bolič's Walther.

He let the light drift over to the large picture window. There was something he hadn't noticed before. A video camera on a tripod. He walked over to the device and examined it. Tangled cables lay at the tripod's feet, and hidden in them like an egg in a nest was a large red footswitch. Without hesitation, Ondragon stepped on it. Sudden bright light glared, blinding him. But not in the room, outside, where the garden looked like it was in broad daylight.

A floodlight! Ondragon looked out. The light illuminated every detail with cold precision: the gravel path, the swimming pool, the bushes and trees, the pond, and the small garden shed at the far end. Someone had installed a battery floodlight in the garden!

"Hey, Ecks, what are you doing?" he heard Rod ask behind him. The Brit and Green stepped up beside him and looked out as well.

"I don't know what that's for," Ondragon said, turning off the light again. Abruptly, night fell back on the garden. "Did you find anything upstairs?"

"No, nothing. No secret room either. Just rumpled beds and dirty clothes."

The three turned their heads as the Madame came through the door. "I didn't find anything either, except dirty dishes and takeout wrappers piled up to the ceiling. Our two mailmen weren't the cleanest. What was that light?"

"Stern and Ellys have illuminated their garden and turned it into a stadium," Ondragon countered.

"Stadium for what?" asked the Madame.

Ondragon shrugged and looked around the living room. "Where the hell did they hide the stuff?" He walked over to the TV, which was equipped with a DVD player, but he couldn't see any movie cases lying around. Strange. Then why did they need the player? His eye fell on the patterned Indian rug in the center of the room. It looked far too small for the large area and seemed somehow out of place. The mailmen didn't seem to be very talented interior decorators either. Following a hunch, Ondragon bent down and pulled the carpet off the floor with a jerk. Underneath, wooden floorboards appeared and the cracks of a neatly cut square. A trapdoor.

Rod whistled through his teeth as Ondragon lifted the door and shone his lamp into the black hole.

"The simplest hiding place since the dawn of time!" he said, dangling his legs down into the darkness. "I think we've found the secret room."

The lamp between his teeth, Ondragon dove down. In the low cavity, crisscrossed by supporting pillars, he found a small warehouse, which was in no way inferior to the inventory of the other secret rooms: weapons in aluminum cases, ammunition, various pieces of equipment, and two black sports bags. Ondragon crawled over to them through the dust, opened one of them, and found what he had been looking for. A fake passport for Stern and a driver's license lay on top. Underneath were wads of cash, papers and folders with the Darwin Inc. logo, clear plastic boxes with a dozen USB sticks inside, and small bags of corn kernels. He opened the other bag. Its contents were identical, except for the fact that the passport bore Ellys's photo. The two mailmen had taken precautions and each had put together a small security package.

Ondragon took both bags and heaved them out of the hiding place into the living room, where Rod, Green, and the Madame received them. Then he pushed another oblong metal case after them, got out of the hiding place, and wiped the cobwebs from his face.

"Nice catch!" said Rod, looking in the bags. "And what's that?" He pointed at the case.

"My precision rifle. The vultures stole it from my trunk!" Ondragon stroked the case almost lovingly, then took one of the small plastic boxes out of the bag and carried it over to the TV. "This DVD player also has a USB port. Let's see what's on the sticks." He put the first one into the player and waited for the device to read the data. The TV screen turned blue and a list of files popped up:

Lab-III-IsoBox-01-Jan-11-2010-1200-1300
Lab-III-IsoBox-01-Jan-11-2010-1300-1400
Lab-III-IsoBox-01-Jan-11-2010-1400-1500 etc.

Ondragon selected the first film, which he suspected was from a surveillance camera in the underground lab, and the blue user interface disappeared. Instead, flickering lines ran across the screen and an image in black and white appeared. Although the lighting was different on the recording, Ondragon recognized the room that had been filmed. It was the interior of one of the cells in the experimental wing in Laboratory III, where he had found the dead rats and monkeys. The cell was brightly lit, and an emaciated, dark-skinned man lay on the cot.

"Etienne Dadou," breathed the Madame in surprise.

Ondragon nodded. The man in the cell was clearly the father of little Christine. Now there was no doubt that the employees of the secret Darwin Inc. laboratory had performed experiments on him. Ondragon registered the digital numbers that ran along the lower left edge of the picture. JANUARY 11, 12:01 AM. So the day before the big earthquake.

All four of them looked spellbound at the screen. At first, nothing happened in the cell. Like a scrawny, dark embryo, Etienne Dadou lay on the cot without moving. Ondragon fast-forwarded. The image remained unchanged almost like a freeze frame, except that the digits kept running. Finally, at 12:30, a change occurred. A flat, angular object slid across the floor toward the cot. It was a tray with an indefinable mass and a cup of liquid on it.

"It looks like mashed potato," Rod said.

"Something like that. That's almost certainly mush made with the corn they grow down there. The DWIN 411-Crypt. The salvation of the world!" remarked Ondragon sarcastically. "They fed their test subjects that stuff and checked to see if it had any negative effects on the human organism."

Rod clicked his tongue disapprovingly as he watched Etienne Dadou struggle onto his thin legs, pull the tray toward him, and begin eating with his hands. Afterward, he sank back onto the cot, powerless, and lay on his side. His face looked sunken, and every now and then it seemed as if he was coughing or clearing his throat of too much phlegm; his body convulsed. He didn't move for the next half hour, and finally the film was over.

Ondragon jumped to the nearest file, and they watched as, after another uneventful quarter of an hour, the door to the cell opened and a blonde woman in a white coat appeared. It was the dead woman from the canteen, Ondragon recognized, the one with the scalpel in her chest. She stepped toward the cot, turned Etienne onto his back, and placed a tourniquet around his upper arm. She then drew two ampoules of blood and slid an infrared thermometer into his ear. She noted down the temperature on a clipboard and listened to the heart and lungs of the subject, who was indifferent throughout the procedure. She then disappeared from the picture and nothing more happened until the end of the film.

Ondragon selected a new file, this time one from the day of the earthquake: *Lab-III-IsoBox-01-Jan-12-2010-800-900*. All was quiet in the lab.

The cot with Etienne Dadou appeared on the screen. The man lay motionless. His skin had taken on a strange gray color and bulging protuberances had appeared on his neck. Nothing happened. At 8:13, the door opened and the blonde woman in the gown appeared. She felt Etienne's pulse in several places and then shone a light into one of his eyes. Shaking her head and her shoulders drooping, she looked down at him for a while. Then she turned and beckoned with her hand. Two men in black uniforms like security guards came into the cell. They loaded the apparently dead Dadou onto a stretcher and carried him out of the small room. The image became still again, showing only the empty cot. The only thing that was still moving was the digital time.

"How can that be?" the Madame asked as the screen went black. "We saw Dadou, didn't we, alive? I don't understand."

"I suppose," Ondragon replied, "they thought he was dead and took him from the lab to the surface, where they were going to dispose of his body. They may have done the same to all the others and just thrown them into the forest. The scavengers then did the rest. There were enough vultures around."

"Those filthy bastards!" The Madame was indignant. "They disposed of the bodies like garbage!"

"Well, pathetic. And stupid. They probably threw Etienne over the fence and left him there. For some reason, he returned to the world of the living half-mad and made the area unsafe. How convenient for Darwin Inc. that the priestess of Nan Margot had already started the zombie tale. So there was a great explanation even for such sloppiness." Ondragon selected the last file. He fast-forwarded to the point where the digital readout showed 4:50 pm. For three minutes, they stared at the image of the empty cot. Then suddenly the room began to shake, more and more violently, until the cot flew across the cell and banged against the door. White fault lines cut through the image before the screen was plunged into mute blackness.

4:54 pm. After the quake!

Uncomfortably moved, the Madame looked at Ondragon. "I wish I hadn't seen that."

"I wish that too sometimes, but the world is no bed of roses!" he replied harshly, and pulled the USB stick out of the DVD player. He selected a new one and inserted it into the port. "Are you ready, or would you rather go out while we sift through the footage?"

The Madame folded her arms defiantly over her chest, "I'm staying!"

"Very well." Ondragon selected a file labeled *0-12*. The TV screen briefly turned white, and then a colored image emerged.

Lush greenery.

Birdsong.

The top of a tree.

A mighty swamp oak with spreading branches.

Ondragon frowned. That sounded familiar. He felt his pulse quicken. There was nothing good coming . . . And when he finally recognized himself, hanging on a branch in dirty clothes and with a reddened face, cursing loudly and fishing for something with his belt, sweat suddenly broke out all over his body. These were the shots from his swamp odyssey! The ones Ellys had talked about.

Embarrassed, he wanted to quickly turn the video off again, when the camera panned from him hanging in the tree to what was below him. Ondragon expected to see the jagged back of an alligator on the surface of the water, but with growing amazement he realized it was just a pool. A turquoise swimming pool . . . and bobbing lazily on top of it was a squeaky green inflatable rubber crocodile.

What the . . . !

His amazement turned to speechless bewilderment as he watched himself trying to hit the head of the rubber crocodile over and over again with the shoe on the end of the fishing rod. Slowly, the camera zoomed out and more of the surroundings came into view. With wide eyes, Ondragon realized where he was. It was crazy, but he was actually perched on the tree in that garden he had looked into not fifteen minutes ago. The floodlit stadium!

Watched anxiously by the others, he reeled back from the television. Was it possible? It had all felt different, after all. So real! He had been in the swamp. He had walked mile after mile, suffered thirst and hunger, swum bayous and climbed trees, and been almost turned into boiled meat by the sun. All that could not have been just imagination!

He grabbed his sweaty forehead. What kind of fucked-up madness was this? Was dehydration to blame? Had it deluded him into believing all that?

In his dismay, as he moved backward, the back of Ondragon's knees bumped against the coffee table, where something clinked over. The sound drew his eyes from the video to the table. Slowly, he bent down and his fingers closed around an object. A small glass bottle filled with tiny beads. He held the label close to his eyes.

"'Lysergic acid diethylamide,'" he read aloud, as if talking to himself, and then let out a bitter laugh. "Goddamn LSD!" With an angry yell, he threw the bottle against the wall and ran to the patio door, yanked it open, and rushed outside into the balmy night. With rapid steps, he crossed the dark garden until he stood before the little hut. At his back, the floodlight flared up with a hiss, dousing the wall of the wooden shack with shadowless light. Only his own silhouette loomed pitch-black and as if cut out in front of him. From somewhere he heard Rod's voice.

"Ecks. Wait! Where are you going?"

Where am I going? Ondragon thought with bitter irony, and put a hand on the familiar door.

To the Hotel Bayou!

He gave the door a gentle push and it swung open. The cold light fell through the doorframe and illuminated the room. With two steps, Ondragon was inside the hut, looking around. The stained mattress still huddled in the one back corner, and the battered chair lay just beside it. On the floor in front of him he saw a chair leg and a tin can cut in two. It was unlabeled and empty. He gave one half of the can a kick and it flew, clattering against the wall where a faded poster hung.

Del Monte Peach Halves!

An art print of the famous painting by Andy Warhol.

What kind of crappy trip had Stern and Ellys sent him on?

And all just to make fun of him! Ondragon clenched his fists. No one had ever humiliated him like that! No one! And if the two mailmen weren't already dead, he would have skinned them alive by now! Bitterly, the bile flowed through him. He grabbed the leg of the chair and with a scream of hate he rushed forward and, raging like a wounded bull, began to smash the pitiful remains of the furniture.

Rod watched him do this from the doorway, the worry lines cutting deep into his forehead.

He didn't know how long he'd taken to cool down, but once he'd regained his composure, Ondragon allowed Rod to accompany him back to the house. There, the Madame and Green had graciously turned off the television and were in the process of putting whatever suspicious material was still lying around the living room into their gym bags.

Breathing heavily and avoiding the eyes of the Voodoo priestess and the mailman, Ondragon trudged over to the camera, unscrewed it from the tripod, and smashed it to the floor. His boot did the rest. The plastic housing burst with a crunch and the lens popped out. He then picked up the fragments and threw them into one of the bags.

"What are you going to do with all the material?" he asked Rod, his head lowered belligerently.

"Oh, I think I'll pulverize it," his friend said, throwing him an encouraging smile.

"What, you want to destroy it?" the Madame exclaimed indignantly. "Don't you want to use it to get those swine from Darwin Inc.? Do you want them to be able to keep doing such heinous experiments forever? Innocent people have died!"

"Innocent people die every second in this world!" retorted Ondragon. "And corporations like Darwin Inc. are to blame. But it would be suicide for us to mess with them. Darwin Inc. is a coldly calculating superintelligence with worldwide influence. We would have zero chance. It would be like David against Goliath. And as we all know, there was only one time in history that turned out well. Are you so selfless that you would give your life for others, madame? Think carefully! You have your community, you have your family, and you now have little Christine. Make sure that she and the people around her are well looked after. That is what you can do for this world. The little things, not the big things. You'd better keep your hands off those, or they'll eat you up . . . every last bit of you."

The Madame looked at him inquiringly. But then an amused smile spread over her lips. "That is very wise of you, Monsieur Ondragon. I wouldn't have expected that from you," she said perkily. "You're making progress. Would you like to join my congregation?"

Ondragon was about to open his mouth to reply, when Rod spoke. "Um, I don't want to interrupt your little flirtation, but I would like to say something. If you don't need the material you got from the lab, Ecks, I'd like to destroy that too."

"Out of the question! I'm keeping that. You never know. After all, I need to be able to cover myself in case Darwin Inc. finds out about me one day. Don't worry, Rod, I'll store it safely. In a safe deposit box somewhere abroad. Switzerland, maybe. They say they're thorough and reliable." Ondragon allowed himself a grim smile. "Do we have everything?"

The Madame and Green nodded.

"Good!" Ondragon took his iPhone out of his pocket and turned it on. Before they left the house, he wanted to do one more thing. He had Google Maps show him the satellite map of the area around the house and zoomed in until Chalmette's street grid appeared. He then put the phone away again and looked at his three companions. "Now let's get out of here. This place sucks!"

They crept out of the house and over to the car via the quickest route. Ondragon put the key in the ignition and started the Mustang with a rich roar. A peaceable expression appeared on his face and he hit the gas. The Mustang plowed through the night like a submarine through the black waters of the deep sea, leaving the sleeping houses behind. When they reached the main road, to the great surprise of the others, Ondragon turned not toward New Orleans but in the opposite direction.

"What have you got planned?" asked Rod, but Ondragon did not answer.

Silently, he steered the car along the wide, two-lane road until, after a few miles, it climbed slightly and rose above the dark, marshy terrain. At the highest point, Ondragon stopped on the hard shoulder, turned off the engine, and got out.

He stepped up to the railing of the bridge and listened. Finally, two vehicles arrived, and the sound they made as they passed finally dispelled the last of his doubts.

Clack, clack! Clack, clack!

His trek through the swamps had never taken place.

CHAPTER 36

February 18, 2010
New Orleans
11:17 am

In a good mood, Ondragon poured espresso from the Italian coffeepot into his cup. The case was solved. And so was the mystery of the zombies. Even if it had taken him on some bumpy detours and had clearly worn away his patina, the task Rod had set for him was satisfactorily completed. With a little polish in the form of a few days' vacation afterward, he would survive the whole thing well, especially since he had carefully destroyed all evidence of his involuntary drug trip.

Ondragon took a sip of the strong coffee. They were sitting in the Madame's kitchen enjoying a late breakfast. Rod sat next to Green and was equally in good spirits. He praised the housekeeper, Camille, for her excellent cooking, while the Madame took a bite of her croissant and jam and looked over at him, Ondragon, with a smile.

And for all the adversity of the past few days, this was possibly the most gratifying reward—a truce between two people as different as the two of them. Ondragon was glad to have finally found a level where he and the Madame could get along. True, it was a purely professional level, but that didn't make it any less titillating. He returned her smile, and for the first time, the Madame lowered her eyes in embarrassment. A warm feeling of comfort flowed through him. Maybe one day they would get togeth— No! They wouldn't! It would spoil everything. Better that they remain just friends. He turned his attention to his cell phone, which had been beeping. It was an email from Charlize. He called it up and read it.

Hey Boss,

It all worked out the way you planned it. I let those guys capture me outside my hotel, and they took me to a motel room outside town and interrogated me. They wanted to know why I was snooping around and what I had already found out. I pretended to be scared shitless and told them the story about the paralegal from St. Louis who was researching victim testimonies for her boss. I told them my boss was planning a class action lawsuit against Darwin Inc. over the Oregon Cryptococcosis cases. The guys—real amateurs, by the way—threatened to cut my pretty face if I didn't stop my research immediately. Just ridiculous, but I went along with it, bawling like a jilted teen, promising to try anything to convince my boss to let it go. I made a fake phone call and pretended my boss had agreed. The guys dismissed me with a warning that they would find me and kill me wherever I was if at any point Darwin Inc. received a lawsuit about Cryptococcosis. I assured them that would not happen. One of the pigs then grabbed my breast and they just released me onto the street. I would have loved to cut the bastard's fingers off! And I swear to you, if he crosses my path again, and I'm Charlize Tanaka and not a helpless paralegal, I will!
I'm at Portland airport now. Flying back to LA with a detour via St. Louis, just in case the nutcases come after me.
I'll see you back at the office.

Sayonara, Charlize

Ondragon grinned. Obviously, the trick he had thought up last night and told his assistant about had worked. From now on, no trace of Charlize aka the paralegal was going to lead to LA, or to him or his firm. So Darwin Inc. had no idea how much he knew about DWIN 411-Crypt and the ugly scheme with the genetic corn. For now, that would give him security from any reprisals from the corporation. If Darwin Inc. did one day discover that material from the lab in Haiti had fallen into foreign hands, he had a second life insurance policy in his pocket. He would store the material in a Swiss bank and threaten the corporation that if he died an unnatural death, it would automatically be forwarded to a major newspaper in Germany. The Germans were known to be the least tolerant when it came to dirty dealings with genetic engineering. They would make short work of Darwin Inc. in the press. It would be his revenge from beyond the grave.

Ondragon turned off the cell phone and finished his espresso. He put the empty cup down and rose. "As pleasant as it is to sit here with you and chat, I'm afraid I must take my leave." That was the well-bred diplomat's son talking.

The Madame and the other two also rose. Ondragon took the hand of the Voodoo priestess and breathed a perfect kiss onto it. It tasted of jam and Caribbean mystery. He gave her a mischievous look and said, "Though it may not seem so to you, it has been a pleasure to work with you, Madame Tombeau."

"Mari-Jeanne, please, Mr. Ondragon."

"Gladly, but then you must call me Paul too."

The Madame gave him a radiant smile, marred only by her impossible glasses. "It was my pleasure as well, Paul. I will miss your eternal skepticism."

"To make sure that doesn't happen, I might hire you on a case sometime. Do you also work on a fee-for-service basis?"

"For you, always!"

"Excellent!" He disengaged himself from her hand. "You will take care of the Reverend?"

"*Bien sûr.* His days in New Orleans are numbered!"

Ondragon smirked at the thought of a magical duel between the Reverend and the Madame, and thought he would only too gladly be a spectator.

"I'll tell you how it was," the Madame said with a twinkle in her eye, as if she had read his mind once again.

Ondragon grinned and signaled to Rod that he would see him outside. With one of his "what-goes-around-comes-around" smiles, he said goodbye to Alejandro Green and left the kitchen. As he reached the door, he turned back and said, "Of course, I'll keep my promise once I get to LA too."

"Merci beaucoup et au revoir," the Madame called after him with a gracefully raised hand.

"De rien!" replied Ondragon, stepping through the door into the hallway where his luggage was already waiting. He took the two bags and went out to the porch with Rod by his side. There he set the luggage down again and enclosed his friend in a warm embrace.

"So long, you old warhorse!"

"You too, Ecks." They broke away from each other.

"Will you stay here a little longer?" asked Ondragon.

"No, not for long. I'm flying to the UAE with Green today. After all, I have to track down the mole and give him notice."

"Well, that's a nice way to put it. I hope you catch him. I'll send Dietmar over if it doesn't work out."

"Thanks, that'd be great."

"You're welcome," Ondragon replied, looking into his friend's ice-blue eyes. "It's been an honor to work with you, Spider!"

The Briton pulled a serious face. "No, the honor was all mine." He slapped him on the shoulder. "You're the best damn man I know!"

Now it was Ondragon's turn to look sheepishly at the ground. The older man's compliment touched him.

"By the way, it's also damn decent of you to promise Mari-Jeanne you'll sort out a new passport for Christine," Rod added. "It's good news that the little girl is already feeling better. She'll be over it soon. She'll be fine here in her new home. Mari-Jeanne will make an excellent surrogate mother. You know, Ecks, you two are frighteningly alike!"

Ondragon looked up. "What, me and the Madame?"

Rod grinned. "You're at least as stubborn as each other!"

Ondragon breathed a sigh of relief. Oh, that was what his friend meant. He shook his hand one last time in farewell.

"Will I see you in Dubai sometime?" asked Rod.

"I'd fly there with you right now to help you unmask the mole, but I have some urgent business to attend to."

Rod tapped his forehead with a finger and said, "Understood."

Ondragon gave him one last look, then picked up his bags and walked through the little garden to the gate out into the street.

CHAPTER 37

February 19, 2010
Interstate 10 near Tucson
4:35 pm

After 1,400 miles, Ondragon pulled off Interstate 10 and turned his car north, past the countless gleaming bodies of rotting airplanes. The desert sun glared down from the sky, baking the barren landscape in the shimmering heat. Whistling a ditty, Ondragon turned onto Escalante Road and parked the Mustang by the side of the road. He got out, checked his outfit, and adjusted the dark aviator glasses on his nose. Then he walked at a leisurely pace through the barren neighborhood to a small house. He fumbled an ID card out of his jacket pocket and rang the bell.

"Ah, Agent Otter!" exclaimed Mr. Diego delightedly when he realized who was at his door.

"Good afternoon, Mr. Diego," Ondragon said to the man, putting the badge back in his pocket. "May I come in for a moment?"

"*Sí*, of course. Please, come. But what happened to you? You look quite, how shall I say, *destrozado*."

Ondragon smiled and felt the damaged cheekbone under his sunglasses. "I had an operation that was a little tough. Nothing bad."

"Okay. Do you want something to drink? *¿Agua, cola, limonada?*"

"No, thank you. I don't want to bother you for long, I just have a few questions."

"Ah, did you find out what happened to Señor Ellys?" Mr. Diego planted hands on his hips.

"Well, we still don't know where he is, but we have since found out what he was involved in. What it was, I can't tell you, of course, Mr. Diego. One thing is certain, however, it was not exactly in the spirit of the law. I'm sorry to tell you this, but your nice neighbor was a not-so-nice criminal."

"*¡Madre de Dios!* This will make the children sad."

"It's not like you have to tell them. By the way, where is your daughter?" Ondragon looked at the open porch door.

"Maria is out in the garden."

"May I have a word with her?"

Mr. Diego's eyebrows drew together suspiciously. "What do you want with her?"

"Just asking a question."

"Uh-huh. Just a question." Diego looked him up and down, but couldn't seem to detect anything threatening about the FBI agent, and finally said, "*También*, come on, then." He led Ondragon outside to the garden, where both children were playing in the sunshine on Diego's green lawn. He called his daughter to him, who came running up on bare feet and looked at the visitor with curious brown eyes.

"Hello, Maria, how are you?" asked Ondragon, crouching down in front of the girl.

"*Muy bien, señor,*" the child answered politely, crossing her arms behind her back uncertainly.

"That's a nice necklace you're wearing. Is it Tío Tyler's?" He slid a finger under the jewelry made of strung seeds that the girl wore around her neck.

"*Sí,*" she said, smiling proudly. "Tío Tyler brought me the pearls from a trip."

Yes, from a trip to hell, Ondragon thought, but smiled back kindly. What he was about to do would not please the girl, but he had to do it.

"Do you have any more of those seeds?" he pointed to the reddish corn kernels hanging from the chain among other fruiting bodies.

"No, they're all on here. Would you like to see them, *señor?*" She pulled the string over her head and handed it to Ondragon, who let the grains slip through his fingers.

DWIN 411-Crypt—so inconspicuous and yet so dangerous! It was not to be imagined what would happen if only one of these grains got into fertile soil and sprouted. If it grew into a plant and produced grains again, which in turn grew into plants and produced grains. What this stuff held could wipe out all of humanity. It was literally the seed of doom, designed by a money-grubbing corporation. What Darwin Inc. had done was irresponsible. But it had been even more irresponsible of Tyler Ellys to put the corn kernels in the hands of this child. Ondragon closed his hand around the chain.

"I'm heartbroken to have to say this, but I have to take the necklace," he finally said, watching the child's lips begin to tremble.

"Why, Mr. Otter?!" protested Mr. Diego, taking a step toward him.

"I'm sorry, but these seeds are evidence. Mr. Ellys took them from a breeding program." He stowed the necklace in a clear bag he had brought with him and put it in the pocket of his FBI jacket. In exchange, he pulled out another bag filled with colored glass beads and handed it to Maria. "Here! You can make a much nicer necklace out of these." Satisfied, he saw the girl's eyes light up happily.

"*Muchas gracias, señor,*" she exclaimed, running over to her brother in enthusiastic bounds to show him the beads.

Ondragon turned to his host. "I will mention your cooperation in my report, Mr. Diego. You have been very helpful."

The Mexican smiled.

"I'll leave you alone now. Goodbye." Ondragon left the house and walked back to his car. All the while, his hand was tight around the bag in his pocket. It wasn't until he was sitting in the Mustang, staring through the windshield, that his grip on the bag loosened. He would have to keep this stuff safe. At home in his safe, where he had stored that old diary from the English lieutenant from his last mysterious case. One day he would decide what to do with it.

He started the engine and steered the car back onto the highway. The desert sun was gradually sinking toward the horizon, promising a magnificent evening. Ondragon slipped a CD into the player and listened to "Anyway the Wind Blows" by Eric Clapton and J. J. Cale, while he rode off into the sunset on his little horse in good old Western movie style.

CHAPTER 38

February 28, 2010
Los Angeles
5:58 pm

At a steady pace, Ondragon jogged along the concrete path, enjoying the steady rhythm of his breathing. It was a perfect 70 degrees Fahrenheit and calm. To his left, the sun was setting over the Pacific Ocean, turning the Santa Monica boardwalk into the literal California Dream. And to his right, the fireball was reflected in the windows of the beachfront apartment buildings. As always, the palm-lined promenade was busy. Tourists, joggers, cyclists, people on in-line skates and roller skaters were out and about. Each was more sporty than the last. Out on the water, surfers were catching the last of the waves, black silhouettes against the blood-red evening sky. Ondragon looked ahead to the Santa Monica Pier, the start and finish of his usual loop to Venice and back. The lights of the Ferris wheel on the pier were just coming on, pulsing in psychedelic patterns. Whooping cries drifted over from the amusement mile.

Arriving at the pier, Ondragon bought a cold water at one of the food stalls and allowed himself a short break. After his pulse had returned to normal, he went to the parking lot on the pier, where he had parked his matte-black Honda Hornet. He pulled a sweater over his head and put on his helmet. Normally, he liked to ride without it, but for what he was about to do, he needed anonymity. The bike's license plate wasn't real either.

He got on the bike and turned on the ignition. The souped-up machine made a rich sound, and Ondragon took off at a good pace.

He passed the ramp and the archway of the pier and roared straight down Colorado Avenue to 4th Street, where he merged onto the still-empty Santa Monica Freeway. The traffic quickly became denser, however, as he switched to the northbound 405. There, cars were bumper-to-bumper—the everyday madness of Greater Los Angeles. But that needn't bother him. Ondragon ducked over the handlebars and hit the gas.

This was where the fun began!

In a sporty slalom, he circled the honking obstacles and left Chevies, Chryslers, and the others behind. He made good time and his mood jumped another notch on the urban pleasure scale. Traffic-jam hopping was really a joy! Especially with this fast and agile machine between his legs.

With a daring maneuver, he cut through a closing gap between two cars; behind them the lane was clear for the motorcycle. Ondragon glanced to the side and realized he had a playmate. Another motorcyclist, dressed in full gear and helmet, slid expertly through the dogged line of cars. The guy glanced over at him briefly and nodded. Ondragon nodded back and opened the throttle. The unofficial race was on and promised a nice adrenaline rush at the end of the day.

Ondragon sped through the traffic jam at a murderous pace, with the unknown man in the lane next to him, stubbornly keeping pace. On either side of him, the queue of stationary and slow-moving vehicles slid dangerously close, stinking exhaust fumes seeping into his lungs. He barely scraped past a wing mirror with his right knee.

No matter, Ondragon thought, this sport was unhealthy in the long run either way.

Suddenly, a vehicle swerved in front of him, and he would have collided with it if a gap had not opened up at the last moment through which he was able to swerve. Cursing and laughing at the same time, he drove on, his brain intoxicated by his body's own drugs. He risked a glance to the left, where his opponent was driving two lengths behind him, staring intently ahead.

Shortly afterward, the guy caught up with him. Level with each other, they passed the exit to Wilshire Boulevard, where Ondragon swerved into the far too narrow emergency lane to overtake a truck.

The driver sounded his horn angrily, drowning out the howl of the Honda's engine.

When the motorcycle duelists finally reached the exit to Sunset Boulevard, the traffic gradually flowed more smoothly and they were able to accelerate without restraint. With the tachometer in the red zone, Ondragon pushed his machine to 140 mph. The wind tugged at his clothing, and the machine lurched viciously at every bump in the highway, but still he didn't let up. In the rearview mirror, he saw his playmate gradually getting smaller. Obviously, he did not dare to interpret the speed limit as generously as Ondragon. Or his machine was no good.

A victorious smile on his lips, Ondragon pulled off onto Mulholland Drive a few miles later. He made his way at a leisurely pace up the winding road to Laurel Pass and finally reached Sunset Plaza Drive via Wonderland Avenue, where the garage where he parked his motorcycle was located. Sunset Plaza Drive was above Doheny Drive, where his villa was, but there was no connection between the two streets. Only a narrow trail led down the slope to his house. This was Ondragon's number one escape route and the motorcycle was his usual getaway vehicle. Doheny Drive had far too few branches to allow for escape in an emergency. Mulholland Drive offered much better options.

Ondragon locked the garage door and descended the path to his garden in the dark, entering through a back door. Crickets were chirping everywhere, and the freshly manicured grounds were an idyllic sight with their myriad small lanterns and illuminated pool. Whistling cheerfully, he strode to the terrace and went into his villa through the side entrance. Inside, he switched on the lights and headed straight for the bathroom, where he treated himself to a hot shower.

Having freshened up, he went to the open-plan kitchen and living area, where his housekeeper had prepared a light dinner for him.

Lupita Lopez was Mexican, of course, but that was as far as the stereotype went. His Lupita was different. She was thirty-five, of stocky build, toned like a bodybuilder, and could knock a bull off its hooves. Lupita was a Lucha Libre and very successful in Mexican women's wrestling. Mostly, he needed her to keep the house in order and maintain some semblance of a normal middle-class home. In Hollywood, just about everyone who was anyone had maids, just as everyone had a psychotherapist. A bachelor like him would only stand out if he didn't employ staff. Oh well. Life was complicated. But it also had its pleasant sides.

Ondragon grabbed a cold Desperados and Lupita's salad with the chipotle dressing from the refrigerator and sat down on the comfortable sofa, with a breathtaking view of Los Angeles at night. While he ate, he looked through his travel documents, which were on the coffee table. His flight to Zurich left the day after tomorrow and his appointment at the bank was the day after that. And while he was there, he would head to St. Moritz after taking care of business and relax for a few days of powder snow and après ski. Charlize would hold down the fort as long as he was in Switzerland, and then get time off to chill for a week in Hawaii.

Ondragon placed the empty plate on the table, where the Madame's Voodoo candle stood in a plain holder. A small memento of the crazy zombie hunt in New Orleans. With an amused smile, he pulled out his cell phone and checked his email for the last time that evening. He furrowed his brows, perplexed. Half an hour ago, Charlize had sent him an email. It was a forwarded message from captainzombieshop-neworleans@xmail.com with no text but a jpg file attached. A scan from a newspaper clipping. Ondragon glanced at the grainy black-and-white photo next to the article. It showed the face of a Black man, but it told him nothing. He read the short article.

Who knows this man?

New Orleans—Yesterday afternoon, an apparently confused man (photo) of African descent was apprehended on Interstate 10 westbound in the Maurepas Swamp Wildlife Management Area. He was dressed only in underpants and could not provide any information about his identity. He was initially taken to the Lake Shore Mental Hospital for evaluation of his mental condition. The authorities are asking for any information. Does anyone know this man?

A vague memory flashed through Ondragon's mind. Hastily, he searched his emails and found a message he had received from the Madame three days before. Or rather, a photo. He opened it and stared at it for quite a while until he finally understood. Simultaneously shocked and amused, he leaned back. The photo was of a gravestone. Ondragon didn't know what cemetery it was in, but he knew the name that was engraved on it: PATRICK FOUILLES SEPTEMBER 4,1964–FEBRUARY 21,2010—OUR REVEREND

So the good Reverend Zombie had gone through the earth! He had received his Haitian punishment and had been dug up again. What an ironic twist of fate! The Reverend had been beaten at his own game . . . and was now walking through life as a zombie. *C'est la vie!*

With an amused snort, Ondragon rose from the sofa and went to the basement, where a special Sentry safe was hidden behind a folding TV screen in his gym.

He opened the safe with a six-digit secret combination and removed an addressed envelope. On the front was written Mme Mari-Jeanne Tombeau, 616 Ursulines Avenue, New Orleans, LA 70116. He reached into the envelope and pulled out the blue document with the stamp. It was a US passport. He opened it, looked at the photo and the security holograms, and read the name: Christine Dadou Tombeau, born May 25, 2001, in New Orleans.

The photo was not very good, you could still clearly see how much little Christine had suffered, but it was sufficient for the purpose. Otherwise, the passport was an excellent job and indistinguishable from a real document. Satisfied, Ondragon packed it back into the envelope. He would send it by courier to New Orleans tomorrow, along with a forged birth certificate, and look forward to the Madame's call when she received it.

His hand rested for a moment on the Darwin Inc. records, which were in a black folder. In three days they would be in the safest safe in the world. Ondragon pursed his lips. Maybe, he thought pensively, if I'm planning my big exit one day, maybe I'll blow the whistle after all. A reckoning with the world, so to speak, a global swipe.

Opening Pandora's Box . . .

Yes, he liked the idea. He closed the safe again and went upstairs to the living area, where he sat down on his sofa with another drink and turned on the TV.

At 11:30 pm he went to bed. More than ever, he was reminded of how happy he would be when he finally deposited the material in Switzerland. He had to admit that the stuff in his safe worried him more than he had assumed it would.

He closed his eyes and tried to fall asleep. Soon he was dreaming of the Swiss Alps, of snow and glaciers. He skied down a wonderful slope on brand-new skis, making elegant turns toward the valley station, where he sat in the lift and enjoyed the panorama of snow-covered mountains with hyacinth-blue sky above him during the ride. At the top, he gazed out over the white mountain peaks and plunged down the deserted slope. The skis glided through the snow as if over butter and Ondragon felt the rush of speed tingle in his veins. The tall fir trees flew past him left and right, including the orange slope boundary and waving zombies.

Ondragon paused and frowned. Zombies? He turned his head and sure enough, he saw a line of zombies standing at the edge of the road. Stern and Ellys were there and so was Bolič.

Ondragon shook his head and drove on. Did zombies go on skiing vacations?

Suddenly, another skier of a very small stature appeared next to him. Ondragon watched as this one approached him, making daring turns. Finally, skiing parallel to him, the small skier pushed his goggles up his forehead and grinned at him.

It was Per!

Ondragon looked at his brother in amazement. Per Gustav was not skiing; no, he was riding two inflatable rubber crocodiles down into the valley.

"Hey, surprise, huh?" Per called over.

"What the hell are you doing here?" asked Ondragon as they shot down the mountain together.

"Someone sent me to you. A certain Madame Tombeau! You know her, don't you?"

"Yes, but . . ."

"I'm supposed to give you a message!"

Ondragon became angry. Couldn't the Voodoo priestess leave him alone, even in his dreams? "Tell her to stop bothering me with her nonsense!" he hissed at Per, whose face turned serious. In their schuss, neither of them noticed the fir and zombie forest getting denser and the slope getting narrower like a funnel. More and more Sterns, Ellyses, and Boličs flew by.

"It's important though!" shouted Per urgently

"Oh yeah?" snapped Ondragon back. Now the slope was only a narrow alley. Shoulder to shoulder, he and Per raced down, the arms of the zombies reaching for them.

"Really!" affirmed Per, casting an anxious glance at the end of the slope, where fir trees as prickly as thorny bushes awaited them. And zombies.

"Oh, shit! Then tell me and get the hell out of here!" Ondragon ordered gruffly.

"All right, my dear Paul, the message is: Wake up!"

"What?"

"WAKE UP, DAMN IT!"

Annoyed, Ondragon ducked to the side as the first twigs and fingernails threatened to scratch his face. Per fell behind him on his crocodile skis, the slope so narrow now. Did his brother have to mess everything up for him?

Ondragon uttered a loud curse and unwillingly opened his eyes. The slope disappeared and the dark shadows of his bedroom appeared, the wardrobe, the lamp, the chair, and the person.

The person?

Even before his adrenal glands could release the adrenaline, Ondragon reached for the gun under his pillow, pointed it at the intruder, and pulled the trigger without hesitation.

Click.

A dirty laugh rang out. "Hey, that's my gun, isn't it? It doesn't always work!"

Ondragon felt the cold barrel of a silencer pressing against his temple. Slowly, he lifted his gaze to the face of the figure looming beside his bed. The hot wave of the stress hormone finally took effect, and his heart began to race as he realized who it was.

Kaplan Bolič was standing there looking down at him. He was wearing motorcycle pants and a white T-shirt. A grinning Bugs Bunny reached up from the Bosnian's forearm and gave him a hard punch in the face.

Bright stars framed the cartoon bunny, and Ondragon spat out blood.

"What do you want?" he asked the intruder, who he had assumed was lying dead in the Arizona desert. But that's how wrong you could be, and it was probably his turn to have a hole in his head now.

"I want the stuff from the lab and the other things!" said Bolič.

Ondragon blinked. "Is that my gun?" He jerked his chin toward the Sig Sauer in Bolič's hand.

"Don't deflect, smartass! Where do you have the material?" The muzzle of the silencer came dangerously close to Ondragon's cheek, but he did not allow himself to be impressed. Instead, he thought. He was in his own house, he knew his way around. That was his advantage. But Bolič was not just any opponent, he was an experienced fighter who was possibly his equal. After all, he had tricked his alarm system and was also significantly younger than he was.

"If you shoot, you'll never know where I hid it!" said Ondragon calmly at last.

"I know that, but I can hurt you to get you to tell!"

"If it amuses you, Captain," Ondragon replied mockingly, meanwhile calmly considering where his nearest weapon was. One pistol was taped under the dining room table, there was a second in the drawer in the study, and the sawn-off pump shotgun was in the top dresser drawer in the living room. The third pistol was in the safe, but Bolič would surely suspect that, because it was a standard hiding place, after all. Ondragon continued to ponder. The pepper spray was hidden in the lampshade and the baseball bat under the sofa. The Japanese swords were in the hallway on the antique armoire from 1900. There were knives too, of course: in the kitchen, but also under the carpet in the living room and bedroom, above the door panel in the study, and in the gym on the ergometer. That was possibly the only one that was realistic. But did he want a knife fight with a Bosnian war veteran? Not really.

Bugs Bunny sped toward him again, and Boličs fist crashed into his head, exposing a swastika on the inside of his upper arm.

Ondragon raised both hands placatingly. "I'm coming. What do you want with this stuff anyway?"

"None of your fucking business!" Bolič dragged him to his bare feet; he was obviously not moving fast enough.

"Aha, now I understand!" exclaimed Ondragon. "How could I be so slow. *You* are the mole at DeForce! *You* knew about the mission and about the potential to blackmail Darwin Inc. And you knew Ellys before, didn't you?" He pointed to the tattoo that looked exactly like the swastika emblem on the White Power Movement flag he had discovered in Ellys's secret room. So there was the connection!

"You guys met at a White Power meeting, and Ellys advised you to apply to DeForce, right? And Spider didn't know about any of this. There wasn't supposed to be any connection between you."

"Shut up!"

"So I'm right!" Ondragon grinned and received a kick in the calf from behind, which brought him down. Bolič grabbed him roughly by the hair and pulled him back to his feet.

"Ouch, that actually hurts," Ondragon joked.

"I'm about to do some other shit to you, motherfucker! Come on, show me where the stuff is now." Bolič pushed him brutally out of the bedroom toward the stairs.

Ondragon let it happen and descended the stairs provocatively sluggishly while asking the Bosnian constant questions. "You told Ellys about your planned inside sellout because he was the only one who would be able to get the material, and he brought in Stern as support against Green. But why weren't you in on it when we busted them both along with that shady Reverend? Hmm, let me think. Ah, I've got it! You just used Ellys and Stern to get them to do your dirty work, and then you wanted to get rid of those pesky accessories and rake in all the dough yourself. Pretty clever."

Bolič laughed spitefully. "Well, and I didn't even have to get my hands dirty because you came and got them out of the way for me. That was extraordinarily kind of you."

"And you really thought your plan would work?"

"It did, didn't it?" Again, the Bosnian laughed.

"What about Spider? Are you going to get rid of him too when this is over?"

"We'll see. Now shut the fuck up!"

They had reached the foot of the stairs. To the right was the kitchen and the living room and to the left the study and the other rooms . . . and the stairs to the basement. Ondragon hesitated. Where should he lead Bolič? Should he risk a knife fight with an uncertain outcome, or would it be better to try a firearm? The nearest one was in the dresser, not ten steps away from him.

But Bolič was not stupid; he noticed his hesitation and guessed what he was going to do. Again, he received a painful kick in the calves with the motorcycle boot.

"Don't even think about it!" the Bosnian hissed. "For sure you have hidden weapons everywhere here. After all, I know who you are!"

"Yeah, yeah, a bullshit legend. Thanks for the flowers!"

"It wasn't a compliment, you ass! I just wanted to make it clear to you that you don't have to try any nonsense. Now what? Which way? And no detours, if you please. For every step you take me in the wrong direction, I'll shoot a finger off your hand. Since it's your gun, you know you got enough ammo for seven fingers and your head. Seven fingers, seven steps. So? Think it over."

Shit! He wouldn't make it to the dresser like that. He had to give in to Bolič whether he liked it or not. Even though it seemed ridiculous in the face of death, he didn't want to go to the afterlife without his fingers. He turned left to the stairs and slowly descended, followed by Bolič.

"Always be a good boy, Mr. O, and maybe I'll leave you whole before I kill you."

Ondragon felt the adrenaline in his bloodstream begin to ebb and his attention lessen dangerously. He bit his chapped lower lip. He had to keep his brain running at full speed, it was the only way he would have any chance of success against this bull of a man. Eager to keep the flame of his anger simmering, he thought of ugly things he would do to Bolič if Lady Fortune showed mercy and turned the tide after all. Meanwhile, he slowly walked to the end of the corridor, where the gym was located.

They were soon standing by the door.

"Come on, what are you waiting for? Go in!"

Ondragon did as he was told, focusing his mind on the knife attached to the ergometer's handlebars with Velcro. The fitness machine was not far from the screen behind which the safe was hidden. It was his only chance; he had to take it.

Bolič switched on the ceiling lamp and pushed Ondragon into the room. In the bright light, the knife seemed to flash from afar. Damn, he hoped Bolič hadn't seen it.

Not letting on in the slightest, Ondragon walked toward the wall with the screen and came within two arm's lengths of the ergometer. Bolič still had the gun trained on him; all his strained senses were telling him so. All he had to do was distract him for a moment. But Bolič was certainly carrying a knife as well.

Never mind, Paul Eckbert! Fight or flight! You have to try. Otherwise he'll have won.

At this thought, his jaws ground hard against each other.

The great Mr. Ondragon has been executed in his own home, wearing his pajamas, by a Bosnian fighting machine. Just great. But at least his executioner was a consummate professional.

He squinted inconspicuously at the shiny blade on the ergometer. He only needed to make one movement and he would have it. But he would also have three bullets in his back!

With his eyes closed, he counted to ten in Japanese: *ichi . . . ni . . . san . . . shi . . . go . . . roku . . . shichi . . . hachi . . .*

kyuu . . .

juu!

He reached for the button on the wall and let the screen swing forward. Behind it the safe appeared, and Bolič gave a delighted sound, which meant that at that moment his attention was focused on the safe and not on him.

Ondragon reacted with lightning speed. He raised his leg with a mighty swing, spun around, and kicked the weapon out of the surprised Bolič's hand. It flew in a high arc across the room and landed with a thump behind the weight bench. A professional through and through, Bolič made no attempt to dive after it, instead pulling a matte military blade from his boot with a fluid motion that indicated how well-trained he was in hand-to-hand combat. With a shout, the Bosnian lunged at him.

Ondragon dodged the blow and tore the knife from the ergometer's handlebars. In the same movement he whirled around and just managed to ward off another well-aimed stab at his stomach using a Krav Maga technique.

Bolič was not surprised that his opponent was also skilled in hand-to-hand combat, and even seemed to have expected it, as he effortlessly slowed his forward motion and turned around smoothly despite his body mass.

Now the two opponents were face-to-face like gladiators, a knife in their right fist, the other ready to smash teeth and bones. Unfortunately, Bolič had the advantage of the door at his back.

Ondragon glanced quickly at the weights bench. It was impossible to get to the Sig Sauer behind it with the Bosnian's speed.

"Kurva!" he heard Bolič curse in his native language. "You son of a bitch, I'll kill you!"

"No false promises!" retorted Ondragon belligerently, directing his gaze at the center of his opponent's body.

The Bosnian attacked out of nowhere, and the force of the impact forced the air from Ondragon's lungs. They both crashed to the ground, and Bolič buried Ondragon under him. The Bosnian grabbed his wrist and forced it down, while Ondragon struggled to lift the meaty arm of the man, which weighed at least 40 pounds. Strained gasps filled the room, and inch by inch the Bosnian's matte blade lowered toward his opponent's unprotected chest. Ondragon felt his hand threatening to fall asleep around the knife as Bolič squeezed the blood from it. His numb fingers were losing strength. He fought with all his might against the Bosnian's weight, tried to get him off him with a leg technique, but Bolič remained on top of him giving ugly laughs and pushing his knife down with merciless determination. The tip touched Ondragon's chest and cut the skin, but met resistance and drilled into a rib. With a scream, Ondragon did the only thing that remained to him. He pulled Bolič down toward him with a jerk despite the penetrating knife, took advantage of the mass that the surprised Bosnian was unable to control, and slammed his forehead into his nose.

Bolič howled in shock, and finally Ondragon managed to throw him off with a leg scissors maneuver. With a quick leap he was on his feet and plunged his blade into Bolič's back. But the blow was not firm enough because of the numbness in his fingers. The Bosnian reared up, roaring like a stuck pig, and thrust with his knife. Ondragon felt the pain in his side as the blade tore at his skin, but he grabbed Bolič by the arm and broke it with a crack over his knee. The knife fell to the ground. Grunting, Bolič threw himself around and rammed the elbow of his other arm into Ondragon's stomach. Ondragon collapsed forward and spat out what was left in his stomach, right onto Bolič's back.

This bastard can't be broken! he thought, while the bile burned in his throat and he looked at the door with his one eye. For the bull Bolič, he needed more than a little knife. He dodged an uppercut from the Bosnian and dashed for the exit. With long strides, he ran for the stairs. But Bolič came rumbling after him with frightening speed.

Taking the stairs three at a time, Ondragon leaped upward. The wound in his chest had begun to bleed profusely. The red liquid was already running down his leg and threatening to make him slip on the stone steps. With one last great leap, crying out in pain, he reached the landing, but Bolič was right behind him. Like a predator, he threw himself at him and caught him by the foot. Ondragon tumbled, fell lengthwise, and banged his shoulder against the armoire. Something on it began to sway and fell down on him. In desperation, Ondragon grabbed it. He saw Bolič coming at him, like a steamroller run amok, his massive body tensed and the fist of his healthy arm clenched. Bugs Bunny smiled back at him, and Ondragon saw the Bosnian grab his back and pull out the knife.

Hastily, he scrabbled at the elongated object in his hands and found the handle. Bolič stomped toward him, mighty as a giant, the knife in his hand and an expression of triumph on his face. The ground literally shook under his steps.

"Son of a bitch, now it's your turn!" Bolič dropped toward him, knife tip first.

More unconsciously than anything, Ondragon rolled over, got to his feet, and automatically unsheathed the long blade. With a flowing movement, he struck.

Bolič's head rolled down the hallway, leaving a bloody trail. His body crashed to the floor like a felled oak. A moment later, Ondragon's feet were bathed in a rapidly spreading pool of blood.

"Lucky this place is tiled," he said softly, wiping the blood from the 17th-century samurai sword and putting it back in its scabbard. It had fallen from its stand on the dresser right into his hands.

Bushido!

Lady Fortune knew the way of the warrior after all.

Ondragon grinned into the darkness of the hallway. Good girl!

He looked at the mess on the floor and sighed. He would have to ring Lupita and wake her up. And he would have to take a night-time trip.

He walked, leaving bloody footprints, into the living room where his cell phone lay. He pressed Rod's number.

"I got the mole!" he said curtly. "You can stop looking for him. It was Bolič!"

"Kaplan Bolič?" asked Rod, aghast. "But he's dead!"

"Yes, indeed he is now."

"Are you going to tell me what happened?"

"Not now."

"Okay, another time, then."

"Yeah, that'd be better." Ondragon hung up and dialed another number. He spoke briefly to the man on the other end and then hung up, before informing his housekeeper of her extracurricular assignment. She agreed to come without a murmur. Ondragon tossed the phone onto the sofa and headed back into the hallway, where he set about preparing Bolič for his hot grave . . . in the kiln at the Riverside cement plant. Not a micron would be left of the Bosnian. And his atoms might serve a good purpose after all, perhaps in the foundations of a California family home.

ABOUT THE AUTHOR

Anette Strohmeyer is a German crime writer. She began her career illustrating comic books but unfortunately never developed the skills to rival her role model, Jean Giraud aka Moebius, so she decided to focus on the speech bubbles instead.

Now, Strohmeyer is known for her fiction writing and meticulous, often immersive research work. She has participated in a voodoo ceremony in Haiti, eaten termites in the jungle, generated lightning in a high-voltage laboratory, and trekked through Japan's infamous Aokigahara Forest along the edge of Mount Fuji.

Since 2018, Strohmeyer has lived in Denmark, where she splits her time between Copenhagen and the island of Møn. She also writes as Anne Nørdby, author of the bestselling Tom Skagen thriller series.

Podium

DISCOVER MORE

STORIES UNBOUND

PodiumEntertainment.com